I0819171

ALSO BY JANE SMILEY

FICTION

Lucky

A Dangerous Business

Perestroika in Paris

The Last Hundred Years Trilogy:

Some Luck, Early Warning, Golden Age

Private Life

Ten Days in the Hills

Good Faith

Horse Heaven

The All-True Travels and Adventures of Lidie Newton

Moo

A Thousand Acres

Ordinary Love and Good Will

The Greenlanders

The Age of Grief

Duplicate Keys

At Paradise Gate

Barn Blind

NONFICTION

The Questions That Matter Most

The Man Who Invented the Computer

Thirteen Ways of Looking at the Novel

A Year at the Races

Charles Dickens

Catskill Crafts

FOR YOUNG ADULTS

The Horses of Oak Valley Ranch Series:

The Georges and the Jewels, A Good Horse, True Blue, Pie in the Sky, Gee Whiz

The Ellen & Ned Trilogy:

Riding Lessons, Saddles and Secrets, Taking the Reins

LIDIE

LIDIE

THE

Further Travels

AND

Adventures

of

LIDIE NEWTON

⊱◆⊰

JANE SMILEY

ALFRED A. KNOPF ◆ NEW YORK ◆ 2026

A BORZOI BOOK

FIRST HARDCOVER EDITION PUBLISHED BY ALFRED A. KNOPF 2026

Published by Alfred A. Knopf, a division of Penguin Random House LLC, 1745 Broadway, New York, NY 10019.

Knopf, Borzoi Books, and the colophon are registered trademarks of Penguin Random House LLC.

Library of Congress Cataloging-in-Publication Data

Names: Smiley, Jane, author
Title: Lidie : the further travels and
adventures of Lidie Newton / Jane Smiley.
Description: First hardcover edition. | New York : Alfred A. Knopf, 2026.
Identifiers: LCCN 2025029545 | ISBN 9780593802298 (hardcover) |
ISBN 9780593802304 (ebook)
Subjects: LCGFT: Novels | Fiction
Classification: LCC PS3569.M39 L53 2026
LC record available at https://lccn.loc.gov/2025029545

penguinrandomhouse.com | aaknopf.com

Printed in the United States of America
1st Printing

The authorized representative in the EU for product safety and compliance is Penguin Random House Ireland, Morrison Chambers, 32 Nassau Street, Dublin D02 YH68, Ireland, https://eu-contact.penguin.ie.

LIDIE

I

PERHAPS MY SISTERS would say that my sojourn in Kansas and Missouri, and then all the way to Massachusetts to visit my dead husband's family, chastened me. But when they saw me upon my return from Medford, they didn't say anything like "I told you so." They welcomed me kindly, and sorted out my living arrangements. My sisters, Harriet, Alice, and Beatrice, actually were my half sisters, the daughters of my father's first wife, and considerably older than I was. They seemed to me more like aunts than sisters. I was the only surviving child of my father's second wife. Alice told me that I would stay with her and her husband, Frederick, as I always had, because, even though Beatrice had more space, she had too much on her mind, what with Christmas coming on and all the business she had to attend to at Lorton and Silk, her husband, Horace's, emporium, and Harriet was very busy on her farm, mostly because she didn't trust others, including me, to take proper care of the chickens. It had always been a pleasure to me that Alice's house was farther from the center of town, more modest, quieter, since my nephews that Alice had called "hooligans" were out of the house, and the remaining two, Larry and Fred, behaved themselves, and actually did errands. And I knew the neighborhood well, which was comforting.

Now, I was more willing than I had been before I went to Kansas to help my niece, Annie, who was a year younger than me, do all the housework Alice burdened her with. When we were growing up, the only thing I didn't mind was stirring the washing in the tubs, and, because I was tall, I never minded wringing out the laundry and hanging it on the lines, but I didn't do it often enough for my sisters to think that I was "of use." I hoped that helping Annie would be a way I could renew my connection with her – helping her, but not telling her much about what had happened or how I felt about it.

I wore my black mourning dress; Alice understood that the death of Thomas Newton, abolitionist or not, was a tragedy, and that it was unlikely, given my plain visage and wayward nature, that I would find another husband, and so I might be starving them out of house and home forever. But all three sisters were sympathetic, perhaps more than they might have been if I had told anyone about Lorna. Not even three months before, I had attempted to get Lorna out of Missouri to a free state, and because of my incompetence, I had failed. I didn't tell anyone in my family about this, because some of them would sneer at my incompetence, and others would shake their heads at my foolishness. What I thought that I learned in Kansas Territory (we'd called it "K.T.") and in Independence, Missouri, was to keep my eyes open. I did wonder more than I had about my brother-in-law Roland, who was from Kentuck, and swore up and down that he hated "d — ned abolitionists," but had never owned a slave, though he said his cousins in Kentuck had a right to. My eighteen months in K.T. and Missouri showed me that this slavery issue was a messy nightmare that I wanted to stop thinking about, at least for a while.

Only a day or so after I moved in, Annie walked into the parlor and handed my sister Alice a bit of paper. Alice turned it over in her hand, and then she stared at Annie as if she were seeing a specter. The piece of paper turned out to be a ticket to the theater on

Maine Street, where Annie and I had once seen *Dombey and Son* and a bit of *Macbeth.* It was a free ticket to a production of *A Christmas Carol,* because Annie had a role in the play, the role of Ebenezer Scrooge's betrothed, Belle, who appears in Christmas Past, and is quickly excised from the story. Somehow, Annie had gotten herself out of the house and to the theater while keeping up with her work. I thought that I shouldn't be surprised, because I remembered how much Annie had enjoyed everything about the *Dombey and Son* play. I wondered if seeing that one was what had inspired her to act onstage, or simply to find a way to get out of the house.

About an hour later, when we were carrying water for the washing up, I teased the information from her – where had she gone the night before, when I heard the back door creak and peeped out the window at seven-thirty in the cold and misty night? She explained about the rehearsals she had sneaked away to, and that there were to be two performances, one two nights before Christmas and one the night before Christmas. I threw on my shawl, got out the door, and headed down to the theater to buy myself a ticket. I must say that I hadn't felt as perky, or maybe a better word is "hopeful," since I could remember, and for a brisk fifteen minutes, as I walked, I thought nothing of what I had left behind in K.T. and Missouri.

Of course, Mr. Dickens was a great celebrity in Illinois, and not only because of his stories – he'd been to the area once, though not to Quincy. I dare say, there were plenty of folks in our town who couldn't understand how he missed us after finding himself in Cairo, of all places, and why did he take that trip down the Ohio River instead of a much more pleasant trip through the northern lakes and then to Chicago (though Chicago wasn't much in those days, it was more than Cairo)? And then he wrote his book that related the horrors of that trip, and was anyone surprised? He just didn't have the gumption, was what everyone said who happened to know the book. Even so, this play, made out of his *Christmas Carol,* had become a customary performance in Quincy. I'd never seen it. I arrived at the theater, handed over my four bits, and got myself a ticket up in the back rows, then walked home.

It wasn't a bad day for December. The streets were gritty and covered with horse dung, because no one had cleaned them since before the last snowstorm, but they weren't slippery, and the eaves of the houses glittered with icicles, though not as many as there had been in Medford. It was about two in the afternoon, the best time of day in the winter – the sun convinces you that light is warmth after all. The bare limbs of the trees shook in the wind, a sound I liked because it made me look beyond the houses and therefore the arguments folks were having in the streets about this and that, and also what this mess in Kansas was doing to our nation, and what folks thought of Senator Douglas, who had created that violent mess by introducing the Kansas-Nebraska Act, which allowed states, even those north of the Mason-Dixon Line, to decide on their own whether to allow slaves. Of course, everyone in Quincy knew Senator Douglas personally, or said that they did, but I had never even seen him, as far as I knew, and if I were to see him, I thought for a moment, I would have a thing or two to say to him, but then I stopped, shut my eyes, and thought, "Enough of that!" I was walking down Maine Street, and he wasn't.

I turned up 20th Street toward Vermont. Things got quiet. Mrs. Abercrombie was squatting on her front stoop, using the sunlight to candle some eggs. She had more chickens than we did – maybe ten, and a rooster, too, that sometimes woke me up. Everyone in the neighborhood liked her eggs, and my sister Harriet said that she didn't ask what she should for them. But money is chancy – our county bank issued some one-dollar and two-dollar notes last year, and some five-dollar notes this year, and no one trusted those notes. Alice gave Mrs. Abercrombie strawberries from our garden in the spring and jam in the winter, and, at any rate, we were never without eggs. She glanced at me, and I waved to her. She waved back, and I might have told her about the play, but then her two girls ran out on the stoop, slammed the door, almost knocked Mrs. Abercrombie over, though it looked like she saved the eggs. She shouted, "You girls settle down or I'm gonna give you a whipping!" But I could tell they knew she wouldn't. They ran down the stoop and around the back of the house. Mrs. Abercrombie heaved herself up, wiped her hands on her apron, gave a sigh, and carried her basket of eggs into the house. I fingered my ticket and kept walking.

That evening, just like it was nothing, as if she had used no energy making the beds, shaking the blankets, sweeping the floors, and sorting through the vegetables, looking for rot, then making supper, Annie said, "I'm going to the rehearsal," and walked right out the front door, and no one made a peep. Alice and I did the supper dishes, and Fred just wiped his mouth and grunted. I understood then that I should have bought tickets for Fred and Larry, up there with me in the back. Alice's other boys were safely grown up – either married or employed, and in Quincy, which was a rowdy town, that was the best you could hope for. And then there was Harriet's boy, Frank. Harriet was bound and determined that Frank was not going to end up like me, and Alice and Beatrice agreed with her. They thought that clearly it fell to me that Frank had gone so astray in K.T. But when I saw him, he seemed glum to me, and resentful, and there was no seegar in evidence anymore. But he was quiet. He was reformed indeed, which I truly regretted. Yes, in K.T., he had been almost impossible to handle, and he had gotten into a good deal of trouble when he joined a gang of Mormon boys who had been kicked out of Utah. Maybe they had told Frank they were going back to Nauvoo, which wasn't far from Quincy, but what they really did in K.T. was try to steal what they could. They had some horses, but then the horses ate some poison hemlock, and three of them died, including Frank's. He had to walk back to Lawrence, and then Roland had made his way to K.T. and taken him back to Quincy. The only thing he'd said about those boys was that they had no idea what they were doing. I would like to have talked to him, to have found out more about his shenanigans, but also about what he thought about K.T., and all the issues we'd discovered there.

In the week that passed (with only one snowstorm) between Annie's presentation of the ticket to Alice and the first performance, Annie changed day by day into a girl I had never yet known. On the first day, Alice and I were sitting in the parlor, beside the window, doing some needlework – I was clumsily mending an old quilt so that it might get through one more winter, and Alice was neatly setting cuffs into Roland's Sunday jacket. Harriet should have been the one to do this, since she was Roland's wife, but she didn't have the needlework skills that Alice did, and since the death of our father, Alice had taken over some of Harriet's tasks. Roland had a habit of wiping his nose with the cuffs of his coat, and a coat is a nightmare to clean up, so Alice made the best of her abilities and replaced the cuffs whenever she had to. I don't know what Annie had been doing, but she must have been out of doors. She came into the parlor and tossed her gloves on the table and said that she needed money for a new pair – she was going to Lorton and Silk, and would Alice please give her the money. In a resonant voice, she said, "I am fed up with these old bits of rubbish. My hands nearly freeze off every time I go out."

Alice glanced at me and lifted her eyebrow, but she is, underneath all the remarks, a kindly soul, so she went to her drawer and took out some bills and put them in Annie's hand. Right then, Annie reverted back to the grateful and quiet self I'd always known. She took the money, blushed bright red, gave Alice a kiss on each cheek, and crept out of the room. The gloves she came home with were dark-brown kid, and went up under the sleeves of her coat. "Why not a muff?" muttered Alice. "A muff is warmer anyway." But she kept her opinion to herself, so as not, I think, "to encourage her." Alice and Harriet were great believers in not encouraging us.

The next day, Annie came to me when she was about to dress herself to go to her rehearsal, and beckoned me into her room, which was right beside mine – the two rooms had been one, but Roland had put a wall down the center, and, yes, they were small as could be, but private. Annie's was neatly dusted, and mine was not. She shut the door, took off the gown she was wearing, and said, "I want you to lace this corset as tight as you can."

I said, "It looks tight to me already. I can't imagine that you'll be able to say a word if it's any tighter."

It was a long corset, not like the one I wore, which Alice had made for me, just a lined cotton band with a loose waist and some tucks that held me up. Annie's went a good deal below the waist, with boning. She stared at me, then said, "The director says I need to cut a better figure." I supposed at the time that if I was going to collude in her stage career, such as it was, I had to collude fully, not hold back. She stood up, turned her back to me. I measured the distance between two edges of the corset, from between her shoulder blades down to her hips and then I pulled the strings. She put her hands around her waist and pushed in whatever flesh was there, which wasn't much. I pulled again. In the end, the two sides of the corset almost touched. I helped her get her gown on. Was she uncomfortable? She didn't admit to it, and, indeed, when she descended the staircase, her step was light. Late that night, though, when I helped her out of it, I saw bruises on her back, where the rods had poked her. She said she didn't feel them. I was glad that by Christmas Day she would no longer have to undergo what looked to me like torture, but, indeed, the whole experience reminded me of Lorna and Helen, the daughter of Lorna's "owner," Mr. Day. Helen was always pestering Lorna to pull it good and tight, and Lorna would roll her eyes and glance at me, as if to say, "Ah don' see no diff'rence, do you, missy?" and I would smile to myself, because I didn't see a difference, either, but Helen had to have her way, at least in small issues of vanity, and if Lorna or Mr. Day gave in, she was happy and agreeable about everything else.

The next morning, day three of Annie's transformation, I heard her through the wall between our chambers, talking in a peculiar voice. I put my ear to the wall and listened. Her tone went up and down, loud and soft, but the odd thing was the words: "Oi" for "I" and "Moi deah" for "My dear." When she said, "Dahhhling!" with a long trill, I laughed out loud, she heard me, and she fell silent. I waited for a moment, then knocked on her door. She opened it. She looked a bit abashed but also annoyed, and Annie never looks annoyed. I said, "Tell me."

"Tell you what? I'm practicing my lines."

"But you sound peculiar."

"That's my – " She tossed her head, took my hand, and drew me into her room, and, yes, she has the larger window. She'd gotten the pleasant side of the original chamber, and why shouldn't she? But I noticed. I always notice. She coughed, and said, "A fellow showed up for last night's rehearsal, all dolled up, I must say – top hat and everything. But it turned out that he's come from England, some town – what would it be? – oh, London? Have you heard of that town?"

I nodded. I might be the only person born in Quincy who has.

"He showed us how to talk the way the characters in the book talk, and it was terribly funny. Made us all laugh. But then Mr. Lake, that's the director, made us practice our lines talking that way, and" – her voice changed – "Oi must sy, it was a greet plaasure."

We both laughed, and after that I sat quietly on her (already made) bed and listened to her run through her lines. She got smoother with each try, and added in some facial expressions – joy, sadness, annoyance – that also would have made me laugh if I had let myself. I jumped off her bed, planted a good kiss on her cheek, and said, "I can't wait for this show! I can't wait! Already, it is whisking me right out of this place, this room, this town!" I ran out of the room and down the corridor with my arms in the air, pretending I was going to take off like a bird.

Later, I was standing in the kitchen, about midday, when Roland came storming in from somewhere, and when I say "storming," I don't mean that he was angry, only that he was covered with snow and dead leaves and waving his arms and talking a blue streak about something or other that I didn't pay any attention to until he said, "Lydia, girl, I need ya to come with me to the horse auction, cuz there's two steeds I've heard about just now, and you've got a good appreciation of horse flesh, better than my own, I admit, so git your shawl or your coat or whatever, because we got to git over there." I dried my hands on a rag and took my coat off the hook. I didn't say anything, but there's never a moment when I would refuse to look at a horse, or a pair, or a whole herd galloping down a hillside.

They were chestnuts, well matched, tall and brightly colored. But the bidding went higher than Roland could afford and they weren't cart horses, anyway, they were carriage horses, and, I thought, would be humiliated at the very sight of Roland's wagon.

The next day was a Saturday. I woke up thinking of the pair of chestnuts, and then I gave a sigh for my Jeremiah, who had indeed been curious. When I rode him, he was the one who kept a lookout, ears pricked in this direction or that, or one ear swiveling toward a noise I couldn't hear and the other pricked forward. But he had, as I did, a basic trust in humanity that turned out not to be justified by experience. It was a man who shot Thomas as he sat beside me in our cart, but it was a boy who shot Jeremiah, letting out a great exclamation of pleasure as Jeremiah collapsed in the traces. My gaze had spun from Thomas to the man to Jeremiah to the boy, even as Jeremiah's collapse pulled the reins from my hands. So my last sight of the killers was of the boy, maybe thirteen, thin, no facial hair, a look of happy triumph on his pale face, his mouth open in glee, a perfect demonstration that there is no innocent childhood, no inherent goodness to be perverted by experience. But I was tired of having every thought go down this road, so I took a deep breath and hoisted myself out of bed.

Annie had gotten up much earlier, quietly. She had cleaned up the fire pit and started the cooking fire, and was already serving the corn mush to Alice, Frederick, Fred, and Larry. I greeted them, sat down, got my helping, saw that I had missed the ham. Fred glanced at me as he forked his last bite between his lips, but I don't mind missing ham, and it looked as though there was no apple cake to miss – it must have been finished off the day before. Alice's apple cake is tasty indeed, but rare, so, as with all good things, we give thanks, but don't beseech. I ate my mush. Annie had stirred some bacon into it. After we cleaned up, Alice came in from the parlor and handed Annie a list of items she was to get from Lorton and Silk. I went back to my room to read a book I'd found that Thomas had once mentioned – *The Three Musketeers* – while there was some sunlight. A few chapters after Annie departed, Alice came into my room and handed me a note: I was to go after Annie to Lorton and Silk and pick up the trotters that Alice had forgotten to write down on Annie's list. Trotters were Frederick's (and Roland's) favorite Christmas treat (Roland said that that was a Brereton family habit), and though no one else liked them, Roland and Harriet were coming to town for services and so, as always, they would be served up on Christmas Day, at noon, along with some biscuits and the much-preserved fruitcake that Alice and Harriet put together in September and hid in the cellar for three months.

I put on my boots and my shawl, and wandered down 20th Street, glancing here and there; sure enough, when I turned onto Maine, there was Annie, and, lo and behold, her arm was tucked behind the arm of a well-dressed man who was walking along beside her, and her hips were swaying gracefully, and all of a sudden, she tossed back her head and gave a laugh that I had never heard out of my Annie's mouth – high and gay. I glanced around; the street was busy, and there were horses and carriages or wagons everywhere – the last Saturday before the last Sunday before Christmas, indeed – so I turned back up 20th, and scurried down Hampshire to 16th, then back to Maine. Because of the press of our citizens, Annie and her escort hadn't made it far – I could see them as soon as I turned the corner, laughing again. The transformation was this, that, in spite of her plain coat and her hair pulled back from her face, and her worn-out shoes, and a demeanor that I had never seen, and in some ways did not trust, she looked graceful and even beautiful, her eyes open and bright, her face flushed, her lips spread into a large and – how shall I say this? – well-constructed smile, a smile where the upper lip has two little peaks and the lower lip arcs downward, and there are the teeth, Annie's teeth, white and shiny. It wasn't a put-on smile, it was a truly happy and pleased smile. And then her hand, I saw, squeezed the wrist of her companion and they parted – she turned in to Lorton and Silk, and he kept walking, his stick dangling from his arm.

I paused long enough so that I could get close to him. I ran my gaze over his person. Forty, I would say, or slightly older, neatly made auburn curls cuddling about the nape of his neck, a very stylish bowler hat perched on the top of his head. He was shorter than me, dapper and trim, curled mustache, and everything about him said that if he *had* looked at me his gaze would have passed over me as over an unsightly shrub, untrimmed, uncared for, unimportant. I carried my note into Lorton and Silk, which was also jammed, and waited near the rack of spices and tobacco. I glanced around for Beatrice and Horace – Horace more or less ran Lorton and Silk, and Beatrice sometimes helped behind the till – but I didn't see them. Now Annie came walking in my direction. She was back to her old self, stepping aside for everyone else, performing her task, fading into the mêlée. As she paused, looking at her list, I said her name, and handed her the note. She read it, made a little face, then smiled at me. She said, "What money do you have?"

"Two bits, four bits, six bits, a dollar."

"Enough for some cabbage, then. I'll cook up some cabbage soup to go with the trotters. My papa hates cabbage soup." We shared a subversive roll of the eyes. I helped her find the other things, and we carried them home without saying much, just huddling against the north wind that had come up and was blowing in our faces.

The wind was not a good omen. Just before supper, a howling snowstorm blew in, and rattled the windows even after Alice closed the shutters. Once it was dark, the few candles we lit kept blowing out, so we all went to our rooms and snuggled under the coverlids, thinking our own thoughts – Annie, too, who must have assumed that her rehearsal was canceled. I passed my time imagining the thoughts the others were thinking (because I didn't want to imagine any of my own). Their thoughts were lifting out of their heads up to the ceiling and then shimmering through the roof and into the falling snow. Alice was thinking of the cellar – was there enough flour, barley, cornmeal, beans, dried meat, and cheese to last a month, should the house be buried under twenty feet of snow? Fred, I imagined, was doing what twelve-year-olds do, which was tiptoeing around the house, opening drawers and closets. Larry had crawled under his bed, and was imagining an ugly duckling wandering around in the snow. Harriet, on the farm, was wondering if Frank was truly in his bed, or if he'd sneaked out, only to find himself frozen in the snow, his feet blocks of ice, and how long might he live as the snow covered his face? The tip of Frank's nose was poking out, then Frank himself curled downward and made his way through the snow as if he were swimming (and all the boys in Quincy are good swimmers; I was, too. We just couldn't help ourselves). This thought led me to Frank. I imagined him rolled up in his quilt, keeping warm, rolling back and forth, over and over, getting himself dizzy just as a way of passing the time until it was truly dark and he knew that everyone was sleeping. It was then that he would creep out the door and swim into the snow, all the way to the river and across to – But then I stopped my imaginings, because I never cared to imagine Missouri.

I fell asleep before I got to Annie, perhaps because Annie was so quiet, even though right next to me, as it were, but then I woke up in the deep dark, no telling what time it was, and I had rolled onto my stomach so that my ear was right beside the wall. I could hear her sobbing, soft but sure – sob, sob, then a sniffle, then sob, sob, then a very quiet blowing of her nose. I imagined that she had sneaked out to meet that man in the darkness and that: (1) He had revealed the wife who would soon be arriving from wherever he lived. (2) He had frozen to death because he had no idea what to do with himself in a snowstorm. (3) He had made a mistake and spoken to her in his true language, which was Kentuck all the way down to the ground, and then he'd offered to marry her and take her off to (what might be the worst place in all the world?) Texas. I didn't want to invade her room and demand to know what was going on, as Alice might have done, so I lay quietly in my bed until long after she stopped crying and, I suppose, fell asleep.

When I went to breakfast, she was herself, and the snow was hardly to the windowsills. After we ate, Fred and I went out and shoveled a way to the street, and also the back stoop and some of the back area. The sun was bright, the air was cold, and Alice did say that there were plenty of provisions, whatever might happen. Late in the day, we walked out to church – this time the Congregational church, which Harriet preferred – which was closer to the house than the Methodist church that Alice preferred, or the breakaway Methodist church that Roland preferred. Everyone preferred the church that their friends attended. We walked carefully in the snow, and got there in time for the sermon and a few hymns; as we walked home, I sidled up to Annie and took her arm. I said, "Tell me how you are, my dear. I heard you weeping in the night."

She glanced at me as if she didn't know what I was talking about, then said, "Ah, Lidie, yes, that was in the morning, terribly early, because I got to sleep right when we went to our rooms and then woke up well before dawn. So I whiled away the time practicing my scene. I was trying different forms of weeping. I see," she said with a cocky look, "that you were convinced! Thank you." And she brushed my cheek with a sweet kiss.

By Monday, the snow was just something that had to be dealt with. I spent about two hours in the morning pushing it here and there, mostly because the weather was warm enough to melt it a bit. I swept the walks as clean as I could, because sunset would turn the melt into ice. Annie left as I was finishing up – two rehearsals today, to make up for the lost one. She tripped along, waved gaily to us as she headed down 20th Street. I thought, "She has earned her freedom."

I wished I might follow her and see what this rehearsal process was. I was indeed grateful that she was drawing me out of myself. After the shoveling, I helped Alice with various tasks – balling wool, dusting the parlor, sorting through the potatoes, looking for sprouts and green patches. Potatoes are poisonous, according to Alice, and it's a shame they've become so essential, but if you are vigilant, you might survive a serving of fried potatoes one more time. Frederick liked potatoes at every meal, so that was a serious breach in their marriage; Alice yielded but was vigilant. We checked on the fruitcake twice. It was fine both times. Alice was sure that the rats in the cellar were after it, and even that they had moved the tin she'd stored it in. I could see it – Christmas loomed, and therefore Alice sensed danger in every dark corner. Frederick set the traps. Alice wouldn't even look at them, but as we wandered about the cellar, I saw that the rats were in greater danger than the fruitcake. We washed up very carefully when we came out of the cellar, and so, of course, as we were washing, Alice shook her head and lamented how quickly the yellow fever might be coming up the river from New Orleans, and we wouldn't know about it until we were done for, and did I remember the cholera six years ago – fifteen people in Quincy, hideous way to go, but what isn't? People always commended their luck in living by this river, this famous busy river, though it was muddy and got much too warm in the summer. Of course, there were plenty of goods to buy and people to meet, and you could take a steamboat just about anywhere, if you really wanted to, but who did? Once you'd been to St. Louis and seen that rabble – well! Alice shook her head.

I said, "Being shot by a Border Ruffian isn't as bad as someone watching you being shot."

She sighed and looked at me, and I could tell she was thinking that I'd brought that upon myself, but it was not her place to say it. She did stop talking about epidemics.

I was amazed that, as old as she was – fifty-three now – she still had any fears left. I thought they would have been battered out of her long ago.

What I learned about Annie on this day, Monday, two days before the first performance, was that the whole time I had been gallivanting about, either off to Kansas or running around our town like a restless dog, Annie had been not only doing the work, but also listening to Alice (and Harriet, too) unload their worries and fears and concerns and opinions and judgments, and she had hardly said a word in response. I saw now that it was not because she couldn't talk, or didn't like to talk, it was because no one, not even her own folks, not even I, Lidie, inquired after her views, and, sure enough, she had plenty of them.

That evening, maybe because she'd sparked her own fears for Annie's safety, Alice sent both Fred – because, even at twelve, he was rather tall and sturdy – and me to bring her home from the theater. It was true that Maine Street was full of rowdies, though it wasn't much past eight, according to the church bells that rang while we walked. The saloons were wide open, and carts and men on horses were running hither and thither.

Annie was a bit affronted when she came out the door of the theater and there we were, but she, too, was intimidated by the crowds. She and I linked arms and walked just behind Fred, who didn't hesitate to elbow his way through the press, and of course Alice had been fearing the worst, and had to pat her brow with her kerchief after she welcomed us into the house. But she had made some lovely chamomile tea from the store of dried chamomile in the cellar, and as I drank it, I wondered why this day of all days had seemed so lengthy. I saw, of course, that it was because of the housework, and I thought that, even though I was obliged to, as a female, I was not going to prolong my life in that way.

Tuesday was the day of the dress rehearsal, to take place at the same time of day as the play would be presented on Wednesday, that is, beginning at eight o'clock, though Annie had to be there, corseted and ready, by seven. Alice gave her some supper around five, and then I heard her marching around her room, saying her lines in some sort of accent, though how was I to know whether it was truly Dickensian? At half past six, she knocked on the wall between our rooms, and I knew what she wanted – I went in and tightened her corset until she gasped and had me stop. Then she closed her eyes and took some deep breaths, and she said, "You know, Edgar Smedley, who's playing Scrooge, he's wearing a corset, too, because Scrooge has to look as though he's been a skinflint even with himself. He's done some stage work in Springfield, and he had a small part in something in St. Louis. He says actors corset themselves as a rule." I didn't ask if Edgar Smedley wore a bowler hat and affected an English accent when he was simply walking around Quincy. By then she was talking normally, even a little boomingly – she was thrusting her jaw out a bit, and her words emerged rounded and full, as if they would float anywhere, including all the way up to the back of the hall, where I would be sitting the next evening. She also told me that women acting women's parts was rather a new thing, at least in England. In all of those plays by that fellow William Shakespeare, boys played the women's parts. Then she surveyed me up and down and said, "I wish I looked like you. I would play the men and the women. The men's parts are so much more varied." Then she deepened her voice, and one of the men's lines from the play rolled out: "If these shadows remain unaltered by the Future, none other of my race will find him here. What then? If he be like to die, he had better do it, and decrease the surplus population."

"Who says that?"

"The Ghost of Christmas Present, talking to Scrooge."

"Sounds like a Border Ruffian."

Annie wriggled into her gown, handsome and shiny, but with evidence that it had been taken apart and sewn back together many a time, as a costume would be, I suppose. I helped her with the back fastenings, and then, maybe because he needed to get off the farm, Frank showed up to take her to the theater, and he was instructed to stay there and under no circumstances leave. He nodded. I supposed that someone would do her hair and pin on her cap once she got to the theater. After she left, I contemplated how naturally she did it all – dressing, speaking, preparing herself, heading out into the evening darkness, giving Alice a peck on the cheek and me a conspiratorial smile. By the time she and Frank returned (he would spend the night with Fred and Larry, whose room was a large one), I had put myself to sleep reading *The Pathfinder,* which I'd found on the bottom shelf of one of my father's old bookcases, dusty but, I had hoped, promising, since I had long ago enjoyed a book by the same author told from the point of view of a pocket kerchief. I'd only read a few parts of that one, in some old journals, but it made me laugh. This one did not, but it gave me a good sleep, and so I was bright and alert the next night, when I went by myself, took my ticket, and found my seat.

I would have said that I had nothing left to learn about Annie. My sole intention was to watch the play, enjoy the story, which I might have read if I'd been able to find the volume anywhere. As I remember, Thomas had read two of Mr. Dickens's works, *David Copperfield* and *Oliver Twist,* but he left the copies behind in Medford when he came with the Emigrant Aid Company and the Sharps carbines to our neck of the woods. I remembered that he had enjoyed the works, but then I put him gently out of my mind and stared at the stage. The lights went down, and the play began.

If I'd had any ambitions as an actress, I would have chosen to play one of the ghosts. There are four of them. The first one, Scrooge's former partner, came banging onto the stage dragging chains. He was short, with a big belly and a booming voice, and no wonder Edgar Smedley looked terrified enough so that I doubted whether he was acting. I looked around the stage and suddenly remembered a moment of that production of *Dombey and Son* Annie and I had seen before I went to K.T. One of the actors was holding up a candle, and just before the curtain caught fire, another of the actors noticed, and, smooth as silk, stepped over and moved the first actor's arm. I could have played the second ghost, the Ghost of Christmas Past. The fellow who played him wore a long gown and had a high voice. He took Scrooge to his first employer, who was a kindly man, and Annie appeared very briefly, her hair done beautifully and a happy look on her face, when she and Scrooge were falling in love, and then, maybe ten minutes later, here came Annie again, for her big scene, she alone with the young man that she, apparently, had set her cap for. But it was not to be. Scrooge was now a miser. It was a long scene, where she tells Scrooge that money has changed him for the worse, and she is breaking their engagement. Annie said,

"If this had never been between us, would you seek me out and try to win me now?" She shook her head and looked down, then said softly, and yet loudly enough for everyone in the theater to hear, "Ah, no!" She put her face in her hands.

Edgar Smedley was looking at her, then turned his face to the audience. He looked not sad, but angry and insulted. I was impressed. As for their Dickensian accents, they did the best they could.

But my surprise was in the third part, where Scrooge gets his just due – he is shown what happens after he dies, how no one cares for anything except his money. And there was Annie, not onstage, but in the wings, sobbing. The sound of weeping gave that scene a truly eerie feeling, much more so since Edgar Smedley played it up a bit, cocking his head toward the sound from time to time, shaking it off, hearing it again. The ghost shows him the horror, but the grief of Annie's sobs convinces him of the sadness.

The show was a big success, and there were four curtain calls. Annie, as the youngest of the three actresses, got some shouts and some hoorays, and she did a thing that I'd never seen her do: she lifted her chin, smiled that huge smile, and "acknowledged" the praise, which was not the same as being grateful for it. Something in her demeanor told us all that she knew she deserved it. And the applause got louder. Edgar Smedley turned toward her, took her hand, kissed it. She tipped her head, and then the curtain came down the last time.

I made my way out of the theater slowly. I wanted to hear what people had to say, especially since the citizens of Quincy can be very particular. But almost everyone was happy and satisfied. The worst thing I heard about Annie was, "Now, there was a girl I never expected that sort of thing from." I glanced toward the speaker. It was a woman who lived in our neighborhood whom I'd never spoken to. She went on, "Such a quiet girl as a rule." Then the woman clucked and gave her companion, who looked like her own daughter, perhaps, a sweet embrace around the shoulders, and I saw that maybe her daughter was also a quiet thing, and Annie was being cited as a model. A few people who knew me smiled and nodded. As I walked along, the thing I was most grateful for was that the play, and watching Annie onstage, had driven K.T., Thomas, Jeremiah, and Lorna completely out of my head for several hours. And then there was Alice, up and peeping out the door when I got home. She said, "Oh, my heavens! How did it go?"

I told her about the show and about Annie's success, and Alice closed her eyes and said, "Thank the Lord! I was so afraid."

"Of the theater burning down?"

"Heavens, no! Of the gossip! What would they say about my child exposing herself like that, and of me allowing it? Aghh." Then she grabbed my shoulders and kissed me on the cheek and said, "If you do something like this and your neighbors like it, then you needn't worry ever again, because your neighbors are your worst critics. If you can impress them, you can impress anyone."

She was entirely serious, and, I thought, entirely correct, and the next night, Annie managed to impress Frederick, Harriet, and Alice, and Roland, too, though he swore up and down that he couldn't understand a word they were saying. On Christmas morning, as Annie and I were carrying buckets of water into the kitchen for the day's cleanup, she happily told me about the various tiny ways that she had changed her presentation between the first performance and the last one in order to give her character more feeling. And she did not envy the woman who had played Fan, Scrooge's sister, even though she had the death scene, and everyone who goes onstage loves a death scene. Fan had drawn it out so long both nights that the other actors were vexed. Annie talked to me about the show for maybe four days, and then, I think, she finally realized that it was over. On New Year's Day, Edgar Smedley showed up, and Annie asked him in for tea. He was off to Indianapolis, he said, having landed a part in a brand-new play about a shipwreck that had just had a very profitable run in New York, and companies all over the country wanted to try it. Edgar Smedley said, "There are four women's roles. I wish . . ."

But then he didn't go on. I wondered if Annie felt as I did—I'd heard of Indianapolis, but I could not begin to imagine what it might be like there. Nor did I ask her about that most mysterious character, the man with the accent and the bowler hat. I feared that, given her demeanor when I saw them walking together, she had hoped to attract him and he had betrayed her. I hadn't seen him in the play or at the theater. To think of the way she'd squeezed his hand and walked along laughing and close against him made me think of Thomas, made me think that true love is fated to be destroyed, made me think that what lasts are these marriages like Harriet and Roland's, where the husband spends all of his time out of doors and the wife manages the household, and if they can remember one another's names, that's the best you can hope for. I knew very little of Alice's marriage except that this small house in town where I now lived was once a chaos of boys, and whether she and her husband, Frederick, ever said a word to one another back then, I didn't know. These days, Frederick was still a rather impatient man, especially with the two boys, and so perhaps Alice was relieved that there wasn't much communication. I thought of my own child. I might have been standing here, looking down at my own giant belly, or I might have been sitting in a chair, listening to Alice give me advice that I should have, but would not have, paid attention to. I remembered thinking that when I lost the baby I lost every aspect of my relationship to Thomas. What did I wish had happened? And then I thought that the baby might have died after being born, as my six brothers and sisters had. I sighed. Indeed, the unending depths of January, with nothing to look forward to, do induce you to think as little as possible, because the thoughts that draw you are as dark as the winter landscape.

Once or twice, I imagined spring pulling me back to Independence, where I would find Thomas's killers and give them their due, but most of the time, I didn't know what to imagine, though I did get into the habit of saying a little prayer for Thomas and a little prayer for Lorna before I fell asleep and after I woke up. And then, one night, I heard Annie talking through the wall, and the next morning, when she was off to Lorton and Silk, I sneaked into her room and found a bound copy of a play beside her bed. It was entitled *The Willow Copse*. I read a bit of it – lots of words like "Nay!" and "Pray, tell me," and "ye." Of course Annie would be interested. I set it where I'd found it, carefully, leaving no evidence. But I did listen to her for the next three nights, attempting both the men's dialogue and the women's. That she had gotten the play from someone reminded me of the small lending library in Quincy, and I did go there and borrow a Charles Dickens book, not *A Christmas Carol*, but one Thomas never mentioned, *The Old Curiosity Shop*. It took some getting used to, but eventually it drew me in, not so much the story as the words and how I could use them to imagine a place completely unlike K.T., or even Quincy. Thinking of those words and settings let me forget that, exactly two years ago, the death of my father and the appearance of Thomas Newton were unforeseen, unexpected. The nature of my life then, right here in this room, was simply dreary and dull, and all I'd looked forward to had been crocuses and then daffodils and then lilacs. I knew I had nothing to look forward to now, but I kept reading in order not to think of that.

2

HORACE AND HIS FATHER, who owned Lorton and Silk (Mr. Silk was long gone), no longer posted those bills about K.T. that I had found alluring – lovely villages on perfect hillsides with all the amenities one might care to have, villages that had sprung up mysteriously all over K.T. once the Kiowa and the Osage were driven off. We all knew better now, and not only those of us who'd been there. Horace, too, had been fascinated with the idea of K.T., and after I came back, he asked me a few friendly questions. I told him what I knew – that is, what had happened to me and Thomas (though nothing about Lorna) – and he lamented that everyone, including the Emigrant Aid Company, had gone about things so clumsily. Look at Illinois. In Illinois, all sorts of folks got along, didn't they?

Once in a while I dared to pay a bit of heed to events in K.T. – I looked at the papers in a vain attempt to see if the friends I'd left behind had been killed. The Emigrant Aid Company did report killings, but news of them only showed up in Massachusetts. Perhaps papers in Quincy didn't dare to say much about K.T. – Geary, a man whose first name I didn't know, who was very young but had already straightened things out in gold country, had been sent by President Pierce to cool things down in K.T., and maybe he did. Two things were said of him in Quincy – that he had single-handedly prevented a band of Border Ruffians from burning Lawrence to the ground (How many? Five? Five thousand? Reports differed) and that he had turned away a considerable sum of money that some d — ned abolitionists sent to their colleagues in Lawrence to help them get through the winter (Five thousand? Fifty thousand? Once again, reports differed). But if you wanted to talk about K.T. in Quincy, you kept your voice down and your eye out for eavesdroppers. For my own sake, I didn't bring up the subject, and as much as I could, I stopped myself from looking for the face of that boy who had shot Jeremiah. No reason on earth for that boy to be in Quincy, but once in a while, I imagined seeing him from behind, walking up to him, and throttling him to death right there on the street. This was about as believable as the sight of Jeremiah trotting down 20th Street, looking for me and whinnying; we all have our fantasies, especially in January.

Some folks said, though, that Geary had gone completely over to the Free State side, and had sent a bill to the President proposing that K.T. be admitted to the Union as a free state, with its capital in Topeka, but it was impossible to ascertain if this was true or not. And that is all that I will say about Kansas, as anyone who might be reading this narrative will already know the outcome.

It was a cold winter. Roland complained that his stock of hay was smaller than it had been the year before, and he was beset with indecision – whom could he best do with less, horses or cows? The horses produced the energy that ran the farm, and the cows produced the product that would keep the farm in business. There'd been cold winters before, but he was d — ned if he remembered what he had decided then. Why was it that every year on a farm was completely new?

Beatrice kept quiet about how Lorton and Silk was thriving. If you were a citizen of Quincy, and you had a few bits to spend, you would spend it. Highly rectified whiskey, it was said, at least made you feel warm while you were freezing to death. On the coldest night, when the temperature got so low that Annie and I huddled together under all of the coverlids we could find, with stockings on, and gloves, too, a boy did freeze to death down by the river, and when some folks found his mother roaming about, searching for him, she said that he'd been out looking for some wood, anything he could find, and she'd known he shouldn't be doing that, but she had three little ones – what else might she have done?

The next morning, when I got up sometime after Annie did because I was dead asleep and she is the quietest girl in the world, so I didn't hear her leaving to stoke the cooking fire in the kitchen, I noticed an envelope lying on the floor of her room, half pushed under her chest. I of course picked it up and of course turned it over. There were many postage stamps on it, and I therefore looked at the return address, and there was the word "England," though not "London," but, rather, "Liverpool," and where that was I had no idea. My fingers trembled, but I refrained from removing the sheet of paper from the envelope, and instead pushed it back under the chest, upside down. Perhaps my unspoken question about the man in the bowler hat was answered, and perhaps, in order to know the answer, I would have to speak my question aloud, but days went by, and the weather warmed a bit, at least enough for a good snowstorm, and I said nothing.

On the Sunday after the snowstorm, Beatrice said that she'd heard from some shoppers at Lorton and Silk that the graveyard where our father was buried had suffered some fallen branches in the bad weather, and that we had to go down there and see if the headstones of our mothers and our father were dislocated or damaged. Except for a prayer or two at Christmas, we never said a word about our father from one day to the next. He was eighty-two when he died (he was thirty-three years older than my mother, his second wife, and, indeed, a good deal older than his first wife, though how many years exactly I never knew). He was three years old in 1776, his own father survived the War of Independence, and he'd been born in the place that eventually became New Jersey, but that was all we knew about him other than his name, Arthur Harkness. Some families have fathers who tell stories and joke about all their escapades, good and bad, but not so Mr. Harkness. Did he have anything to cover up? We never heard any rumors about that, either. He was like a long storm that has come and gone, leaving no visible trace.

We made our way, the three sisters with Frank in the lead, carrying a shovel and a pick. Harriet walked in front with Beatrice; I walked slightly behind Alice, carrying the broom. Beatrice greeted everyone, Harriet had a thing or two to say, and Alice nodded and smiled to the women that Beatrice greeted, but not the men – Alice is always suspicious, and says that you must be, with all the drunks, cheats, and grifters who float up and down the river. "Quincy is prosperous and therefore a . . ." And I don't remember what else she said. I looked down, because the muddy streets were frozen and slippery and I seemed to be more worried than my sisters about slipping and falling. Seeing Frank from behind was interesting, too, all shoulders now and big feet, hunched forward with his tools in his left hand.

In the summer and especially in the fall, the graveyard was a pleasant one, overlooking the river, planted with trees, full of grass and plenty of weeds, like dandelions and clover, which I liked. Some of the ladies belonging to the churches nearby (it was far from our house, but the one that my father preferred for his own wives) tended it like a garden, so it had patches of jonquils and irises in the spring, and a threesome of lilac trees. I'd walked there several times on my restless treks about town, but even though I knew where the Harkness gravestones were, I didn't visit them. The wives' stones were low and square, with their names etched in, and their birth and death dates, but nothing more. I gave Mr. Harkness the benefit of the doubt, and thought that that was what he could afford when they died. Beatrice and Horace could afford more, so my father's stone was a white spire, maybe four feet tall, set into a white square. On the side facing the river were his name and dates, and on the left side a quote, "Lord have mercey upon my soul, Amen." And if there was a Lord, I hoped he had. Thomas's remains went back to Medford. His gravestone read, "For the Lord loves the just and will not forsake his faithful ones," all words spelled correctly and, perhaps coincidentally, facing south, and for some reason, I found those words comforting. I was fond of graveyards, because they were as well tended and fragrant as parks, but also almost empty of visitors.

Father's gravestone was tilting slightly – perhaps we'd not have noticed the tilt if we hadn't been looking for it. The soil above the river was wet. Our mothers' stones were covered with icy snow, and I helped Frank shovel and sweep it away. We looked up at the limbs of the nearest chestnut tree. One had broken off, and another was cracked. The one that had broken off was a few feet from the grave; we dragged it closer to the trunk of the tree. The cracked one seemed more of a threat, but it was twelve or fourteen feet off the ground, and no one understood what to do with it. My sisters walked around and looked up; Beatrice kept glancing toward Frank, as if he were still that wild boy who would clench his seegar between his lips and run up the tree like a squirrel, but Frank paid no attention, except to gauge the height of the branch and, I saw in his face, decide that he couldn't reach it. If I had been on Jeremiah, I might have – but then I averted my gaze from that thought and surveyed the graveyard. A few stones had been knocked over. It became clear that my sisters hadn't made their way to the graveyard to do what they could for the gravestone, but, rather, to discuss Annie, and they did, not knowing or perhaps caring that I was eavesdropping. Perhaps my task was to tell her what they were saying?

Alice began by saying that Annie wasn't as attentive to her household tasks as she had been, and of course this was a bad sign because . . .

As Beatrice said, would she ever find a husband in Quincy, because . . .

As Harriet said, . . . the prospects for a husband, a *respectable husband,* were slim at best, what . . .

As Beatrice said, did she have to offer? No dowry, of course, who had that, and no . . .

As Alice said, Skin and bones.

I thought of how tightly I had laced her, how beautiful she had seemed on the stage. I opened my mouth. Alice glanced at me, and the look on her face said, Well, if Lidie can find a husband, perhaps . . .

And Beatrice said, No thought of anything besides . . .

And Harriet said, Frivolous, frivolous. She glanced at Alice.

And then there was silence.

But no, I thought, the girl in the show who delivers that news to Mr. Scrooge that he has lost her love through greed and selfishness, and her sadness has changed her forever, cannot be frivolous. I opened my mouth again, but I didn't know what to say. They had been at the play. If they hadn't seen it, how could I describe it?

Alice said, Most young men find spouses in their congregations. Perhaps. But which congregation, I thought, Alice's easygoing one, Harriet's harsher one, or Beatrice's congregation of merchants?

Now Harriet glanced at Alice and Alice glanced at me, and all three of them eased away from me, but of course they underestimated my eavesdropping abilities. I stayed where I was, staring down at the gravestone of a woman named Martha Abernathy and her five babies, Ethan, Edna, Elliot, Ethel, and Edith, all born between 1849 and 1854 (and Martha's death date was the same as Ethan's) with my ears pricked. The name Beatrice came up with was Johann Krebsner, a man from Germany, but . . .

Alice said, Germans are very industrious, however isn't he . . .

Harriet said, . . . actually from Switzerland?

Everyone tossed their heads: What did such a thing matter?

Johann Krebsner was known about town – a tall man with a hook nose, some funds, whose origins might or might not have been in Switzerland, and who had relatives in Ohio – Columbus, Cincinnati.

Beatrice said, I admit that he is a bit . . .

Harriet said, . . . hard to please, but what man . . .

Alice said, . . . is not?

Thomas, I thought, and bit my lips, not wanting to make any sort of cry.

Harriet said, Our Annie is surely not . . .

Beatrice said, . . . going to make up to him. His feet are unusually large.

And I turned my head to hide my smile. In the distance, Frank was industriously shoveling snow off of gravestones, and a hawk rose from the top of one of the maple trees and was swept westward over the river, wings spread and dark against the clouds.

Beatrice said, decidedly, She has to do something. This itch . . .

Harriet said, . . . she has for the . . .

But no one said the word "theater."

Beatrice said, Herr Krebsner would . . .

Alice said, . . . quash *that*.

And then they nodded and sniffed, and moved back toward me.

Harriet said, in a louder voice, "Well, first things first, back to work." That afternoon, Harriet told me that I was to come out to the farm to live. She said, "Roland needs some help with the horses." So there was the carrot rather than the stick.

It took me four days to alert Annie to their plan, because I thought their conversation had been so idle that it wasn't in fact a plan. But on Sunday we walked to Beatrice's church, the Congregational one, which alerted me, as well as the fact that, though Alice didn't tell Annie how to dress, my three sisters more or less herded her down Vermont Street to the church. The best thing about the Congregational church, other than the building, which was tall and thin, odd-looking for Quincy, was the choir, well known to have the best director. I paid attention to the hymns until, during the "Gloria," about the time when everyone was announcing, "You are seated at the right hand of the Father," I saw a man across the aisle and two pews ahead of ours turn his head several times and look toward us. At first I didn't recognize him, but then I did – about my height, twice my weight, long coat, dark hair parted down the middle, enormous mustache, small eyes. Johann Krebsner. He did the responses in a booming voice that caused the woman sitting beside him to edge away. I looked at Annie. She yawned, covered her mouth, then sang along to the next hymn, "Rock of Ages." Krebsner did, too. He had a melodious voice. I judged him to be about thirty or so, maybe ten years older than Annie, three or four years older than Thomas had been when he came to Quincy with his case of Sharps rifles. The next hymn, after a pleasantly short sermon, was "Amazing Grace," which Thomas had told me was by an Englishman who had turned away from the slave trade some years ago. Krebsner knew this one, too, and the fact that this congregation sang that hymn with such verve indicated their opinions on the goose question. Maybe, as a Swiss, Krebsner knew what he was singing, and maybe he did not, but I began to think that my sisters' plan was not so bad. Annie didn't know all of the words to "Amazing Grace," and neither did I, but, thinking of Thomas, I mouthed them as best I could. "I once was lost, but now am found." Well, not really, but maybe someday.

I counted the times that Krebsner looked at Annie, and gauged how he responded to what she did. When she fiddled with her bodice or her skirt, he glanced away. When she sang, he watched her. When she yawned during the sermon, he smiled, and it wasn't a bad smile. When Beatrice coughed and Annie handed her a kerchief, he nodded approvingly. Annie didn't notice him even for a second. She was looking at the choir, at the preacher, at the building, at me. He did not come up to us after the service – perhaps she hadn't passed muster, as Roland would say – but my sisters did let her walk her own way back to Alice's house – down Maine Street rather than Vermont. The weather was now rather pleasant. We were still wearing our gloves, but we could unwrap the shawls we were wearing around our caps. I didn't open up until we were almost home. Then I said, "Did you notice that fellow who kept looking at you?"

Annie said, "No. What fellow?"

"He was across the aisle, two pews toward the front."

"That mustache?"

"Yes."

"He kept looking at me? I didn't notice that."

I tried, "I thought he was a presentable sort."

She tossed her head. I remembered the letter under the chest, the man in the bowler hat. I suspected that Annie wasn't as worried about her fate as my sisters were, and so I blurted out, "Beatrice has picked that fellow for your husband!"

Annie stopped and stared at me, then walked on. I don't know what I expected, but that she would say nothing wasn't it. Nor, indeed, did she say a word about it for the next week. And Herr Krebsner didn't show up at the house, either. Roland did, to tell me over a pleasant supper that, once the snow cleared, he would be ready to start his three-year-olds, two in the traces and one under saddle, and how he ended up with three of them he couldn't tell me. He'd kept trying to sell the saddle horse, but then no one offered what Roland thought she was worth, and the two driving horses were so mild-mannered that he could get more for them if they were finished, and the market was, indeed, improving, but any number of horses is too many, and all together, with the plow horses and his own pair and the broodmares, he had ten, and he was a d—ned fool, was what he was. Though, judging by his demeanor as he talked, a happy fool.

By now it was mid-February, and the weather suddenly let up. I enjoyed going down to the bluff above the river and watching the sun sparkle on the ice. The Mississippi doesn't ice over every year, but sometimes the ice is so thick that people drive their carts to the other side and back. There was a story going around that a few years ago the ice was so thick that a train with some cargo to unload up north at a town called Moline went right over the ice to a barge that was stuck there, and unloaded the cargo, then backed up to the track again. But, like most stories in this neck of the woods, you can believe it or not, whatever you wish. This year, the ice was deep enough to stop the riverboats, to skate on, and, for some people, to drive their sleighs across, but it was beginning to break up. I could see some boys hopping here and there and laughing, but I heard no cracking, and the boys didn't seem in danger. Quincy loved it when the ice broke up, and Horace and Beatrice did, too, because commerce resumed and they could stop twiddling their thumbs and wondering when they might run out of bolts of cloth and boxes of boots.

One of those days, I was walking home. There's a pleasant upright brick house that no one talks about anymore where Dr. Eels lived, who got in trouble for harboring slaves who crossed the river. He passed on a few years later. He was fined a lot of money; thanks to the mercy of Mr. Day, I was not, but when I walked past that house, I thought of Lorna and pondered about why it is criminal to save a life and not criminal to destroy a life. I didn't recall that Helen treated Lorna like a slave – she treated her like an older sister to be evaded and argued with – but, as I learned during Lorna's and my attempted escape, how Lorna was treated was not what she cared about. She ached to get to her husband, who, she thought, had bought his freedom, to live on her own, and to have a say. And if I didn't understand that right down to the ground, I wouldn't be me. Just thinking of Lorna gave me a sick feeling – no telling where she was now. Slavery seemed to me to be a deadly disease, no matter how much Senator Douglas and all his ilk went on and on about this great nation. Anyone who might have known Lorna, including Mr. Day (everyone called him "Papa"), would have understood that she was as smart as a whip and as canny about such things as how to grow and fertilize and harvest and make do and put together and maintain as anyone else, or more so. You could close your eyes and ask Lorna a question, and if she felt like it, she would answer you in her own talk, or in Papa's talk, easy as you please. A few times, I found her in the pantry reading a book (and, I have to say, no one minded that). So why did she have to be told what to do all the time and then sold down the river because she didn't like it? She was pretty, too, with a better figure than mine and a riveting look in her eye that said a thousand things in one glance. Some ruffian could have told me a hundred times about the Bible and Canaan and I wouldn't have believed a word of it. When I looked around our town, I could see that every church had a different tale that resulted in the members of *that* church prevailing over the members of all the other churches. I thought that if you proposed to do evil in the name of the Lord, then you soiled His name, indeed, but I kept that to myself, too.

At any rate, I had these thoughts as I was passing Dr. Eels's old house, and then, in the park, I saw Annie, all by herself, and she had a letter in her hand. I paused and watched her. She read it top to bottom, then turned it, read the crossing lines, flipped it over, finished it, started again. She bit her lips, smiled, put the letter in her bag, and walked across the park to Hampshire Street. I caught up with her at the corner of 8th Street. I didn't say a word, even about the weather – in Quincy, we always begin a conversation with a remark or two about the weather. But I just walked along beside her. It seemed to me that she was bursting with something that she didn't dare mention. She walked in an erratic manner, sometimes putting her hand on my forearm and then taking it away, sometimes glancing toward me, and then up the street. But we got to Alice's, and Alice was beside herself about the dishes, so we went to work.

The next day was pleasant, too. Roland appeared first thing in the morning on his gray horse, leading the older bay, all saddled up, and he lured me out to his place to look at the youngsters and have a talk about how we would set about starting them. I was tired and also lulled. I got home late, went to bed, slept like a rock, and did not hear what was going on in Annie's room.

The thing that surprised me when I passed the door to her room was seeing Annie's chest, normally pushed against the wall beside her window, now, though still closed, dragged away from the wall, a little skewed to the left. When I came to the top of the staircase, I knew that Annie was making her escape. At the bottom of the staircase, in the spot Alice called "the tea room," really a small nook with a round table pushed into the corner, Alice was eating a bit of cake and drinking some tea, reading a paper. Annie came to her with the pot; Alice waved her away with her finger, didn't even look up, then sighed. Alice said, "Goodness me, well, I guess it has to be done."

I said, "What is that?"

Alice said, "You might get up at a decent time, Lidie."

I said, "I might."

Alice said, "Frank has been giving his teacher a bit of trouble. I promised Beatrice I would go to the schoolhouse and sit in, since she has more work to do."

"Why would he give the fellow trouble if you or Beatrice were around to keep an eye on him?"

"That's the very thing I said, but Mr. Sallow wouldn't take no for an answer. So much of this life seems like a vain endeavor, if you ask me."

I said, "Don't let Beatrice give up on Frank."

Alice shook her head.

I said, "All day?"

"That's what they wish."

She tossed back the last bit of tea, hoisted herself out of her chair, and made her way to the parlor. I stood there. A few minutes later, the front door closed, and I went into the kitchen. Annie was wiping the dishes with a clean rag. I said, "Take me with you." I did not say, You are my escape from these last two years, but I did have a fleeting picture of Thomas's face and Lorna's face receding into the distance.

Annie set the cup she'd been wiping on the shelf, draped the rag over the back of a chair. Then came the surprise. She said, "I've been wondering how to ask you, but I didn't dare."

"Because you thought I would tell Alice."

"No, because I didn't dare speak aloud what I wanted to keep as my secret."

"When are we leaving?"

"It has to be today. Alice will be gone for four or five hours. The Aurora has a car to Chicago at one."

I said, "Where are we getting the funds? I have almost nothing."

Annie said, "Mallory sent them."

I said, "Who is Mallory?"

"Mallory Cunningham, my investor."

I made myself shut my mouth, which was hanging open.

"He believes I have good prospects on the English stage." She tossed her head. "No, he is not my suitor. He has a wife and several 'offspring,' as he calls them. But he runs a theater company in Liverpool. He doesn't want me to travel unaccompanied, so I told him that you would come with me, that you are an experienced traveler and can handle both a horse and a pistol if need be."

"Did he send you a pistol?"

"No. I bought one. He's a generous man."

"Does he wear a bowler hat?"

Now Annie laughed. "Yes! He does! So put your things together.

I'll write Alice a note. Likely, she'll be happy to be shed of us once she thinks it over."

I thought about Roland's horses, but the only thing I said was, "Is Edgar Smedley going to meet us there?"

Annie smiled a bit of a sad smile, then shook her head. "Mallory says that there's no market on the English stage for men, much less American men, but everyone wants to see a plucky female."

I didn't say that I'd never thought that that female might have been Annie, at least not until I saw her in *A Christmas Carol.*

What did I have to take along? A shawl, two dresses, a pair of walking boots, unmentionables. One book to read along the way – I chose the longest one Alice had in her stack, *The Lamplighter,* said to be composed by a woman, but no one knew. Once we had crossed the Atlantic, there would surely be far more books to read than I could possibly manage. There were plenty of temptations, but the biggest lure was the knowledge that K.T. would get farther and farther away, and that my thoughts and longings and regrets about Thomas, Lorna, and Jeremiah would shrink into that distance.

Yes, step by step, we prepared ourselves for absconding, and then we absconded, merely by walking out the front door, carrying our cases, and tramping down 20th Street to Maine, waving to our neighbors as we passed (Mrs. Abercrombie was again candling eggs in the sunlight, and her girls were again racing about the front stoop). We did not pass the schoolhouse – Annie diverted our route as we got near. I saw that, with a few precautions, any plot can be accomplished, not with a furtive look, but with a smile and an appearance of intent. I mimicked her, and at 1:00 p.m. we took our seats on the car and at 1:20 the bell rang and we headed to Chicago. I opened my book, but I didn't read; rather, I stared out the window and bade adieu to this landscape that I knew so well – flat, not yet spring, all the trees leafless and rattling in the wind. As soon as we were out of Quincy, the clouds rolled in from across the river, dense and gray, reflecting the snow covering the fields, such as they were –

I could discern that most of the farms were like Roland's, partially cleared, as if the settler had started out eager and full of plans, then had given up and decided to do what he could with what he had. Of course, there were no crops, only snow and clouds. Some horses and cows were nosing through the snow or picking leaves off trees, not exactly abandoned, but loose, because, as Roland would say, fencing was d—ned expensive and the stock was likely to push it over anyway, so why have it? Jeremiah would have enjoyed being unfenced, but he was also so friendly that, I imagined, he would have come to me if I whistled. Roland did have fences, at least for the youngsters. Alice always said that Roland poor-mouthed all the time, and had gotten Harriet into it, too, though Harriet had always looked on the bright side when she was a girl. Here and there we passed through some sleet that hit the windows of the car with a snapping sound.

Every so often, I cast a look at Annie, but she was dozing, her head on the back of the seat, or perhaps she was feigning it. If you are bound and determined, not exactly to leave, but to appear as quickly as possible in a distant world you have never seen, why stare at the one you are leaving, or watch your own trudge? Better to dream until you pop out of the magician's hat in your new spot. I looked out the window again. Most of the time when I thought of K.T., my thoughts were not of quiet mornings with Thomas in our cabin, looking through the unfinished roof at the canvas that rippled in the wind and blocked some of the sun, or at the Biskets' more elegant place in town, holding Thomas's hand surreptitiously under a fold of my skirt (our secret, which made us smile at each other). Most often, the thoughts running through my head were of the dry scrub, the forbidding hills, my fears of being on what they called a road – really a path – trying to get somewhere without being shot, and then my failure, both with Thomas and with Lorna. But on the train, heading into the distance, I allowed myself a few of the pleasant thoughts.

No Border Ruffians or shouting drunks came on the car in Springfield or any other towns; it was all decent fellows dressed in buttoned coats and their wives and mothers in bonnets and shawls. And no one was talking about K.T. or the goose question. One woman did board the train with her Negro maid, perhaps a slave. The girl looked about fourteen, the woman about forty. When other passengers glanced at them, the woman stared them down, took her seat, indicated to the girl that she was to sit beside her. I saw at once that the cars presented a dilemma, threw the goose question right into everyone's face, even for those who pretended that it was of no import. I smiled at the girl. She did not smile back, though she looked me in the eye. I felt embarrassed and turned my head to look once again out the window. When we arrived in Chicago, the woman pushed her way to the front of the line while the rest of us were managing our cases, and then I saw her poke the girl to get her off the car, even as the girl looked down at the gap and hesitated. But the girl didn't fall, or stumble. She kept her head down, carrying the case and the two packets they had with them. She walked behind the woman, who held her head up.

Evening had settled in, and perhaps we should have considered where we would be spending the night. I touched the pistol, which was in my pouch, for luck. Annie was wide awake now, bright-eyed and pert as she could be. I said nothing about my concerns, because the railway station was loud. I looked up – the roof was high above, and the shouts of the passengers and the cab men and everyone else seemed to bounce up and then drop back, my first experience of such a thing. I had been to St. Louis, but, for whatever reason, the inhabitants of Chicago had more to say, or, rather, scream, and they spent a lot of time doing it, but no shots were fired. I took Annie's arm, and we stepped out of the station and nearly fell down in the mud – something we hadn't been told about. Down in Quincy, you heard all sorts of things about Chicago, mostly about how many rail lines were meeting up there and how many ships were taking goods from the lake to the Mississippi via a canal they had built in six days (or so they said) back in the forties, and, indeed, Horace was happy to get that merchandise at a cheaper price than he might have if the canal hadn't been built – from the lake to the Illinois River, which runs down to Alton, and then the riverboats take it back up to Quincy, which, yes, is the long way round, at least if you live in Quincy. "But you get what you get," said Horace as the carts dragged the goods up the hill to Lorton and Silk.

The mud seemed likely to suck off our boots, though we had tied them tightly, and here and there I could feel it seep through my stockings. We did our best to hold our skirts up, but when we finally found ourselves a carriage with wide wheels and heavy horses, which moved slowly across a bridge and then to a hotel called Briggs House, we could see that filthy hems were standard in Chicago, and you had to wonder what in the world they were going to do about this mud if even in a cold winter (and it was cold) there was no ice. There was a wind that blew right into our faces, so that we wrapped ourselves as tightly as we could. Whatever misgivings I had had and pushed away now surfaced (for one, what was Alice thinking?), but then the carriage pulled up in front of a large building, maybe as large as I'd ever seen before, nicely lit and very agreeable, and we didn't have to step into the mud – the hotel had laid out a long wooden walkway that led to a stone staircase. Annie paid the driver, and we carried our cases into the entryway, and how was it, I thought, that a pair of donkey bumpkins such as ourselves would be allowed to stay here?

But the well-dressed man behind a long desk was friendly, especially after Annie flashed the money and a note from Mallory Cunningham, who had stayed there for some weeks on his last visit, introducing us, and so, mud and all, we were shown to a pleasant room with plenty of tapers, which the well-dressed man lit for us. I had put my book in my case; I took it out again, but, as before, it was much more interesting to stare out the window than read the book, to listen to the shouts and calls and laughs on the street just below us.

According to the clock in the front room of Briggs House, we were settled just before eight, and, what with looking out the window, chatting (though not about Alice, not yet), attempting to read (Annie had a volume, too, which was called *Much Ado About Nothing,* though that was all I could make out on the cover), attempting to use one of the pitchers of water in the room (there were three, set next to a large basin) to clean the hems of our skirts, we whiled away the time for a good bit. I would have guessed almost till midnight, but still the noise on the street below did not subside; indeed, it got louder, no doubt the effect of highly rectified whiskey or some other intoxicant. Even so, and in spite of her nap, Annie fell asleep well before I did. She continued in her dream. If anything, our day out in the world had brought out those qualities she'd shown on the stage – beauty, verve, self-confidence. I hoped, indeed, that she would never have another dish to wash in her entire life.

Once it was full daylight, we got ourselves out of bed. The streets were still bustling – I couldn't stop looking out the window. We were very hungry, and after we put our cases together, we went downstairs and discovered that there was a table set out with all sorts of items – not only muffins and biscuits (with plenty of apple butter and blackberry jam) but also boiled eggs and slices of ham. We stood and stared at the table until a kindly woman in a neat blue dress (with no mud around the hem) whispered to me that the items were free for the taking, and well they should be, given the expense of the hotel – three dollars per night (something Annie hadn't told me). I ate my fill; Annie picked at a few things, but for the first time she seemed agitated. We got up and went out onto the street. For me, there was something about the bustle of the city, and the elegance of Briggs House (which I gazed at as we stood in the street), that was unlike anything I'd seen in K.T. or Quincy, and that I found soothing. The whole time I was in K.T., I had felt our conflict, between the abolitionists and the Border Ruffians, as a larger conflict that could begin at any moment and envelop everyone. In Medford, in faraway Massachusetts, talking with Thomas's friends and relatives, I had felt the same. But here in Chicago, there were too many buildings being built, too much money passing from hand to hand, and, frankly, hardly a slave in evidence. No wonder Wisconsin, which I understood was only a few miles north, had been Lorna's dream. I counted fifteen Negroes as we walked around the neighborhood, but they were out, as everyone else was, doing their business, and no one stared them down as if to push them off the pavement into the muddy streets with only a glance. But then, thinking of Lorna, I wondered what would be the greatest sin: some folks were agitating for a conflict, desiring to kill one another for what they considered "conscience," while others, thinking of their bank accounts, were avoiding the conflict (and, no doubt, that included Roland). If you talked about original sin, as the pastor at Harriet's church did and the pastor at Beatrice's church did not, which was the original sin – running your hands over your rifle and imagining pointing it at someone you disagreed with, or running your hands over your money, wishing for more?

We passed an opera house, too, and Annie looked at it, but I knew without asking that she didn't have a sponsor in Chicago, nor would she be the novelty here that she would be in Liverpool. I prayed that we would get out of here soon, so that I would not get stuck in this very alluring mud. Farther away – Liverpool – would be even better.

We could not take the cars all the way to New York from Chicago – too many lakes in the way – but we could take a steamboat from Chicago across the lake, get off the boat in Michigan, and get on the cars, and there you were (there we were) crossing Ohio, exactly the way I had gone on the cars from Quincy to Medford. It took me two days to question Annie about it. She laughed, and said, "Lidie, surely you realize that taking the cars is exactly what Alice would have expected of us once we vanished, and the first place she would have sent Roland or Frank to look for us would have been that rail line? But who would be so foolish as to go to Chicago? Now she has lost us for good and all, and when we are about to board that steamship for Liverpool, I will send Alice the letter I've written, explaining how we eluded her."

I looked from one end of the car to the other, and said, "Did Mallory Cunningham come up with this plan?"

"No, indeed, but he described the Briggs House, and he said that it might be a good place for me to accustom myself to more luxurious accommodations than we've been used to in Quincy."

I said, "Annie, my darling, I believe you have been underestimated for your entire life, and I am assuming that you started walking about the house when you were half a year old, but you only did it after everyone was safely in bed."

Annie said, "It may be, Lidie, that one day you will learn all of my secrets." We embraced one another, then arranged ourselves on the benches, and, once again, I engaged in my favorite activity, which was to look out the window at the crusty landscape.

I cannot say that we felt continuously at ease on the cars. The journey took a little more than two days, with stops and changes, since there were many lines that crisscrossed, and none that went all the way. We were on the cars to Cincinnati until late one night, then sat up in the depot, sometimes yawning and sometimes looking about for that thief or murderer who might do us in, but perhaps in the middle of the night in Cincinnati all the thieves and murderers were sound asleep. The only man who approached us did so with a crutch and his cap out – he had but one leg, was thin as a rail, and asked us for a few bits so that he might eat something in the morning. We gave him a dollar, and he bowed kindly and hobbled away. The next morning, on the cars, in the bright light of day, a younger, handsomer man, well dressed and carrying a book, was the one who would not leave us alone, or, rather, wouldn't leave

Annie alone. He poked her in the arm, grabbed her knee, asked her what she was doing in the cars, stuck his mug in her face. I thought it odd that he didn't seem even to see me until I reached over, and just as the car rounded a turn, pushed him so that he fell between the benches, and then I changed places with Annie. The others in the car, three men and two women, looked away as if they felt that he deserved it, or, indeed, that we deserved it for traveling alone. After a bit, the fellow hoisted himself to his feet and staggered past me, his hand a fist, but when he held it up, I stood and grabbed it. He was not as tall as I was, and looked up at me with something like fear in his eyes, and then he staggered to the other end of the car and sat down. A few minutes later I could hear him snoring, and thought perhaps he had spent the night consorting with highly rectified whiskey, and this was the result.

Our time in Cincinnati reminded me of my other aunt, Miriam, the youngest of the sisters, the one whom Beatrice, Alice, and Harriet often spoke ill of because she had left Quincy when she was twenty and spent her life as a teacher up north in Yellow Springs, first of youngsters in fashionable schools and then of escaped slaves who passed through Cincinnati on the Underground Railroad. She was my favorite (though I didn't know her very well). She was the first to pass on, but I suspect that she aided many more Negroes than were aided by Dr. Eels, because, however those Missourians and Border Ruffians brag about their allegiance to Negro servitude, they have got three or four slaves, whereas the planters in the South have got thirty or forty or three hundred or four hundred. Mrs. Stowe lived in Cincinnati, and I hoped that she was Miriam's friend or mentor, but I had no idea – it was not a thing to talk about. Miriam would have liked Thomas, but, even so, she might have given him a spelling test or asked him a few questions about participles, just to be sure he was well trained (and he was).

It was late in the afternoon when the hills began to curl up and bulge – more snow, more trees, a lowering sky, cabins visible for a moment here and there – and then it was dark, and we were in Pennsylvania. All I saw was Pittsburgh – the river, steep hills all around, smoke and fog – and then we stopped and waited in some town I did not know the name of, and then got on another car at dawn. More passengers were on this one, and when some rowdy fools jumped on and started yelling and waving their arms, two other men tossed them off the car onto a hillside. Fortunately for them, we were going slowly because of a sharp curve. I did look out the window and see them roll to their feet. Our window was closed, but it looked as though they were still laughing. The two others who had been with them heeded the warning and never said another word all the way to Philadelphia.

I wished that Annie would sleep the whole time, but she didn't. She read a bit of her book, looked out the window, closed her eyes, mouthed some words I could not understand, and in every way seemed entirely at ease, not even annoyed by having to get on and off, hefting our cases. I thought of asking her whether she knew anything of Alice, Harriet, and Beatrice's two oldest sisters, Hannah and Ella Rose – how old they might be now, whether there were ever any letters back and forth between the sisters in Quincy and the sisters in – I paused. I knew they were somewhere in New York, somewhere in the countryside, which I had always imagined as being like Quincy but colder and windier. I thought and thought. The name of the town that came to me was "Horseheads," but it was hard to believe that that was actually a town. I knew from the school I'd attended for a few months, but Annie had never gone to because it shut down, that there was also a town in New York called "Buffalo." I looked out of the window and wondered which would be the most peculiar. The closer we got to New York, the sprightlier Annie was. She read Mr. Cunningham's letter twice, put it back in her bag. When we crossed the river (the "Hudson," she told me), she was entirely prepared.

3

BY THE TIME we arrived in New York City, I would have to say that I was too fatigued to decide whether this town was more or less crowded and busy than Chicago. All I noticed was that it was not quite as muddy, not quite as cold, and it was impossible to hail a cab. For whatever reason, we would wave our arms and they would pass us right by, empty though they appeared to be. The horses would look at us, but the drivers would not—perhaps they were as sleepy as we were, since it was early morning. Annie was awake enough to notice the street names, and, I suppose, Mallory Cunningham, given how long his letter was and how small his writing (I peeped at it but didn't read it), had told her how to get from the station, such as it was, to the hotel, named "St. Nicholas." Indeed, the building was white as snow and more luxurious than any Yuletide gift I'd ever received, or seen. When we first walked in, the man at the desk surveyed our garments, then informed Annie that applications for housecleaning work were being taken on the other side of the building, and he lifted his arm (though in a kindly way) to redirect us, and then Annie gave her name and Mallory Cunningham's name and he nearly knelt before her. He did glance at me, but I lifted both of the cases, and he thought that I was Annie's maid. That was acceptable to me, since I saw myself as her protector. He asked if I would be staying with her, or if she would like a separate room for me in the servants' quarters, and Annie assumed a kindly benevolent air – if only she'd had a lorgnette – and said, "I do not care to be parted from her, thank you." Our room was on the third floor, and I did not have to carry the cases – a fellow appeared at the ring of the deskman's bell and showed us to our room. Perhaps the main difference between this room and the one at the Briggs House was that there were four pitchers of water rather than three, but we didn't wash anything; rather, we flopped onto the beds and fell into a deep sleep.

When I woke up, around noon, Annie had changed again. This time, she greeted my awakening with pleasure, and began to pour forth information in a way that I had never heard before. She said, "Lidie, love, I am so glad you got some rest! Now, listen to this. I have saved it all for now, because I thought that we had to see this city ourselves before we might understand everything. Mr. Cunningham wrote in his letter that he went back and forth about what shipping line to choose for us. Three years ago, the first time he came to America, but only to New York and Philadelphia, his ship was the *Pacific,* on an American line, Collins, I think it is, the fastest and most luxurious ship in the world, but then, in a subsequent voyage, the *Pacific* disappeared! There were a few dozen passengers and many more crew lost, and this on top of another ship that went down some years ago, though he didn't say what the name of that ship was. Last year, he came on the *City of Manchester,* but there were no rooms on that one for us, so he has fallen back on a line called (and here she adopted an English accent) '*Cunard.*' It does go straight to Liverpool, but we have to wait three days or more, depending on the weather, for the ship."

We looked around the room. The wait did not seem as though it would be a trial. I slipped beneath my coverlid. She exclaimed, and in her Quincy voice, "No, get up! We have something to go see that Mallory says we cannot miss."

I sat up and glanced at the window. Before I went to sleep, we'd pulled the drapes closed, but Annie must have opened them. I could see a bright sky. Annie said, "Here is what we must do to be cautious. I must walk proudly to the fore, with my nose in the air, looking about and nodding as if I know everyone on the street, and you must walk slightly behind me, as tall as you can possibly be, with a sour look on your face. And you must keep your hand on your bag . . ."

"Because that's where we will have the pistol."

Annie nodded.

We got ourselves dressed, and I did pull Annie's corset tight, and once we were out on the street, I not only feigned keeping my eye out, I did keep my eye out – for pistols, especially, but also for truncheons and other weapons. However, if those citizens of New York had any, they had, as far as I could tell, left them at home. We walked the whole way – I gauged about two miles, maybe a little more. As we were used to walking, it wasn't difficult. I, of course, kept my eye on the horses, and there were plenty of them – riding horses, cart horses, carriage horses, even a group of youngsters being ponied somewhere, one a dark dappled gray. Annie's head was turning back and forth, too. What I noticed on the women was the layers and layers of flounces. Beatrice liked a flounce, and she liked selling the bolts of cloth for flounces, too, because she made more money off of more material. But here in New York City, a skirt that was wide enough to brush against you, even if you could hardly make out the face of the woman wearing it, had at least three and sometimes four flounces. Even older women with serious demeanors wore three flounces, though they would be gray or brown instead of green or pink. They were also wearing coats, not shawls, which is what we wore in Quincy, and what even Mrs. Bisket wore in Lawrence. The coats were layered, too, and appeared to me to be constructed of wool, though with elaborate decorations. They came about halfway down the skirts. One I saw was made of felt, and possibly homemade, since the hem was uneven, but after I stared at it, I smiled at this woman and acknowledged her skills. She lifted one eyebrow and smiled a bit at me, too. As for bowler hats, they were everywhere. It looked as though the men of New York City had tossed their top hats into the Hudson River and were glad to be quit of them. They were wearing dark coats and cravats, and carrying sticks. A few had pale trousers on, but mostly they were black or dark gray. They would stride along, dangling their sticks from their forearms, and perhaps their sticks were their weapons.

Yes, there were plenty of folks – men, women, children, dusty with grit and clothed in blackened rags – and some of them were huddled beside the buildings, hiding from the wind, their hands tucked up under their arms and their faces buried in whatever rags they could find. The buildings we passed were sometimes hovels and sometimes castles and sometimes plain wooden houses of the sort Alice lived in in Quincy. This was the lesson I learned in New York: You may observe whatever you wish, for the entire world is before you. If you care for fashion, then the best is on display. If you care for the poor, then the poorest are on display, also. If you care for horses, then every breed, every color, every temperament crosses your path. If you are hungry, the odors waft past you – bread, cakes, roasts, soups. Men and women of every shade cross your path – you may notice them or not. I glanced at Annie; she was noticing them and, perhaps unknowingly, mimicking some of their facial expressions and mannerisms. That was what I noticed – Annie's eagerness to take in her fellow humans, male and female. Thomas had been to New York one time, and spoken to me of his contempt for the bankers there, for their eagerness to invest in the slave trade and yet to allow no slaves in New York. His description of this city had not prepared me for what I was observing.

The spot we were seeking was a destination for others, too – it was called "the Crystal Palace," the site of a famous exhibition (even in Quincy, we were familiar with the words "Crystal Palace," though I'd never seen a picture, and neither, I'm guessing, had

Annie). The building was huge, entirely made of enormous panels of glass, topped by a dome, with a grand entrance. The famous exhibition itself was long in the past, and we could see, as we walked around, that some spaces were empty and some surfaces were dusty, and there were mouse droppings here and there; nonetheless, to be inside this domed sparkling building on what was becoming a chilly and windy day in February was a pleasure. Children ran about, laughing, and one man used his stick to point out to his two companions where the famous cabinetry had been, and the fire engine and the cotton gin. A large mirror was still in place, and a conical white tower that looked to be made of clay, but turned out to be made of rope (cotton, not hemp, which was the sort of rope we had in Quincy). The figure of a bird was perched on the apex.

There was, alas, nothing to eat, and since we had not eaten at the hotel – had not even noticed whether there was any fare set out for guests – we were now, I would say, famished, so we exchanged a glance and hurried out of the Palace. It was late afternoon, and there were two carts not far from the Palace. One was selling small loaves of bread and cheese, and the other was selling various dried fruits. We bought some of each, and went back to the grounds of the Palace and ate them. Both were excellent, especially the dried apples, which had been spiced, something Harriet did not do when she dried apples for the winter.

Once we'd been refreshed, Annie led me back down Broadway toward the spot, I saw at once when we arrived, that she had been aiming for all along, a place called Niblo's Saloon, which was not far from our hotel, and so we had passed it earlier, but now it was full of activity because it was actually a theater, and a large one. Of course, the staff at Niblo's knew Mallory Cunningham, and we were welcomed inside – someone, perhaps Mr. Niblo himself, came out from the back area and met Annie and took her hand and said to give Mr. Cunningham his greetings. He also looked me up and down quizzically, and I bowed, mimicking his own bow, so, perhaps, he was actually speculating about whether I was male or female. The top of Mr. Niblo's head came to my chin, and I have seen that men of smaller stature are more likely to wonder about me than men of greater stature. We were shown to the dining area, where we ate some chops and a few potatoes, and then we went to the theater and watched a show, not a play, but a variety show of the sort that were sometimes presented in Quincy, especially in the summer, when there was a lot of river traffic. I enjoyed the show – bright costumes and many tuneful songs, sung by women and men and one even by a child with such a deep voice that I suspected she was in fact a male dwarf, not a ten-year-old girl, as she was advertised to be. Annie was disappointed to have missed the play, a production of *Rip Van Winkle,* which would have been an appropriate show for New York City. Another play, said to be more spooky and less amusing than *Rip Van Winkle,* was in preparation, but no one knew when it might come upon the boards. Annie seemed disappointed; perhaps Mallory Cunningham had led her to believe that she would see some productions in New York. But the food was good – after the variety show, we ate some coconut cake, something that I'd never heard of and that tasted delicious, and I sincerely hoped that Liverpool would be more like New York than like Quincy. At any rate, Annie and I were both impressed by Mr. Niblo's ambitions; his building was enormous and beautifully styled, with great boxes and balconies, and, indeed, an array of plants that were thriving even in the winter.

As we were leaving, the man came out again, let's say Mr. Niblo himself, found us (I saw him looking around and then sighting me and rushing over), and pressed a note into Annie's hand with a smile. She thanked him, and we went out into the streets. We were two blocks up from the hotel, and even in the darkness (that, indeed, flickered with the lights that shone from the windows of all the buildings along Broadway), I could see it, pale in the distance. When we got safely to the hotel (I did contemplate purchasing a stick for myself, to hang from my arm and flourish from time to time), Annie showed me the note. There was a place to go to, said Mr. Niblo, run by a friend of his named Barnum; it was neither a theater nor made of glass, but as long as we were in New York, we should see it.

That night, as we were lying in bed in the dark (we had pulled the blinds down), I finally asked Annie if she remembered my sisters, her aunts Hannah or Ella Rose. Here we were in New York, should we have . . .

She said, "The only thing I remember about Hannah is that my mother and Beatrice could not believe that she just turned sixty. When was that? Oh, in October sometime. I would guess they think that time will stretch and stretch so that they never turn sixty."

I said, "How old is Ella Rose?"

"Fifty-eight."

"I should have kept my eye out for nieces or nephews when we were gadding about today."

"We can look tomorrow."

We slept soundly, and on the following day, we were more canny. We ate our morning meal at the hotel, and it was plentiful and not inedibly sophisticated. We noticed that the hotel was worth exploring, so we walked up and down the corridor that ran from our room to the staircase (also marble) and sneaked upstairs to another corridor. Perhaps I had never seen so many rooms in one building. In Lawrence, there had been rooming houses, but so ramshackle, because they were put up in haste, that you dared not look at your feet, especially going up and down the staircases, because you would clearly see what a dark, damp hole you would fall into should the steps collapse. There was a shop in the hotel itself, where we investigated the apparel on offer, and though Annie stared at a coat, and turned it over, the price on it was twenty dollars, a price we had never seen before in our lives. What we were paying for our room, with Mallory Cunningham's money, I did not dare ask.

When we left the St. Nicholas, just before midday, the weather was gloomy, and we walked down Broadway, as we had the day before, with Annie looking haughty and me looking (I hoped) dangerous. A certain odor flickered around us, not quite the odor of meat or bread, but salty. Though the breeze was decided, it was not the sort of piercing wind I had known in K.T. As on the day before, there were people everywhere, maybe more in rags than in flounces, but still of all kinds and colors, and, indeed, speaking to one another in tongues that I had never heard. But that would include all tongues other than English. As I listened, I understood that perhaps I was getting out of town in more ways than one, and I felt pleased, of course, since K.T. shrank even more, but also a bit abashed for the first time since we left Quincy. Then, somehow, in this soup of ambling thoughts, I realized that the salty fragrance in the air was the ocean, the very thing I had heard of all my life, read about in books, understood that our very own river, the Mississippi, ran toward, that I had taken for granted, and yet never been close to – even in Medford, where Thomas's father told me the "bay" was about ten or twelve miles from their place, though they hadn't taken me there. I took some deep breaths, and right then it flashed through me that Annie and I would be on that great body of water in two short days, and though I could swim (and had swum the width of the Mississippi), Annie could not, and these stories of ships disappearing, like the *Pacific,* or simply crashing and going down as others had done, now had something to do with me. And here we were at Barnum's American Museum.

The place was a large building – white, like our hotel, with five or six rows of windows, dominating the corner of two streets, and plastered with self-announcing red letters. The citizens of New York and, judging by how they talked, the citizens of many other nations, were rushing in, and we did have to wait for a bit, some of that time in the street, Broadway, itself, because the walk in front of the museum was so packed with customers. I stood close to Annie and stared down the hawkers, whose hands were full of the muffins and trinkets and slippers and other sorts of goods that they were yelling about. When we got inside, it was as chaotic, and Annie and I decided to hold hands, only because it seemed as though one or the other of us could be swept away in the flood and lost forever. The place we went to first was something called a wax museum, with many figures of odd characters, including a mermaid and a figure of two men attached to one another. In another display, there were snakes and an elephant (I had heard of those, but never seen even a picture of one), as well as a lion and plenty of fowl, some of which were similar to those that ran about in our neighborhood in Quincy. Indeed, Mr. Barnum's museum was a mishmash of the very strange with the very familiar, and not, for those of us from Illinois, all that different from New York City.

We stood for a while in front of an exhibit about phrenology, which is popular or not in Quincy, according to who comes to town and gives a lecture, some saying it is the new science of humanity (Alice) and some saying that it is d—ned balderdash (Roland) and some tiptoeing out of the house and looking the other direction (Beatrice, the only one of my sisters who could have afforded such a thing – and then she told me about it just after it had been done, since she knew that I would not tell her secret, and it must have helped her, because she went about smiling for several days). The afternoon passed, and I was less amused by the various exhibitions than Annie was, but perhaps, indeed, what amused her was her fellow viewers, for she watched them carefully.

At three, the theater in the museum put on a show called *Dred,* made up from one of Mrs. Stowe's novels. The theater was in the upper story, very light, and, once again, much more elaborate than any I had seen before. I had thought the play would be about Dred Scott, a famous Negro in Illinois, Missouri, and K.T., whom Thomas once told me about. He was taken about by his owner to several free states, including Illinois, and perhaps Wisconsin, and when he was in one of those states, he married and, it was said, his wife had a child. Then his owner died, and he tried to buy his freedom from the owner's wife, but she would have none of it. The most important thing Thomas told me (and he had raised his voice, which was unlike Thomas, but the whole thing made him hot with anger) was that the law in Missouri did state that if a slave lived in a free state for more than two years, he could be free, and, as well, that Dred's child, since it was born on a boat on the Mississippi, which is free territory, was born free. Thomas said that the case was tried many times, and every time the woman who claimed Scott lost, but I suppose she had plenty of money, or the support of Border Ruffians with plenty of money, and so she kept taking the case to court. At any rate, that's what I thought the play would be about, since I hadn't gotten hold of a copy of Mrs. Stowe's novel, but it was not about that. It was about two families who have plantations in North Carolina, and there is a Dred, but he's not Dred Scott, he is a rebel slave who lives near the plantations, in a "dismal swamp," where, I gathered, the escaped slaves are able to flee to, because no one can follow them there. The very words "dismal swamp" made me think of the Mississippi, which indeed has plenty of bluffs, but also some low-lying, mucky areas where even Frank never went to play. Then, I imagined Lorna's husband, unbeknownst to Lorna, buying his own freedom (he was talented with a saw and a chisel) and then showing up at one of those auctions in St. Louis and buying Lorna—just waving the money in the auctioneer's face and walking off with his wife, then, let's say, getting on a boat and going north to Wisconsin. Mr. Day had said that he sold Lorna down the river, but maybe auctioning her in St. Louis would have been, he thought, more profitable.

I sat quietly, listening to the players, watching them onstage. I do not know how well the play adhered to the book, but there they were, plantation owners, arguing back and forth about beating slaves, finding slaves, how to treat slaves, and my head began to throb. Dred showed up, but not often, though he was allowed to speak for himself, but the main question seemed to be who of the slave owners might marry whom else, and how they would get along, and toward the end, one of the owners did what I did in K.T., which was finally come to an opinion against slavery. I imagined Mr. Day doing that. And then I imagined Helen and Mr. Day, whom in spite of myself I did like and was grateful to for their kindness to me, giving each other a hug and themselves being grateful for having been delivered from the work of the devil through no act of their own. Thanks to Thomas, I believed that this slavery *was* the work of the devil, and the sign of that was the ferment that it stirred up on all sides, the hatred it brought down on everyone who had an opinion against or for, and the conflict that was coming, though no one talked about that except the tobacco-spitting gun toters who couldn't wait for license to shoot whomever they wanted. The voice I kept hearing in my head was Thomas's voice, not at all like the voices of the actors onstage, his gentle Massachusetts voice, kindly yet sharp, loving yet decided. I heard it in a way that I hadn't heard it since my return from K.T., since, perhaps, the day he was shot. The tears began falling from my eyes. I wiped them away with my kerchief, and then put my face in my hands and sat as quietly as I could, though I knew my shoulders were shaking. Annie put her arm around me, and the woman on the other side of me moved away a bit.

I would have said that I had mourned Thomas after his death, for I had wept and regretted all the disagreements, large and small, that we had had (which, indeed, were not many). I had thought of him often and even spoken to him in my mind, and asked all about him when I visited his relatives in Medford. Had I turned away from him (and Lorna) by leaving Quincy with Annie? I'd never imagined I would regret that, but as I was watching this play, it seemed as though he had returned. I felt myself both welcome his return and be frightened and overwhelmed by it.

That day, both of us had been so simple-minded – walking along beside the wagon, in the hot sun, talking about the town we'd just visited. Then I saw Jeremiah's gray ears flick and his head pop up. I saw the two men and the boy, and I heard them shout about "d — ned abolitionists," but I didn't imagine . . . and then it seemed like it took me forever to understand that Thomas and Jeremiah had been shot. My body knelt down, my arms reached out to Thomas, then Jeremiah, but my mind seemed gone. Now I let myself picture Thomas's face – his eyes blinking. Then I allowed myself to remember breathing into Jeremiah's nostrils as he lay on the ground.

I looked up and stared at the stage, and perhaps I was trembling. Annie held me a little tighter, and leaned toward me. I clenched my fists, then sighed.

Annie whispered, "Do you want to leave?" I shook my head. We were too deep into our row of seats, and I not only didn't want to disrupt the other members of the audience, I didn't want to stagger and stumble about, as I feared I would do. Once she took her arm from around my shoulder, Annie placed her hand on my knee for the rest of the play, and sometimes I touched it, just to remind myself where we were, New York City, not K.T. At the end of the play, the most famous actor came on in some part. He was a tiny fellow named Tom Thumb, and the audience gave him a great round of applause, but I would say that if Barnum's American Museum had taught me one thing, it was that I wanted to leave this nation and never to return.

There was a mad rush and crush to get out of the museum, and I did listen to the comments that members of the audience were making. Most of them were haughty and sneering, some because the play didn't adhere closely enough to Mrs. Stowe's book, others that the ability of plantation owners to come to their senses was much exaggerated, and a few, quieter ones (but I have excellent hearing) lamenting that these issues were constantly brought up when it was much better to let things ride, no good could come of looking for a fight, and even though no good had come of Thomas's looking for a fight, these were the ones that I wanted to give a shove to.

We walked up Broadway in the dusk, and when we got to the St. Nicholas, the last light of the day seemed to shine from it, rather than upon it. Annie was famished. We went to our room, and she had me loosen her corset, and then we went to the eating hall, and while she was putting away potatoes, legs of chicken, boiled carrots, pieces of bread, and a large serving of blancmange, she told me what she thought of the play – which players had projected their feelings as if they were true, which had overacted (Tom Thumb), which had been graceful, which had spoken too softly (one of the female plantation owners), which had seemed bored to tears and eager to leave the stage (Dred himself). I nodded, ate a bit of this and that. I knew what I was going to do once we were in bed, and after a walk around the block, we did go to bed, though with our tapers and our books. Annie read. I did not.

What I did was scour my memory for every image of Thomas that might be in there. The first one that came to me was from a night on our claim. It must have been before we completed the roof and on a moonlit, clear night, because what I remembered was waking up, turning over, and seeing his profile, etched by the light, his eyes closed, his dark hair falling back, his prominent nose and his cheekbones in bright relief, his chin thrust up. As I looked at him, he gave a snore. I remembered that I had been overtaken by a sense of pleasure and attraction that no one in my family had ever spoken of – here was the handsomest man in the world, right next to me, and I might have kissed him all over his face, as you would an infant.

From there, I pushed myself backward: What had I thought of his looks when I first saw him? That is, when Harriet's neighbor brought Thomas to Roland's place one hot afternoon as I was helping with the clothes washing. He was pale and quiet. Harriet's neighbor, Roger Howell, was more interesting to me than Thomas at the time, because he was over the moon in love with a mare he had bought from across the river. The first thing I noted about Thomas, after his paleness, was that he said he was not a horseman. He was quiet and appeared thoughtful, and did I find him physically appealing? I would not have said so, but when he and Roger Howell walked away from us after we had a bite to eat, I saw his grace, the way his body swayed smoothly and lightly with every step as he turned to look here and there. Roger Howell, by contrast, was stocky and sudden with every step. Perhaps, if there hadn't been such a difference, I wouldn't have noted Thomas's grace. The next memory came right on top of the first one – encountering Thomas on Maine Street, him touching my elbow, and me turning, as if I couldn't help myself, to walk along with him. I noticed then that he topped me up by an inch or two, and just as I was thinking that, he said, "I've heard something about you, Miss Harkness," and what I was sure he had heard about me was that I was a lazy and useless sort of girl, who did her best to avoid every household task, for something that we understood in Quincy about folks from Massachusetts was that they were endlessly busy and useful, the men out in the fields or on the ocean, and the women in their homes. And then he said, with his very own sudden smile, "You have swum across the river." My secret, told to Mr. Thomas Newton by Frank, the only other person who knew what I had done.

I spent the whole night dredging up memories and did not sleep at all, or the memories faded into dreams and then I would wake up and find more memories. I truly did not remember that I was in New York City, though, which perhaps was the strangest thing. Once the memories were pulled up, I made an effort to preserve them, even the one where I discovered why Thomas was so concerned with the large, heavy wooden box we took with us to K.T. It was filled with Sharps carbines, a new sort of weapon that the Emigrant Aid Company hoped would give them an advantage over the Border Ruffians. This memory linked up with the one where Thomas was not present – the time Frank went with me along the bluffs, the sun to the west lighting them up and Frank mouthing one of those seegars he so enjoyed, though he was just a boy. Frank had an errand, and, as I found out later, that errand was to give some money to Lorna, who had crossed the river and was hiding in a cave. Or that was what she told me, that she remembered seeing me on that day. I always believed her, because her resolution to escape was solid to the core, and she was quick and strong enough to have done it over and over. I bit my lips and sighed, allowing myself to deplore, once again, my inability to save her. And it was Lorna who told me, when I first got to Day's End Plantation, that I had lost my child (mine and Thomas's). I'd known I was with child, but had put it out of my mind, because of all the chaos. I now let myself remember the surprised look on Lorna's face, and then I let myself grieve for the child, not because it was mine, but because it was Thomas's.

And then I remembered a green field with a path running through it, and Thomas sitting awkwardly in the saddle, one hand more or less holding the reins and the other with a tight grip on Jeremiah's mane. I was walking along beside him, my hand on his leg, looking up at him, telling him to take some breaths and relax, and just when he did, Jeremiah shook off some flies and Thomas's eyebrows went shooting up to the brim of his hat. I did wonder at that very moment how he had planned to make his way in K.T. if he could not ride a horse, but he could drive a cart, and he picked up riding bit by bit once we were living on the claim. One time, he even said that he liked it, and leaned toward me to kiss me on the lips.

That boat we took, up the Missouri, was something of a wreck, and crammed with passengers, all sleeping cheek by jowl with one another at night, and fighting over the provisions during meals. Thomas was amazed at the amount of spittle in the spittoons, and

I hardly got to spend any time with him, but I did have a memory from the second day, of a moment around dusk, of his profile against the sunset as he leaned his elbows on the railing of the deck and stared up the river. In my memory, he looked thoughtful, even for Thomas, and I do hope that he was not regretting his choice to come to K.T. or his choice to wed himself to an unruly, untrained Illinois girl. There was another memory, too, from one of those noonday meals, when I was sitting across from him at the table, and the man beside him, dressed in a leather coat and wearing his hat in the dining room, forked the chicken leg right off of Thomas's plate, took it between his fingers, and gobbled it down, and Thomas stared at him in disbelief. I saw right then that Massachusetts didn't prepare a man for Missouri, much less for K.T.

And then I allowed myself to recall again the sight of Thomas stretched out on the grass, his chest bloody and his head turned to one side, and the man who came along, David B. Graves, the very one who later betrayed me. We got Thomas to Lawrence, but he was full of shot, and nothing could be done for him. Whatever skills physicians may have elsewhere, they didn't have them in K.T.

In the middle of the night, with Annie asleep, breathing heavily in the dark of New York City, I held on to that memory in a way that I had not dared to before. And, yes, it did reinforce my hatred of this vile nation. Was it more precious to me for that reason? Perhaps it was.

But I made myself go backward again, and rustle up another, less fraught image, the image of Thomas sitting on a chair beside the fire at the cabin, a book propped on his knee as he read it aloud. It was a book of poetry by a man someone in his family knew, Emerson. Most of the poems he read were beyond me, but one was about such a simple thing, snow, that I loved it and asked Thomas to repeat it three times, and then I borrowed the book and memorized it, because we had plenty of snow in K.T. The lines I loved the most were, "Hides hills and woods, the river, and the heaven, /And veils the farm-house at the garden's end."

Annie rose, yawned, pushed her hair out of her face, went into the toileting room, came out, looked at me in the morning light, and then picked up her kerchief and very gently wiped the tears off my cheeks. She squeezed my hand. She said, "Lidie, dearest, I must tell you that when Mallory Cunningham was talking up this journey, he did say that he was frightened for this country, frightened of the mess we were making for ourselves and the politicians were making for us. I didn't quite understand what he was saying, but, indeed, your experiences point in that direction, and so I think we have to turn our attention to departure. The fellow at the wharf said that tomorrow is the day, did he not?"

I nodded, letting my memories of Thomas fall to the back of my mind.

"Let's make our way to – what is it? – Castle Garden? The man at the front desk told me it's down at the tip of the island. That will be a pleasant walk, anyway, I am sure." I sat up.

Well, it was not, in itself, a pleasant walk – the streets were seething with a mix of hawkers, sleet, pickpockets, horse wagons, yells, and elbows, so much so that I had to stand tall, look menacing, hold Annie's arm, but it was invigorating, and I didn't mind it, even the sleet, which, as we got closer to the tip, softened into rain. But hardly any wind – at least there was that. It took us a while to find the offices of the Cunard Line, but we did, and, yes, they were happy to say, the ship had arrived from Liverpool, was now being done over and supplied, and would leave promptly the next day at midday, so we should be ready to board at 10:00 a.m. I now remembered that I had forgotten to look for the nieces and nephews, but, indeed, it was no wonder, as there had been more things to look at in New York than I had ever seen in my life.

4

ANNIE AND I might have given more thought to our voyage, but she entirely trusted Mallory Cunningham, who had crossed the Atlantic three times in all, the first as a boy on a sailing ship, and the voyage lasted six weeks. We went from the St. Nicholas to the nearest post office, and Annie posted her letter to Alice, which she had read to me the night before. In the letter, she apologized for slipping away, and apologized for taking me with her, but she said that she couldn't go out into the world without me. She said that we were safe, and about to embark on a ship, though she didn't say what ship or what line. She said that she was looking forward to "learning her trade" and hoped that she would prosper. She did not include a return address, but said that she would write again when we got to Liverpool and give Alice one then. It was a short letter, decided but decent, I thought. A good opening to the possibility of future forgiveness.

At last, we were actually standing on the deck of the ship, a much larger and more sturdy vessel than the riverboats I had been on. The man who helped us up the gangway said, laughing, "Aye, miss, I 'ave gret 'opes for this journey. May we see the bergs but miss 'em! Bit early in the year ta be crossin'. Money has got to be mide, though, and folk will go back and forth and back and forth." Another laugh, and then he sent us with a much quieter boy to our accommodation –

cabin, as they called it – on the second deck, small enough, but only in comparison to the St. Nicholas Hotel, and, indeed, every accommodation is small compared to the St. Nicholas. Just at midday, the horn blew, and the ship, named the *Arabia* – and referred to always as "she," which I found confusing – carried us out into the blue and windy ocean, and, I thought, how did they know what direction we were going, without riverbanks to show them?

But, indeed, the *Arabia* was luxurious, especially in the common rooms, and there was a library, well stocked. As for spittoons, one or two here and there, nothing like the vast sloshing tubs on the riverboats, which tipped and spilled and stained the hem of your dress and had made Thomas, perhaps more than any other thing, wonder what in the world he was getting himself into, going to K.T.

I understood by keeping my ears open that the *Arabia* was an unusual ship because she had only two masts, one toward the "bow" and one toward the "stern" – no "mizzenmast," which was why the saloon was so large. It also had a lovely cupola that let the light in, and the passengers, as I saw over the course of our seven-day voyage, did not rush in, throw themselves into the seats, and gobble everything down in three minutes. The first evening, as we were calmly sitting at our assigned table, enjoying some mutton stew, I told Annie about the memory I had had of the man on our boat up the Missouri snatching Thomas's chicken leg, and out of the corner of my eye, I saw that the woman beside me was smiling, and so, a few minutes later, I turned to her and introduced myself, and she was friendly. She was an older woman – she looked about forty-five, but lively and intelligent. Her name was Hermione Gallant, and she and her husband had been in America since September, mostly in Philadelphia, for business purposes. They were returning to Liverpool and then going home to Leeds, where he had two rope factories, and then I told her about the rope exhibit I had seen at the Crystal Palace, but not about the money we had made in K.T., selling rope. She said that she had seen that, too, and then, the next day, when we were far enough out to sea so that a walk about the deck showed nothing but bright-blue water and horizons, I happened upon her again, and we walked along in a friendly way. She seemed calm even when a swell lifted the front of the ship so that I had to reach for the rail, and, since that morning Annie had taken to her bed and had me bring her a bun and an apple, I decided to take Mrs. Gallant as my model and only worry if I saw her forehead wrinkle or her eyes grow wide. Another swell. She drew a breath, looked out over the blueness, and said, "Do you see that?"

I did not.

She said, "It was a whale breaching – far away, hardly visible to the naked eye, but I have good far-sight."

We continued walking around the deck. I said, "The deck is so empty."

"On the first day, most of the passengers are subject to ocean sickness. My husband is, though he was a sailor for five years before I knew him. But, for some reason, I am not. I fully enjoyed our crossing to the west, and I have been looking forward to our return for two months. That's why I prevailed upon him to book our passage on the earliest ship of the season. We shall see if I regret it." She said this last in an utterly calm and reasonable tone of voice.

We were not especially chilled, as we were standing on the sunny side of the vessel and there wasn't much of a wind. The sails above us were slack and pale in the sunshine, and we could hear the engine below us grinding away. Mrs. Gallant said, "Might I inquire if you are from New York?"

I said, "You might. I am not – I'm from . . ." Here I paused. It was on the tip of my tongue to say "St. Louis," but my memories of St. Louis were too dark. I said ". . . Chicago."

She said, "Indeed! That seems to be an up-and-coming sort of spot!"

I said, "It will be, once we get ourselves out of the mud. It is dragging us down."

Now she laughed and said, "I feel the same about Norfolk; that's a spot in the east of England where I spent my childhood. Where we live now is full of hills and trees and, true enough, coal smoke, but lovely out of town. Every spot has its disadvantages."

I thought of K.T., then Quincy. I said, "Is your family still in Norfolk?"

She said, "My father died years ago, and my mother lives with my sister and her family in Hampshire. Her husband has a small estate there. My brother is in the East, in the service."

I said, "You are well traveled."

She said, "Once you begin, my dear, it is very difficult to leave off." She lifted her chin and took a deep breath. The sea air didn't smell, to me, as salty as it had on the tip of Manhattan, but perhaps I had gotten accustomed to it. I might say that I continued conversing with Mrs. Gallant because she was pleasant, but it was also to enjoy her manner of speaking, which somewhat reminded me of the *Christmas Carol* performance, and the attempts of all the actors to generate an English way of speaking. Perhaps what struck Mallory Cunningham about Annie's performance was not that she did the best imitation (she did not sound the way Mrs. Gallant now did), but that her imitation had a musical quality to it that projected it out over the audience, and I may have detected that at the time, since every line she'd spoken pleased me. And it was true that, for the entertainment of the family, Annie had been mimicking everyone for years – even Roland laughed when she deepened her voice and spoke of the "d—ned cutlery" she had to scrub. Thinking of this made me smile, and Mrs. Gallant said, "My dear, pardon me for being so forward, but I can't help myself. You have a lovely smile."

I said, "Thank you."

Now we turned and walked for a few steps, and then she paused, looked at me, and put her hand on my arm. "Women of stature can be forbidding, and what you may not know about my countrymen is that we hold ourselves back. Only the lower classes grin or laugh. But, nevertheless, we always respond favorably to a bright and sincere smile. We feel sorry for you, yes, but we also like you." And then she smiled, and then we both laughed. The next thing she said was, "English citizens love a laugh, and don't let our sour looks tell you otherwise."

I said, "That must be why they love Mr. Dickens's works."

"Oh, yes. He is quite the character, and so strange that he excites much gossip, which keeps him on our minds and sells the journals and books as well. I appreciate him. But have you read *The Newcomes,* by Mr. Thackeray?"

I said, "I haven't heard of that one."

"Or *Vanity Fair*?" Thomas had mentioned it, but only in passing. I shook my head.

"Well, Mr. Thackeray's wit is like the tip of a knife, compared to Mr. Dickens. But you may have *The Newcomes*. You will lighten my load." We continued around the ship, looking here and there, and even though there were a few considerable swells, I felt no rumbling of the guts. I hoped that Annie would meet Mrs. Gallant, and learn to imitate her way of speaking.

That evening, not many were gathered in the saloon, but Mr. and Mrs. Gallant appeared, and he seemed in a pleasant mood. He was talkative, and in his presence Mrs. Gallant was less so, but she had a way of commenting on his remarks with her eyebrows and her lips – smile, grimace, frown, but not as evident as those words make it appear. I "inquired of Mr. Gallant" what he thought our speed was. He said, "Fourteen knots or so."

I said, "What is a knot?"

He said, "You might look off the stern of this *Arabia* and see a slab of wood and a reel of rope, or a 'line,' as they term it, and the line will have been regularly knotted. As she is moving forward, the line unreels, and one of the sailors counts the knots running through his fingers, while one of his mates holds the sand-glass and tells him when to begin and when to stop. As we've been out of the harbor for some thirty hours now, I would say we've made four hundred and fifty miles or so."

I said, just thinking of this for the first time, "How many miles is the journey?"

Mr. Gallant smiled, then said, "That depends on luck, my dear girl. As the crow flies – well, let's say, as the tern flies – some three thousand miles or more, but ships are more erratic than terns."

In other words, our journey could be ten days, or more.

He said, "If we get a good wind off the stern, though, the sails will speed us up. This time of year . . ."

Mrs. Gallant's face was like a small flag, flickering with this response and that one. Now she pressed her lips together and gave a little sniff. I liked her. She would not be my friend, because I understood that, to make a friend, you have to reveal yourself, and I could not and would not do that, but I would be appreciative of Mrs. Gallant. I also understood, from our conversation and from watching her, that I had embarked upon an acting career similar to Annie's: my job was not to be myself, but to be a woman (no longer a girl) who had left her past behind. Yes, Chicago. My trip over the ocean would be where I concocted and memorized my history that did not include K.T., or even Quincy.

Mr. Gallant said, "Which nation do you think is due east of us?"

I said, "I hope England."

He said, "No, indeed. You would arrive in Portugal."

I had never heard of Portugal. Mrs. Gallant seemed to understand this, though whether her husband did I could not tell. But after our meal, she took me to the library and showed me an atlas, and there it was, and there were so many other countries, and all of them larger and more interesting than K.T. My hopes of reducing K.T. to nothing in my mind were coming true.

The volumes of *The Newcomes* she gave me looked as though they would last a lifetime. I took them back to my cabin and stacked them on a small table. I also took some provisions for Annie – rolls and tea and a couple of raw carrots. She seemed to have gotten used to the rolling of the ship. She was no longer as pale as she had been, and she told me she'd gotten up, sneaked out of our cabin, and thrown her spewings over the side of the ship. Now she was well rested, and hoped that I could take her for a bit of a ramble about the ship, and I did, even though it was dark, and afterward, I was glad I did, because that was the last sight we had of a bright dark sky, no moon, sprinkled everywhere with stars, and I would have said that the stars themselves reflected on the surface of the ocean, which was calm. We walked on every deck and looked into whatever windows ("portholes" is what they called them) or doorways that were open, though of course I had to remember to watch my head, as the lintels were low, and down below, the ceilings were, as well, or the "overheads," as they called them. Even in our cabin, I might have hit my head if the boat had bucked like a horse. At first, I did feel confined, but the sky and the sea seemed to release me when I needed them to.

On the third day, we passed what looked like an island, which one of the sailors told me was "Nova Scotia." I saw long stretches of green pine forest, some icy-looking beaches, and plenty of rocks. It took us a while to pass, and, perhaps because of the wind, it seemed to me that we skated a little too close to some of the rocks, but none of the other passengers were gripping the rails and staring, and the sailors seemed in good humor. That night, sometime when I had awakened, I lit my candle to read a bit of *The Newcomes,* and then looked out of our tiny porthole when the candle went out. I saw what Mrs. Gallant told me the next morning were "the northern lights," a straight rainbow, wide and pulsing, that fluttered against the darkness. I awakened Annie, and we looked at it for some time, then fell back asleep and missed the morning meal. What woke us the next day was the storm that blew in, cold, windy, snowy, icy, the very thing that everyone had expected and hoped to avoid.

Annie mostly curled up in her bed with the coverlid over her head, but I made myself look out the window from time to time, and I saw that we were passing another island, I thought, but, because of the rocking of the vessel, I could not make out anything about it, and sometimes the snowy fog was so thick that I couldn't see past it, anyway. I sincerely hoped, and, let us say, prayed, that the captain, or whoever it was that was steering the *Arabia,* could.

In order to distract myself, I concocted my new identity. In K.T., when I was looking to revenge myself for Thomas's and Jeremiah's deaths, I had made myself up as a young fellow. Lyman Arquette, I called myself, and perhaps because I had seen so many fellows swaggering here and there, I would say that my swaggering was something of a success. I did attempt, just once, to put a seegar between my lips, but then I decided that my coughing would give me away. I was used to carrying a rifle and riding a horse astride, and so I pulled it off, if I could remember to lower my voice when I opened my mouth, but of course I was uncovered at Papa's plantation, in more ways than one. I might have greater stature than most men, but I hadn't the shoulders or the hips. My new self hailed from Chicago – which meant that I was sturdy and ready for anything. Annie had met me on the train, and, seeing how I comported myself, had hired me to attend to her. My mother and father were dead (indeed, they were), and I had no other close relatives, as they had died of (here I thought about epidemics) yellow fever when I was away at school, and so I had been kept at that school until a year ago, when I had – here I paused to think of where I might have gone – been sent to Wisconsin. Now I attempted to think of any town I had ever heard of in Wisconsin, and remembered Roger Howell, who was from a town called – and then I paused again. Wawsomething. Let's say Wawbeshaw, I thought, and hoped that the real name would come to me. "Wawbeshaw" was a small farming community, and I worked there, sometimes in the barn and sometimes in the kitchen and sometimes caring for the four boys

(Abraham, Isaac, Martin, and John) for a year, until . . . I paused. Oh, yes, until the old man sold the farm and moved his family back to Chicago, which had certainly grown in our absence! Oh, my goodness me! These thoughts made me laugh, and I practiced my tales of the mud in Chicago, and how much more difficult the work was there than in "Wawbeshaw," for precisely that reason. Was there really a time when I stepped off the wooden walk and sank up to my knees in the mud? Well, perhaps that was a story that would make an Englishman laugh.

The ship continued to reel, so much so that sometimes I had to grab hold of the edge of my bed, but still no spewing, and the night did go by, and in the morning (no sleep) the storm had blown past us, and we were away from that second piece of land, which, over breakfast (which was served all morning), Mr. Gallant told me was named Newfoundland, but I misheard him and thought he said, "The New Found Land," a name I thought was most appealing. In his many travels, without Mrs. Gallant, Mr. Gallant had been to Canada, though not to the New Found Land. We were now, he said, east of Ireland, and with luck we would be carried by the Gulf Stream, as he called it, south of that island and up to Liverpool. The storm of the night before had seemed more unruly than it was – it had, indeed, sped us up a bit, and nothing had been lost except some bags of maizemeal, as they called cornmeal. I worked for a while on my name. Mrs. Gallant knew my name was Lidie Newton; Mr. Gallant may have not known my given name at all. But that was another reason to bid the Gallants good-bye as soon as we docked in Liverpool. I toyed with going back to my maiden name, Harkness, but I didn't want to be reminded of it. In the saloon and in the library, I listened to what my fellow passengers called one another – there were many Johns and Charleses, a few Williams, even a Mr. Brereton, though he didn't look a bit like Roland. Of the women, I saw four or five Janes, a June, a Mary, a Marie, a Maria, two Victorias, and a Lizzie. None of them appealed to me.

The surname I liked was Baron, but then I realized that the man whose name I thought that was, was really named Foxman. Baron was his title. One of the sailors was named Woodson. I took that one, and practiced saying the name "Helen Woodson," but then I remembered that governor in K.T., after Shannon, whose name was Woodson, and who had declared that K.T. was "in a state of insurrection," which meant the pro-slavers could do whatever they wanted. I didn't want to think of that whenever I said my name. Who was someone I respected? I closed my eyes and thought for a moment, then remembered reading *Pride and Prejudice*. There was a place in that book named "Longbourn." I thought of adopting that – "Long born." That was certainly me. So that was the one I chose. "Helen" – I liked the sound of it. I paused, though, thinking of Helen Day, Papa, and Lorna. Then I thought that maybe Helen was one of those girls born in a slaver family who might be won over, because of her fondness for Lorna, and her respect for her. So I stuck with Helen. "Helen Longbourn" – rather elegant.

After we ate, Annie went for another stroll around the ship, and I went into the library. I must say that, somehow, the library was well taken care of, because the books, even with all the reeling, were on the shelves, hardly at all disrupted. I did pick one up off the floor, behind a chair, and perhaps whoever had cleaned up the library hadn't seen it. It was thin. I opened the cover and saw that it was another novel, called *Emma,* by Miss Austen. I sat down and read a few pages. It was amusing. While I was reading, two men entered the library and sat near me. Whether they saw me or not, I had no idea, but they were much enthused about something, and because I could never resist eavesdropping, I soon knew that that something was horses. "Do you know, Charles," said the first man, "that the Cure Mare has foaled out?"

"I did not. What is she now? Nine or so, I would guess. I would have put her out to pasture a couple of years ago."

The first man laughed. "She is out to pasture, and a nice one.

Lord Durham has always fancied her. No reason not to give the girl a chance. Doesn't cost him anything."

"Except the stud fee."

"He might get around that."

"Who's the sire?"

"The very boy you would choose, Charles. West Australian."

"Aye. The very boy every man in Britain would choose. That could be a nick, indeed."

This made me smile, and I must have moved or made some noise, because the second fellow now looked my way. He said, "I say, Charlie. We've been spied upon!"

I held up my book.

The second fellow strode over to me and took it from my hand. "Ah," he said. "Miss Austen. She had many readers. My mother and aunt were among them."

I held out my hand. "Helen Longbourn."

He bowed, not seeming to notice that I had stolen my name from Miss Austen. "Rafe Hammond."

I decided to be bold. I said, "I was listening to you talk about horses. I'm very fond of horses."

"You may listen to me at any time. I am sure that the turf will be the death of me, but it will be a good death. Are you familiar with racing, then?"

"Only a bit. I had a horse when I was living in" – my pause was very brief – "Chicago. My nephew stole him away one morning, and when I finally found them, he had just won a race. I believe the purse was seventeen dollars." This, I made up.

"You don't know his breeding, do you?"

"That is a mystery in Chicago. But he's a leggy, strong gray." I pretended to myself that Jeremiah was still alive, out to pasture, enjoying himself.

Now the other man turned his chair so that I could see him. He had a big smile. He held out his hand. "Charles Dorsett." He ducked his head.

Mr. Hammond said, "If there is anything we talk of apart from horses and jockeys and the turf, I cannot think what it is."

I said, "Why were you in New York?"

"Oh, indeed," said Mr. Dorsett. "There is that. Business. Rafe and I are in the clothing trade. We take samples of our wools and linens to American merchants and force them down their throats." Now they both laughed. They were so good-natured that I could not imagine them forcing anything upon anyone.

I said, "If you please, you may now go back to discussing horses, because I would like to go back to listening to you."

"Here's the difficulty," said Charles Dorsett. "If you live, as we do, in Lancashire, there are so many tracks and so many meets that you may say to yourself that you have other things to do, but then you do not. Was the race your horse went in a jump race or a flat race?"

"Flat."

"If you want a bit of real excitement, then, you must get yourself to Aintree, which is two leagues from the harbor where we will dock. I think the run this year is in about three weeks, but I haven't kept track. You may watch them run and jump, or you may put your hat over your eyes the whole time." He shook his head. Rafe Hammond laughed, then said, "I say, have you noticed?"

"Noticed what?" said Mr. Dorsett.

"It does not appear that we are about to be tipped into the sea."

"No, indeed, but then those bergs do sneak up upon one. Most of the mass is underwater – what is that, eighty percent or more – so they can be a surprise." He turned to me. "We avoided one on the way to New York in November, but just by a hair. I saw the first mate, and he had gone white overnight."

Rafe Hammond said, "I am not going to contradict you, Charles.

It was a frightening experience. However" – he turned to me – "I've been told we're taking a more southerly route this time, and on the trip west, they only saw a few in the distance."

I said, "I thought they were going to hit the New Found Land."

The two of them both chuckled. Rafe Hammond said, "Indeed, the fellow in the cabin down from me must have been hoping for that, because he was praying all night. But, my dear, Newfoundland" – which he pronounced "Nufnnlnn" – "is hardly paradise. It's a peninsula where we had to dock for two days, and, with regard to the weather, it was quite like the Shetland Islands."

Charles Dorsett glanced at me with an informative look, and said, "A set of long-lost islands in the North Sea."

I said, "No horse racing?"

"Precisely," said Mr. Dorsett, smiling.

That was a good reminder, because now they began to tell me about this horse West Australian. He had won nine out of ten races, and was second in his first, which he ran as a two-year-old, just before he turned three.

"But, you see," said Charles Dorsett, "he's but fifteen-point-three hands, not the leggy big fellow some of them are, so he came into himself very quickly."

"And," said Rafe Hammond, "Scott didn't push him all that hard. After that first race, he was off for a good while, and then ran in the Two Thousand, and it was pouring – "

Just then, perhaps because I was so entertained by Mr. Dorsett and Mr. Hammond, Annie walked into the room without my noticing, and she said, "Ah, Lidie. I've been looking for you!" The two gentlemen turned their heads, and even though she addressed me as Lidie, thereby undercutting my attempt to play my role as Helen, both of their faces lit up. And Annie did, too, showing me that, whatever we had thought of her in Quincy, we had been utterly wrong, and Mallory Cunningham had been utterly right. Both men jumped up, held out their hands, escorted her over, and, good for me, I was forgotten in a moment.

She saw that they noticed her, too, because she loosened her shawl a bit, lifted her chin, and smiled a playful smile. I would have thought that lifting her chin would make her look snobbish, but the smile counteracted that, and the length and elegance of her neck were on display. Charles Dorsett went to bring a chair over for Annie. When he sat down again, I jumped into the fray and said, "Mr. Hammond, Mr. Dorsett, this is my employer, Ann Harkness. I am accompanying her to Liverpool."

But neither of the men looked at me. Rafe Hammond nodded slightly, and said, "Miss Harkness, what might you be doing in Liverpool?"

Annie's smile widened as if she were making a joke. She said, "I will be going onstage there. I have a sponsor, Mr. Mallory Cunningham. It's, perhaps, a gamble, but worth the trip, and I'm very grateful to him."

Charles Dorsett said, "I think I have never been to a stage performance in my life, but I shall have to change my habits."

Rafe Hammond said, "Indeed, the theater is very popular in Liverpool."

I said, "Except during the racing season?"

"Yes," said Mr. Hammond, "except during the racing season. But those who have leisure must do something with it, don't you agree?"

I thought of Annie at the sink or mopping the floor. She was certainly the one person here who might never have had a bit of leisure in her life, but now, in her simple but flattering gown, with her shawl that Beatrice had given her as a present after her Christmas performance, and her hands in the calfskin gloves, she convincingly nodded, then turned to me and said, "Darling, did you find a book?"

I held up the copy of *Emma*.

Rafe Hammond said, "That is appropriate reading for ladies."

I handed it to Annie, who took it, and then said, "The book I brought along was too brief. I've had to read it twice."

Charles Dorsett said, "And what book have you been reading? Mrs. Trollope often appeals to young ladies."

Annie said, "It is a play, entitled *Much Ado About Nothing*. I've enjoyed it, but not as much as I enjoyed *The Taming of the Shrew*."

Now both young men fell silent. Annie smiled and opened *Emma*. Because I'd looked at the last page, I said, "There must be more. It seems as though this is only volume one." And so Annie got up and went over to the shelves, where she gracefully searched for the rest of Miss Austen's novel. When she found it, she went over to the ledger where you were to write your name, your cabin number, and the titles of the books you had borrowed, then glided back to us and said, "My dear, don't overlook your victuals." I got out of my chair. She took my arm, and we nodded to the two young men.

Once we were outside of the library and on the deck again, I said, "Annie, I've forgotten to tell you that I changed my name. It's Helen Longbourn. You hired me in Chicago to accompany you. I am an orphan." She didn't ask why, or look offended that I had severed our relationship. She only nodded and said, "I've done much the same thing – I added an 'e' to my name, and when we get off the ship, I will be Anne, not Annie. 'Anne Revere.' Mallory chose the last name, he said, to give a little poke to English audiences. But I like it. It has a nice rhythm."

And so, there we were, in the middle of the Atlantic, soon to be Anne Revere and Helen Longbourn, reborn, or you might say, refreshed. The next time I ran into Mr. Dorsett – who was friendly but evidently shortsighted, because he would look up at me and squint his eyes – he did ask why "the lovely actress" had called me Lidie when my name was Helen, and I said my job was to keep a lid on her fancies so that we might arrive in Liverpool with a few pennies at any rate, and that made him laugh, whether he believed me or not. The two young men continued to be friendly in their distant, English way. I saw that it was only racing that opened them up. They were like the Gallants – if you happened to get them going, they had plenty to say, but as a rule, they held back – and I decided that Helen Longbourn would behave in the same manner.

Sometime around that point in our journey, it seemed to me that I had lost track of not only where we were – how would I keep track of that? – but how long we had been at sea. The nights and days jumbled into one another, not because of the light and the dark, but because of how random our sleeping was. One afternoon, I took a nap, woke up after dark, and didn't realize until I looked at the provisions that it was suppertime and not breakfast time. Annie, or Anne, seemed to be reacting in a similar way, and she made me promise not to tell anyone that she spent some minutes viewing the sunset, then, when clouds covered the light, came into the cabin and told me that she had seen a lovely sunrise, but why were we headed west, away from it? Was the ship attempting to avoid something? I told her it was a sunset, and then we both threw our hands in the air and she said, "I do hope Mallory Cunningham has someone lead us about for at least a few days. Otherwise, I don't know how we are going to overcome our thickheadedness."

And we did see an iceberg – not terribly close, but I was mindful of what Mr. Dorsett had told me. It was a clear night – after midnight, I suspected – cloudy but not foggy, and so no brilliant stars, to my disappointment. I had just turned away from the rail when the ship turned, also, and I saw it as we moved to avoid it: pale, two sharp triangles, one pointing to my right, one pointing to my left, rough and ragged over the top. If no one had alerted me, I might have thought it was an island of some sort. The surface of the ocean was silky smooth, and I did think that I saw the paleness of the berg slip beneath that edge. In the morning, I happened upon the sailor who had welcomed us onto the ship when we boarded so many days ago – I now knew that his name was Daniel Smack, that he had crossed the Atlantic seven times and also traveled to the east as far as India. I asked him if he had seen the berg, and he said, "Ow, you mean the one lite last night, ehh? That was a luhvly thing. Kept to itself, 'e did. The captain wasn't a wee bet nervous with that one. Now, don't ye go askin' me about the one two dies ago." He shook his head and laughed. I had noticed nothing, not even a lurch.

There was another day of bad weather, bad enough so we didn't want to go out onto the deck, but the wind was from the south, rather warm, and the swell regular. I stayed in the cabin, curled up in my bunk, reading *The Newcomes*. I enjoyed it – not because I understood it, but because I did not understand it, and so making my way through the observations and references was similar to walking round a town I'd never been to and trying to figure out which way was north and which way was south. Mr. Thackeray wrote in an amusing, friendly style. One passage made me laugh out loud: "'Gad,' the dear old Major used to say, 'if we were not to talk freely of those we dine with, how mum London would be! Some of the pleasantest evenings I have ever spent have been when we have sate after a great dinner, *en petit comité*, and abused the people who are gone.'" This so reminded me of Quincy, of Alice and Beatrice and Harriet. And I also enjoyed those strange words, "gad," "mum," "sate." In the course of that day, I finished the first volume, and since there were so many, I made up my mind to leave each one behind as I completed it, so, the next morning, Anne and I walked to the library after our morning meal to leave the volumes there. She crossed out her name in the log book – I saw it was still "Ann Harkness" – and that was symbolic, too, I thought. I set the first volume of *The Newcomes* beside the log book and wondered where I would leave the second.

We walked around the deck and came upon Daniel Smack again. He smiled in a friendly way, and we paused. I wished him a good morning, he touched his forehead, and I said, "Where do you think we are, then?"

He said, "Well, now, should be ayble ta get a peek at Barleycove, if ya keep yer eyes open. Off t' th' left thar." He waved his arm.

"Barleycove?"

"Aye, County Cork, in Ireland. Wee bit of a town. Then it's up the Irish Sea, Ireland to the left, Wiles and England to the right, and if there's n' starm silin' through, we can avide th' rocks." He laughed and zipped away. Anne and I leaned over the railing and watched. I saw some humps, no green, nor any snow, but, then, it was March now, the beginning of March, though I had no idea what day. If I had ever given any thought to Ireland in my lifetime, I don't know when that was, but, looking across the gray-blue water, I remembered some people I had known in Quincy – the Shaughnessys, and another family, too – I thought for a moment – the O'Haras. I said to Anne, "Do you remember the O'Haras?" She shook her head. It was said around town that the O'Haras had come to Quincy straight from Ireland at the height of the famine, but what had happened to them before they came no one ever mentioned. What was that? Ten years ago now. And as I looked for the coast of that island, I vowed, once again, that Helen Longbourn would not be the careless fool that Lidie Newton had been, always unprepared, uninformed. Anne didn't ask who the O'Haras were, but she did stare as intently as I did. We agreed to go back to our cabin and pack up our things, so that we might spend the day on the deck, reconnoitering, or, indeed, enjoying the perspective. There were rocks and there were cliffs and there were curved, pale sandy coves where the blue waves flowed back and forth, and let me say that those bits, where the ocean and the land came into quiet contact, were the part that I liked best, that no one ever talked about, and they reminded me of some of the places where the boys of Quincy did play, but the lapping of the Mississippi, such as it was, was brown, not blue-green.

Anne got excited, and turned into the person I had once known, who was bobbing up and down on her toes and laughing.

It took all day and most of the night to get to Liverpool. Anne said that the ship stopped at one point, after I fell asleep, but she was still awake, and perhaps the purpose of the stop was to enable our docking by the first light, which would make sense. At any rate, our bags, such as they were, were packed, we were swaddled in our shawls, and we were the first ones off the ship. I had no idea what time it was. I longed for my watch – Thomas's watch – but I had sold it in order to get some provisions when Lorna and I were on the run. For a moment, I imagined having Lorna with us, how the other passengers would look at her – some wrinkling their brows, and others admiring her grace and her way of telling Anne and me what to do (she was good at that). Perhaps she had escaped after all, like the girl in Mrs. Stowe's book. I hoped so.

The sun had risen just behind the hills above the harbor. Once we disembarked, Anne looked at me and said, "Thank you, Helen dear, for accompanying me on this journey. Don't let me forget to send Alice another letter, telling her that we have arrived safely, though heaven only knows how it might get there." And then we looked about, and the principal thing we saw was piles and piles of coal heaped on the docks, and very little else.

We stood still, perhaps a bit dumbfounded, and then a boy came up to us and said, "I say, is one of you Miss Revere?"

Anne nodded and said, "I am Miss Revere."

The boy said, "Good 'nough, then. Mr. Cunningham sent me to wait for the ship, and said to bring you back to his home when I might find ye. I'm guessing 'e's still asleep, though. Most of 'em are, this time a day." The boy led us between two of the piles of coal to a cobbled street where another boy, slightly older, was standing with two dark bay horses that were harnessed to a pleasant-looking carriage. I could not help myself. I petted the horses, and one of them ruffled a little sigh out of his nostrils. I said to the older boy, "What day is it? I'm a little confused."

He said, "Miss, six March."

Ten days at sea.

I had expected that Mr. Cunningham would live in the countryside, in some such gloomy estate that I imagined from my readings of Mr. Dickens, with creaking trees bending over the roof and thick, uncared-for bushes covering the front of the house, but he did not. The horses trotted up a hill, and then kept trotting, the older boy in the front of the carriage, Anne and I side by side on the seat, and the younger boy sitting behind us, humming to himself. Once we were on our way, the trip took very little time, and, in accordance with my vow, I did my best to pick out the names of the streets, as they were written on the buildings – Park Lane was one, Upper Parliament Street, and Hope Street. There was a park, too, though not on Park Lane – rather, next to a cathedral. But the house, large, brick, square, was on Canning Street, and I hoped that this was not an omen that Anne and I were destined for housework. It was still early when we arrived at the house. The man who opened the door for us and bowed but did not smile, and was much better dressed than we were, stepped aside and waved us in, pointed to a clock when I asked him what time it was. It was ten after nine. Then the man showed us to our rooms – mine downstairs and Anne's upstairs, mine pleasant, with two windows looking out at the trees, everything, including the walls and the floors and the coverlid, shades of gray and brown.

5

I SET DOWN my bag and went out into the entry hall. No one was there, and the place was, indeed, very quiet, so I slipped out the front door and went for a walk around the block, not forgetting to stare at the signs on the corner – Hope Street and Canning Street. The sixth of March. This weather – balmy, cool, wet but not misty or raining – would have been called pleasant at this time of year in Quincy and ideal in K.T., but there was no one walking on the street. I reminded myself to ask Mr. Cunningham why that might be after he rose. Other than the weather, though, there was absolutely nothing familiar about this spot. On each side of the street (I did stare at the horses and carriages and carts going by – there were plenty of those), a row of brick buildings ran into the distance, three stories high, with white steps and white trim, and black wrought-iron balconies across the second-story windows. They were severe and elegant, and no rag-bedecked men and women and children were seated against them, as they had been in New York City. Every step around the block was clean and elegant. I turned the corner to the right, and went down "Percy Street." There was an offshoot that looped into a busier, dirtier area where horses were standing, one of them being shod, I could see as I passed, and there were also people pushing carts and carrying loads. I watched until one man looked at me, and then I walked on. I did get disoriented a bit, but the greatest pleasure was walking beside the park, and noting that some of the flowers in there were already set to blossom.

But the park turned out to be a cemetery; when I peered through the bars of the high fence, I could look down upon rows of gravestones standing upright, none of them terribly ornate. I did want to get in, but there was no gate along Hope Street, and I feared that I didn't have enough time to go all the way around to the other side, as the cemetery seemed to run along Hope Street as far as I could see. I went back to Mr. Cunningham's sturdy house and rapped on the door. The man opened it again, as if he had been standing there waiting for me. I asked him what time it was, and he said, "Ah. Miss Longbourn. It is half ten. Mr. Cunningham and Miss Revere are awaiting you in the dining room." I nearly looked around to see whom he was talking to, but I smiled my best smile and dipped my head, then followed him to the dining room, the very thing Alice had always wished she had.

The table was made of large, dark, shiny wood and had elaborate carved legs. Anne was sitting at the far end with an entirely bald man who stood up at once as I came in and said, "Ah, Miss Longbourn. Welcome!" He stepped around Anne, came to me, held out his hand. I saw that he was the man in the bowler hat, and I also saw that he did have some hair around the bottom of his head that was gray, like his neatly trimmed beard. He said, "I ask your pardon that my wife is not here to welcome you. She and my daughter have gone to Bath for a month. My two sons, are, of course, away at school, and so the house is a bit lonely." I sat down in the chair he showed me to, across from Anne, and the provisions began to arrive – something that looked like biscuits but were chock full of dried fruit, three or four slices of ham and a very black sausage that I later found out was made from blood (I ate some; it was tasty, and if you have been to K.T. you will eat anything), fried eggs, a large pot of tea. Anne ate a bit, I ate a lot, Mr. Cunningham watched over us with a pleasant look on his face and the top of his head shining in the sunlight.

Because I was too low-class to know any better, I said, "Mr. Cunningham, why does everyone get up so late?"

"Ah," he said, "those who are flush with money and time eat late, stay out until at least two in the morning, and are lucky to be up before noon. Those who make their way by the sweat of their brow are up early and hard at work by nine. It's a peculiarity of the English. You might tell how much a man has to live on by what time of day that he is yawning."

I saw that Mr. Cunningham had a sense of humor. I judged that he was perhaps fifty, and I guessed that he understood British manners by having seen them from all sides, up and down. The man who had let us in, who I later understood was the butler, Barnsby, was more elegant, handsome, and standoffish than Mr. Cunningham, and I did see that Mr. Cunningham was rather intimidated by him, though he tried not to show it. When I went into the kitchen from time to time, though, I saw that the cook, Berta, wasn't intimidated by the butler at all, and ordered him around like a dog. One time, she even swatted him away with her wooden spoon.

After our meal, Mr. Cunningham showed us about the house. It was not a castle – it only had twelve rooms, of which his wife's chamber was the most elegant, and was not the same as his, which was simpler and more spare, though with plenty of hats on a rack beside his window.

The chamber he had given Anne was nearly as elegant as the wife's, with carpets and drapes and chairs and a four-poster bed with a silk top, everything shades of green and blue. Her chamber also had a delicious scent, which I traced that night after I had undone her corset and she was lying on the bed, to an empty box that was sitting on her side table. I picked it up and smelled it so many times that, after a day or two, she handed it to me, and I took it to my room downstairs. The box turned out to be made from sandalwood, smooth and reddish, with no decorations. Barnsby eventually told me that the wood came from India and was very precious. He seemed to be itching to take it out of my room, but I told him that Miss Revere found it offensive, so I was keeping it for her.

Mr. Cunningham's plan was to put Anne to work at once, in a play entitled *Not So Bad as We Seem*. Rehearsals had begun two days before, and opening night was scheduled for March 17. Anne was to play the daughter, Lucy Thornside, and that very morning, she began working on her part. For about two hours, I sat with her in her room, reading the play back and forth with her. We both had manuscripts, and sometimes I would read her lines to her, and sometimes she would read them back to me. She said that hearing them engraved them in her brain better than reading them herself.

Most of the characters in the play were men with some funny names – Hardman, Softhead, Thornside, Easy. Anne was one of two young women; the other was "Barbara Easy." Anne did not appear until Act Two. It was evident from the beginning that her job was to be wooed, but not too readily. Or, rather, it was "Lucy's" job to be wooed, and Anne's job to appear worth wooing. As we went through the play, and, following that, three more times through the second act, I could see that Anne was trying out various ways, not of talking – perhaps Mallory Cunningham or the director would coach her in that (already, my experience of the Cunard ship and Liverpool, such as it was, had shown me that the manner in which English men and women differentiated themselves when they talked was careful and precise, and, indeed, I thought it was best for me to stick with my flat Quincy pronunciation, so as not to look as though I was aiming for some sort of higher status than those that I spoke to might give me). She moved about the room, carrying her papers and saying the words, sitting here and there, walking, turning, bending, lifting her chin, tossing her head. So, I thought, this was what she'd been doing on the other side of that thin wall between us in Alice's house. She seemed to me to flicker into and out of the person of Lucy, who was sometimes meek and sometimes sassy and sometimes turned inward and sometimes open.

As I read the other lines to her, I tried to recall what she had been like as a small child. It was not really true that she had begun washing the dishes and mopping the floor by the time she was five years old, and, indeed, she had learned to read and write much more quickly than I had. But all I could remember was watching her trip around the side yard when I was about six and she was four or five. Alice had flowers and various vegetables planted out there, and it must have been spring, because I watched little Annie, holding her skirt to keep it out of the way, jump back and forth over the rows and laugh. I said nothing, so it took Alice a while to find her, and when she did, she told the poor child, three times, to settle down, and then slapped her on her rump. I never saw Annie run about like that again, but let's say she did.

At some point, the housemaid came tapping at the door. I opened it, and she said that Mr. Cunningham would be ready to depart for the theater in a quarter of an hour, and did we need any help dressing? I was about to say we did not when the maid handed me what she had been carrying over her arm, which was two dresses, a pale mauve one, small, and a brown one, large, both some sort of wool, I guessed, though mixed with something smoother. No flounces, for which I was grateful. She handed them to me, and Anne and I took off the gowns that we had been wearing for two weeks now, without, I may say, hardly noticing, since in Quincy, in the winter, you wore anything you had that would keep you warm, and no one, except perhaps Beatrice, cared a whit. In K.T., it seemed to me as though nothing would keep me warm.

The gowns were neatly done – Anne's fit well, mine was short in the waist, but long enough in the skirt. Mallory Cunningham met us at the bottom of the stairs, and he looked only at Miss Revere. I could tell by his smile that he now felt that the odds of success on the bet he had placed to get us here had shortened, and he was happy about it.

The theater was an easy walk. The streets were, indeed, more lively now, the walks full of men and women in all forms of dress, and the street full of carriages and carts. There were also some young girls. We passed a long brick wall as we walked up Hope Street, higher than my head, with tree limbs just beginning to leaf out leaning over the top. As we came to the end of the wall, Mr. Cunningham pointed to the gate down the next street, where more girls in simple dresses, all alike, were waiting to enter. The girls looked about eleven or twelve, some of them older. Mr. Cunningham said that the building, which we could now catch a glimpse of, was a famous one in Liverpool, formerly owned by a slave dealer, now by an abolitionist, who did not live there, but sponsored it as a school for girls. "Indeed," said Mr. Cunningham, "there's a poke in the eye to the former owner. Unfortunately, he's too dead to feel it." But he laughed so loudly that a few of the girls glanced our way. Then he turned around and pointed to a building we had passed on the other side of the road, less imposing, and said that that was the "Mechanics Institute," which was a boys' school for learning various trades. He seemed in an excellent mood. Anne looked here and there, as he told her things, but I could see her lips moving as she quietly recited her lines. We paused, and Mr. Cunningham said to me, "Even though I expect you to accompany Miss Revere to the theater, I do not believe that walk is dangerous. Our part of town is relatively new. The gangs, and there are a few, are out and about on the far side of Tithebarn Street." He waved his hand to the right – the north, I thought – then said, "Miss Longbourn, you should take care, but it is also true that you have an imposing appearance. I do not fear for you."

I said, "I will try to be observant, Mr. Cunningham."

He nodded and smiled.

The theater was down a shorter street, and was, indeed, small. I could see that Mr. Cunningham was hedging his bets, and well he should. Once again, there was a man there to open the door for us, and just as we got inside, another man, this one a bit rotund, grabbed Mr. Cunningham by the elbow and said, "Mal, old fellow, where've you been? Everyone's been sitting around for the last half-hour!" But he didn't sound angry, only eager. He didn't even wait for an answer, but spun toward Anne, Miss Revere, and stared at her. Anne held out her gloved hand and gave him her best smile – not brilliant, not snobbish, not shy, but intriguing, playful. The man took her hand, squeezed it. Mr. Cunningham said, "Indeed, Ellis, calm yourself. Miss Revere, your manager, Mr. Thomas Ellis. Mr. Ellis is playing Softhead. An appropriate part."

Mr. Ellis's laugh pealed out through the hall, and he now turned to me, and said, "Sir, you must be an actor, too, a young man adept at ladies' parts." His eye was twinkling. I glanced at Mr. Cunningham, who looked a little taken aback, but I was not offended. I said, in a rather high, sharp voice, "If that were true, Mr. Ellis, I would be most content with my life, but, indeed, my job is to put up with the disadvantages of both masculinity and femininity."

"My sympathies," said Mr. Ellis. We exchanged a smile, and I saw that there would be teasing, and I vowed not to be shy in giving as good as I was to get.

The other actors were milling about onstage. Nothing about the place was grand. The seats were velvet, but a bit worn, and there was an upper level, but only one. I guessed that the capacity of the theater was four or five hundred. There were no boxes, as there had been at Barnum's. But even so, to the eye of an American woman, the place looked appealing – not elegant, but formerly elegant. Mr. Cunningham and I found seats in the stalls. Ellis escorted Anne up the stairs and introduced her to the others. I especially watched the other actress, who was playing Barbara Easy. She was older than Anne by a good many years, but she sorted her actions so that she did seem to be about Anne's age. Her hair was tied back, and just before everyone took their seats and they began going through the lines in the sections that Anne was in, a wig was brought to her by someone who had been backstage. She set it on her head – golden blond, with a cap, in exactly the style I had seen on some of the better-dressed ladies as we were walking up Hope Street. Everyone settled down to their work, and went about it industriously. Ellis sat beside Anne and whispered things to her. She nodded agreeably and, evidently, did her best to follow instructions. She had learned her lines, at least for her first act – she made only one mistake that I saw.

It was meant to be an amusing play. The act began with Lucy Thornside's father becoming suspicious of his servant once he realizes that the servant knows that Thornside has stashed away some money in the library. Both actors were about the same age, and both hammed it up a good deal – Thornside turning to the audience (Mr. Cunningham and me) with terrified and angry looks on his face, the other actor, playing Hodge, talking in such a broad accent that I could barely understand what he was saying, but acting so respectfully toward Thornside that I thought he might fall on his face and kiss Thornside's boots. After Hodge fell silent, Thornside looked to the right and then made a move as if he'd been shot, he was so startled. He waved his arms as if he were grabbing a sword and then poking at something, and his line was "This is the fifth bunch of flowers that's been thrown at me through the window – what can it possibly mean?" I was the one that laughed out loud, and Mr. Cunningham nodded. Thornside and his friend went back and forth for a bit, and then there came another line that made me laugh, though I controlled myself better. Easy said that the flowers must be from a woman, and Thornside said, "A woman! – my worst fears are confirmed! In the small city of Placentia, in one year, there were no less than seven hundred cases of slow poisoning, and all by women."

The new man was the one named Easy, and he was very relaxed and good-natured in the way he said his lines. They went back and forth about Lucy, and the fellows who were after her, and as they did, I saw Anne lean forward, paying close attention to what they were saying. Just before Anne said her first line, Thornside declared that he had plans for Lucy, but then she said, "O, my dear father, forgive me if I disturb you; but I did so long to see you." I understood that she had been listening closely to the fellow playing Thornside, because her way of speaking sounded very like his. Perhaps other actors noticed the same thing, because they were, indeed, looking at her. From the audience, I could not see her face – all the actors were sitting in a circle, Thornside and Hodge facing me and Anne's back toward me – but she went on smoothly, saying her lines and sounding for all the world as if she actually cared for the crazy fellow, and perhaps she knew how to do that, as she'd always been openly fond of Roland Brereton, and had laughed at remarks the rest of us drew back from.

Lucy's job was to be the sensible one, because she pointed out that the howling dog, from the night before, was howling at the full moon, but then Thornside, again turning to look at Mr. Cunningham and me, indicated that her very act of knowing that the moon was full was suspicious, because she must have been looking out the window! I laughed again and I saw Mr. Thornside's eyebrow flicker as if he heard me laugh and appreciated it, but everything else about his face remained the same. I was impressed.

The lines went back and forth. More of the men spoke up, and Mr. Easy produced a very loud and amusing sneeze on command. Anne's job, as Lucy, was to confuse everyone but herself about which of the eligible men she actually preferred. There were five acts, and all of them long. I wondered how she was going to keep the mystery going, especially as the one who played the nobleman was by far the handsomest. Later, after the rehearsal was finished, we were taken for a late supper by Mr. Cunningham. We then walked back to his house, where the plan was that I would work with her on her other scenes. I asked how she planned to do it, and she said her only thought on this was that she had looked at the actors who were playing the various suitors, and she herself did not know whom Lucy should choose. Mr. Cunningham seemed pleased but not elated. I thought of those men on the ship, who had told me about the Aintree racetrack. Perhaps Anne had gotten over the first few jumps successfully, and that was enough for Mr. Cunningham.

The next day was Sunday, no rehearsals, but we did go with Mr. Cunningham to his local church, St. James, an imposing, dark brick building with a square tower set in a large, already grassy graveyard shaded by many trees. It was a pleasant walk, in spite of some mist, and we could hear, as we had fairly steadily since installing ourselves into Mr. Cunningham's house, the horns of ships as they entered and departed from the dock area, carrying mostly coal, as I had surmised when I'd seen the mounds. Liverpool, I thought, was a strange place, and this church, St. James, rather epitomized that – the rows of brick buildings and parks and trees and hills made you think that you were solidly on the ground, and yet the blowing horns and the mist and the winds, the screeching of birds flying everywhere, made you feel that you didn't know where you were. You might walk through the streets when they were quiet, or you might walk through the streets when they were bustling, you might see rows of gravestones, or you might see rows of bushes budding out and ready to flower. You might hear a man or a woman talking in a beautiful, expressive voice, or you might hear a man or a woman saying words that you could not understand at all.

One person that I could not understand was the minister who gave the sermon in the Church of St. James. The hall was big, there were statues here and there, and the pews were filled. We sat about halfway back, and Mr. Cunningham nodded right and left to everyone he saw. Anne smiled, I, perhaps, did not, but, then, I was so afraid of falling over the children who were running up and down the aisles that I didn't notice. At some point, the children were herded away, I suppose to Sunday school, but then there were others – old people mostly, who also presented a hazard. All in all, I was thrilled to return to Mr. Cunningham's, have a bite to eat, and then get down to our work, which was to go through the entire play, beginning to end, because the rehearsals were to begin again the next day, and there were only nine days of rehearsals before the opening night.

Mr. Cunningham said that Barnsby would keep us supplied with provisions so that we wouldn't have to take time for dinner or tea, and indeed he did, or Berta did, and perhaps Anne had told Berta what she preferred, because there was bread and butter and muffins and some sort of lamb, but Berta also contributed something I'd never had – crumpets, with her own apple butter. We ate and recited and recited and ate, and Anne walked about her room so much and cocked her head so often and lifted her arms so gracefully that she seemed well fueled by what Barnsby called "the comestibles." I eventually came to understand the play, and I saw that it was meant to raise a laugh, and I certainly hoped that it would. We stayed up late enough to light candles, late enough to hear the revelers in the street, to exhaust ourselves, and then sleep until Mr. Cunningham was already risen, but Anne did learn her lines, and so I was, in a polite way, dismissed. My services were no longer needed, and I was free, as both Mr. Cunningham and I realized, to meander about the town and see what I could see. Before he took Anne off to her Monday rehearsal, he handed me a stick, made of another wood I'd never heard of, East Indian rosewood, with an ivory handle. He said, "And I know you won't hesitate to use it, nor should you." He also handed me some coins, and told me that I had earned my wages, and more. Indeed, I thought, he was a generous man, and if getting out of Quincy was my salvation, then Mallory Cunningham was my savior.

It must be said that when I went out that afternoon with my stick and my wrap, as they called shawls in England, I did not quite know what I was going to do, and then I turned up Canning Street and walked along, away from the harbor, and what I did was look at the horses. Perhaps it was that thought of "Aintree" that fixed it in my mind. I also kept my eye out for those fellows from the ship – Hammond, tall, and Dorsett, short – but if I saw them, I didn't recognize them. As for the horses, first I looked at the grays. A lovely group of four trotted by; Mr. Cunningham later told me this was called a "four-in-hand," and I had seen four horses hauling wagons in America, but nothing like this high-stepping, arched-neck group, dappled all over, seeming to trot in a unified rhythm, and the driver with his head up, a bowler hat on, and the whip lifted in his hand but never descending upon the horses. I wasn't the only one to stop and stare: one man near me exclaimed, "Percherons, no dat, but Ay nivver saw none that light! Fella must've bred'm 'imself." There were also several gray ponies harnessed to small carts. The ones I saw I couldn't help comparing to Jeremiah, and he always came out ahead, especially as I was reminded of the time, after he was stolen, when he reappeared, came to me, and sniffed the back of my neck, then followed me – such a pleasure.

I walked for four hours, got soaking wet. When I later told Barnsby how far I had gone, to a place called Croxteth Hall, he was impressed with me, perhaps for the first time. He paused to chat, I suspected, about Croxteth Hall, but I said, "There are so many beautiful horses. I couldn't stop staring at them, and I suppose they led me there."

He now let out a little grunty noise that I realized was a laugh, and then said, "Might Miss Longbourn be a horse aficionado?"

I'd never heard that word, but I knew what it meant. I said, "I am."

"Might Miss Longbourn enjoy the turf?"

I said, "I think everyone likes a grassy field."

Barnsby said, "I am referring to horse racing."

I said, "I do."

"Indeed!"

He said no more, but all I had to do the next morning was tell him a bit about Jeremiah and the race he had won in K.T., and Barnsby's demeanor changed completely and permanently, for it turned out that if there was anything Barnsby liked to do, it was to place bets (he said always small ones), look over breeding records, go to races important and unimportant, chat about sire lines, and look at pictures of famous horses. He showed me the four that Mr. Cunningham had in the smoking room, one of a filly named Blink Bonny, a slender dark bay with a large white star. He said that, the year before, she had done something no horse had ever done before, much less a filly – won both the "Darby" and the "Oaks," two days apart. I said, "Did you place a bet on her?"

"For the Oaks, yes, for the Darby, no, but I do have a great fondness for her dam, Queen Mary. Poor thing fell in her first race, and never raced again, but she's produced one great horse after another. And Melbourne is a fine beast, too."

I said, "Is he related to West Australian?" And then Barnsby was won over to my side forever, because he was a great fan of West Australian. I said, "What is this race at Aintree?"

"Ah, Miss Longbourn," he said, "you have missed it this year, I am sorry to say. It was run the day you and Miss Revere arrived on the ship."

"Did you get to go there?" I wondered why those men on our ship had been so wrong, but I didn't say anything.

"Alas, no, but I was fortunate in placing a small bet on the winner, a handsome ten-year-old named Little Charley. I won't say I have an instinct, but I have had some good luck of late." I asked him about the horses I'd seen, with large eyes and slender noses, and he said, "Oh, the Arabians! They are the absolute source of horse racing!" And then he told me about Byerley Turk, Darley Arabian, and Godolphin Arabian. I said, "Were any of them gray?" Barnsby shook his head, then said, "But there are plenty of grays now. I placed a bet on Chanticleer for the Doncaster Cup some years ago, and won a fair amount, but he is said to be a nasty sort. There was a gray mare, Miss Belvoir, oh, perhaps a hundred and forty years ago, who is said to be the ancestor of all the grays we have today, but I cannot say if that is true." I did wonder if perhaps Jeremiah had been a Thoroughbred, given his elegance.

Here is how I discovered that in England I was a member of the servant class: not only did I have a small, plain room on the bottom floor of Mr. Cunningham's house, and eat in the kitchen, and not only did the visitors who came throughout the week call Anne "Miss Revere" and me "Helen," but Mr. Cunningham, Berta, and the housemaids also began calling me Helen. Only Barnsby called me "Miss Longbourn," but he did so with a twinkle in his eye. And, then, I was asked to do errands, at first a few, later on a regular basis – to the apothecary, to the greengrocer, to the meat market, to the dressmaker (who came to Mr. Cunningham's to measure Anne, but I had to go there to pick up the three gowns Mr. Cunningham had ordered). If Anne was to go out and about, and Mr. Cunningham was busy, I (and my stick) were to accompany her. I still had my pistol in my bag, but I saw that such a thing was not appropriate in Liverpool, as it had been in K.T., or even in Quincy. And why would it be? Even though there were thefts and fights and sailors and drunks, there was also an air of civilization that we did not have back home – not in K.T., but also not in Chicago or New York City.

Part of my discovery that I was a servant was that that was the best thing to be. The other servants were interesting to chat with, the errands kept me out of the house and exploring the town, and there were plenty of servants to blend in with. Even wealthy women in places I'd been to in America were not as restricted as they were in Liverpool, and I sometimes wondered how they passed their time here. Of course, I heard shouts and even insults on the street of the sort that "fine" women were not subject to, or perhaps didn't hear, since they moved about in carriages and hardly ever walked. But these shouts were nothing compared to what I had heard from the Border Ruffians in K.T. or from the gamblers and grifters that went up and down the river in Quincy. Once, when I was walking up Rodney Street, someone shouted, "Look at that horse-faced hussy!" and I laughed aloud, and then the man who had shouted it laughed with me, gave me a wave, and did not draw a pistol, as he might have in K.T. I told Barnsby about this, and he was amused.

In other words, as a servant girl, I was free, especially after Berta put me to work for an hour slicing beets and parsnips and discovered that not only could I not do it correctly, but I was in constant danger of slicing my own hand, and then she said she hoped the best for me, as I was a "daycent gal," and sent me off for some halibut she had ordered from the fishmonger.

Anne also treated me like her servant – pointing at things she wanted me to hand her, waving me out of the room, never saying thank you but only tipping her head, walking in front of me – but we knew that she had to, because she could not be who she had been in Quincy and at the same time who she wanted to be in England, and that she had to practice. At one point, she apologized for asking me to pick up a hairpin that she had dropped, and I said, "I know you must practice. I have to, also. It's very hard for me not to call you 'Annie.' "

I kept my eye out for a letter from Alice or Harriet or Beatrice in response to what Anne had sent in New York, and also the first day after we'd gotten to Canning Street. The post came every day, but nothing from Quincy. I did look at the return addresses when I could – if, say, Barnsby had set one of the letters on a shelf beside the door – and there were a few from America (Philadelphia and New York), and one from Toronto, Canada, but I couldn't tell when they had been sent without asking Mr. Cunningham. I didn't know what I actually thought about our family's cutting us off in response to our cutting them off – Alice, had, after all, been kind to me, and so had Beatrice and Harriet, in their own ways. But the only person I knew who had left his relatives was Thomas, and he did so because they believed in the Emigrant Aid Company, and sent him. If anything, when I met his parents in Massachusetts, they seemed to be even more avid abolitionists than he was.

Since I did the errands, I was given money to pay for what the others had ordered, or to pay off accounts that they had with the merchants. After a week, I still had not spent any of the coins Mr. Cunningham had given me for my own use, but I did come to know what English money was – a pound, a shilling, pence, sixpence. I didn't know how those compared to dollars, nickels, dimes, and bits, but as I came to understand my coins, I saw that I had more money than I had realized, and took it out of my bag and put it into an inside pocket I had sewn into my new dress. I didn't want to be away from it, to leave it in my room or in my bag. I put a kerchief in with it, to prevent it from jingling, and I also held a few pence in my hand as I was walking to give to beggars, especially child beggars, as, depending on the district where I walked, there were plenty of those.

In fact, I walked so much that I wore out the sole of one of my boots, and had to find a shoemaker, which I did. The sole was not worn through, it was simply flapping, and the shoemaker, whose name, he said, was "Mr. Boots," charged me two shillings to sew the sole back together. As it was morning when I turned up, and he was only starting his work, he did it right then, and that was how I came to know another servant, Reggie Scofield, who was bringing in three pairs of boots that his employers had broken up by mistakenly running over them in their carriage. They were fancy boots – two pairs tall and shiny black, one pair smaller, with heels, a dark-brown color. The first thing that struck me about Reggie Scofield was that I sensed him standing behind me without hearing him step into the shop, and then I turned around, my hand on my stick, and I was only facing his Adam's apple. I looked up. If I had ever seen anyone who was "horse-faced," it was Reggie Scofield, who had a long, sharp, pointed nose with large nostrils, large brown eyes, and thick eyelashes. Thinking of that expression, "horse-faced," must have made me smile, and Reggie Scofield smiled back. Mr. Boots now came out of the back room and handed me my boot, took his two shillings, and said, "Mornin', Reg."

When Reggie Scofield handed him the three pairs and told the story, I was lingering in the window of the shop, where there were a few samples on display, and of course I eavesdropped on the whole thing – Mr. Furnish hadn't realized that he'd lost the bag with the boots in them until he entered the front door and Mrs. F. rifled through the things he was carrying and asked him where the boots were, and then they'd gone out and found them round the side of the house, where he'd dropped them just before the stableman led the horses off to the stable. The paving there was cobbles, which was why they were so scratched and broken up, and . . .

All this time, Mr. Boots was handling the footwear, and when Reggie Scofield finished his tale, he said, "Ten shillin's ought ta cover it, but I don't know when I c'n get to it."

"Make it twelve, Mr. Boots."

"I'll see to it tomorrow."

I set down the lady's boot that I was holding, and Reggie Scofield turned. I preceded him out the door and down the steps, but he caught up to me on the walk and said, "I'm thinkin' you're mee sister."

I said, "May it be so."

It turned out that Reggie's employers lived on a street not far from 2 Canning Street, in a similar row of houses, called Falkner Street. I'd not seen him before (I would have noticed) because the family he worked for had just returned from Glasgow, where Mrs. Furnish had relations. We walked up Duke Street, not exactly as if we were walking together, since I was carrying some parcels and he was, too. I did not, for example, have my hand on his arm. But we were near enough to one another to chat, and the first thing I said was, "Am I your younger sister or your older sister?"

He paused and looked me up and down. Then he said, "Looks to me as though we might be Irish twins."

I said, "What are those?"

"Pair o' babes within a year o' each other."

I said, "And what year were you born in?"

"Thirty-five."

I said, "Indeed. I was, too!" Then I said, "What's your favorite thing to do?" I assumed that he would say placing bets on horse races, but he said, "Tendin' the gard'n, I spose. Gettin' around town. I came in here from Giggleswick. Lovely spot, but not much trouble you can get into there." He smiled.

I said, "Does everyone laugh there? I am from a town called Quincy, and everyone there winces."

Now he did laugh. A few minutes later, we came to Mr. Cunningham's large brown house. I had started heading for the kitchen door rather than the front door, and now I stopped at the gate of the grounds and turned to him. I said, in my brash American way, "I would like to see your garden."

And he said, "I would like to show you a fair few of the parks they 'ave here." We both nodded, and he turned and continued up Canning Street. I watched him for a bit. He had a long stride, stood up straight, looked out for the other people in the street. I would accept Reggie Scofield as my brother, indeed.

Perhaps because of the ease with which I joked with Reggie and he with me, I allowed myself to think of Thomas – not because the two of them were alike, but because of my comfort that they were dissimilar. Nine months since Thomas was shot, and Jeremiah, too, and nearly two years since Thomas and I met when I was tending to the washing with Harriet.

I was carrying something to the kitchen, and I passed my reflection in one of the many mirrors in Mr. Cunningham's house. When I paused to look, I did not see much that was different about my outer self compared to two years ago. There should have been signs of care and grief on my face, but, mostly, my face looked plain and blank – this very spot, far, far away from K.T., was where I had come to push those thoughts away, and now I saw in my visage that they were rising up, and I felt them overwhelm me. I set what I was carrying on the sofa and turned and walked out the door, and then around the block, allowing myself to remember Thomas's smile, his touch, lying next to him in our cabin outside of Lawrence. And this new me, this older me, said, "Darlings, what were you thinking? You were fools." But, then, I knew that if we hadn't been fools we would not have married, known each other, had those brief moments together. I stopped and stood, listening to the horns blowing up from the docks. I knew that I was cherishing these memories, and that this moment would pass. Somehow, that, too, made me weep.

On Wednesday morning, Mr. Cunningham found me in the dining room, polishing the table, as Berta had asked me to do, and he handed me a ticket to Anne's opening night. He looked bright but edgy. I hadn't seen Anne yet: she had gotten in so late the night before that she was still, as far as I knew, sleeping. I said, "How – "

"Terrifically! Far beyond my expectations. The fellow playing Thornside had me falling from my seat laughing. Ellis is out of his mind with great hopes." He closed his eyes tight, shook his head suddenly, and knocked three times on the table I was wiping down. Then he said, "We'll walk over together. The curtain goes up at half eight."

When I saw Anne most of that day, she seemed the way she always did, and she even wanted to go for a short walk with me, perhaps to get away from Mr. Cunningham, whom we could hear pacing back and forth in his study. Only once, just after tea, when I was in her room about to lace her corset, did she lose her calm. She suddenly leaned forward, put her hands over her face, moaned, then turned toward me and threw her arms around me, saying, "Oh, Lidie, oh, Lidie. What in the world have we done?"

I embraced her, saying nothing, and after a bit, she pulled herself together and stuck herself back into the person of Anne Revere.

Mr. Cunningham and I set out for the theater just at eight, and all the way over, the streets were bustling. The drinking establishments, which Mr. Cunningham had told me were called "public houses," all had their doors open, but I supposed that it was too early in the evening for the drunks to be rolling out into the street. Even so, Mr. Cunningham had me put my hand on his forearm, and he put his other hand over mine, as if to prevent me from being yanked away. The theater was quieter, alas. There were a few people standing near the ticket office, and some others in the entry hall, and a few more in the seats. We presented our tickets, and Mr. Cunningham led me to the fourth row of the stalls. He looked gloomy, but said, "This is why we open midweek, you know. Tonight's performance and tomorrow night's performance are really for rehearsing in front of the audience, so that there will be no missteps on Friday or Saturday, when the house is fuller and more opinionated. But, then, in Liverpool, I dare say, the house is always opinionated." He walked off.

I sat quietly, wishing I were up in the balcony, where I had been for *A Christmas Carol* in Quincy. People went to their seats. The curtain rose. The acting was good enough so that I got caught up in the story and laughed at the right times. I was, indeed, taking a liking to Mr. Thornside, because he was so colorful. In Act Two, I realized that I was mouthing some of the words, I knew them so well, and then Anne Revere made her entrance, and the same thing happened that had happened in Quincy, not even three months ago – she lit up the stage, looking beautiful and riveting. I glanced around. No one near me could take their eyes off her. The rustling of papers and the shuffling of boots and the coughing and the sly remarks subsided. It was interesting to compare her to the woman playing Barbara Easy, much more experienced and entirely a mistress of her role. She flubbed no lines, and Anne flubbed one, by pausing in the middle and then spitting out the rest. But the woman playing Barbara Easy played her character as an English woman would, and Anne played Lucy as an American was meant to, with lively grace and a sense of curiosity and freedom that went through her body and her lines in waves. I saw that Mallory Cunningham had known exactly what he was doing when he brought her to Liverpool, and he saw it, too. Every time she was onstage, he would stare at her, then look around the audience, then stare at her again, then gauge the audience response again. All through the play, from beginning to end, there was no telling which of the suitors Lucy was going to choose, because Anne's Lucy looked like she might do anything at all and be glad of it. And her voice, the voice I had known for most of my life as low and sweet, though melodious, rang out through the theater with enough of our flat, Quincy twang to make sure we knew that she was a Revere but with enough English to make herself understandable to everyone. That, I thought, was her greatest accomplishment, but I doubted that anyone in the audience noticed it other than myself.

The play did go on forever, and toward the end the audience got a bit restless – we weren't out of the theater until half eleven, and a paper I saw on Mr. Cunningham's front table the next morning complained that the show "must have been intended to give the audience a good night's sleep," but Miss Revere was called "a great find" and a "lively presence."

All day Thursday, Anne and Mr. Cunningham were at the theater, and, though I didn't go to the show that night, I noted that they were home and I was unlacing Anne by eleven. She said that they had cut here and there and speeded up the action onstage a bit, and the audience seemed more content. Of herself, she said nothing, but when I left her in her room with a cup of mint tea, closed her door, and was walking toward the stairs, Mr. Cunningham, who had just come up the stairs, threw his arms around me without a word. I was not in the least offended, though I was glad Barnsby wasn't there to see the spectacle.

But the success became pleasantly routine rather than exciting as everyone got used to it. The show was to run for "two weeks," which was actually nine days, Wednesday through Saturday, then Tuesday through Saturday, but the audience grew, and so they put on three more performances during a third week, Thursday, Friday, and Saturday. Mr. Cunningham was pleased by this, and I overheard him say to some visitor, "Well, at last a bit of profit, Cranston, and why are we in this business again? Please, tell me." The papers declared it "something of a success." I did not see it again, but Anne came home with stories which she laughed about as I was helping her to bed. On the first Saturday night, Mr. Softhead stumbled over a stool, grabbed the hat rack and made all the hats fall to the floor, played up his softheadedness, got a laugh, and so incorporated this bit into the play for the rest of the run. On the Tuesday night, Anne herself stepped forward too quickly in the second act, onto the hem of her gown, which then ripped open around the waist, so that for her later act she had to wear her own gown, not a costume. Since the play was set in the time of King George, she looked quite out of place. On the second Friday night, the curtain dropped before the end of the third act, leaving the actors to shout their last lines in the dark. But they finished on a high note – for the last three performances, the house was full, no mistakes were made, and the cast got three curtain calls, with, Mr. Cunningham told me, a standing ovation on Saturday night for Mr. Thornside and Lucy. The next day, when we went to church, he spent the whole service kneeling, his eyes closed, his hands raised in prayer, and I doubt if he heard a word of the sermon, which was about a war going on in China that in America I had heard nothing about.

When we got home from church, we sat down to a lovely meal

that Berta had made, a roasted goose with vegetables and a delicious pudding, which seemed to me was really a sort of fruitcake. After we ate our meal and toasted Anne's success with a bit of port, Mr. Cunningham became very serious, and said to Anne, "Now, my dear, I am going to share with you what we may look forward to, so that you may prepare yourself."

We sat quietly in our seats. Anne was looking down, with her hands in her lap, nodding slightly. I was on the side of the table facing the windows, and I was looking out into the grounds, at the branches of the trees, which were now fully green and thick, not like any trees I'd ever seen in Illinois, much less K.T., and I said to myself, Not much can go wrong when we are surrounded by such trees as these.

"Ladies," said Mr. Cunningham, "the theater in this land is a lesson in boom and bust. The more beautiful or magnificent the show, the more it costs, and the more it costs, the more likely it is that the investors will go bust, and if they do, they will fall to bickering and even to suing one another. Three years back, I put on a performance that included three large trained canines, who did lovely tricks, such as walking on their hind legs, and even turning about as if they were dancing. They looked alike, because all three were from a single litter, and it was a great success, until one of the dogs leapt up and bit an actor who bumped against it, bit him on the cheek, and drew blood, and the actor proceeded to sue me for including the dogs, and though I was not ruined, the suit was a profound distraction, not least because there was a long battle in the papers about whether the dogs should ever have been included, and how did we know whether the dog had hydrophobia or not, and all sorts of nonsense."

Anne continued to nod.

I knew what she was thinking, that, boom or bust, her only alternative was to return to Quincy, and what was there for her?

Helen Longbourn's alternative would be to return to Chicago, but, indeed, what was there for me? No Longbourns.

Mr. Cunningham continued. "Even if you go from one success to another, my dear, and there are those actors who have, especially if they do not invest in the productions but only act in them, there is the constant travel. Liverpool cannot support you, Manchester cannot support you, Leeds cannot support you, and nor can London itself, as expenses are high there. You will have suitors and proposals of marriage, and everyone around you, including myself, will have opinions about your acceding to or rejecting those proposals. But no man is predictable, no matter how lovely his country seat might be. If anything, the tale played out in *Not So Bad as We Seem* is an optimistic one."

Anne said, "Mallory, I understand, and I have thought through all of these issues." She said this in her Annie voice, soft and direct. Then she raised her head and looked him in the eye for a long moment. The sun continued to flicker through the leaves of the trees. Mr. Cunningham said, "Well, then," reached over and squeezed her hand, glanced at me with a small smile, and stood up from the table.

6

ON THE MONDAY after the last performance, Mrs. Cunningham returned from Bath with their daughter, Evelina. I came upon the mistress of the house in the kitchen, where she was speaking to Berta. Berta turned and said, "Aye, ma'am. 'Ere she is, 'elen Longbourn, 'tis. She's bin a gret 'elp ta me with all o' this 'at's bin goin' on." Mrs. Cunningham was wearing a green silk gown, and it did have a flounce, though only one. She looked to be forty, and if she wasn't more tightly laced than Anne I would have been floored, as I had heard Berta say. I smiled, tipped my head. I said, "Thank you. I enjoy doing the errands, Mrs. Cunningham."

Mrs. Cunningham didn't smile in return. She said, "I understand you have been a useful girl, Helen. And, indeed, getting the errands done is a difficult task, I must say, when there is so much else to think about around the house." She said nothing about the play, or Anne, and I understood at once that her goal in leaving town was to avoid the whole thing. I saw Evelina later, sitting in the parlor doing some needlework. She was slight and perhaps shortsighted, as she had her needlework up by her face, and when she reached out her hand for her cup of tea, she knocked it off the side table. Fortunately, there were only a few drops left in the cup. I stepped into the room and said, "May I help you, miss?" I leaned down and picked up the cup, used the kerchief in my pocket to wipe away the moisture. And I did press my elbow against my pocket to prevent the jingling of my coins. She said, "Are you Helen?"

"I am." I stood up. She looked up at me and stared. I said, "Is there anything else I can do for you, Miss Cunningham?"

She said, "No. No." Then, "Thank you," in a very soft voice, and if I had ever seen a shyer or less prepossessing girl in my life, I couldn't remember who it would be. My heart immediately went out to her, and I recalled the time, two years before, when I had been upstairs in my father's old house, listening through the air vent as Alice, Harriet, and Beatrice discussed my exceedingly tiny prospects for getting married, or, at least, getting off their hands. I softened my voice and said, "That is beautiful needlework you are doing. I've never seen such a thing before. May I ask what it is?"

"It's tatting." She held it up. The piece she was making looked like a collar made out of snowflakes, two rows of delicate white lace circles. I said, "It looks almost finished." I thought, who was that woman I saw who was tatting? In K.T.? Kansas City? But I couldn't remember.

"It is. It's for Mama." Her voice was soft but not high or babyish, and I raised my estimate of her age from eleven to fourteen or fifteen.

She said, "Mama says you are doing the errands."

I said, "I am. It there anything I might do for you?"

"Not right now, but tomorrow, if you could bring home an issue of *Punch* or *Household Words*—that's a weekly. There might be something amusing in that one."

"Of course. I suppose Barnsby will tell me where to find one . . ."

"Please, don't ask. Mama says they are too racy for me." She paused and glanced up at me. Sighed.

I said, "Would you like to go with me? Your father gave me a stick . . ."

"Here in Liverpool, I don't go out on the streets. The coal smoke is too thick."

Had I not noticed? Perhaps I had, but smoke – wood in Quincy and coal here – is thick everywhere. Maybe there was one good thing about K.T., then, though the smoke had been noticeable in Lawrence. I said, "Your father sends me to the news seller's. I will look there." She smiled, said a very soft thank you. Then Mrs. Cunningham walked in. I saw at once that I had misunderstood Mrs. Cunningham's manner, because she was affectionate with her daughter, and seemed to have softened toward me as well. I bowed slightly and left the room. Evelina Cunningham gave me a conspiratorial smile and then showed her mother her tatting. Berta later told me, when we were out in the garden, harvesting some spring cabbage, some radishes, and some sorrel, that Miss Cunningham was consumptive, had been for three years now, in spite of the trips to Bath and Blackpool and even Bournemouth. "Aye," she said in a low tone. "Such a bright little thing she was, and then . . ." She shook her head.

I was sent out to pick up some parcels at the meat market the next day, and I passed the news seller, where I bought the two periodicals Evelina had asked for. When I came out of the salon after I arrived back at Mr. Cunningham's and gave them to her (she received them with pleasure and handed me a shilling), Anne was pacing around the front hall with a letter in her hand. I saw that it was thick, and even before she showed it to me, I knew that it was the one. She handed it to me, and I took one end but she didn't let her end go. We simply stood there, staring at one another. Anne had written a third letter home and sent it only two days before, telling about the play, and her success, but that letter had certainly gotten no farther than the Liverpool post office, if, indeed, it was there yet. She let go. I held it in one hand while she grabbed my other hand, and we ran up the staircase to her room.

We closed the door and went over to the window seat. It was a misty, gloomy day, and the horns from the docks were even louder than usual, but the trees seemed to huddle around us in a comforting manner. I ripped open the envelope and two letters fell out. I picked up one – from Alice – and Anne picked up the other one – from Harriet. Anne said, "You go first."

The one from Alice read as follows:

Dear Annie –

I simply don't know what to say. Everyone has been out and about looking for you, and the weather hasn't made it any easier. Roland was sure you had been taken off by some fellow – he thought there were boot prints on the back stoop, and he went all over Quincy looking for some sort of large boots, and then he prowled about the railway station, asking the fellows who work there if they had seen you. But I knew all along that it was Lidie who spirited you away. If I had known of her intentions, then I wouldn't have had her in the house once she got back from those escapades in Kansas Territory. I knew all along that they made her soft in the head, and I do have sympathy for what she went through, but I see now that she cannot be controlled. Here I always thought that Frank was going to be the problem child, and yet Harriet says he is doing well at school and has taken employment at Lorton and Silk, thanks to Beatrice. So, you never know. I realize now that Lidie must have talked you into that thankfully brief play you went in, and then that turned your head, and she was able to keep after you. Well, I hope she doesn't live to regret it, because even though she is foolish, I know that deep in her heart she is very fond of you. I did get her letter that she sent, but it made no sense as far as I can see. All the same, I was glad to hear from you. Things aren't the same without you, and I can't say that I am up to filling your place about the house. But enough said about that. Except to say that when you come back, as I am sure you will, we will welcome you with open arms. My hand is cramping up now with all this writing. I wish I could say more but I can't.

Affectionately,
Mother

After I was finished, I looked at Anne. Her expression was a mix of sad, angry, and amused. All she said was, "I guess she will never blame me for anything. Never did, never will."

I said, "What did you ever do that was blameworthy? I mean, apart from breaking that plate?"

"Don't you remember that I ran off when I was six or so? I got all the way to Maine Street. She thought I was going to throw myself in the river and drown, because that's what six-year-olds do."

I laughed. I did not remember that. I was eight at the time, but maybe everyone hushed it up and didn't tell my father or me.

Now Anne read Harriet's letter:

Dear Annie and Lidie,

I will say that Alice is fit to be tied with all this running off, and I was, too, for a few days, but then Frank came to me and told me in secret that he saw you get on the train when he should have been at school, so what was I supposed to say? I didn't know whether to sit and stew or tell your secret, so I was very glad when your letter arrived from New York, and to tell the truth, I knew that Alice would send Roland after you if I told on you, and I didn't want him to go after you because I knew he would find you and drag you home, and what is there for you here? Even in the time since you left, it's just one thing after another about the slave issue, and now Mr. Lincoln is accusing Senator Douglas of betraying the Republican Party, and there's no telling how that will turn out. Last week at Lorton and Silk, two men were looking for some rope and one of them said to Harold that it was for a hanging, and Harold was shocked, even when the man laughed and said he was fooling around. Given your views, Lidie, that you picked up in Kansas, I don't see how you would have stayed out of trouble, what with all the things that these men and some of the women are saying, too, and it isn't all on one side. Mrs. Cowran, you might remember her from Alice's sewing group, said right out loud that she didn't see anything wrong with race mixing, they do it all the time on plantations down in the South. Well, I won't say the other ladies have shunned her since, but to say such a thing in this world, at least in Quincy, with all the folks who come over from Palmyra and all and have their ears wide and their eyes open for slaves trying to escape, and more of them are doing so by the day. All in all, Illinois is not the place to be these days, though they say things are quiet enough up north in Chicago, but who can tell how long that will last.

My only wish is that you will keep sending some letters, because I truly would like to know what you are doing and what you are seeing, and although I love the farm and am thankful for my life here, it is sad to think of how old I am, turning fifty in three days, and I've never even been to St. Louis. I did look at Liverpool on a map, and after I got your letter, I ran into Sally O'Hara in the street the other day and told her where you are, and she said she had never been there, but knew someone when she lived in Navan who went back and forth, and always spoke highly of the town. And so, though I have never envied Mrs. O'Hara in my life, for all the things that she has gone through, I do now, just a bit. The truth is, when someone you love leaves town, your heart does follow her, and your fancies do, too, and that is a fact.

Love to you both,
Harriet

There are times when family disagreements work in your favor.

. . .

Mrs. Cunningham evidently had different feelings about Anne Revere than Mr. Cunningham did. She was polite to Anne, but didn't treat her as a friend, or even as a guest. She was polite to her but not, should I say, "respectful." The problem for Anne was that now she didn't have much to do. I didn't take her with me for my errands, but twice she went with me to the graveyard along Hope Street, which in this season was truly a park. Barnsby told me that it was "simple folk" who were buried there, but the stones were well cared for, and the peacefulness of the place was a pleasure in the bustle of Liverpool. Anne said that Mr. Cunningham was casting about for another production to showcase her, and then he hired a singing master for her, and for two hours a day, I could hear her in the salon, doing her best. She seemed to be enjoying herself, but Mrs. Cunningham did say "she was no Jenny Lind." Even in Quincy we had heard of Jenny Lind, as she had gotten to St. Louis on her tour, and everyone knew someone who had gone down to see her there, or said they did. You could tell who really had. If they hadn't, they said she was wonderful in every way, and if they had, they said she was a little piercing or had gone flat in one of the songs, was, indeed, fairly good, but not quite as impressive as Aunt Martha or Cousin Louise.

After a few days, the music master (who also played the piano) shifted her repertoire, as Anne called it, to popular English ballads, such as "John Barleycorn" and "Mary Hamilton." Where she would ever sing any of these songs onstage I had no idea, but I loved listening beside the door. My favorite was a song about the devil coming to a young girl and threatening her, but then he asks her some riddles, and when she answers them all, he leaves her be.

I thought Anne's voice was pleasant, and once she was singing melodious, simple songs, the music master would sing along with her. They sounded good together. They seemed to enjoy themselves, and Evelina and I certainly enjoyed them. One day, Evelina showed me the fiddle that she had played when she was younger but no longer had the strength for. She was very matter-of-fact about her illness – how she disliked its effects and knew the pain it was causing her mother and father, and, furthermore, she knew how it would end. But a young man she knew, the older brother of a friend of hers, had been killed in the Crimean War (which I'd never heard of), so she knew there were "worse ways to go," as she said. I knew that, too, of course, and I was tempted to tell her about Thomas and Jeremiah and what I now understood as a war in K.T., but I was *Helen,* I dared not crack the brittle wall around Lidie or, I thought, the whole thing would come tumbling down. Evelina showed me her chamber, which was next to her mother's chamber – there was a door between them, which was closed when I visited Evelina's chamber. The space was not elaborate – the more furnishings and drapes, the more dust. The chambermaid, whose name was Jane and whom I hardly ever saw, had to wipe it down twice a day, and she wiped down Mrs. Cunningham's chamber once a day, so that Evelina could go there, at least briefly, to spend time with her mother. As for Mr. Cunningham, he was kind to his daughter, but it was from a distance, as if he were afraid of her, or, indeed, of damaging her. He acted as if he were a clumsy fellow in a room full of glassware. I saw in that why he liked Anne: she had a kind of American sturdiness to her that he could relax around, and perhaps I had that, too. He offered me some more money, not as much, for my services around the house and the neighborhood, but I said that I'd only spent a bit of the money he had already given me, and so he needn't bother. My pleasures were sufficient payment.

It was now almost May, and Barnsby, who always treated me in a friendly way, came to me at the breakfast table one morning, and asked if I wanted to see some horses. I set down my fork. It was a beautiful warm day, he said, and there was a day of racing, not at Aintree, but at a training track for flat races not far away, as the horses had to practice a bit before the commencement of the principal season. There might be betting and there might not, depending on which of the bookmakers showed up. I said, "I should ask – "

Barnsby smoothly interrupted me. "Mrs. Cunningham thinks it might be a pleasant excursion for you."

I found my shawl and my sturdier boots, as well as a bonnet, which I tied securely around my head, and a small bag, though my kerchief and my coins were still in my pocket. We could not walk there, because, like Aintree, it was two leagues from Canning Street, but in a slightly different direction. We went to the corner of Hope and Canning, and a cab came past that had rounded the turn from the bottom of the graveyard. After we got in, the driver said, through the top, which was open, that he had delivered three families to the graveyard today, two for one funeral and one for another, and so a lovely trip to the racecourse, called Calstead Farm, "'ud bay plaasnt indaid." The taxi made good time, the horse trotting briskly along. There were brick buildings, but soon we were into an area of parks, trees, and flowers, and then into high, flat countryside, full of fields recently planted and now green with shoots of – Barnsby told me – wheat, barley, oats, turnips, beets, grass for hay. The fields were neatly surrounded by hedges, and there were several breeds of horses and cows – the horses mostly Shires and Cleveland Bays, the cows mostly Herefords and Ayrshires (which Barnsby preferred for their butter), but a few red ones with long hair that Barnsby said came from the highlands of Scotland, and were fancied by the family who owned the farm we were passing merely because they liked unusual breeds. Barnsby had never tasted their cream or milk.

Barnsby was informative but not conversational. I asked him about this war in Crimea, and he told me a few things – it had been started by the Russians, over on a peninsula that, according to a map he had seen, looked more like an oak leaf than a willow leaf. The plan was to get rid of the Turks, but neither the French nor the Brits thought this was a good idea, and so armies had been sent.

Things seemed to be going well enough. That was all he said. He would answer each question knowledgeably, or, if we were passing something unusual, he would point it out, but he could go for quite some time without saying a word, and during these times, I heard the cabdriver calling out to his horse or humming a tune. I was reminded of the pleasures of the countryside – we had those even in Illinois, where the land was flatter and rougher than it was in England, and no wonder that Mr. Cunningham's house was full to bursting with paintings of the countryside, as the memories of what you were passing, of two cattle touching noses and the brilliantly white puffy clouds floating in the dark-blue sky behind them, and then, for a moment, the branches of a tree entered the picture and you attempted, as hard as you might, to engrave this into your brain, and it flashed away the next moment, when you saw three chestnut horses come galloping over a hilltop and slide to a halt beside the fence, only to start grazing in the thick grass. And then Barnsby was looking in the other direction, at a pair of hawks floating over a tree, and the only thing he muttered was, "Healthy oak, I must say."

There were plenty of people at what they called the racecourse. In fact, it was an unfenced winding way that had been mowed into a large field. The first, wider part went up the hill, across a small ridge, and then wound down again to the shorter, flatter part, which ended where there were two flags. The starting line was near the finishing line, but separated from it by a meadow. The first race was about to start as we got out of the cab. We could see the horses – I counted eight – milling about in the small field. The riders were just being hoisted up. They were wearing colored shirts to distinguish themselves from one another. There was a single gray horse in the race, darkly dappled, nearly black in the tail and mane. Barnsby went to a man he knew who was standing not far from where the cab left us, and received a list. The gray was named Lord Alfred. When I pointed him out to Barnsby, the man behind us said, "Ah. Bad-tempered fellow, that one." I decided to keep my eyes open and my mouth shut.

Once all the riders were hoisted up, they walked and then trotted around the meadow, and the gray was a little grumpy, but one of the dark browns was worse – he reared up and dropped his rider. They hoisted the rider on again, and just after that they lined up as best they could at what Barnsby called "the post." Two men, one on the inside of the mowed path and one on the outside, held up a long white strip of cloth, and when the horses were more or less along it, they dropped it and the crowd started yelling.

It was, indeed, a lovely place to watch a horse race, because the hills made the horses visible from a distance, and I saw that mowing the course made for good training – if a horse veered into the unmowed area, he knew it, and would, of his own accord, go back to the mowed path. The other interesting thing was seeing Barnsby's reserve slip away as the horses gathered speed. By the end, even though he didn't have a bet, he was rooting for a chestnut called Brave Boy. I could see that Brave Boy was a good horse, but I would not call him a brave boy, as he opted to stay away from the others and make his bid on the outside, stretching and galloping as fast as he could to make up time around the tighter curve. He "came third," as Barnsby termed it. I asked if there was purse money, and he said indeed there was; he supposed Brave Boy would have won fifty guineas.

As we walked around in the course of the day, I saw that there was money, indeed – the owners were well dressed and prosperous-looking, and the horses were shiny and well taken care of. The men far outnumbered the women, but the women who were there had flounces and silk gowns and fur on the collars of their wraps. The horses in the later races of the day (there were six races in all) were, Barnsby told me, aiming for the Ascot Gold Cup, and as it was over two miles, a race for stayers; the horses would run twice around the circuit, the last race of the day. Perfect for Jeremiah, was my first thought.

Of course, I was reminded of Jeremiah's race in K.T., the year before, the time when Frank spirited him away and I found them outside of town, in a huge field, running heats. At the time, what struck me, other than Jeremiah's success, was the fact that all sorts of men were consorting in amity, whether they were sound on the goose question or abolitionists – all they were interested in was the racing and the betting, though who was taking the bets I didn't know. What I remembered now was how rough the field was, how burly and unsavory the men gathered there. Frank and I fit in perfectly well with them, to a degree that I was embarrassed to talk about to Thomas when I got home, though I did show him the few dollars that Jeremiah won. Thomas would have disapproved of this gathering no less – he thought gambling was dangerous – but he might have tolerated the order of it all, the way that even the two bookmakers who showed up were neatly dressed and reserved. And well they might be, since everyone on the course, even a few of the women, knew who they were.

Barnsby placed two winning bets, one in the third race on a horse named Right Honourable, a plain bay with a long stride who won by a length, turning Barnsby's four shillings into a pound. In the last race, he put his winnings down on Fisherman, a dark bay with an alert look and a lively manner. But, then, so did everyone else, because Fisherman, though only four, already had a following. Apparently, his owner took him about everywhere, because the horse loved to race, and so why spend the money on training when he could be trained and raced at the same time?

When they were being saddled and mounted in the meadow, Fisherman seemed entirely uninterested – he wanted to put his head down and take a bite of grass, and after a minute or two, his trainer let him. Two bites were enough. He lifted his head, pricked his ears. The rider took a light hold, and they ambled to the spot where the tape would be. Barnsby told me that the trainers picked numbers out of a hat for what he called "post position," and Fisherman was exactly in the middle, five horses to the right of him, five to the left of him. The chestnut on his right did attempt to bite another horse, but not Fisherman – he looked as though he didn't dare. The tape went down, and the horses took off. They all left Fisherman behind as if they didn't know any better, and his rider let him gallop along, stretching and easing into ever bigger strides. The ones at the head of the group ran like they were fighting it out – tossing heads and tails, pinning ears, but Fisherman, about four lengths behind the last horse, just galloped along. I thought he looked as though he might pause for a healthful bite of grass. They came toward us around the smaller end, passed through the meadow, which was clear of horses and people, and then passed the post again. It was just as they were coming out of the first turn that Fisherman lengthened his stride even more, sped up, and began to take an interest. I had never seen a horse in such perfect physical condition. As he passed the other horses, they seemed to be hopping up and down, while he seemed to be swimming through the air, his neck stretched, his legs working like a metronome. One by one he passed them, until there were only two left, a chestnut on the small side and a brawny bay with a white face. The rider began beating the brawny bay with his whip, and the bay did make an effort, but Fisherman galloped past him. Now they were in the last turn, which was good for the chestnut, because it was tight and he was small, with a quick stride. He looked as though he was fit, too, and he did speed up. His rider leaned a little backward, as if to push him out from under his seat, and smacked him one time. All Fisherman's rider did was lean a little forward and put his hands along Fisherman's neck. They turned toward the finish line, and everyone was screaming, some of the women loudest of all. One woman was holding her parasol in her hand and hopping up and down. Fisherman galloped past the post, his rider sat up, and Fisherman came down to the trot in the meadow. The small chestnut was much more agitated. His rider leapt off and he and the trainer walked the horse around and around. Fisherman's rider let him take a few bites of grass before they came for the prize, which was a hundred guineas. Barnsby said, "Agreeable beast, eh?" and went to retrieve his winnings. Because of the odds, his pound had turned into only twenty-two shillings, but he didn't mind.

It was now about four in the afternoon, judging by where the sun was in the west, and Barnsby knew that we had better get back to 2 Canning Street before supper. He seemed a trifle worried, but when we got down to the road, our same cabdriver was there, told us he had stayed most of the day – back and forth to nearby houses, because everyone had to have enough of funerals at some point. On the way home, Barnsby showed me his list of the horses who had run, the marks he'd made on it, told me a bit about breeding, and seemed, for him, animated. I watched the fields and the trees and the streets again, and thought about how much I'd enjoyed my day. We were at 2 Canning Street in plenty of time, and as soon as we got out of the cab, Barnsby was entirely himself. Even when Mr. Cunningham showed up at the front door with a big grin and demanded to know how we had done, Barnsby said, with a slight, stiff bow, "Rather well, sir," and went off to the pantry.

After he left, I said, "Have you put him onstage as a butler yet?"

Mr. Cunningham said, "My dear, he is too perfectly behaved to be convincing."

Later that evening, when he was sorting through some things in the "drawing room," as he called it, I was reminded of how well dressed so many people at the racecourse had been, and I commented on this to Barnsby. He looked at me with an amused expression and said, "Well, many members of the upper class socialize at the races, and to do that, they must be well turned out, especially the aristocrats. One might have lost a hundred pounds in, say, the first running, but he wouldn't dare show that. The first thing he would do in such a case would be to go to his horse boy and tell him to polish his boots."

We both smiled, and Barnsby went back to work for a moment, then said, "It is my understanding that, in your country, there is quite a difference between how the Southerners live and how the Northerners live."

I said, "If you mean slavery . . ."

But he shook his head a bit, and then said, "Not precisely. You must know that those who went to Virginia and other spots in your Southern lands were escaping from our own fracas in the sixteen hundreds. Are you aware of Cromwell?"

I shook my head.

"Miss Longbourn, he was a rabid Puritan, and labored hard to overthrow King Charles, which he did. The royalists and anti-Puritans had to flee to somewhere, so many of them took ship to Virginia."

He put away the last of the items he was sorting and closed the door of the cabinet, then turned to me and said, "They, of course, wanted to live as they had before the wars. My feeling is that this conflict you are having these days is the offspring of those conflicts that our ancestors endured two hundred years ago."

I remembered the man at that saloon in Kansas City, and said, "Were they 'cavaliers'?"

"Yes, indeed. Obviously, that meant that those were the ones who rode horses in battles, but they could afford horses because they were the ones with funds and, often, estates." I didn't know what else to say. Even in Quincy, we had been taught in school that perhaps the greatest thing to happen in the history of civilization was the discovery of America and the enlightened knowledge that the English and even the French had brought with them on their ships.

The next day was Sunday. Evelina was not feeling well, so I

stayed home with her when the others went to church. She did not want to eat the porridge Berta made for her, but I went out into the garden and found a ripe apricot, peeled it, took the pit out, cut it up, and sprinkled the bits over the top of her bowl and she did eat most of it. I had continued buying her copies of *Household Words,* so, after she had eaten her porridge and also taken a cup of tea, she read me some pages of a story written by a female called "My Lady Ludlow." It was interesting enough, but on the same page, as I saw after she let me look at the paper for myself, was a piece I thought more interesting, about not only gardening and farming, but also about fishing and forests. That evening, Anne came to me and said that she was sending a letter to Harriet, with a note for Alice and another note for Beatrice. We knew that, of course, all three of them would read everything, but they would think twice about responding to what Anne might say in the notes addressed to others. She asked if I wanted to send along my own letter. I went down to my chamber, lit a candle, and wrote it. It read:

My dear sisters,

I do wish I could be sending you some sketches or pictures of where we are. I went a bit out of town today, to watch some horse racing, and if I have ever seen such lovely fields, I do not know when. The horses were beautiful and so different from one another that I could not stop looking at them. The man who took me is a butler in Mr. Cunningham's house, a confirmed bachelor, and a kind but strict man who makes sure that everyone, including me, behaves properly about the house. His name is Barnsby. I do not know if Annie has described the house to you. It is in a real city, not like any place I've ever been, with lots of streets lined with houses built of brick, all in a row. There are backyards, which they call gardens, and a few people do grow some vegetables and a few fruits, such as blackberries and raspberries, and, of course, apples – the back garden here has three apple trees, and this year they have budded out beautifully. I am sure that Harriet would be envious. They have plenty of rain here, but not much in the way of storms, and no tornadoes. I asked Barnsby about that and he said, "What in the world is a tornado?" When I described it, he said that they do have whirlwinds, and plenty of them, but they are nothing like the ones we have.

Annie may not have told you what a great success she was in the show Mr. Cunningham put on. Just because of "Anne," they did three extra performances, and she did get standing ovations each of the last nights — by which I mean that the main male character held out his hand while the audience was clapping, invited her forward, and when she took a bow, everyone started shouting and clapping even harder. One good thing about the theater here is that the people in the audience aren't talking all the time and the actors don't have to shout over the audience members in order to be heard. The lines in Annie's play were witty, as they say here, and the audience had the sense to see that and laugh. No one had to fall off the stage in order to get the audience's attention. I was impressed. Now Mr. Cunningham is casting about, as they say here, for another good opportunity for Annie to show off her many skills, as well as her beauty and her "appeal," as Mr. Cunningham calls it. She has been taking singing lessons. She is very good. Do you remember Mrs. Stone, who sang in the choir at Harriet's church, and went about offering lessons to girls? I am so sorry that Annie didn't get a chance at those. Or at playing the piano. It's a shame when a piano goes unplayed, as yours did for so long, Beatrice. I blame myself, because I knew that I didn't have any musical talent, so I never thought that Annie might, either. But now I know.

As for me, I am happy to go about, doing errands, as I did at home. You know I like being active, and this city is a wonderful place to be active. Every few days, I walk down along the docks and look at the ships and the ocean. They come and go at all hours of the day and night, and I suppose that they have to, because there are so many of them that must get in and get unloaded. It took me a while to orient myself, and to realize that the docks are not actually on the ocean, but, rather, along the banks of a river, called the Mersey. Perhaps I was confused, because the river is blue, not brown, like the Mississippi. I have a bit of money, and I have thought of buying myself a horse of some sort. If I did that, I could explore more, especially up the coast along the Irish Sea.

I stopped there and did not sign my name, because I didn't want them to know about Helen. After I reread it, I saw that it was not a kind or affectionate letter. It was, in fact, a breezy, small-minded letter. But it seemed like the real me, and I thought they should see who that was. I didn't show it to Anne – she didn't show hers to me, either. The next morning, she shoved them all into the envelope, and we went to the post, where we put together enough money to send them. The man at the post office said that it might arrive in two weeks, especially this time of year, when the weather is fair and there are lots of ships crossing to New York and Philadelphia. Then he asked, in a pleasant manner, where Quincy was, but as he had never heard of Chicago, or even St. Louis, all we could say was that it wasn't Kansas, which he had heard of, because the shootings at Marais des Cygnes, which was termed a massacre, had been so horrifying that they even got into the English papers. Some Border Ruffians came to K.T. and rounded up some Free Staters – how many I did not quite understand – and took them down into a hollow and shot them, even though they had no weapons on them, much less any Sharps carbines. None of the English papers named the victims, though, so I had two choices – to imagine that all of them were Free Staters I had known or to imagine that none of them were. I chose the third alternative, which was, once again, to turn away all thoughts of K.T. as best I could.

On the way back to 2 Canning Street from posting the letter, I was hailed by that tall fellow with the horse face, Reggie Scofield. When I waved back, he came trotting over and asked how we were in a very friendly manner, took Anne's hand, dipped his head, said his employers had seen her in her show and chatted about her all the next day. He had no idea that Anne and I were friends. I said, "I'm her maid," and he dipped his head again. He believed me. As 2 Canning Street was on his way back to where he worked, he did as he had done before, and walked along near us, keeping up a one-sided conversation about the garden he tended, how much lettuce and spinach he had harvested already, how the strawberries were doing, and what he considered the best manure for fertilizing – "'T's roight thr in the street, you tike a good-soized cart, and you walk along of a mornin', and you my pick whatever you wish. I can tell what th' harses eat easy as you please. I never pick up what 'as oats in it, because they pop up as weeds j'st loik that. And the ones from the country who're j'st atin' grass, they don't 'ave much to offer a berry bush. The ones as are atin' a mix of grass, barley, linseed, and some hempseed, the plants j'st eat that up. Even in the winter, before plantin', I go lookin' far s'm bits of turnip and beet and parsnip, though it is true that they bile those before feedin' 'em to the harses, so that tikes awy a good dale of their strength." On Upper Duke Street, appropriately enough, he went out into the muck and kicked at some droppings with his boot. He said, "Tike a look at theys grane ones. They're too fresh to use roight off, but I'd put them in mee cart soon enough, and age 'em. I've got a goodly pile out the back corner o' mee garden."

I could see that Anne was enormously amused by Reggie, and I was, too. He was the kind of enthusiast who makes the best use of everything he learns, and, in order to learn it, tells himself and everyone he knows all about it. Since we weren't carrying any parcels and had some time, we skirted 2 Canning Street and went along with him to the house where he worked, on Falkner Street. The Furnishes were away again, this time to London, and Reggie was alone there, doing his own cooking and watching over the garden, which, it was evident, the Furnishes cared about, too, because it was beautifully managed. I spent so much time walking about and admiring it (and Reggie seemed to like flowers as well as fruits and vegetables) that Reggie said I was welcome to come by whenever I wished and have a look, whether he was nearby or not. He acted toward me with the same mix of kindness and familiarity as he had before, and on the way home, I told Anne about the incident when he asked me if I was his sister. She laughed, but I thought, I will be.

The next day was a Tuesday. Anne, Mrs. Cunningham, and Evelina were sitting at the dining table, and I had just brought some raspberries in from the back garden. I had them in a little bowl and was about to give them to Mrs. Cunningham when Mr. Cunningham came rushing in and said that Sarah Wakenfield had fallen ill and could not go onstage; his friend, the fellow who was financing the play, had come to him almost in a state of madness and asked if there was any way "that girl you brought from New York" could take up the part, as they didn't have any one backing up the actress. They might forgo one show, on Wednesday, but Anne had to be ready by Thursday, and she would be paid handsomely, as the theater was a large, popular one, with two tiers in the balcony, maybe a thousand seats in all, great acoustics, a few boxes up to the right. . . .

Did Anne have the opportunity to turn him down? If so, she didn't take it, or even think of it. She was already out of her seat. Mr. Cunningham nearly jumped onto the table, he was so happy. He beckoned me, and the three of us ran out of the room. I was handed two copies of the play, and we went straight up to Anne's chamber.

The play was called *The Vampire,* by a man whose name I could not pronounce, and Anne's was the principal female role, another Lucy. Anne had heard of it in New York, where Mr. Cunningham said he had seen it, though there they called it *The Phantom*. Mr. Cunningham's friend had chosen to produce the play as it was originally written. It had a castle, an inn, many people who were killed and then rose up again, and its goal was to get the audience screaming in fear rather than laughing in pleasure. By Thursday, midday, when Anne had learned all of her lines and practiced dying maybe twenty times, I was sick of the whole thing, and was very glad I did not have to accompany her to the rehearsal and then her installation into the performance that night. But I was wide awake, waiting for her in her chamber when she returned, and I could tell that she was excited and had enjoyed herself. As I undid the back of her gown and then her corset, she told me how all of the actors seemed out of their minds, which was exactly what the audience wanted. She had played her part as she thought – properly – with some elegance and reserve – but she was not going to make that mistake again. Once she was offstage and watching, she saw that the actors were enjoying themselves very much, especially when they were keeling over from fright, and afterward everyone was in a good mood. The man who played the main character, named Raby, a demon, advised her to "put it on a bit, my dear," and so we practiced one more time, on Friday. This new Lucy nearly pulled down the drapery on one of the windows of her chamber in her agony of fear. Evelina heard the noise, and came knocking, so I let her in, and she was so impressed she was torn between laughing and shouting. I was afraid she would then have a coughing fit and collapse, but the whole thing seemed to perk her up. When Anne was ready to leave, Evelina and I walked her to the door and hugged her good-bye.

Then Evelina, still in great humor, took me to one of the corner shelves in the library and showed me a book that she said she was not supposed to know about, but that she had read twice, called *Varney the Vampire,* and where had she found it but right here in her mother and father's library, though whose it was and how it got there she had no idea. Evelina explained to me that vampires sucked people's blood, and if they couldn't get any, they died, and for a while after she read this book, she was afraid even to look at the back garden through her window because it was winter and the garden was dark – one time, when she had been looking out her window, an owl flew right at her. She fell down in fright, but she still remembered enjoying the book. She put it into my hands, but after she left the library, I put it back where I found it.

Anne's play ran for five weeks, and the best thing to be said about it, since it was roundly denigrated in the papers, was that it made a lot of money, and Anne was well paid. She got along excellently with the other actors, who were also well paid, and if, as people say, lots of activity is a benefit to one's health, well, her health as well as her pocketbook thrived. She handed me a pound note as thanks for helping her rehearse, and now it might be true that I did have enough to buy a horse. As for Anne, she had enough to buy two silk gowns, one a pale yellow, almost golden in the sun, and the other a creamy white, as well as a new pair of boots, just the latest fashion, and a parasol that went well with both. This, I would say, was perhaps a necessary expense, because many more people recognized her on the street than had after *Not So Bad as We Seem*. Every time we went out, someone would come up to her and say that he or she had seen her in the play and how heartrending her death had been, or how gracefully she had fallen to the stage. Even Reggie Scofield saw the play – his employers gave him a ticket. Evelina was not allowed to go to the play – Mrs. Cunningham didn't approve of that sort of thing, and thought it would be too much for Evelina – but she did get Anne to say some of the lines and fall to the floor just for her.

In the end, the whole thing was so exhausting that Mr. Cunningham, his hands jingling the coins in his pockets, took Anne, Mrs. Cunningham, Evelina, and Jane, Mrs. Cunningham's maid, to Torquay, another resort town with pleasant weather and not much smoke, for a fortnight, as Mr. Cunningham called it, then brought Anne back and left Mrs. Cunningham, Evelina, and Jane there, as Evelina seemed to be perking up. Once they got back, the singing master returned and the daily lessons, and then a dancing master showed up, and Anne spent an hour a day learning how to dance about the salon with a kerchief in her hand, her chin tilted upward, her back straight, her arms always in a graceful position, and her feet moving in perfect time to the tunes that the singing master was playing on the piano. One time, I overheard him saying, "My deah, good thing you are but a youngster." I saw that part of the reason English ladies did not get out of the house was that they had so many skills to master that they had no time for walking down the street.

7

WHILE ANNE'S PLAY was running, I had my own melodrama, as you might call it, because I knew that the anniversary of Thomas's murder was coming, and as much as I wanted K.T. to vanish from my mind like a mote of dust, I also wanted to honor Thomas's memory in some way. It was the weather that reminded me of the killing every single day, not because it was like the weather in K.T., which had been hot and windy, but because it was cool, damp, and breezy. Everything in Liverpool contrasted with everything in K.T., and so, when I thought of Thomas, I would, in spite of myself, completely enter that world and remember the details – how we had walked along beside the cart for a while, Thomas talking, me looking at Jeremiah's long tail swishing back and forth because of the flies, and thinking about how I should trim it, or at least comb it, and then that moment when something I hadn't realized I could hear alerted me anyway, so that when the three Border Ruffians come galloping out of the trees, I felt that I had known they were there, known they were coming, but I hadn't had the sense to reach for the Sharps carbine – and it should have been me who reached for it, because I was a better shot than Thomas, and we both knew it. The moment the biggest of the three Ruffians opened his mouth, talking like he came straight out of Arkansas, I should have shot him, but I didn't. Sometimes, I would think these thoughts.

Other times, Thomas lying on the ground would come back to me, how I undid his coat and saw the two wounds, red oozing out of his chest, oozing out of his shoulder, life itself departing, his face almost unrecognizable because it was blank with pain. Knowing what I knew now, I would have stretched myself against him, hugged him, kissed him, stroked his forehead, at least for a few moments. But I didn't do that then. Why not? Because his pain had been like a glass window surrounding his body, and I was afraid of breaking the glass. Or I remembered how I saw him when I was looking over my shoulder as I was checking on Jeremiah, and then my closing Thomas's open eyes also came back, as well as the sight of his feet, neatly shod, large, sticking up, and his hat lying in the grass.

Something I had forgotten in the intervening year was my hemming and hawing about finding help. How could I leave him? How could I not leave him to find a doctor? Back and forth. He had told me to leave him, and I finally did, but one night, the very anniversary of his shooting, I lay awake for hours trying to pinpoint how much time I had piddled away with my indecision: Five minutes? Half an hour? An hour? If I had broken that glass window and lain down beside him, just for a few minutes, could I have departed more expeditiously?

In honor of him, I allowed all the memories to flow in and out. On the anniversary of his death, Anne came to me with a handful of flowers, tears in her eyes, and hugged me and kissed me before leaving for the theater. She asked if she could do anything for me, and all I said was, "Keep it between us." And she did.

I did block out some memories, the memories of Thomas's rescuer, David B. Graves, because he was the same man who doomed Lorna to her sale down the river. Of all the people I met in K.T., including the man who shot Thomas and the boy who shot Jeremiah, he was the one I could least bear to have in my mind.

In order to reckon with these memories, I did make my way to Reggie Scofield's place. When I got there, he was, sure enough, standing beside his pile of horse manure (and every other kind of vegetable peeling or other refuse), sticking his spade into it and turning it over. He welcomed me, literally, with open arms, and I enjoyed that thing I had never known, a brotherly hug by a man who was taller than I was. He had a huge wide smile that turned his horse face into beauty. After I had received such a welcome the first time, I had gone more often, not for Reggie's pride and joy, the berries (or the cherries or the apples or the pears), but for the scent of the flowers, and there were many of them, roses, but also sweet peas and irises and a short, brightly colored plant Reggie called "violas." My favorites were the freesia and the lilies of the valley. One day, I'd asked him to show me his thumbs. He laughed, held out his hands. His thumbs were green, but so were his palms – he had been trimming some of the plants by hand.

When I was wandering around the Furnish garden, the first face that floated into my head was not Thomas's – it was Evelina's, thin and pale, and then her mother's, reserved and blank. It came to me that Evelina knew she was soon to die and accepted it, but that her mother was as I had been the year before in K.T., struck dumb, and pushing the very thought away as energetically as she could. She had taken that collar that Evelina tatted for her and had it sewn onto one of her favorite gowns, replacing the previous one. I often saw her touching it. Her finger was like a metronome, counting the thoughts she was having of her daughter even when she was engaged in routine tasks like making lists of shops for me to visit. But if she saw me noticing, she would scowl, so I didn't dare seem attentive or sympathetic. I recognized that, too – after Thomas was killed, my only thought was to find the killers and shoot them. Reggie let me walk around as I pleased, and was so busy sorting through the pile of remains that when I left he only waved and smiled.

A few days later, now a year and a week after Thomas's funeral, I asked Anne if she wanted to come with me. I saw that she had something on her mind, and I hoped she would tell me, but she shook her head. When I got there, the gate was slightly ajar, a sign that Reggie was elsewhere. I sneaked in and walked quietly around, only to discover, after about ten minutes, that there was a woman sitting on the bench reading a book. Reggie must have told her about me, because she looked up calmly. I dipped my head and said, "I apologize for intruding. Reggie Scofield said – "

The woman nodded, and said, "I understood that a young friend of Reggie's has been coming by. I am Elinor Furnish. I don't mind our Reg showing off his skills. But I do worry that if some posh fellow comes around he will snap Reggie up and give him a larger scope for his ideas. I have forgotten your name, though Reg did tell me."

I said, "I am . . ." I almost said "Lidie Newton," because I'd been thinking of Thomas, but "Helen Longbourn" did pop out, as I had trained myself thoroughly. Then I said, "I work for Mallory Cunningham."

"There's a character," said Elinor Furnish. I wasn't sure if she was speaking in Mr. Cunningham's favor – Americans can never tell with English people.

I said, "I'm entirely mesmerized by your garden."

She said, "I wish it were mine, but it isn't. It belongs to my cousin and his wife. Mine consists of three geraniums and a very delicate pot of lavender that I tend to assiduously."

She seemed to be good-natured. She looked to be three or four years older than I was, evidently unmarried, since Furnish was her name. I said, "Do you live in the neighborhood?"

"I once did, but now I teach at a girls' school, and live there, so even though it's but a short walk, I only come from time to time."

"The one behind the wall?"

"Indeed, if you mean the one on Hope Street."

"The former slave-merchant's house."

She shook her head. "Yes, but we are doing our best to clean the place out."

Now neither of us knew what to say, so I stepped away and looked up into the trees. After a bit, I heard her close her book again, and say, "Mr. Holt, the gentleman who bought it from the slave dealer and started the school, was a lovely man. He died when I was eighteen, but I knew him because he was a friend of my parents. I've never met such a kindly person, or one who did more to account for and repudiate his sins. Do you know the tune 'Amazing Grace'?"

I nodded.

"Well, indeed, that one tells the story for many of the best folks in Liverpool. I would sing it for you, but I haven't a voice."

I said I knew someone who did, but I didn't say it was Anne. I said, "How about Reg?"

She said, "Reg might, but he's a tad bit shy on that score, too." We let the subject drop, and I asked what she taught the girls at the school.

"Reading. Handwriting. Domestic skills. But, indeed, the thing they need to learn the most is how to get along with one another."

She sounded as though she would teach the girls to be patient, if only by example. She seemed a kindly woman, simply dressed, but something about her made me feel awkward as I wandered through the garden, so I cut my visit short and wished her goodbye. She went back to reading her book, and I did manage to see the title – *North and South* – but I was too shy to ask her anything about it. Later that evening, I went into the Cunninghams' library, but I didn't find it there. I was curious, because I suspected that it was an English novel about the goose question, and I was very intrigued about what someone like Mr. Dickens would say about that. I couldn't get it out of my mind, though, so, a few days later, I mentioned it to Reggie, but he had not heard of it.

The singing master did sing that song, "Amazing Grace," to me, and I hummed along. The singing master was quite fond of it. And it had a lovely tune, but, thinking of Lorna, I disapproved of a song that was all about a man being forgiven for his sins but makes no mention of the people he had sinned against or the pain he had caused.

Some days later, the Cunninghams returned from Torquay, and Evelina did look a bit better nourished and brighter. Along with them came the two sons, one older than Evelina, Peter, and one younger, Caleb. I saw nothing of interest in them. I was friendly in a Barnsby sort of way. Whenever Barnsby was to serve Evelina, I could see his demeanor soften and become more welcoming, even though his words remained the same. With Peter and Caleb, he was reserved and correct. Berta told me, "Ye mayght disapprove o' them boys" but she didn't say why. I understood a few days later, when a man showed up with a horse that Peter had purchased, evidently without his father's permission. It was a mare, a riding horse, bright chestnut with a glistening coat, very tall, only three years old. The man handed her over as if he was glad to be quit of her, as Berta might say, and as soon as Mr. Cunningham's groom led her into the stable, she squealed and kicked out at the two geldings he kept in there for the carriage. I overheard Mr. Cunningham question Peter about her background, and Peter was grumpy. He didn't really know; a friend of his said she was a lovely horse, fifty pounds did seem like a lot to spend, but he was sure she was worth it; some of the other boys at his school rode to hounds, why shouldn't he?

"Because those boys have had a country upbringing and are entirely familiar with country ways."

No response.

The very next day, I was out in the back garden with Berta, holding the basket while she picked beans and spinach for supper, when Peter came walking out of the stable, leading the filly, who was tacked up. He mounted fairly easily, but then her ears went back and she kicked out, shifting Peter to the side. She threw up her head as if she planned to rear. I dropped the basket and went over, stood in front of her, took a rein in each of my hands, held her until I felt the tension ease out of her front end. A moment passed. I said, "Might I ask if you rode this one before you bought her?"

He shook his head.

I said, "Well, she is a beauty. I can see why you were drawn to her, but . . ."

He was not especially gracious. He said, "How would you know?"

I said, "I've been riding all my life."

Out of the corner of my eye, I noticed Berta, standing with the basket – she must have picked up whatever I'd dropped. She had her hand on her hip. She turned and walked toward the house, and that gave me an idea. I let go of the reins, stood there for a moment, then turned and strolled down one of the garden paths. The filly (later I learned that her name was Toffee) followed me, either to get to the plants in the garden or because she needed someone reassuring to follow, and I walked for about a quarter-hour, here and there, the filly close enough behind me that every so often she bumped me with her nose. Peter was still on her, and, step by step, he got easier, too, and began to sway with her movement. One time, he lifted the whip he had – I think inadvertently – and her head popped up. I looked at him, and he dropped the whip into the bed of purple flowers. By the time we were back to the stables, Toffee seemed calm, but, more important, Peter seemed to have completely relaxed. Nor was he as grumpy. He shook his head, pushed his hair back, and said, "Don't tell, please, Miss Helen. It was a gaming debt. I owed the fellow seventy pounds, but he said he would take fifty if I also took the horse off his hands. He hasn't been able to do a thing with her. He bought her as a yearling, but she wouldn't race and she's been hard to manage. That's why I didn't try her out."

The easiest thing, I knew, would be to send her to the knackers, as they called it here in England, but she didn't seem to be a mean thing – rather, a frightened thing – so I said, "When do you go back to your school?"

"St. Matthew's day."

I said, "That might be enough time."

I will say this for Mallory Cunningham: he did not interrogate either me or Peter about the horse or about what we were doing or why, though I did see him looking out the window sometimes (I also saw Caleb looking out the window). We did it as if it were a secret: in the morning, before everyone was up, before breakfast. I didn't ride the filly – I didn't have the clothes for it – but Peter got on her every day. He stayed out very late on the Friday night after we began our regime, but he got on her anyway the next morning, then got off after fifteen minutes and puked into the manure pile, and he must have learned some lesson, because every night after that, I heard him come home well before midnight.

Peter was not a bad rider, though he was irritable. Toffee soon persuaded him out of that, because she could sense everything, and if a flash of impatience ran through him, she would pin her ears instantly. I suggested that if he felt himself getting annoyed he should remember that she was young and virtually unbroken, take a few deep breaths, and relax his hands and shoulders. That did seem to work. I walked with them here and there, kept my eye on her, moved in on them when she looked edgy, moved away from them when she lowered her head and relaxed her ears. After a few days in the garden and the stable yard, we went out onto the road, which was fairly empty early in the morning, and then to a small nearby park. Peter got more confident and also more patient. One time, she almost dropped him, when a starling flew out of a tree, but he managed to stay on, and then to calm her by walking her in small circles. The other thing I did was have him give her hay twice a day, not leave it to Lester, the groom, because I wanted her to look at him and think of something pleasurable. Once in a while, Caleb came to the stable and watched Toffee. He seemed more pleasant than Peter, but also more shy. I asked him if he would like a horse of his own, and he said, "I wouldn't mind driving a horse. Have you seen those ponies that came from Ireland? They can do anything, and if you fell off one of them, I don't think it would hurt."

I said, "Does their breed have a name?"

Caleb said, "They come from a spot called 'Connemara.' That's all I know." He glanced at me and smiled a bit, then went back to the house.

I enjoyed the hours we spent with Toffee, and a few times, I persuaded Evelina to go to the garden and pet her, which both of them seemed to enjoy. Of course, in my mind I compared her to Jeremiah, a steady boy if ever there had been one, but, then, he was older – by his teeth, we had estimated that he was seven or eight, a grown horse. And he was not a Thoroughbred, though he had that look. At any rate, he hadn't been as full of beans as Toffee, so she intrigued me. I had thought that Barnsby would take an interest in her, but, other than discovering her breeding, which he said "wasn't much, indeed," he didn't seem to care. And it was true that he let the groom do all the tending and the driving. All Barnsby liked about horses was the racing – he had made a point to take me aside in June and tell me that Fisherman, the horse we'd seen win with such ease, the horse Barnsby had gotten maybe two shillings on, had won the Ascot Gold Cup, with the Queen and all of her family watching.

Caleb was a kindly, bookish boy and good friends with Evelina, who read aloud to him every day. He was friendly to me, asked me more than once about life in America, and said that he wished to go there someday, especially to Niagara Falls, which one of his masters at school had read of in Mr. Dickens's book about his visit to the United States. I told him about the Mississippi, said that when I was living with my parents outside of Chicago we had taken a boat down the river. I was tempted to tell him about the Missouri – a much more interesting river, in my opinion, and not only for the dangers of the rocks and the rapids – but I knew that once I began he would start asking me questions, and I would drop a bit of information that I didn't want to even exist, much less be known. We laughed about the mud in Chicago – perhaps I exaggerated a bit. I told him about Mr. Barnum's museum in New York, and the Crystal Palace. He said that there was one of those in London, too, and he had agitated off and on to be allowed to visit, but his mother didn't like London and his father hadn't the time, and . . .

Caleb seemed to think that I might step in here, and offer to accompany him, but the very thought of London – of the London I had read about in Mr. Dickens, of the London Barnsby had left, of the London where Mr. Cunningham would have loved to stage a production but didn't have the wherewithal for it – those Londons intimidated me. Peter had been there when the boys in the class he'd just finished were taken on a school trip to London by rail. It wasn't much of a journey from Liverpool, by rail, and they were shown Westminster Cathedral and the Houses of Parliament and Buckingham Palace, and they walked about Hyde Park of an afternoon and went to the British Museum, which was maybe a mile from the hotel where the boys were put up, Brown's Hotel, and of course it was all very stuffy, and two of the boys – not Peter, he *said* – had run off one night and seen more things going on in the streets than they had ever seen before in their lives, but Peter wouldn't tell Caleb what those things were, except they *said* they had gotten down to the river, which was a bit under two miles, running all the way there and all the way back. Caleb looked at me very seriously and said, "I like to think of myself as an explorer, and I feel I should get started. Do you know Sir Francis Drake?"

I shook my head.

"He was eighteen when he went to the Bay of Biscay, twenty when he went to Africa, twenty-three when he went to Boston. And, you know, he fought the Spaniards, but we don't have to do that anymore. He went around the whole world. Took him almost three years!"

I said, "Where would you go?"

"Australia first, then south. The South Pole."

I said, "I hope you get the chance," but I didn't mean it. My own explorations had not been pleasant, but at least I was accustomed to the out of doors. The same could not be said of Caleb. But he and Evelina did pass the papers I continued to buy for her (on the sly, I admit) back and forth, and he was not at all consumptive or subject to ill-health in any way. One place I accompanied him to was the docks, where he walked back and forth surveying the ships and telling me which ones he thought looked most "seaworthy." Several of the boys in his school, he said, had not seen their fathers in years because of their foreign service in India, and one boy had lost two of his brothers in the war in Crimea. It turned out that there was a poem that Evelina had memorized about that war, and she recited it to me one day when we were in her room and I was holding out my hands so that she could roll her hanks of yarn into balls. "Half a league, half a league, / Half a league onward, / All in the valley of Death / Rode the six hundred." I listened politely, but the only lines I cared for were, "Theirs not to make reply, / Theirs not to reason why, / Theirs but to do and die," and I thought, over and over, why do men do this? There was nothing in the poem about any of the sons of the Queen leading them into the valley of death, just as Thomas Newton went to K.T., and so, for that matter, did those Border Ruffians, but you never found Senator Douglas or Franklin Pierce galloping into any valleys that might be dangerous in any way. Well might they have second thoughts about starting wars if there were cannon to the right of them and cannon to the left of them, but all they ever heard were the birds in the trees. Though I did not express these thoughts, I saw that they made my hands tremble in anger as Evelina was rolling the balls, so I took some deep breaths and relaxed my shoulders, as I had been telling Peter to do when he rode Toffee, and it worked well enough.

One thing that was amusing, to Mr. Cunningham as well as to the rest of us, was the sight of Peter making up to Anne. He was three years younger than she was, and exactly her height, though he would stretch himself a bit when he approached her. He was attracted to her in both her yellow gown and her ivory-colored gown, and he frequently asked her if she would go with him for a walk in the park. She did not. But after she and the dancing master had a little chat with both Mr. Cunningham and Mrs. Cunningham, he was allowed to join her for the dancing lessons, and, as with the riding, he was awkward at first but was observant enough and limber enough to catch on after a few days. Once he was dancing with Anne, the dancing master could follow them about and help them correct their steps or their rhythm, and he thought it a good thing if sometimes Anne – the lady – led and sometimes Peter – the gentleman – led. The purpose of switching back and forth, the dancing master said, was that quite often there were so many couples dancing that you could not follow your intentions, and you had to be prepared to step up or move out of the way. If you sometimes led and sometimes followed, then you learned to attend to your partner as well as to your own thoughts. Another thing he did that was effective was to set up barriers and items that they would stumble over if they were not alert. By the end of the month, the two of them were quite something to watch – leaping about or gliding smoothly here and there, twirling each other, moving backward, moving forward. And after a solid hour or more of Anne every single day, Peter lost all of his romantic thoughts.

Anne and I agreed this was a good thing, because Mallory Cunningham's goal for his older son was a proper English marriage into a large income, a beautiful estate, and a willingness to invest in theatrical productions. I wondered what his goal for Caleb was, but maybe it was putting him on a ship and waving good-bye.

All in all, I enjoyed the two boys more than I had thought I would when I first met them. Perhaps the only boy I had ever known well was my cousin Frank, who was of an age with Peter, but who had been much wilder and had learned his lesson. When he was wild, in K.T., I couldn't keep track of him and felt fear and guilt, and when he became much more standoffish back in Quincy, I felt that he resented me, and perhaps blamed me for many unnamed things. The Cunningham boys had a kind of willingness and flexibility that was appealing. I would say that my job as a servant to the Cunninghams was the best thing that had ever happened to me, because it kept me busy and it also kept me on my toes, as each of the Cunninghams was so different from the others. When you are living with your own family, you don't pay much attention to them, because you are used to them (too used to them) and you think that you know all about them. If you are a girl like I was in Quincy, your chief intention is to get away from them, and so the only thing you watch them doing is watching you. How did Harriet get along with Roland? Well enough if he stayed out of the house – that was all I might have said.

How did Mrs. Cunningham get along with Mr. Cunningham? Over breakfast, she was attentive – she asked him how he was enjoying the provisions, she asked if the ham or the bacon seemed as tasty as it had last week, she thought perhaps the meat man was salting it too much lately. And the scones? She thought they were light enough – did he? But then she would move the dish of scones or the bacon slightly out of his reach, move the bowl of fruit a little toward him, glance at his belly, at the way the buttons on his waistcoat were straining their buttonholes. She escorted him out of the dining room, and spent the rest of the day attending to Evelina. Sometimes, Mr. Cunningham would chat about a project he had thought of. She would listen, smile, nod; then, later in the day, I would see them in the garden, walking back and forth, Mrs. Cunningham speaking to him with a directness I never saw when they were in company. So the way she got along with her husband was intelligent and complicated. She had ideas about what he might do, what he should do, but instead of throwing up her hands, shaking her head, or snorting in anger, as Harriet would have done, she eased him here and eased him there. She also believed him. The project of promoting Anne had been entirely his idea – she had never been to America or seen Annie before we arrived, so I also saw that he could not have done that if she hadn't supported his idea. If she had been pretty when she was Anne's age, that was gone now. She was gaunt; her lips had thinned to nothing; she was evidently shortsighted, because she leaned forward slightly and stared when she was talking. Her hair was graying. But Mallory Cunningham could not do without her, and perhaps that was the reason that he never flirted or made any sort of overture to Anne – all of Alice's fears blown away.

Toward her boys, she was a bit different – more ready to laugh at their antics and their observations even as she was warning them to stay out of trouble. Toward Evelina, she was as caring and gentle and remote, all at the same time, as a woman could possibly be. Toward Anne, she was polite and encouraging; toward me, she was grateful – I had taken on tasks that she didn't have the knowledge or energy to do – but also reserved, as if, were she to encourage me, I would "forget my place."

I watched all of this with fascination, and, no, I would never forget my place, because my place was the best place in the house: I was active, free to come and go, free to make friends like Reggie, free to observe the boys and Evelina and Barnsby and Berta and Jane and Lester and Toffee, not to mention visitors and guests, and to come up with my own opinions. And I had no stake in the outcome of any single thing, other than Toffee's tossing Peter off her back and injuring him.

At the end of August, Anne began rehearsing for a production that was to open in late September, when, Mr. Cunningham said, the weather would be chilly again and everyone would be back from their country or seaside retreats and ready for some diversion. I gathered that the question was how to make use of Anne's profitable turn in the melodrama without consigning her to a career exclusively in melodramas. Three fellows who were putting on plays about ghosts and castles and witches and demons came to him and told him, as he related to us at the dinner table one night, that they admired her ability to swoon, how she looked up, threw back her head, and then collapsed gracefully to the stage – even her hair fell gracefully around her cheek. But Mr. Cunningham thought there was more to Anne than that, so he kept looking until he chose the very thing that, perhaps, Anne herself might have chosen, a short run of a William Shakespeare play, *Macbeth* – we had seen a bit of that a couple of years before, both fascinating and scary, since one of the actors nearly set fire to a curtain with his torch.

There were more characters in the play than there were actors in the company that was to put on the play, so everyone had to take on two or three roles. Anne was to play Lady Macduff (of course the one who dies) and one of three witches, or "hags," but the manager of the play decided to have each of the witches represent a different stage in women's lives – a grandmother, a mother, and a girl. Anne was to be the girl. It was set in Scotland – everyone in the audience would know that – so Anne had to learn a Scottish accent (not difficult for her) and a witch accent, that sounded, when she spoke to me in it, distinctly French, which made us both laugh. The promise was (Anne told me privately) that if she did a good, or even a passable, job, they would hire her for a play that they planned to put on in the spring, the very one she had been reading on the ship, *Much Ado About Nothing*. This *Macbeth* was not a long play and easy to understand – Macbeth kills the King, mostly because his wife wants him to, and he regrets it long before she does. I would have liked to see Anne as Lady Macbeth. If they had asked me, I would have said that she was his second wife, much younger and more ambitious than the first, and he killed the King because he couldn't resist her, and she got him to do it because she was selfish and impetuous and didn't know any better. Like that boy who shot Jeremiah, or several of the Border Ruffians I saw who looked younger than I was. Or a few girls I knew in Quincy who took up with men who got off boats going up and down the river because those men looked to be so much more promising than the fellows we had around town. People say that there's no telling what a boy will do when he's young and brash, but I would say that there is no telling what a girl of the same sort will do, either. And then I would look in the mirror. However, no one asked my opinion, and the woman who played Lady Macbeth was from London itself, willing, because it was considered to be such a great role for a woman, to stay in Liverpool for three months just to do it. She was famous enough that when they put up the advertisements for the play, her name, Miss Lucas, was above the name of the man who played Macbeth. There was much of interest, but as I helped Anne learn her parts, I thought, what was the difference between this and a melodrama, except the poetry?

Once again, I did my tasks at home but did not go to the theater, especially after Peter took Toffee off to his school, and so, once again, I had time to myself after I had run all my errands. Reggie Scofield's garden (but he told me to call it "the Furnishes' garden") was, if possible, even more beautiful in September, and I didn't mind for a bit helping Reggie harvest the apples at the end of the month and carry the baskets to the portico at the back of the house, sort through them for good ones, bad ones (for making cider), and mediocre ones (for making apple butter). We also pulled up turnips and carrots and beets and parsnips and onions and leeks. My compensation for working with Reggie was that the Furnishes gave me a peck of apples to take home to 2 Canning Street (which pleased Berta, as she liked Ribston Pippins, and the Cunninghams had only Norfolk Pippins, which weren't ripe until almost November, and didn't taste "a bit as good as 'em Ribst'ns").

I did miss Toffee, as she had turned out to be a friendly enough filly. Sometimes, she pinned her ears for no reason as I approached her, but if I backed off, she would put her ears forward and come toward me. Like all horses, she had her quirks, but when they left (and they went by train, which was not uncommon in England), she and Peter seemed to be getting along well enough.

The Furnishes' house was now fully populated, and I began to meet them in the garden. Reggie had told me when they were at home or when they were away, but he hadn't told me how many there were, or what intrepid travelers they were. Like most of the travelers I had met over the years, they were friendly – even to me, a servant girl – curious, ready to chat. The ones who asked me questions were Mrs. Furnish's nephew and his cousin. I told them bits about Chicago and New York, but not about K.T. I visited the garden, sometimes, to read my book – I had returned to *The Newcomes,* and there was plenty of it to pass the time (if I happened to be sitting in the garden at the Cunninghams', I could be readily interrupted and sent on an errand). Both the nephew and the cousin asked me what I thought of Lincoln or Douglas. I said that I had no idea who they were. Both of them looked surprised, then treated me to some tales of their experiences in the Cape Colony, which turned out to be on the southern tip of Africa, and of buying and shipping cotton from Egypt, a place I had heard of in church. The nephew had helped to bring telegraphing to India, and the cousin had established a sheep station outside of Dunedin, which was in New Zealand.

One of the Furnish daughters was a teacher, like the cousin Elinor, though she taught at a school in Canada, in Wingham; had I ever been there? Not so far from Chicago, was it, though the teacher, whose name was Ruth, had only gotten as far into the United States as Detroit, and what did I think of this Kansas thing? I said I had no idea what she was talking about, that people in Chicago didn't care two bits about – what was it, Kansas? Or was it Arkansas? I could never keep the two of them straight. So she went back to her own story: her husband was a Scot, from Glasgow, they had met right here in Liverpool, he had taken her to Ontario, sadly, she had no children of her own, though there had been two. . . . And here I started to cough and cough and cough, and I put my book down and gasped out that I needed some water, and she went inside and got me a cup, and so I pushed off all thoughts of stillborn babies.

I saw that if you grew up in Liverpool, like Caleb, you didn't have to leave the house in order to be infected with the desire to explore.

It seemed as though the Furnishes had a fair number of relations who were Scottish, and when I told Barnsby about this, he said that that was not unusual in Liverpool – there were fair numbers of all sorts of people, including the Irish, of course, as they spread everywhere like a plague, but Spaniards, and dusky folk from the Antilles, and even a Swede or a Dane here and there. It was all owing to the shipping; you never knew what the cargo would be, who would sign on as a boy to clamber up the mast, which was a dangerous job, and only a boy with no sense would do it; had I been to Toxteth? Once a lovely spot. Giant deer park, Barnsby didn't know how many acres, but now it was all small houses and rubbish and, of course, smoke, as was the case all over the city, but, indeed, so many houses were crushed together in Toxteth that there were more chimneys, more burning coal, and possibly, though Barnsby could not directly attest to this, not so much of a breeze as we were used to on Canning Street. As he knew I enjoyed walking about the cemetery off Hope Street, he thought I might enjoy the one that ran along Smithdown Road, sizable and pleasant. Only about a mile and a half. And then there was Wavertree, that was a walled botanic garden up to the north a bit. I appreciated how Barnsby rambled on as if he had no intentions, but once I went walking over to Toxteth, I wondered if he did, because, in addition to the cemetery and the garden, there was a large population of, as Barnsby had said, "dusky folk," and they were all walking about as if they were both quite at home and quite at ease.

Here it was, I thought, the place Lorna should have fled to, the place perhaps her long-lost husband *had* fled to, but when I walked about, pretending to be striding down the streets with some sort of purpose, my ears wide open, I didn't hear anyone who sounded American – all of the accents were new to me, some of them shades of British, some entirely unfamiliar. I then went to the cemetery and the botanic garden, and was once again impressed by how thriving and beautiful this city was. There might be riffraff in some neighborhoods, and there might be smoke. Some days the smoke was, indeed, a stinking fog, and Mrs. Cunningham would be in her room with Evelina, the doors and windows shut up tight and the curtains drawn, planning another escape. But, other days, because of the winds, it was brighter. Everywhere I walked, there was not only something to look at, but also a spot of greenery or an attempt by someone to plant a few flowers. I'd read in Mr. Dickens's books about young boys and girls forced to work for nothing, and I did see some of that, but that was true in America, too. Harriet and Alice sometimes talked about the little children, orphans, sent out on trains from New York and Philadelphia to Illinois – the ones Harriet heard of were in Meredosia and Mount Sterling – not more than five or six years of age, supposedly adopted by families who had farms there, but, really, just put to work, not taught reading or writing, and what could a five- or six-year-old do? Alice had heard they were at least ten years old, but that would mean they'd been stuck in those orphanages, and which was worse? Indoors scrubbing floors all your life, or getting a little fresh air? All of this prattle while Annie was setting the teapot on their table, and they hardly looked at her. I saw that I was now one of those persons who became angry at everything I thought of. If I hadn't been able to walk it off, I don't know what I might have done.

After three weeks, the time came for the dress rehearsal of Anne's play, and Mr. Cunningham said I could attend. Anne told me that I was to be her critic – my job was to watch the play and think up the worst, most sneering things I could about her performance and then tell them to her when I was helping her out of her corset and her dress that night. She was deathly tired of praise, because she had gotten a lot of it, and she felt that it set her performance in stone. Every time she was crossing the stage and remembered a compliment the director or one of the other actors had given her, she felt her face freeze or her body tense up, if only slightly, in order to preserve that compliment forever. My own view of this, which I didn't mention, was that, having grown up with Alice, who never hesitated to criticize, Anne was suspicious of praise, thought the compliments were lies. But I went, and I took a small journal and a pencil to write down whatever disparaging remarks I could come up with.

I was taken to the theater by Mr. Cunningham in his carriage, and I saw that it was the same pleasant, large one where they had put up the melodrama. The weather was now cooler, and the doors of the saloons along the way were closed, which meant that there was less of a fracas on the streets, and by the time we got to the theater, I was in a quiet mood. Mr. Cunningham related to me that Peter was continuing to behave himself at school, and, apparently, so was Toffee. Peter took her out every day, round and about, with some of the other boys who had horses, and she was frisky but well behaved.

As always at a dress rehearsal, there was no sign outside the theater that anything was going on, but, inside, everyone was busy with last-minute tasks: set builders, seamstresses, cleaners, men putting up pictures, women sweeping. This time, we sat toward the middle of the rows, and I pulled out my pencil and my notebook. Anne was in the first scene. Of the three witches, she was the one who, at first glance, didn't look like a witch. The other two were made up to look ill-kempt and ugly, but the only thing that looked strange about Anne was the long fingernails they had attached to her hands somehow, and the redness of her lips. In the first scene, they were standing around a steaming cauldron, and Anne's job was to speak last – every time another witch suggested some evil deed that had to be done, Anne suggested something worse, and the other two looked at her in a motherly way, as if she were doing her schoolwork just as she was supposed to. I wrote down, "Miss Revere is far too appealing to have been cast in this role."

The fellow who played Macbeth was in many ways perfect for his part, because he was a well-intentioned man who kept looking about as if he couldn't figure out a thing. His companions treated him with a bit of disdain, and whenever the folks backstage worked up a noise or made the wind howl, he looked startled. He convincingly had no idea what was coming.

Then there was another witch scene. The older two spoke like classic complainers, and then Anne called out that Macbeth was approaching, so the three witches presented themselves. Macbeth more or less hid behind his friend, whose name was Banquo, and Banquo laughed at the witches and asked them about their beards, which, as far as I could tell, they did not have – all they had was boldness. But they seemed insulted, and so they got evidently more intent and more ruthless. Anne's job was to step up to Banquo, stand in front of him until he backed away, and then tell him a lot of things that he didn't understand, including that his children would be kings of Scotland. Anne looked slightly different than she had fifteen minutes before: still the fingernails and the red lips, but now her hair was standing on end, and her eyebrows had been extended. She also looked crueler – she delivered her news as if it was, indeed, a curse, and Banquo reacted to it in that way. I wrote down, "Miss Revere will certainly never receive any marriage proposals if she continues in this manner."

The woman who played Lady Macbeth had a lot of scenes, all of them nasty. She was made up to look slightly frayed, as if she had been living beyond her means and was tired of having to mend her own skirts. I did see her point of view, though, every time she said that she wished she'd been born a man.

Now came the ghostly parts, but it was evident that the company putting on the play could not make things like a knife appear in the air, except perhaps by dangling it from the catwalk, but then the lights might have shown the string. At any rate, they settled for letting Macbeth sound unhinged, and he did a very good job, saying things, and then looking here and there, and then opening his mouth as if he wanted to say something else. All the murders took place offstage, for which I was very grateful.

Anne's next witch scene was meant to be the most spectacular, and they did their best. The fellows behind the scenes were making so much thunder noise that I had to block my ears. They also flashed pieces of bright cloth to mimic lightning. In this scene, a fourth witch appeared – the actress who played Lady Macbeth, which was evident from her voice, though she was completely veiled in diaphanous black. I wrote in my notebook: "Fortunately for the audience, Miss Revere was not able to steal the scene, though she made so many facial expressions that it was evident she was trying."

A little bit later, the stage went completely dark, and at first we heard only sounds of hissing and boiling, and then some light came up, but only around a large pot, of the sort we might use for boiling laundry. In this scene, Anne still had the fingernails and the eyebrows and the red lips, but she was swathed in a similar black fabric to the fourth witch's in the previous scene, and her hair was pulled back, as that witch's had been, indicating that Anne's witch was to be the favored one. The witches were making a stew, and when Macbeth showed up, looking much worse for wear, they gave him a taste, in a cup, and then three predictions. Anne's was showing him the limb of a tree, and telling him he was to be king until some trees moved up a hill to stop him. For this scene, I wrote, "Miss Revere's ability to say unbelievable things defies this critic's belief."

In the next scene, I could see why they had wrapped her up, because she came on as Lady Macduff, no fingernails or red lips, an entirely normal young woman who watches her child get killed and runs away as the killers chase her. Of this scene, I wrote, "Miss Revere seemed so terrified in this scene that I feared she would fall off the stage. I worry for her professional future."

After that, the play moved along very quickly. I glanced at the audience, and only a few were fidgeting. Most were staring at the stage, and not in the way that they had at the melodrama. There was a look of dread on the faces of some of the people I could see. It was also true that the actors looked to be deep into their roles in this play, not entertaining themselves by hamming it up. Even the witches had a kind of sinister reserve when they spoke their words or, indeed, glanced at the audience, as if to tell us this could happen to us.

8

THE PLAY WAS a moderate success, and the theater was about three-quarters full for the entire run, ramping up a bit, but not as much as the melodrama had. Anne got some money, enough but not what she earned for the melodrama. The critics in the papers especially appreciated the actress who played Lady Macbeth, and referred over and over to her successful career in London. They said that Macbeth himself was "adequate for the role, in that he delivered the lines in an understandable fashion." They enjoyed the witches, and appreciated, as I did, the little witch society that came of making the witches different from one another rather than all alike. One critic said that he was taken aback and had to check his playbill when he saw Miss Revere as both a witch and Lady Macduff – he was amused by her witch and found her Lady Macduff "heart-wrenching." Anne and I agreed that this was the best compliment she had gotten in her brief dramatic career. "That," she said with a laugh, "is almost as good as being told that I will never receive any marriage proposals if I continue in this manner." I saw that we both appreciated our independence.

Sometime during the run, I asked Mr. Cunningham if there had been a real Macbeth, and as he was saying, "There was . . . ," Evelina piped up, and told me that he had lived in the eleventh century, had I heard of William the Conqueror, who came over from Normandy in 1066, but there were also the Vikings, who were in Scotland and all along the east coast. Did I know anything about the Middle Ages? They were very interesting, and she went into the library and found me a book, *Ivanhoe,* which she said she liked very much. It was long, but not as long as *The Newcomes*. I hoped I would get to it eventually. Though I didn't mention it to Anne, these discussions of Scotland, of Scottish people and Scottish ways, made me think a bit of the Harknesses. As Helen Longbourn, servant to Anne Revere, or, indeed, as Lidie Newton, I had distanced myself from the Harknesses, who we'd always known came to America from Scotland at some point, but we had never known when or why. There were no ancient dusty tartans lying in any trunks in Quincy, nor were there any stories about Duncans or Alistairs in our family tree. Perhaps the Harknesses had decided to fob themselves off as English, or, indeed, just to put all of that behind themselves. They had been in America for a least a hundred years, but how they came and why they came no one ever said. My father would have known, and might have cared, but he was far gone into old age by the time I came along, and so he had nothing to reveal. And my sisters never talked about him. Perhaps he had never talked about himself, because there was no discussion about where he was born, only that he was born in 1774 (I seemed to remember that when I was a small child, his birthday was celebrated sometime in the late summer). No one said whether he came to America as a child to the colonies or as an adult to the new nation.

The next time I was at the Furnishes', I hoped that the cousin, Ruth, might be there, but she wasn't. Now that my desires were frustrated, they became more intense, and so, the next day, when Berta sent me to the meat market and the vegetable seller, I passed the girls' school where Elinor Furnish was employed, and I looked for her on my way to the shopping. On the way home, I passed the gate, paused, looked around, walked to the end of the street, turned back, passed the gate, and looked around again. This time, my persistence paid off, because Elinor was just emerging from the front of the school with a group of girls. She marched them in two lines toward the gate, and on the way, she pointed at various plants and trees, and the girls called out their names – rowan, elm, lilac, brambleberry – and then she saw me, smiled, and waved. She brought the girls to the gate, still identifying plants, and I asked her if she planned to go to the Furnishes' any time soon. Sunday was the day, she said. I nodded. I hoped I could get there. I thought I might weasel out of the Cunninghams' usual visit to that crowded and unpleasant church. Berta didn't have to go, Barnsby stayed home. Perhaps, if I sat in my room evidently mending something, they would let me stay home, too. But in order to mend something, I would have to rip it, and I hesitated to do that, especially as my mending capacity was very minimal.

Even though Anne didn't get paid much for *Macbeth,* her fame did expand, and the woman from London who had played Lady Macbeth and was staying in Liverpool until after Christmas, took her here and there in her brougham, sometimes to parks, where they would go walking, and sometimes to tea parties, where, Anne said, Miss Lucas never ate more than a bite of anything, no matter how much cream it had or how many cherries were upon it. Anne ate modestly, too, as indeed, she had to, given how tightly laced she was now, even during the day. When she was out on the street with me, I walked behind her and kept my eye on the men who would pause, bow, tip their hats to her, and say, "Ah! Lady Macduff!" They were, as Berta would say, "o' th' better sort!" not like the ones who had complimented her after the melodrama. Then they would run their glance up and down me, as if my height made me such a freak that I should have expected it, and Reggie Scofield told me that this happened all of the time to him, too; in addition, some women actually turned and hurried away if he stepped too near them. I must say that I didn't see Reggie as often as I wished, now that so many Furnishes were about and his duties were plentiful, but I did bump into him once on the street and ask him if "Scofield" was a Scottish name, and he said it was not.

Just before the beginning of December, Miss Lucas asked Mr. Cunningham to put on what she called a harlequinade for Christmas. The theater, she said, the same one that had put on *Macbeth,* was open, because the play after *Macbeth* was to close on the 21st. They could rehearse in Mr. Cunningham's own parlor – it was big enough, if they pushed some of the chairs and tables out of the way, and the singing master and the dancing master could help them come up with the program. They could take, she said, some fairy tale, like "Cinderella," and redo it to give it a Christmas theme, with lots of songs. And then she turned to Anne, and asked her to sing "I Saw Three Ships," which Anne had asked her music master to teach her a few days earlier – I knew by this, and the way she practiced in her room, that she and Miss Lucas were in cahoots, as Roland would say, but why not? Miss Lucas was a lively woman, evidently loved the stage, and perhaps wanted to get Lady Macbeth behind her. She said, "Indeed, what else is there to do on Christmas? Better to go to a production than sit about with all the kinfolk you can barely tolerate, and twiddle your thumbs." Mr. Cunningham looked skeptical, but Evelina looked excited, and so he gave in. The fairy tale they chose was "Jack and the Beanstalk." How they would turn this into a Christmas story I had no idea, but Mr. Cunningham, Miss Lucas, and Evelina put their heads together for a couple of days, and then invited the singing master to join them; Evelina copied out the script, which was only five or six pages. Anne was to play Jack – Mrs. Cunningham rifled around in Peter's clothing and came up with a pair of trousers and a vest and shirt that fit her well enough, along with an old felt billed cap they called a shako – it was so tall that they could pile Anne's hair on the top of her head and push the cap down over it. They also wrapped her around the chest. They got a friend of Mr. Cunningham's named George Graff, who was a big man but agile, to play both the cow and the giant, and Miss Lucas, of course, played the giant's wife. Another actress played Jack's mother, but she was young, so she played her as Jack's sister, because children in fairy tales are always orphans. Their version of the story began five days before Christmas. The two orphans have no money, so Jack takes the cow to sell it so that they may buy two coverlids for warmth and a goose for roasting and a Yorkshire pudding in honor of the holiday. A stranger stops him, offers him magic beans for the cow; he takes them, of course, and when he gets home, his sister declares they are useless and throws them out the window. The beanstalk appears the next morning, which is the winter solstice.

There was no way to install a giant beanstalk for rehearsing in the Cunninghams' parlor, but they hung a heavy hemp rope with knots from the upper banister in the front hall, so that Anne might learn to climb it. There were to be three simultaneous sets on the stage – the cottage, stage right; the beanstalk, center stage; and the giant's castle, stage left. The music master was to play his piano in the pit, and the singing master was to lead the audience from downstage left as they sang the carols. The first one they sang was "I Saw Three Ships." The beanstalk would be the same thick hemp rope with knots for her to grip that Anne practiced with, but woven with green, hanging from the catwalk.

Once Jack had pulled himself up a few feet, the lights were to go down, so Anne could stop climbing and then reappear, tiptoeing about the castle. George Graff was good at walking about, sniffing, and saying, "Fee, fie, fo, fum, I smell the blood of an Englishman!" in a gruff voice, and as soon as he did, the piano started playing, and the singing master led us in "We Wish You a Merry Christmas." While the song was being sung, we saw Jack being hidden in a closet by the giant's wife, and then the giant went offstage, looking for his figgy pudding. The giant's wife gave Jack a bunch of gold coins. When he got back to the cottage, he showed his sister the money, and they talked about buying a goose, but there were no more to be had in the village. The next day, Jack climbed the stalk again. The giant's wife helped him steal a small harp, and when he got down, he handed it to a man who had appeared next to the singing master. The song we were to sing now was "Hark! the Herald Angels Sing." The next scene was on Christmas Eve, still no goose, and Jack climbed a third time. The giant's wife gave him a goose, and when he stared at it, she said that, even though it was Christmas, the goose could not be eaten, no matter how hungry Jack and his sister might be. He carried it down the beanstalk under his arm, told his sister, set it on a pile of straw in the house. Jack and his sister now looked very hungry, and as they lay down and went to sleep, the carol we were to sing was a very quiet version of "The First Noel."

The next day, Jack and his sister, whom he called Jane, woke up in their beds and sighed. The sister went and got the last of their small stock of porridge, which they ate quietly, and then the goose made some goose noises, and the sister went over to the nest. She brought back three golden eggs, and Jack and his sister were amazed. Of course, everyone in the audience knew that they were golden eggs, but, just to be certain, Jack and his sister had to show that they could barely lift them, they were so heavy. The carol was "It Came upon a Midnight Clear" as they looked at the eggs and rolled them about on the small table, and then the door of the cottage slammed open, and there were the giant and his wife. Jack and Jane leapt from their chairs – Anne was to knock hers down. The giant was carrying parcels and the wife was carrying a large platter with roast beef and a pudding, and they all sat down and ate as the audience sang "Oh, Come, All Ye Faithful."

I must say that it was not easy to put this together, as willing as everyone was. Anne had a difficult time climbing up the rope even a few feet, and fell once, but eventually managed to do it. The goose was sometimes cooperative and sometimes uncooperative, and George Graff kept improvising his lines, which annoyed Mr. Cunningham, though he didn't show it. But Miss Lucas remained good-spirited and patient, and Barnsby was very cooperative about the mess everyone made in the salon as well as keeping an eye on Anne as she practiced her climbing. And then, in the last week of the play that was onstage, and which had spare sets, the theater allowed our company to rehearse around midday, which put everyone in a good mood. The morning after the play was over, Mr. Cunningham hired a fellow with a large cart and four assistants to move the sets he had put together in the salon over to the theater. It took them four hours, and they worked well enough.

In the end, Miss Lucas prevailed upon Mr. Cunningham to charge only twopence per ticket, which meant that, for the two nights it ran, the theater was full and everyone was singing so loudly that people outside the theater could hear them. It was said that plenty of folk, including the ragged and impoverished, sang along, and the papers pronounced it a success, and "not only as entertainment for those who rarely can afford to be entertained." I went to one performance, I sang along, and I may have been the only member of the audience who was deeply satisfied that Anne didn't have to swoon or die. It was a year since Anne had acted in Quincy, in *A Christmas Carol.* She had now acted in a witty comedy, two melodramas if you considered *A Christmas Carol* a melodrama (which I did, since I was now extremely knowledgeable about the theater), a tragedy, and a harlequinade. In this whole time, she had forgotten one line, stumbled and ripped her skirt one time, and not fallen from the rope. When Miss Lucas bade adieu to Anne after the second performance of *Jack and the Beanstalk,* she was very affectionate and also in excellent spirits. She kissed Anne once on each cheek, embraced her, and said, "My dear, I shall see you in London." One glance at Mallory Cunningham revealed that he agreed with her on that.

As for me, the harlequinade caused a change in my life, too, not one that I expected. On the evening I left the theater, there was a man coming out into the street just as I was. The doors were wide, so several people could go in and out at one time. I stepped onto the pavement and slipped, because there was some ice, and this man grabbed my elbow and prevented me from falling. When a few steps revealed to us both that I had twisted my ankle (and the blame was my own, since I had purchased this pair of fashionable boots for myself only two days before), he offered to walk home with me. He assumed that neither of us had the means for a cab, and, indeed, we did not. For the first block or two, he was quiet, only offering me his arm, and I saw that, because I was the lady, it was my task to speak first. I glanced at him two times. He was my height, with a square jaw, some whiskers but not too many, and a well-used top hat, not a bowler. He was better-looking than Barnsby, but not as neatly dressed, and he had a thoughtful look on his face. My reserve fell away. I said, "You are a good Samaritan. Thank you."

He said, "I would have accompanied you even if your abode was not on my way home, but, as it is, I only take credit for my curiosity."

I said, "Then please ask me a question. But first, let me give an answer. Chicago."

Now the fellow laughed, and he was one of those men with a melodious, good-natured, pleasing laugh that turned a decent-looking face into a handsome one. I could not help myself: I laughed, too. I said, "What is your answer?"

He said, "East Kilbride by way of Belfast, but I've been in Liverpool for twenty years, so I doubt anyone who knew me in Ireland or Scotland would know me now."

I said, "Did you enjoy the harlequinade?" Then I winced, because my ankle gave me a sudden shot of pain. He said, "I was pleased when the giant was redeemed." I should have noticed that. But I was looking for praise for Anne. I said, "What did you think of the players?"

"The young fellow who played Jack was amusing and lively."

I said, "I thought so, also. I wondered how old he was."

"No doubt fourteen or so. Hasn't gotten his growth yet, still thinks all will turn out well." Now, as we walked, I mouthed these words to myself, so that I could relate them to Anne as soon as she got home. I ventured, "I understand the lady who played the giant's wife is very well thought of."

He said, "I know nothing of that. Perhaps I haven't seen a play in seven or eight years. But . . ."

"Twopence," I said.

"Twopence is indeed affordable."

At the corner of Upper Duke Street and Hope Street, I stopped, thanked him, and said that I could make it alone from here. He nodded. I thanked him for his company, and he saw that he had to walk off. He tipped his hat and turned on his heel, and I did watch him for a bit before making my way to 2 Canning Street and letting myself in through the garden gate. The walk, I was pleased to note, had healed my ankle, but I gave the boots to Jane, and she said that they were "big enough for two o' me, but I'll stuff the toes with rags and wear 'em proudly." And Anne was immensely pleased to find out that she had played Jack so skillfully that it was a matter of course that a member of the audience saw her as a boy.

Nevertheless, the fellow had watched me, because a few days later, I was letting myself out of the gate to fetch some goods from the vegetable seller and a few other spots, and here he was, and he said, "You are Miss Longbourn, aren't you?"

Another fellow who was passing must have heard the name, because he looked me up and down and smiled – born long, indeed.

I admit I was taken aback by the man's greeting (and I did not understand whether he was an Irishman or a Scotsman). This must have shown in my face, because that smile opened up his visage once again, and he said, "One of the Furnishes told me who you are, and that wondrous gardener of his, Reggie, told me you are his sister and where I might find you."

By daylight he was even more appealing. The sun, such as it was this time of year, glinted off his light-colored hair and his wide smile. His thick woolen coat looked frequently mended and, perhaps, handmade by his mother, as the sleeves were set in a bit unevenly. His stick looked handmade, too, as if he, or someone, had gone out into the back garden, cut off a useful tree limb, and carved it into a good enough tool for walking about. As I was back in my frequently repaired but remarkably comfortable boots, I appreciated that he was the sort who made use of his goods and cared little about his appearance, a rarity in Liverpool. "I understand that you are an avid walker and an excellent horsewoman."

I let this lie. I said, "I'm not Reggie Scofield's actual sister. I wish that I were."

"That he claims you is an excellent recommendation, though. I don't know a landowner in Liverpool who wouldn't give his eyeteeth to snatch Reggie from the Furnishes. He is that well thought of."

I said, "Who are you?"

"John Hegarty."

I said, "Is that an Irish name or a Scottish name?"

He said, "Irish."

And now we were walking toward the church and the graveyard along Hope Street, and to do so seemed as natural as the breeze off the river that carried the blasts of the horns entering the harbor, or the rustle of the leafless tree limbs above us on the street.

How had I felt the first time I saw Thomas, now dead for eighteen months, almost double the time I'd known him? For the first time since leaving Quincy, I felt capable of pondering this, and so I did, looking around this place that was completely alien from K.T., and letting Thomas appear. My initial impression had been neither good nor bad. Our neighbor, Roger Howell, couldn't stop going on and on about his new mare, the weather was hot, we were boiling the laundry, it was evident to me that Harriet was ready to marry me off to anyone passing through, and then, when I handed Thomas the dish of cakes that Harriet *said* I had made, he dropped them into his lap. But the next time I saw him, I thought he was appealing and intelligent. I remembered that I knew nothing about attracting a man, or being attracted by one. Very quickly, I saw that this Mr. Newton was evidently, and openly, a good person, even to Roland, who repeatedly referred to him as a d — ned abolitionist. He was quick to turn in on himself, and sometimes, when we were at Charles and Louisa's house in Lawrence or on our own claim, I remembered him looking out the doorway or up toward the roof, and feeling him depart from me even though he was sitting right across from me. I had no idea what this meant, but I did think it was preferable to the times I had seen Roland throw something (though not *at* Harriet) and rage out of the house. Thinking of this, I sighed.

The only memories I had of my own mother and father were of her in her room or the nursery, and him by the fire, staring blankly. Beatrice and Horace Silk got along well – she told him what to do behind the door; then he came out and did what he was told, and their emporium prospered. One time, before Thomas came along, Beatrice had said to me that it was best not to be too enamored of your husband, because the resulting size of the litter would send you to an early grave, and though she said this lightly, I only had to look around Quincy, and, indeed, my own family, to see that this was the case. And so I'd thought our marriage was perfect – building itself ever more sturdily on shared principles and adventures, but only moderately building itself on being enamored. Thomas was kind to me and did his duty, and I have always been certain that he would have welcomed the baby, had he lived. Had it lived. When he was shot, I was devastated, but there was also a way in which I was not surprised. If you live among Border Ruffians long enough, what surprises you is that you survive, not that you are shot.

But Helen Longbourn was not Lidie Harkness, and as we walked along in the gloom toward the Furnishes' garden, just to see what might be there in the deep dark of winter, Helen surveyed the supple demeanor and the cheekbones and the sudden smile of John

Hegarty and was, as they say on the stage, smitten. Whatever was happening, I wanted it to go along slowly, and then more slowly, so whatever information Mr. Hegarty and I might share would drip, drip, drip out, and then, if I were to enjoy a little bit of this and a little bit of that, it wouldn't matter what might happen, because my pleasures would be a sufficient return for my efforts – some pleasant memories to cover the unpleasant ones that were never far from my thoughts no matter how much I tried to push them out. Even as we walked, I asked Thomas, in my mind, what he thought of this, and there he was, glancing up from the book open on his lap, a half-smile on his lips, a full smile in his eyes, giving me a little nod.

It seemed as though Christmas was celebrated in Liverpool in many different ways. As in that Dickens book *A Christmas Carol,* there were some merchants or manufacturers who didn't celebrate at all – I did see saloons and stores that were wide open, and men and boys walking down the street evidently in their work clothes with unhappy looks on their faces. The Furnishes had a family feast and some flowers and tree boughs in the house, but Reggie, at least, was hard at work when I came that afternoon to give him a sisterly gift – a small book on gardening that no doubt he didn't need, but it had lovely plates, so I thought he would like it anyway. And he was prepared – he gave me some Dutch cocoa to be made up as a drink, telling me that I would like it, that it was healthful, and that Berta would know how to make it (which she did, and I did like it, as Reggie had suggested, sharp, almost bitter, without sugar, and with some cream).

At the Cunninghams', Evelina was in charge of Christmas, and as her favorite Christmas song was "The Twelve Days of Christmas," there was some sort of celebration every day, from December 25 (when, in Quincy, the saloons were closed and the men stayed home and ate a roast goose or at least a roast duck, which they themselves would have shot, and you had to be careful about picking the lead bits out of your piece as you ate) until January 5 (when, in Quincy and K.T., most of the citizens were still recovering from New Year's drinking bouts but had to go about their business anyway).

On Christmas Day itself, we feasted at 6:00 p.m., an unusually early time to eat in Liverpool, but when I came into the dining room and saw the feast laid out on the table, I could understand why. No goose, no duck, no wild turkey (which was what Roland liked), but a large roast of beef, and that preceded by fish. There was also an array of vegetables that had been saved in the cellar – carrots, parsnips, turnips, potatoes, beets – cooked in several ways.

These were followed by a figgy pudding, which was dark-colored and flavorful – lots of dried fruits, including some actual figs, nuts of various kinds, chopped apples, molasses (I could taste that), beef fat, which Berta called "suet," and, evidently, rum. I was invited to sit at the table, between Anne and Peter. I don't know whose idea this was, but I appreciated it, and tried to mind my manners. Anne knew exactly how to mind her manners, having watched not only Mrs. Cunningham but also the revelers Miss Lucas had introduced her to over the past month. To sit beside her and see how she tilted her head, how she smiled and laughed and ate sparingly, was to see a truly English woman and not the girl I'd seen the year before, hardly speaking to anyone at Beatrice's Christmas dinner (served at noon) and waiting to be told what she had to do next – clear the dishes or bring in the pumpkin pie, which Beatrice was very fond of, and served up as often as she could.

There were other guests – the singing master, the music master, a cousin of Mrs. Cunningham's from Norfolk whom I hadn't met before, the actor who had directed Anne's first play, and his daughter, who was about Caleb's age and sat across from him. There were three others, a young man and two young women, whose presence I understood after the meal, when Evelina led us into the salon, where seats had been set in rows around the piano. The music master sat down, and the knowledgeable guests took their places – one bass, one baritone, one alto (one of the female guests) and one soprano (the other of the female guests). Every seat had a small sheaf of papers, on which the words of the carols were written out, and the singing master had us hum a bit to him. Then he pointed to the seats we should take; Anne was in the soprano section, I was in the alto section. There were fifteen pages of carols, some I was familiar with, and others I was not. Evelina, who sat in the soprano section, eased her chair away, turned it slightly toward the rest of us. It was evident that she was beside herself with pleasure and anticipation – the sheaf of carols was trembling in her hand. Caleb kept his eye on her.

We began with "The Twelve Days of Christmas," which I had sung many times before, went on to "The First Noel," which we sang much more loudly than they had sung it onstage during the harlequinade, and then "Hark! the Herald Angels Sing," which I think I'd heard a few times. But what Evelina really liked were English carols – "The Cherry Tree Carol" (which Caleb was allowed to sing as a solo), "Good King Wenceslas," "The Coventry Carol," "God Rest Ye Merry, Gentlemen" – which I enjoyed but sometimes did not quite understand. Everyone sang with vigor, and, to my ear, the singing sounded bold and melodious. Evelina seemed pleased at the end, but also fatigued. Her mother took her off for the night, and though there was some Christmas punch, with lemon peels and more rum, as well as other ingredients only Berta knew, we all had but sips, and then the first day of Christmas was over, and I thought about those lines, "my true love sent to me / A partridge in a pear tree," and I wondered if that was a warning that someone like me, who didn't know what a partridge was, and could barely imagine a pear tree, perhaps wasn't prepared for true love.

When we were finished with our breakfast the next morning, called by the Cunninghams "St. Stephen's Day," we were all given gifts that, I suspect, Evelina had chosen, or, in some cases, made herself. For me, she had done a chalk drawing of a horse, a bay with a goodly blaze, and my first instinct was to be critical – the neck wasn't quite right, and the cheeks were too big, but as I looked at it, I came to like the intelligent eye, the alert facial expression. When did she see horses? From her seat in the carriage, or, perhaps, looking out the window. But she was observant. For Anne, she had edged a fine cotton kerchief in tatted lace. For Peter, she had painstakingly knitted a pair of socks, which quite impressed me – I'd seen her going about this, four little needles busily moving – but hadn't realized what she was doing. To Caleb, she gave a book I'd seen her reading, called *The King of the Golden River*. We opened our presents from Evelina one at a time, and I saw Caleb's eyes roll a bit when he saw Peter's socks. When he unwrapped his own book, he looked relieved, leaned over, and gave Evelina a kiss on the cheek. She also had gifts for Barnsby, Berta, and Jane, all of them carefully chosen or made. The next day, she went with her mother and father in the carriage, and took a few gifts to relatives and friends. Fortunately, the air was not as thick as it had been – a hard rain had muddied the streets, but that only meant that the carriage had to travel slowly. She was bundled up when they took her out the front entrance, but she seemed warm enough, and lively when they returned two hours later. And she brought some treats – shortbread, ginger biscuits, scones sprinkled with dried cherries, which we tasted at tea.

On the third day, since the air continued to be fresh, all of the Cunninghams went for a ride in the countryside – Peter and Mr. Cunningham mounted, Caleb, Mrs. Cunningham, and Evelina in the brougham. They brought home some holly and some ivy, and then, around tea, I heard them sing that carol, "The Holly and the Ivy." And so it went. On the fourth day, which was a Tuesday, I'd planned to find a gift for Evelina, but Barnsby said that the shops were closed, as well as the factories, celebrating Christmas when the shopkeepers and the manufacturers might actually enjoy a free day. On the fifth day of Christmas, the day of the five gold rings, Barnsby and Berta sent me to retrieve some parcels they had purchased for Evelina, and I purchased some hanks of cotton wool for her to tat with. So it went, for the twelve days. There was another small feast with a different sort of punch on New Year's Day, as well as roast lamb and one of Mr. Cunningham's favorite dishes from his boyhood, faggots, which turned out to be meatballs concocted of organ meats. By this time, I was eating in the kitchen again, and was thankful that, after watching Berta make them, I didn't have to eat them, though I got a taste of the punch. The twelfth day was when we gave Evelina her gifts.

I had looked forward to the twelve days of Christmas, having never seen anything like that before, and knowing the Cunninghams' talent for entertainment, but when the evening finally arrived, it did appear that Evelina was so exhausted by all of her activities, and perhaps by the smoke and fog that had once again settled over the city to such a degree that the horns blowing from the docks sounded as if they were right outside your window, that handing her gifts and waiting while she slowly opened them was painful rather than pleasant. The question was, why had Mrs. Cunningham allowed her to exert herself so much? Anne and I thought the answer might be a sad one – that she didn't expect Evelina to live to see another Yuletide season. Shortly after the twelfth day of Christmas, she and Evelina departed by ship, something Berta said they had never done before, to a town in France, far away, that Evelina's doctor had proposed, I think as a last resort. It was called Biarritz. One of the Furnishes, of course, had been there – it was originally famous as a whaling port. The next day, Peter and Caleb went off to their school, accompanied by a friend from nearby and the friend's manservant, who was to take them by train and then return. When I was out in the stable area later in the day, I was surprised to discover that Toffee was still in her stall. I'd not heard any ill of Toffee – I had overheard Barnsby and Peter talking kindly about her. Barnsby said that she was filling out nicely and looked to have grown a bit – her withers were now the same height as her croup – and she had a smooth walk with a good overstep. Peter said that he enjoyed riding her with his friends, partly because she was a head turner. Sometimes, he said, he thought she was a bit frisky, but that was better than the horse his friend rode, a stocky bay who seemed right enough, but then, out of nowhere, grabbed the bit and ran off bucking – bucked the fellow off on the green right outside the school grounds. He didn't break anything, but the fall gave him a good headache that lasted three days.

Toffee, of course, was still young, officially four but actually still three – she had been born at the beginning of March – the age of a racehorse in England, according to Barnsby, was determined by what year they were born, not what day. That was why, he said, it was better to breed your mare so that she gave birth early in the year, even if the weather at that time might be risky for the foal.

The stableman saw me looking at her. He put a headstall on her, opened the door, and handed me the lead – he didn't even ask me if I wanted to take her for a stroll, because he knew I did. There wasn't any grass, but, then, she wasn't hungry, having just eaten her hay. She sniffed this and sampled that, but she walked along pleasantly, and just when I was wondering what the difficulty was, and why Peter had left her at home, Barnsby came out of the kitchen, wiping his hands on his kerchief, and joined me. He said, "Ah, Miss Longbourn. You will be pleased."

I thought he had decided to give her to me. I would, indeed, have been pleased, and for the briefest of moments I pictured myself riding Toffee around that walled garden –

He said, "I do believe we've found a trainer."

I said, "Indeed, she seems . . ."

"No, I am referring to a racing trainer. There seems to be a feeling that she has promise after all, as she has done well with Mr. Peter, and seems more muscular and better balanced. I myself believe that four-year-olds do the best on the course – they've more confidence in themselves, and if the jockey asks them to do something unwise, they easily overrule him and do what they need to do in the best way."

I said, "Horses are smart."

He said, "If only they could speak, I'm sure we would learn a lot from them. Ah." He smiled and stroked her neck. "The trainer is Mr. Denham. He is coming for her in a few days. You might attend to her a bit between now and then." I knew I would enjoy that.

Since, at this time of year, the streets were even more empty in the morning than usual – perhaps because the sun didn't rise until the servants were already up eating their breakfast (and, indeed, it went down before tea, a short day, only about eight hours according to the grandfather clock in the hallway, which Barnsby said was rather old, constructed by a man named Lassle or Lassell, who had lived not far from Canning Street, in Toxteth). I took Toffee out first thing and led her about the streets and over to various gardens and even down Upper Duke Street to the entrance of the cemetery. She minded nothing. She was a curious filly. She would sniff the gravestones and stare at the trees and whatever plants were defying the sleet and the cold – close to the harbor, there wasn't much snow, and the ice came and went. I did look around for some hooligan who might try to steal her from me, but they must have stayed up too late and were still "hammered," as Reggie said.

I have to admit that on the second day of our walks, simply because I could not drive that fleeting thought that they might have given her to me out of my mind, I found myself alone with Toffee in the graveyard and led her over to a gravestone, one of the taller, sturdier, and more upright ones, dedicated to a local sailor named Elias Jerkins, 1801–1852, and used it to hoist myself onto her back. She was patient, gave me time to push my skirt backward underneath myself, and thank goodness no crinoline, and let me guide her with the lead and by shifting my weight to the left or the right, something Jeremiah had been very attentive to. Of course, she wasn't as well trained as Jeremiah had been, but she was pleasingly willing. I did not know if that was a good thing in a racehorse or a bad thing, but, eventually, we would find out. I rode her around the graveyard, let her investigate this and that, then out of the entrance and over to Upper Parliament Street, up the hill to the corner, where I slid off and walked her to Grove Street, over to Myrtle Street, back to 2 Canning Street. By then, it was late enough for people to be up and wondering what I was doing, so I took her home, and put her away.

On the third day, I did not expect to take her out – her trainer had said he would show up, but he was delayed, so I took her out again, this time up the hill in search of parks, also early in the morning. We were passing the Furnishes' place, and I was glancing about to see if Reggie might be there, when a familiar voice spoke to me. I halted, Toffee nickered, and I turned around to see John Hegarty offer her a piece of apple, which she took neatly. He then petted her as you should pet a horse, not a dog, a smooth stroke down the side of her face, followed by a smooth stroke down the side of her neck. I resumed our perambulation, and he came along with us, saying nothing. What had it been – two weeks – since I'd last seen him, and in that time, I had been turning over in my mind whether there was anything to think about that might happen between us. I did not experience longing: I knew that Yuletide was for friends and family, not strangers, and in many ways I was grateful for the respite, given my decision to draw out as long as possible whatever intimacy we might share. Now, as he walked along beside me and I glanced at him from time to time, I noted that I remembered his smile perfectly, and the twinkle in his eye, as well as his grace, his cheekbones, his shoulders, his neatly shaped nose, and how his nostrils flared as he breathed.

We did converse – his celebration of Christmas had not been elaborate, but the goose had been tasty and the Yorkshire pudding was always something to anticipate. I told him about Evelina and her generosity, and he said that she sounded like a lovely girl.

On our way back toward 2 Canning Street, he asked me to pause, and he stepped back and surveyed Toffee. He complimented her for exactly the traits I appreciated – her balance, her length of leg, her neat pasterns, her attentive ears, her calm demeanor – and said that it was too bad she was being sent to the racecourse. When he stroked her as we were about to part, I noticed his hands, which were graceful and strong-looking, agile as he touched her here and there, as attentive, in their way, as his eyes were. This was a strange thought that I had never had before. I didn't even remember Thomas's hands except through their actions – turning a page, hoeing our garden. But John Hegarty's hands seemed to have a being of their own. That was what I thought of later, after we parted at the Cunninghams' garden gate, and I put Toffee away, then went about my errands.

9

I CANNOT SAY that Alice, Beatrice, and Harriet were faithful correspondents. They sent us separate letters in single envelopes addressed to Anne – Alice's mostly about Fred and Larry, Beatrice's about the successes and troubles of Lorton and Silk, and Harriet's about the ups and downs of the farm and how Roland was putting up with the weather. Of course, there were a few good wishes that they sent our way, especially at Christmas, and I responded in kind, with bland remarks about how well Anne was doing in her theatrical endeavors and how much I was enjoying this prosperous city and the Cunninghams. I did write a bit about Evelina, in hopes that my sisters would see that I could appreciate a self-sacrificing, delicate girl as well as a misbehaving boy. But then, one morning when Anne was out with Mr. Cunningham, discussing with a group of investors some project they hadn't yet disclosed to me, I was gathering a few of her belongings – a petticoat, a wrap, a bag – and when I opened a drawer to put away a silver-and-amethyst brooch that was sitting on her side table, I saw there a collection of papers with Beatrice's name on them. I lifted them out of the drawer; they were a set of letters that Beatrice had written in the course of the autumn, and I saw that Anne had kept them from me because they addressed the goose question.

The gist was that our state, Illinois, and, indeed, our town,

Quincy, had become a hotbed of debate. I, of course, had seen Senator Douglas on the street, and had heard of Mr. Lincoln, though mostly, as was usual in Quincy, about his looks and demeanor. Those who denigrated him said that he was awkwardly tall and odd-looking (something I could sympathize with); those who admired him said that he was strong and good-humored, evidently a kindly man, and they admired his cheekbones. He was certainly more peculiar-looking than Senator Douglas, but in a positive way: to me, Senator Douglas looked like any self-satisfied and mercenary man of success whose belly stuck out and whose lips turned down because he was in a constant state of envy at the greater success of others. In K.T., the Biskets and most of the other abolitionists detested Douglas, as he was the one who had introduced the Kansas-Nebraska Act, thus opening the can of worms that was the bloody conflict there, and then never showing an iota of remorse. They knew, Thomas knew, that this was a step-by-step invasion of the goose into other states. Douglas was short, indeed – perhaps as short as Mr. Lincoln was tall – and so, in their debates, they must have certainly looked an odd couple.

One of the letters included a clipping from the Quincy paper about what each of them had said. Beatrice said that Horace had attended the Quincy debate, and that Roland had asked to go along, but Harriet stepped in and said that she was feeling very weak and ill, and she did not think she could do without Roland should he go. This was no doubt because she did not want him to get fired up. However, Beatrice said, she did catch a fleeting glimpse of him as she was leaving the debate hall, and Frank, too, though how they had put this over on Harriet she did not know. And there was no mention of Roland getting fired up. My impression of Roland, whom I had known for most of my life, was that he was a constant barker, but never a biter, and perhaps, if he had seen Lorna or another escaped slave (and some did cross the river from Missouri), he would have been more likely to help them than hinder them.

And then I had another thought – perhaps, when Roland referred to d—— ned abolitionists, he did so to divert attention from activities of his own, because, indeed, those activities had to be secret – more and more so, these days. I found this an intriguing thought.

Beatrice herself considered the debate between Mr. Douglas and Mr. Lincoln exasperating – why did they not leave this issue to work itself out, as so many issues do? She admitted that Mr. Lincoln made some interesting observations, and there were plenty of folks, including women, who did not wish to be ruled by others, especially those they considered less intelligent or honest than they themselves were, and who was to deny that those who inherited wealth or domination often did not deserve it? It was all very well for some to say (here she would be thinking of the pastor of Harriet's church) that the Lord above decided who should rule, but, she wrote, with two exclamation points, if you looked around yourself, you had to wonder what His standards were. She and Horace did their best to act reasonably and fairly as the directors of Lorton and Silk, but all you had to do was look up the street or down the street to see others who did not act morally, and who profited as a result. And as I read this, I thought that Beatrice may have had good intentions, indeed, but why did she think that the goose question was about her or her emporium? It was about Lorna.

In spite of myself, I kept reading. In the Quincy debate, apparently, the two candidates simply reiterated the positions they always took – Mr. Lincoln that enslavement was wrong and not to be justified, but to be gotten rid of somehow; Mr. Douglas that the citizens of the states had the right to decide whether it was wrong or not. He seemed to have learned nothing from the troubles in K.T., or at least, he had not learned the thing I had learned – that right and wrong are not decided by principles or debate, but by weapons and passions. One thing I always thought interesting about the Border Ruffians was that, although many of them did not actually have the money to own slaves, they were outraged by the idea that they might be prevented by others from doing as they pleased. Another thing that I thought interesting was that, at least when Thomas and I first went to K.T., it was the abolitionists who possessed the superior weapons. The Border Ruffians were so hotheaded that they always seemed to attack without a plan. That fellow, John Brown, whom I'd heard about but never met when I was in K.T., was said to have committed attacks of vengeance on pro-slavers who had attacked abolitionists. He was savage enough that he might as well have been one of them, and then, when he acted as the Ruffians did, but with more canniness, people who shared his views recoiled. Given my experience, I might not have recoiled. I did note that Mr. Lincoln stated that he was not proposing that Negro people would be made citizens once they were freed – Beatrice considered this a reason to support Mr. Lincoln's views compared to, say, Thomas's (though she dared not mention his name). If Mr. Lincoln had proposed citizenship, his audience might have stood up and walked out. He knew that and I knew that. All in all, what I gathered from reading the clipping and the few things Beatrice said about the debate was that nothing was resolved, and that was why I was here in England – resolving the goose question was as impossible as resurrecting Thomas or Jeremiah.

In the last of the letters, Beatrice wrote, briefly, that Mr. Douglas had won re-election. Of course, Horace had voted for him – Mr. Lincoln was too strange, too willing to bring on heaven knew what. Who had Roland voted for? For my entire life, I would have said Douglas, but now, having considered that perhaps Roland was not the man we thought we knew, I wondered. When I finished reading the letters, I folded them up, but in reverse order to the way I had found them. I wondered if Anne would notice, and if she did, whether she would discuss it with me. It seemed extremely bizarre to me that this long-standing question, this question that concerned the whole nation, East and West, North and South, might be decided in Illinois.

I was still thinking of this two days later, a Monday, when I happened upon John Hegarty again. I was carrying some parcels along Hope Street and chanced to look down at the graveyard from above – there was a spot not far from the corner of Huskisson Street where you might get a good view. It had snowed the night before, and the graveyard was picturesquely lined in fluffy white, but not covered. I knew him at once from his walk and the way he held his head. He came to one of the graves, doffed his hat, and stared at the headstone. I looked away. How old was he? Possibly as old as Thomas – that is, thirty – and in all likelihood the grave belonged to his wife, or, indeed, his wife and child, no uncommon thing in Liverpool or in Quincy. I could not resist looking at him again, and perhaps I cast a shadow, as the sun was behind me. At any rate, he looked up and raised his hand. I continued to stand there for a bit, and then walked slowly toward the corner of Upper Parliament Street. Having lost a spouse was not something that I wished to have in common with Mr. Hegarty.

We fell into step as soon as he met me, along Upper Parliament Street. The first thing he said, and in a lyrical voice, was " 'The boy stood on the burning deck, / Whence all but he had fled; / The flame that lit the battle's wreck, / Shone round him o'er the dead. / Yet beautiful and bright he stood, / As born to rule the storm; / A creature of heroic blood . . .' " He fell silent.

I said, "I noted that you were looking at one of the gravestones."

"Yes, belonging to a teacher of mine when I was a young man in Belfast. He made us memorize many poems. That is one of the two that have stayed with me. He died of the cholera shortly after he returned from Belfast. No one would have expected Belfast to be a more healthful town than this one, but for him it was. He was thirty-two at the time."

I said, "I haven't heard that poem before."

"Perhaps no one in Chicago knows it, then. Most of us in England learn it." He went on for a bit. " 'The flames rolled on – he would not go, / Without his father's word; / That father, faint in death below, / His voice no longer heard.'" He paused.

I said, "A very sad poem, indeed."

He said, "Do you know this one? 'Beside the ungathered rice he lay, / His sickle in his hand; / His breast was bare, his matted hair / Was buried in the sand. / Again, in the mist and shadow of sleep, / He saw his Native Land.'" His mouth was open to continue, but I stumbled and nearly fell. My face was red, and my breaths began to come fast. The last time I had heard that poem was two years before, sitting by the Biskets' stove in Lawrence, and feeling amused by it, even as I watched Thomas stare at Mr. Bisket as he spoke the words. Longfellow, I remembered his name. Mr. Hegarty grabbed me by the elbow, prevented my fall, picked up the parcel I had dropped. I caught my breath. He said, "Slavery was abolished in England twenty-four years ago." Then he halted and turned to me. He said, "Miss Longbourn, is that an issue you care about?"

I couldn't help myself. I nodded. When I looked down, he took my chin gently in his hand, lifted my head, said, "I do, too. Everyone must. Even an American."

I nodded.

And perhaps I trembled, but he stopped there, only squeezing my hand and turning to continue our walk. My hand was trembling, and I put it on his arm. By the end of the block, my heart had settled, my hands were no longer trembling. The sun was now getting quite low. We had gotten as far as the corner of Bedford Street. I said, "Goodness, I lost track of the time. I need to get home."

He said, "May I accompany you? Are you all right?"

But the last thing on earth that I wished was for him to accompany me. I said, in my calmest Miss Lucas voice, with my nose slightly flared and my chin slightly lifted, "No, thank you. I will be fine on my own."

He bowed a bit, said, "So be it, then," touched the brim of his hat.

After I turned away, I heard a brief melodic chuckle, and I was tempted to turn back, but no. I needed to adhere to my principle that interacting with Mr. Hegarty was a sweet pleasure best taken one drop at a time. When I got the parcels to 2 Canning Street, I was able to put the incident out of my mind, because I saw, as I came in through the garden gate, that the trainer, Mr. Denham, was there with one of his men, attempting to take Toffee away, but Toffee was having none of it. I took the parcels to the kitchen entrance, where Berta received them and lifted one eyebrow. I said, "How long have they been at this?"

Berta said, "Too long, y'ask may." I went toward the stable area. Every time the helper led Toffee out of her stall, she pinned her ears and balked. The plan had been to take her on the cars, as they did in England, but she'd been so perverse that they'd missed their train. Mr. Denham stood back. The helper, who seemed my age, looked to me as though he was about to lose his temper. Our groom was standing with Mr. Cunningham, and when he shook his head at me, I saw that, as far as the Cunninghams were concerned, the trainer and his helper had to prove themselves competent in order to deserve Toffee. One more time, the helper pulled her out of her stall, and she went along for about three strides, then reared up and struck out. The helper dropped the lead. Toffee came down, her ears pricked, looking ready to run off, and I went to her and grabbed the lead. She remained alert for a few moments, then stretched her head toward me and sniffed my arm. This seemed to relax her, and I stroked her face a bit. I admit I was surprised. I had not seen her misbehave in months. With Peter and me, both, she was patient and kind. I looked around. The sun was not down, but it was late afternoon, the trees were casting long shadows across the grass, and as there was a decent breeze, the limbs were creaking, and the shadows were flickering. I said, "I must tell you, she doesn't go out at this time of day very often. I've always taken her out in the early part, and I believe Peter generally rode her no later than mid-afternoon."

Mr. Denham came over to me. I said, "She is an observant filly, and intelligent, too." By this point, Toffee's head was lowered.

Mr. Denham said, "And there is a chill in the air. That charges them up." He petted her neck. She allowed it. The helper was pacing back and forth. He did look cross. I ventured, "Perhaps your assistant was handling her a bit roughly."

He said, "Ah, my son. Leo. He is a mite hot-tempered, I admit."

I glanced at Mr. Cunningham, who came over, and said, "Thank you, Helen. Perhaps a bite to eat would settle us down, and we might try again in the morning, if, as you say, she is more agreeable at that time of day."

I led Toffee to her stall, and our groom promptly forked her hay in. She went straight to work, and it is true that some horses are more edgy when they are hungry, quieter when they are full.

Berta had no difficulty rustling up a pleasant and filling tea – not only scones and biscuits, but some sandwiches with a bit of cheese and some cold duck from the night before, a few of the remaining apples, sliced, and some boiled turnips. As everyone was grimy, we ate in the breakfast room off the scullery, and by the time we had finished the ginger biscuits, Leo had settled, and had turned out to be rather charming and talkative. Anne joined us, since that was to be our meal for the evening, and I could see that he set out to charm her – perhaps because she had not witnessed his behavior with Toffee, or perhaps because she was putting on her most agreeable air – and he might have thought he had succeeded, but he did not. After tea, the Denhams and Mr. Cunningham decided to go out and about a bit. Of course I was not invited, and Anne declared that she needed to continue to peruse her script, and so, alas, she did not dare join them. I had heard nothing about a new script, and, indeed, when we were in her room together, I saw that she was reading a bound book by Mr. Bulwer-Lytton, the same fellow who had written the first play Mr. Cunningham put her in just after we came to Liverpool. The book was entitled *The Caxtons*. It was not a lengthy volume. When she saw me watching her read as I was wiping down the surface of the small table in her room, she turned back some pages, and read, "'There was, indeed, a kind of suppressed, subtle irony about him, too unsubstantial to be popularly called humor, but dimly implying some sort of jest, which he kept all to himself; and this was only noticeable when he said something that sounded very grave, or appeared to the grave very silly and irrational.'" She glanced up at me, smiling her brilliant, good-natured smile, and said, "And then he names his son Pisistratus."

I smiled. We both knew that this recalled a word that Roland often used for urinating, much to Harriet's embarrassment, and in front of anyone, male or female. I said, "What's the nickname?"

She said, "Sisty."

"Roland would be disappointed."

She said, "Well, I'm sure that when Frank was born, he suggested . . ." And then we burst out laughing. As if Roland knew how to read anything more complex than a bill of sale. At that moment, it occurred to me to broach the topic of my new suspicions about Roland, but just then, Anne said, "I've been reading it most of the day, while you were out doing errands and Mr. Cunningham was engaged in business. It isn't long. It's very amusing. I think it could be made into a play. There is a bit of a love story, but what interests me are Sisty's parents. The mother is the sane one, and the father is the amusing one. I quite enjoyed how amusing *Not So Bad as We Seem* was. I think if the acting had been better the audience would have found it more amusing, and we might have even had a longer run."

I said, "Is this what you talked about when you had that meeting with the investors?"

"No, indeed. I wish it had been. This is a different one. If it goes over, I am to die in the third act. I am supposed to shove the blade in, pull it out, stare aghast at the dripping gore, and plunge it in again, then lie there dead still as the three young men come rushing in, and the hero carries me offstage. Then seven other players are killed because of my death, and the hero is left to sit with his head in his hands and moan until the curtain falls."

I stood there, not quite knowing what to say.

She shook her head. "It doesn't scare me. They have these theater knives where the blade pushes back up into the handle, and the blood, which is pig's blood that they've treated with alcohol, covers the blade as you press this little switch and lift it out. It takes a bit of practice, but . . ."

I said, "I would rather laugh."

She said, "Why wouldn't everyone? That's what I wonder. But the fellow Mallory met with, he said, 'Blood makes money.' "

"Didn't make any in K.T."

Anne stared at me for a moment, then said, "If only they knew." We went back to our activities, me clearing up and straightening her bed, her reading. Then, since I had already unlaced her and she was sitting in her dressing gown, I left and went downstairs to my room. My candle was new, therefore long, and I still had several volumes of *The Newcomes* to read. I took my candle to the kitchen, where Berta lit it for me; she was putting together a mince pie, which Mr. Cunningham was very fond of. I carried my candle back to my room, wrapped myself, since I did not want to bother with a fire, and picked up my volume. But I couldn't follow the story and soon laid it down again.

The fact was that I had forgotten my morning encounter sufficiently so that, when it suddenly came back to me, all sides of it – the memory of Lawrence, the presence of Mr. Hegarty, and the poem by Mr. Longfellow, which I knew was about a slave wishing to return to his home – my heart started pounding again, and Mr. Thackeray couldn't stop it.

Did my candle light the room? Once I crossed from the chair to my bed, removed my garments, and lay down, staring up at the ceiling, it seemed to me that the candle was the very thing I could not look at, because, if I were to do so, the thoughts I was having would explode, even though I had tried so hard to shrink K.T. to the size of a seed. They were only thoughts. And yet, once again, the thoughts were so powerful that they seemed to push against my skull. I had become adept at not remembering the sound of the pistol, the act of turning my head, the sight of Thomas curling to the side, his hand over his chest, and falling out of our wagon. I had become adept at not remembering Jeremiah rearing up in his harness, and then the sound of the rifle, Jeremiah folding, and the sound of that boy's laugh. Now those pictures seemed to be inside the candle flame, asking me to look at them. And, yes, I could have gotten out of the bed and blown the candle out, but I was shivering with cold as if I were freezing to death, and crossing the room to the candle seemed like crossing a frozen lake – would the floor break away and drop me into the icy water? I can hardly describe all of the pictures that rushed into my mind; one of them was that if I approached the candle my hair would catch on fire. Part of my mind laughed at how ridiculous they were, and part of my mind believed them.

My thoughts moved back and forth, away from and then into the mind of the boy in the poem, longing for his home. He knew that he had been sold into slavery without his parents' knowledge, that they were looking for him, thought he had drowned; he had seen his brother talk back, then be attacked and tossed off the slave ship; he had left his wife behind, after watching a golden-haired slave trader violate her and toss her aside. All the while I was thinking these thoughts, I knew they were mine, not the poet's, born of stories I had heard from the abolitionists I knew in K.T. (and I wished Lorna had told me how she had come to be enslaved, but she never had, and I didn't dare ask), but just the image of him on the ship brought all of these things into my mind. My relatives in Quincy, for my whole life, had shaken their heads, said, "Best not to talk about that," then done what they could to help when some occasion presented itself, the way Frank had, the day we walked down by the mouth of the creek, heard rustling in the nearby cave, left four dollars under a rock for the escaped slave, who I had thought was a man but had turned out to be Lorna.

Nighttime was my difficulty, wasn't it? During the day, I could stay active, look at this and that, step in to handle Toffee, have an amusing chat with Anne, and appear, to everyone around me, as a good-natured horse-faced hussy, and now I had nothing better to do than host every cruelty and evil that I had known or heard about. And why did the image of Mr. Hegarty now present itself as a solution to this difficulty? Only because he was handsome? Only because he had that melodious chuckle? Only because, when he looked at me, he seemed to actually see me? I didn't know, but I was enabled, by holding the picture of his face in my mind, to get up and blow out the candle.

And then there was sleep, another strange thing. I did fall asleep without, in a sense, knowing it. I did sleep soundly, dreamlessly, and I did wake up when the light came through my window – I had not closed the shutters – and I did get up, thinking first of Toffee and ready to go to the stable and discover what they were doing with her. I pulled on my clothes and went to her. She was calmly eating her hay; no one else was around. I suspected that, as the Denhams and Mr. Cunningham had gone out the night before, they would surely be asleep still, and then, as I was walking back toward the kitchen door, I remembered my nighttime terrors. Even in the rather foggy light of day, with the horns from the docks blasting, not a beautiful scene in any way, they seemed distant and ridiculous, and I thought the best thing to do was to pick up my step and walk away from them. It was also a great help that, when I opened the kitchen door, I could smell the loaves of bread that Berta was pulling from the oven. She set them on the table, turned to me, and said, "Now, thar ya go. Ya let that dough rise ahver the night and then knade it down and bake it. A sight chewier and more flavorsome."

Mr. Denham was in the dining room, looking out the window.

He turned to me and smiled. He said, "A trainer's habit is to get up at dawn, as the horses are already awake and pawing for their sustenance."

I nodded, then said, "Toffee seems agreeable this morning. I hope she will cooperate. She has been on the train before."

"I suspect you were correct about the shadows and the time of day. We shall see."

I smiled and was about to leave the room when he said, "Have you considered employment on the course?"

I could see Barnsby in the salon. He must have overheard this, because he could not keep himself from smiling. I said, "I wish I could, but . . ."

"I have some garments I could dress you in. If you scowled every minute of the day, no one would challenge you."

Now we both laughed, and I went to see if Anne needed any attentions.

An hour later, I went out to the stable area and watched as they worked with Toffee. She was entirely agreeable, and so was Leo Denham, who seemed calmer and more graceful in his movements than he had the night before. I helped only a bit, by brushing her down and holding her as Leo wrapped her legs. They did seem pleased with her. As her legs were being wrapped, Mr. Denham walked around her several times, assessing her build, her look, her joints, her length of leg. He was even happier when they left than he had been when we went to the stables. They walked away with her, first down Hope Street. The station was not terribly far, maybe an hour's walk, and, truly, how else might they get her to the course, which was south of London, about five hours on the train from Liverpool, according to Leo?

And Barnsby was pleased, too. After I got back into the house, he said, "I do not think we are going to make our fortunes on that one."

I said, "Why not, she's . . ."

He twinkled at me and said, "The odds, my dear, will be much too short."

Then, a few days later, I went to the Grand National Race at Aintree with Barnsby and watched a very close race, won by a horse that Barnsby didn't fancy at all, a six-year-old named Half Caste. I counted twenty horses in the race, which seemed like too many to me, given the challenging nature of the jumps. I watched much of the race, but looked away when my heart was pounding too hard. It was amazing to me that the horses would fall, the jockeys would huddle until the others had passed, and then horses and jockeys would get up, walk away, though sometimes limping. Barnsby was unfazed and pleased to have put his money on the horse that ran second. In many ways, my days were passing as quickly, or so it seemed, as that long race. There were moments that seemed to last forever, and then they had already sped by.

The project Anne dreaded gained steam, which she seemed to accept – she understood, as the investors suggested, that, were it to do well in Liverpool in the spring, it would be moved to London in the fall, the best time of year for dramatic productions, as those who had the money for the priciest tickets were returning from their months at their country houses and bent upon some entertainment. She did tell me that Miss Lucas, who understood the connection between melodramas and income, had sent the investors to meet with Mallory Cunningham. She also said that she had written a note to Miss Lucas saying how much she was enjoying *The Caxtons,* and Miss Lucas wrote back, "Indeed, my dear, write it up! Who knows what might happen? Every investor prefers a bird in the hand." Anne, therefore, spent the early spring busy in her room, scribbling out her script, then reading to me, and having me read it, asking me to correct whatever spelling errors or inconsistencies I might find. I did what I could and showed it to Barnsby, who was much more bookish than either Anne or I. He was helpful –

reading the book on his own, rearranging this and that, cutting some bits and adding a few others that enhanced the part Anne would play, as the mother. He also had his opinions – this was not Mr. Bulwer-Lytton's best book, but it was short enough, which was a virtue not often to be found in novels (he sniffed). Had she read a book by that fellow Trollope (unfortunate name) about racing in Ireland? Barnsby thought that perhaps he was the only man in Liverpool who had read it, but it was intelligent and funny. I said that I would like to read it, but Barnsby didn't know where his copy was, he might have given it away, since all of his books could not fit in his chamber.

I was busy with this and that all day. I did walk past the Furnishes', where I saw Reggie turning over the heap of manure and detritus that he used to feed his plants. There were plenty of farmers around Quincy, of course, though Roland was the only one I knew well. None of them had been as interested in their work as Reggie was. Roland talked endlessly about expenses and profits and storms and weeds and rot, and, admittedly, his income was precarious, as we all knew, and sometimes it was supplemented by Horace and Beatrice. If a storm blew in, Reggie rushed out to the garden, curious, not afraid, ready to see what the storm might have done, which limbs had come down, how his espaliered trees had held up. Of course, he was careful with everything he planted or constructed, careful enough so that the Furnishes sometimes teased him, and they paid him well, but he was not so much worried as curious, and if something had gone down, he would fiddle about with a solution, and enjoy himself doing it. He saw me watching him, smiled, came over, took my hand in his. I said, "Reggie, you should write a book."

He said, "If only I might. I can hardly write mee own name."

I said, "Why is that?" – thinking that perhaps gardeners didn't get schooling in Liverpool – but he said, "Well, when I was in school, mee teacher used to smack me a good one if I wrote with mee left hand, but I could not get mee right hand to make the letters properly. I can read right enough, but once I took on this work, let's see, I was four and ten, I didn't see the purpose of it."

I said, "Others would love to know how you build such a garden."

"I'll be straight with you, Miss Helen: I hardly know how I do it meeself. I come through the door, I look about, and whatever I am to do presents itself."

"I will write the book, then, and Evelina will sketch the flowers. Evelina Cunningham. She's my employer's daughter."

"Aye." But he sounded skeptically good-humored and went back to digging and turning over the pile, which was dark, dark brown, wet, and fragrant. I continued on my walk. I had been sent by Barnsby to a new bootmaker someone had spoken of to Mr. Cunningham, and since his wife was not around to restrain him, he had already ordered up three pairs of boots: a black pair made of calfskin that he liked very much, but dared not wear out in the rain; another black pair, which could tolerate mud; and the pair I was picking up, which turned out to be a rich reddish brown. The shoemaker's assistant wrapped them in a thin piece of cotton fabric and then in some newsprint and placed them carefully in my bag. I said in a low voice, not knowing if the young man would hear me, "What might the price on these be?"

He whispered, "Five pounds, ma'am," then glanced toward the bootmaker, who was speaking with another customer. Five pounds was a significant sum; the most recent pair of boots Anne had bought cost her two pounds. I should have known what these figures were in dollars, but I had no idea. I walked toward the market area (where I was to pick up a packet of oysters at the fishmonger's and a plucked pheasant at the meat seller's) along streets I was not especially familiar with. Since I no longer had my watch (Thomas's watch, sold for the money that I needed to get away from K.T.), and I was to be home by five so that Berta could get the pheasant into the oven and prepare it for dinner, I had no idea what time it was and sped up.

If I hadn't felt that obligation, I might have slowed down, because, as the sun began to fade, I felt my innards begin to flutter. I was looking here and there, opening my ears and my thoughts so that I could hear what the people around me were saying ("Get on with ye, ye're mad!" but said with a smile; "Ten days in Tenerife, and not even a spot of tea," said with a frown). I looked up at the buildings, over at the trees, into the faces of passersby, even those who themselves looked threatening, standing close to brick walls, looking off to the side, like thieves waiting for the right moment, hand in pocket, fingering a blade or a cudgel. They seemed less frightening than my thoughts, remnants of the night before, gathering with the darkness. I picked up the oysters first, hardly pausing to greet the fishmonger, who was a friendly fellow and gave me an odd glance when I hurried off; then, at the meat market, I received the pheasant, and the fellow who gave it to me said, "Would ye care to have a sit-down, ma'am? You appear to have exhausted yerself." He waved toward a bench, but I nearly ran from the shop. The last thing I wanted was a moment's peace.

It was full dark when I got to 2 Canning Street – only the merest strip of pink glowing in the distance, through the leafless trees, above the end of Hope Street. Barnsby opened the front door, the quickest way in, and swept the pheasant out of my arms. I closed the door and took the oysters and the boots around to the back. When I got there, the pheasant was already in the oven. I gave the oysters to Berta, who seemed not at all put out, and then took the boots to Barnsby. And then there was nothing, nothing, nothing, nothing to do except endure the assault of the very same thoughts, as if they came off a printing press, that I had had the night before.

As there were to be guests for dinner, I was not to appear, either as a servant or as a friend. Often, if the Cunninghams' guests were from London, or of the upper classes, my presence was considered too distracting because of my odd accent and my strange appearance. Anne was intended to be exotic enough to provoke some conversation, but not off-putting, and she played her part well. As a rule, I didn't mind this, but tonight it seemed as though my only recourse was to take to the streets again, until I imagined the faces of those suspicious characters I'd seen during the day, and not only their faces. I saw the cudgels or the knives coming out of their pockets, being lifted up, and if not against me, then against some unsuspecting fellow, and there was another dilemma – would I step in, in such a case, or run off? One thing I did as I wandered about my chamber, in the dark, because I was afraid of my candle, was go to my closet, reach around, and then put my hand on my pistol, hidden away in a corner. I caressed it. It was not so common an item around Liverpool as it had been in K.T. or even in Quincy. It was metallic, cool, familiar, but not comforting. In some ways, carrying a pistol if you were nervous was a dreadful idea, because you came to rely upon the pistol, to think about it, to get closer to using it in a state of panic, and the fact was, you could only use a pistol properly with a cool mind. I removed my hand and closed the closet door.

I could not distract myself with a book if I had no candle, so I attempted to distract myself by standing at my window and looking out. The sky had cleared to the west – there was some wind – and I could see a half-moon, high, bright, and a planet just to the right of it. The back garden of the Cunninghams' place was neither as large nor as elaborate as the Furnishes'. It was mostly grass, a few berry bushes for Berta, and three trees. For a minute or two, it looked peaceful to me, but then the shadows began to coalesce into pictures – a man lying in the grass, dead, or asleep, or knocked out. I shook my head. The wind rattled the branch casting the shadow. I saw the shadow, then it changed again, this time into Lorna, hiding behind the tree, her skirt, made of hemp, dyed blue-green, wavering slightly in the breeze; her eyes were staring. I shook my head again, closed the curtain, went over and sat in the small chair where any normal serving girl would do her needlework, but I was not one for needlework, was I? Unfortunate.

Now I set about another method of distraction, which was to pull into my mind an image of every room in the Cunningham house, all of them full of pleasant memories for me – the dining room, where I was sure amusing conversation was taking place even as I was thinking about it; the library, with its collection of books, both frequently read and dustily forgotten, and its smooth, almost golden carpet from the East somewhere; the kitchen, with Berta cooking and chatting at the same time, turning out a constant stream of delicious provisions – yes, she was our Reggie. I thought of the front hall, the staircase, the large multi-paned windows, and the chandelier made to mimic intertwined grapevines. I walked in my mind as I had on my feet, dusting or wiping this or that, picking up or setting down parcels, listening to Jane, humming a tune as she worked, or even singing a bit of a song to herself – "The water is wide, I cannot get o'er." I did not let my mind go outside, I did not let my mind walk down the street. Everything seemed safe as long as I imagined the rooms in the daylight, the sun pouring through the windows or glittering through the shutters, which I imagined myself throwing open (sometimes I was asked to do this if Mr. Cunningham or Evelina did not want to get up from their seats). But then I made the mistake of entering Evelina's room, which I had dusted every few days since her departure with Mrs. Cunningham to Biarritz, and once my mind went in there, it wandered around, looking at the empty bed, the empty chair, the tatting laid aside, the books closed, the sketches half finished, and of course my mind leapt into the near future, when this would not be a room waiting for its girl to return, but a shrine commemorating a girl lost forever. I got up from my chair and threw myself on the bed.

Now, there were two things that I did not understand. One was, how could I, or, indeed, Helen Longbourn, destroy my happy life by going on like this? I knew that there was plenty to despair of here in Liverpool – you only had to look around to see it – but I had fallen into a piece of good luck by getting out of K.T., Quincy, and a nation heading, as far as I could tell, toward general horror. The other was, how had I diverted my attention from these thoughts, both my own and those of others, for such a while? Of course, I knew that I had run away from them, but that was not what I meant by "how." What I meant was, since so many people had to live those lives, how was it that I had allowed myself to escape? Why had I not continued to pursue those fellows who killed Thomas and Jeremiah? Why had I not sought to find Lorna and buy her freedom, or help her escape again? Why had I not looked about, right there in Illinois, and betaken myself to the office of Mr. Lincoln and offered my assistance in his campaign? Springfield was a day's ride from Quincy, quicker by train. It had never even occurred to me, once I was caught and found out in K.T., to keep at it. If it was me who had been shot, Thomas would have been fired up, would have assembled his allies. He was not Mr. Brown (he would have been more canny than that), but I doubt that he would have run back to Medford, even if he had been jailed, thrown out of K.T. He and his friends in Medford, in the Emigrant Aid Company, would have found a way to keep at it. I began to shake and shiver. I felt as though I understood nothing.

Sometime later, perhaps because the meal in the dining room was over and they had moved to the salon and begun drinking this and that (though the season of punch was past), I could hear them walking, laughing, talking if a voice was raised. I did not hear what they were saying, as I used to do in Quincy when I put my ear to the wall between Annie's room and mine and listened to her practicing her lines, but I heard a burble of noise. This, too, developed into something, an image of myself, such as I might see in a mirror or a shopwindow, standing in a field in K.T. Someone behind me, not recognizable, taps me on the shoulder, and I know I am meant to turn about, to ask him what he (or she) needs, what I might do for him (or her). I feel the tap, light but decisive, and against the K.T. brightness and openness, so different from England and Liverpool,

I see myself pick up my skirt and walk away. This was an image, or a picture, that I could not get rid of, not by rolling over or sitting up or looking, again, out the window. Whatever I did, that "Being," who Roland or Harriet or my mother – rest her soul, who had died when I was eight, fourteen years ago now – would have said was God Himself, hovered in my mind. Years it was that I had been going to church with my sisters – three different congregations, three different pastors, three different sets of beliefs and believers (and now, in Liverpool, still another set, at the chaotic church that the Cunninghams went to when they could make the time) – and I had hardly ever given a thought to God. Everyone saw Him differently. I remember Frank saying to me, back when he was smoking his seegars and making up for himself the life he wanted to lead, "I can't make much sense of all of this stuff, can you, Lidie? As much as they try to explain to me who them Canaanites are, I just don't see it." I didn't know how to answer him, because I hadn't been listening to the sermon (later, I did discover that folks who said they were sound on the goose question maintained that the Canaanites descended from Ham, and God Himself wanted them to be enslaved, but I let that idea slip away as nonsensical, too). But now I wondered, what if there indeed was a God, and behind all of the noise and the images in my mind of the world I lived in and walked about in, it was Him, as my mother would have said, and perhaps His invitation was not about the road to Heaven or Hell, but simply a request to perform an errand, whatever it might be that I could do?

There was something reassuring about this notion, reassuring enough that, as the talk in the salon and the calls of the owl outside my window flowed and ebbed, I did manage to sleep, once again as soundly as if I were dead, and at first light, when I opened my eyes, I knew that what I had to do was find John Hegarty and ask him what he thought.

When I went toward the kitchen to begin my tasks, thinking

about where I had seen Mr. Hegarty and whether I should wander about those spots in an effort to see him again, I nearly ran smack into Barnsby, I was so intent on my thoughts. He stepped smoothly out of the way, and said, "Ah, Miss Helen. I have something to show you that might amuse you." He went to his private cupboard and brought me a leaf of the morning paper. The story was about a man I had never heard of, Congressman Sickles, from New York, who shot another fellow named Key for having an affair with his wife. The scandal was not, perhaps that he shot him – frequent enough in America – but that he did so in broad daylight right in front of the White House. I read it, told Barnsby, who was both shaking his head and hiding a smile, that I didn't know either of them, and was about to step around him when he said, "Ah, we do know this fellow in our country, as he took a woman in to see the Queen under an assumed name, and she turned out to be a notorious harlot." He looked as serious as I'd ever seen him when he then said, "Some folk considered this an educational experience for Her Majesty." He took away the paper, and went back to picking out silverware. The Cunninghams sometimes talked about the Queen – she had nine children, and weren't they a passel of idiots, so said some people, and weren't they a national treasure, so said others, and surviving all those births was not her only piece of luck, said some, look at all of those fellows who tried to shoot her, and their pistols misfired – tell me that isn't an omen? I said, "I'm sure the Queen was very polite to her."

Barnsby lifted his chin. He said, "She always is." I understood that it was hard to determine Barnsby's political leanings, but, then, now that I had reconsidered Roland Brereton, I knew that everyone's political leanings were more complex than I had thought.

I watched him sort the silverware for a minute, then said, "Barnsby, have you ever been in love?" I knew he did not know Lidie, and therefore did not know about Thomas. He knew only that I was a tall plain girl of twenty-three, too old to be thinking of love, at least according to the books I'd read. Without looking at me, he said, "Hasn't everyone?" He said no more, and after waiting, understanding that he *would* say no more, I continued into the kitchen area where the servants were given their morning meal. As I sat down to my tea and my scone and my bit of sausage, I thought: Well, my intentions are not about love, are they? They are about understanding what is right.

I had plenty of errands that day, and in the rain, which came just after breakfast and went back and forth from being steady to being a downpour. The weather had been rather mild back in February, and since then, too, because of, as Barnsby informed me, the Gulf Stream. He also told me something I had suspected from our trip, that Liverpool was closer in what he called "latitude" to Hudson Bay, a place in Canada that I had heard of, than it was to Quincy. I remembered those two fellows on the ship saying that if we had sailed straight east from New York, we would have ended up in Portugal. At any rate, the warmth of the Gulf Stream also carried plenty of rain rather than snow, and on that day, it did a very good job, but Mr. Cunningham was set upon getting his reddish-brown boots back to the bootmaker, along with a note saying that, as the first two pairs fit him perfectly and these did not, the bootmaker must have sent along the wrong pair. I was also to pick up some cheeses, a book at a bookseller's (I intended to spend a fair amount of time there), and some sugar, and to go to the post and get Mr. Cunningham's mail. Evidently, everyone else had decided to stay home, but I didn't mind this, and as I left, Barnsby handed me his own parasol – or umbrella, as he called it – and pointed to the top end, which had a rather sharp metal poker on it. It was as if he had been reading my thoughts. He must have noted this in my face, because he said, "More thieves out and about in a good rain, as folk aren't paying as much attention when they walk down the street."

I thanked him.

10

As I left the house, I thought of turning up Hope Street and looking through the fence at the graveyard again, where I had most recently seen Mr. Hegarty, but I made myself walk the other way, down Upper Duke Street, toward the bootmaker's shop. Perhaps God had tapped me on the shoulder; in order to find out, I decided to place a wager, to go about my business in the most efficient manner, and see if God produced Mr. Hegarty without any efforts on my part. Thinking of Barnsby, I gave God rather short odds – three to one – and dared Him to beat them. The difficulty was the umbrellas – not mine, but those of others, especially the women. As I was tall, I had to watch where I was going, so as not to get a poke in the eye from the umbrella of some shorter person. If there were thieves about, I would have been surprised. Had one of them stolen something, the victim would only have had to scream and all the umbrellas on the walks would have come down upon him – poke, poke, poke – as he was writhing on the ground.

The bootmaker was not surprised to see me; he recognized me at once, and came out, took the packet I was holding, and handed me another. He said, "The man these were for has already been in, miss. Please give Mr. Cunningham my apologies. I believe Sean was confused. He only just started working here." I glanced over his shoulder and saw the young man who had handed me the boots. I smiled at him – he had given me this walk, for which I was grateful. Next, I went to the bookseller's. I had the money with me to buy a book called *The Coral Island,* which I was then to take to the post and send off to Mrs. Cunningham, to be given to Evelina. I wandered about the shop, a little inconvenienced by my parcels of boots. The shopkeeper said I might set them safely in a back corner, which I did. There were plenty of books and journals to look at. One was by that Trollope fellow we had been talking about, concerning a doctor, not a horse. I passed over it. In the end, I bought Anne the January issue of *Blackwood's Edinburgh Magazine,* which contained the last episode of *The Caxtons.* The bookseller asked me if I was Scottish, and I said, "No, sir," in such an American way that he laughed aloud. If Mr. Hegarty had been in the bookshop, I would have seen him, as the cases weren't as tall as I was, and even though there were plenty of customers, his pleasant looks would have stood out clearly. I headed for the cheese monger.

It was then, after I came out of the bookshop and turned right, that my eyes did open, and I saw something I had seen before in Liverpool but had not noted, and that was the dark faces of Negro people making their way here and there, looking no more, nor less, pressed than everyone around them. The thing I noticed was something I had seen before but not paid attention to, which was that they didn't have to touch their hats, drop their gaze, or step off the walk when they encountered a white man or a white woman. In this, everyone was equal – they made their way as best they could, and as long as the ladies and gentlemen were bundled up in their carriages, everyone simply tried not to bump one another or stumble on the cobbles. Certainly, it would be different later in the day, when the gentlemen and ladies were going to their clubs or their parties – the carriages would halt, the attendants would shoo us all out of the way, and the ladies and gentlemen would be swept into their sanctuaries – but even in Quincy, in a free state, the Negroes had to watch themselves. At the very least, some hotheaded Border Ruffian might have crossed the river from Missouri and would take umbrage that he was not "respected." I thought of the peculiarity of Roland again – as much as he d — ned this and that and shouted, if someone looked him in the eye, he was likelier than not to smile and say hello in a pleasant voice. Here in England, it appeared to me as though the upper classes expected to be honored, that is, greeted politely if at all, and they also expected to have their way, but they knew that they were often being made fun of, and when they noted that, they looked off into the distance. Here was another question I would ask Mr. Hegarty: Did he know persons, or families, who were always in a temper? Lived in a temper, waiting to be crossed so that they might strike you or shoot you?

At the post office, I picked up a small packet of letters, and then, coming out, I stepped into a deep puddle, soaking the hem of my dress, which was wool, and also my right boot. Best to pay attention, indeed. I went to the shop where I was to get a loaf of sugar, and it was heavy enough – a "stone," as Berta would say, and, indeed, it felt like a stone. She had a set of what she called "nippers" to cut pieces off the loaf, and then she would pound them down and make her cakes. Sugar was a much rarer and more precious thing in Quincy than it was here. Berta went through a loaf every five months as a rule, but, what with the holidays, this time it had taken only three months. It was interesting to look at the loaves in the shop, set out on a shelf (and because of the wet weather, the door and the windows were tightly closed). They looked like tall, round-headed cones of different sizes; the one for tea was the smallest. The largest was brownish, looked like a pyramid. It was not expensive for its size, but how you might get it out of the shop I could not imagine. The sugar monger wrapped ours up, said, "Now, miss, don't let the rain get to it, and hurry home." I thought, And don't fall into a puddle, either. Altogether, I was more nervous about the ten-shilling loaf of sugar than I was about the five-pound pair of boots.

I did hurry home, as the rain was worse, but my hurry didn't drive off my new way of seeing. Did I look into every Negro woman's face and wonder if maybe Lorna would show up?

Berta was thrilled to see me, and took the precious sugar gently out of my arms. I knew there would be a pudding for tea. I carried the boots to Barnsby, thanked him for the umbrella, and told him that it was on the back stoop, along with my wrap, which I had shrugged myself out of before entering the house, and then I took the issue of *Blackwood's* up to Anne, who leapt from her writing desk and grabbed it out of my hands, not forgetting to kiss me three or four times. Here was the other thing about doing the errands: when you returned, you were always greeted with affection and pleasure. For the rest of the afternoon, I stayed out of my chamber, that home of sinister imaginings. I offered to help Jane so many times that eventually she swatted me away and said I was distracting her so that she didn't know what she'd already done and what she still had to do. I sought out Barnsby and asked if there was any news of Toffee, but there was not. He did say, "Thank you for carrying that loaf of sugar safely home. Sugar, as I am sure you know, has a troublesome history in this country." He smiled, but didn't say anything more. I nodded as if I knew, though sugar was something we didn't talk much about in K.T., and the only time I remembered Thomas mentioning it was to say that he much preferred maple syrup. Finally, I took a clean wet rag into Evelina's chamber and dusted everything. I imagined her tatting or sketching, in this seat or that one, with such determination that, indeed, she nearly did appear – twice I spun around, thinking I had heard her shuffle in her seat. And then, as with that new ability I had felt as I walked through town, I managed to call forth Mr. Cunningham, who came out of his room with a letter in his hand, and he said that Mrs. Cunningham was much gratified by Evelina's increasing good health, whether it was due to the baths or the air or the comestibles, no one knew, but she was active and in a good humor.

Another letter was from Miss Lucas, for Anne, saying that the production of the melodrama was moving along nicely, and she had persuaded the producers to liven it up a bit by bringing a parrot, two greyhound dogs, a large cat, and a donkey upon the stage – for one of her exits, Anne was to ride the donkey "offstage left" in a "distressed manner, turning to look back at what she is losing." To both of us, the melodrama seemed to be getting more and more ridiculous, but, as Miss Lucas averred, "therefore more profitable." In Liverpool, it was to be shown at the same theater as the previous melodrama and the harlequinade; in London, one of the theaters in the "West End" was showing some interest, principally because of Miss Lucas's enthusiasm and willingness to play a part herself, though I hadn't heard what her part would be. Anne said that Miss Lucas was one of those actresses who would play any part, no matter how strange or how awful, just because she enjoyed everything about it – being on the stage, but also learning her lines, helping to sort out the production, finding investors. Ten years before, she had helped produce a melodrama called *Frankenstein,* from a book that Anne had peeped into but I had not. She'd gotten the investors to agree that she would play the monster, and she did, on woodblock shoes that had raised her a good eight inches and made plenty of loud noises as she pounded around the stage. She'd gotten a costume maker to construct a mask out of badger skins, and when she made her entrance, even the fellow who played the lead had gasped, not to mention the audience. At any rate, Anne believed that Miss Lucas knew what she was doing, and was pleased to hear from her as often as she might. Anne herself did not have the best handwriting, but I saw her work on it, as she did on her look, her accent, her dress, her manners. Anne read the letter over a second time, then folded it up and set it upon her writing desk as she sat down to read the last bit of *The Caxtons* in the Edinburgh paper.

I walked to the corner of the room to pick up a kerchief she had dropped, and looked out the window to check upon the rain. It had now petered out – merely a drizzle. I said, now talking to my niece, not my employer, "Annie, have you ever been in love?"

I glanced at her, but she did not look at me. She did say, "Now, there's a perplexing question. Do you remember Donnie Perkins, who used to come for supper sometimes with his mother from down the street – what was her name? – oh, Marjorie? I would stare at Donnie until he made a face at me. Was that love? I don't have any . . ."

And there he was, walking up Canning Street, stopping to peer at the number beside the door, looking up at the house, the same face I remembered so well.

As I looked at this, my niece returned to her current status. "Anne" continued. "I must have been twelve, but even as I say his name, I can . . ."

He was carrying his umbrella folded up, hanging from his arm. Did I see the twinkle in his eye from this distance, the smile that was just about to burst across his visage? He turned, walked away to the corner, not far. I leaned forward, turned my head to follow him.

Anne said, "And then he kicked me one day when I was on Maine Street, carrying something, I don't remember what, from Lorton . . ."

Mr. Hegarty came back up the street, stood in front of the house. Anne's window was the one on the first floor (or, as we would say in Quincy, the second floor) farthest to the left. I might have exited her room, gone down the staircase and out the door in the space of a minute or two, but I did not. I watched him, and I knew he was looking for me. I waited to see if he would come up the step, rap upon the door. He seemed to take a deep breath, but how was I to know that? Then he turned toward Hope Street.

I said, "He kicked you?"

"In the backside. There were other boys around. I was sure even then he was showing off to them. The next time he came with Marjorie, he did look ashamed, but, indeed, I never stared at him again, I'll say that."

I said, "I wonder what he's doing these days."

"Works on a riverboat, is what I heard."

I went over to her and stroked her on the head. I'd noticed that talking about Donnie Perkins, whom I might have remembered, had brought the Illinois back into her voice. I touched her magazine, and she went back to reading it. I thought that might get the Illinois out of her.

I went down to my room and opened my little purse, counted the money: eight shillings, tenpence, a ha'penny, a dollar, and six bits. That meant I owed God one pound, six shillings, sixpence, plus five dollars and two bits. I decided to keep the ha'penny for myself.

The next day was Sunday, again raining, but that was good for me, because Mr. Cunningham decided to take the brougham to church, and only he and Anne would fit inside it. He did suggest that I might go with Barnsby to his church if I so desired, but when Barnsby came knocking on my door, I stayed very quiet until I heard him leave by the back entrance. Who was I, that I would place a bet on God's showing up, and God would show up, and yet I couldn't bring myself to go to church? My reason for staying home was more a feeling than a thought. For one thing, I did not want to be overwhelmed by the chaos of Mr. Cunningham's place of worship – the children running about, the conversations in the pews even as the minister was trying to shout his prayers and sermons over the noise. There was something about the building, though it was a luxurious and beautiful spot, that made it impossible to understand what you were hearing. The minister himself seemed to get more and more annoyed as the time passed, so that when he turned toward the choirmaster, and indicated to him that he should begin one of the hymns, his face said, Save me. The choir, too, was difficult to hear. It was behind the organ, up on a balcony. If the congregation liked a particular hymn, they would fall silent, shush the children, and listen. If they did not, they would keep talking. The minister always stood beside the door at the end of the service and blessed the parishioners who passed him as they went out, but he looked both exhausted and irritable as he did so, and the parishioners, without even realizing it, would hurry by, which annoyed him further. Mr. Cunningham said that he had been transferred from a church in a small town in Warwickshire, and had been unhappy there, too, because he had done well at Oxford, and considered that small church an insult. But it was evident that, however well he had done at Oxford, he was of an irritable temperament, and many people in the congregation were open in their dissatisfaction that he had replaced a much kindlier man who gave shorter sermons, Rector Burroughs. Some of the long-standing parishioners even went up to him and told him what they thought, suggested that he visit old Rector Burroughs and seek some advice. I could just imagine the effect that suggestion might have.

But there were plenty of other churches in Liverpool. The one Barnsby went to was also Church of England, though a longer walk, a bit more toward the countryside, and for that reason, I thought after he left, I should have gone along with him. Certainly, he chose that one because it suited him – and he was hard to suit. Given Barnsby's nature, everything about the church would have been orderly, correct, and thoughtful, and the rector or vicar or curate, whatever he was, would have been well read. But then, as I thought about that, I realized that I probably would not have understood a word he was saying, and would have fiddled in my seat and jostled Barnsby and otherwise irritated him.

And so I did a thing that I would never have thought I would do, either as Lidie Newton or as Helen Longbourn: I went over to the window, lifted the shade, and knelt in the light, putting my elbows on the sill, putting my head in my hands, closing my eyes, issuing a prayer rather than a wager.

What was my prayer? I knew I was supposed to begin, "Dear Lord," but I began, "God." "God, I don't know why you should, since I have been neither faithful nor good nor obedient, since I have done mostly what I wished to do and avoided many obligations, since I deceived, or helped my cousin to deceive, my sister, since I have held on to revengeful thoughts and never forgiven those men who hurt Thomas and Jeremiah, since I do not read the Bible, and so I do not know what your instructions are, but, indeed, please give me some way to sort through my obligations. Please tell me who I should be kind to, or, indeed, what is kindness? Please tell me if it was kind to help Lorna escape and then watch her condition be made worse by my actions? Please tell me if my escape to K.T. with Thomas, who did greatly believe in you, was an act of kindness or an act of temptation? Please tell me what my primary obligation is. Everyone I knew in Quincy thought I was to marry and procreate, but I recoiled from that until Thomas took me off to Kansas. Please tell me if I am wrong. Please tell me if I am aiding Anne in going down some wrong path. Please help me understand. Every time I seek understanding in a church, I come away more confused." I stopped there, then remembered to say, "Thank you, God."

At the end of my prayer, I looked out the window. Every tree, every branch, every sprout, every puddle was exactly the same as it had been. I waited. Nothing except a few blasts from the docks, and then a flock of starlings that settled on the roof of the stable, squawked a bit, and flew away. A thought—a memory, really—flitted like the movement of a starling's wings into my head and then out. I closed my eyes, grabbed on to one fragment of that thought—the wall of Alice's parlor, papered over with something new – pale, printed with images of flowers in a diamond-shaped pattern. I stared at that print, and as I did, it got clearer in my mind, and there were Alice and my mother, sitting in their customary chairs, Alice knitting, my mother embroidering. Sunlight through the window, lighting up the wallpaper, which was why the pattern was so decided, and no fire in the fireplace, and so it was late spring or early fall, and my mother was saying to Alice, "I believe that I saw Jesus." And then, looking at Alice more steadily and speaking more decidedly, "I believe it." Where was I? As I was remembering this, I knew what was in my hands, my rag doll, so I would have been four or five.

What was Alice's response? I didn't look at her – I kept staring at my mother – nor did I hear her say anything. Harriet would have told my mother to be sensible, Beatrice would have asked her if she had a fever, but Alice was more confused in her responses to just about everything. At any rate, I did not remember my mother describing Jesus or saying where she saw him, so, as I was kneeling, I imagined him for her, placing him in the kitchen, having him walk through the backyard, then down 20th Street. I imagined him appearing in the dark, a figure of light, wafting through a doorway and out onto the front porch. However much I concentrated, though, I could not imagine him saying anything to her or even turning to look at her. I could only imagine him going about his own business. Surely because I was so young when this occurred, nothing more about that incident or about my mother around that time came into my mind. After I was born, two more followed, but they didn't survive. Even though I was her surviving child, she left my upbringing to my sisters, and I now wondered if her distance was the product of fear – perhaps she thought that she personified bad luck, and so, if she stayed away from me, I was more likely to survive. Sometime after she died, I did ask each of my sisters what she was like, what they thought of her, and they all said, uniformly, that she was a kind and handsome woman, always good to them, good to my father, who required a deal of care because of his "mental condition." Asking them about her was like singing a song everyone knew well – always the same as the last time.

I thought of my ha'penny. Then I thought, Let's say for now that she did see Jesus, odds, twenty to one. I put my hand in the pocket of my skirt and took out the ha'penny, set it on the sill, right in the middle. I didn't know what might happen that would require me to pay tenpence to Jesus, but I did know that my task was to keep my eyes open and my mouth shut.

One effect of my new way of looking at things was that time sped up. What I began doing to push off the memories of what I had not understood and could not understand was to replace them. I helped around the house, talked to Anne, read letters from my sisters, visited Reggie, chatted with any Furnishes who happened to be home from Natal or the Crown Colony of Western Australia. I walked down by the docks, looked briefly into the faces of everyone I saw, walked slowly past them, whoever they were, listened to what they had to say, understood very little, but it got to be more. The Cunningham boys came home for their "half-holiday" of about a week, and it felt like it lasted a day.

I believe that what caused this was my nighttime ritual, which was never, as I put myself to sleep, to think of anything that had happened prior to that morning – I thought of what we had eaten in the kitchen for our breakfast, I followed myself on my errands outside, on my tasks inside. If Barnsby had given me a silver bowl to polish, I re-polished it as I fell asleep. If I had watched Reggie picking the early asparagus from his garden, I watched him again that night, noting the slender stalks and tiny tips, looking at the plant he put in my hand, tasting it. If I had noted four Negro women on the streets as I walked and three men, I remembered their faces one by one – did they look happy or sad, frightened or angry? Most often, they looked tired or curious or suspicious, as everyone else did on the streets of Liverpool. If I had heard someone speaking French, I tried to recall it, though I had no idea what it meant. If I had heard Mr. Hegarty's characteristic Irish way of speaking, I listened to it again, watched my own head turn two or three times to make sure that whoever was speaking was, indeed, not Mr. Hegarty. It never was. Did I see Jesus? How was I to know? How had my mother known? Perhaps she had been walking down the street and a young man had passed with such beautiful features that her eye could not help going to his face, and when it did, he lit up with a kindly smile that seemed to pour light over her own face, and then he walked on, stepping quickly but lightly, staying out of the way of everyone, only pausing to ask an old lady who was staring down at her feet as she stood on the corner of two streets if she needed aid, and then letting her lean on him as they made their way through the puddles and the mud and the other citizens to the other side, where he helped her onto the curb, she patted him on the shoulder, thanked him, and waved him away. I noticed him, the old lady noticed him, no one else did. That night, as I lay in bed and thought through those few minutes, I decided that he was Jesus, that one of his qualities was that he was everywhere, doing his errands, and he was too busy to be bothered about whether he went unseen. The next day, Mr. Cunningham gave me some wages, and I put tenpence next to the ha'penny on the sill.

I'd noticed that Spring presented itself earlier and in a more complicated way in Liverpool than in Quincy. In Quincy, the ice broke up, the river flooded the docking area, the streets were full of mud, and Roland began complaining about the cost of seed. In Liverpool, the rain drove off the smoke, the fog brought it back in, grass appeared everywhere, including in the tiniest cracks, the wind picked up, and there were all sorts of flowers, especially if you looked up as you passed the buildings and saw them peeping over the sides of the window boxes. The long, narrow, parklike area along Hope Street, facing the cemetery, made itself into a beautiful garden. It was an interesting area. Mr. Cunningham said that it was meant to be a row of houses like the ones across from us on Canning Street, but money had run out, and so they had only built four and were working on the fifth, but slowly. Even so, someone, perhaps people who lived in the houses, took a Reggie-like interest in the greenery across the street, and it was there that I saw the first crocuses and then the first hyacinths and then some lilacs that were blooming much earlier and more beautifully than they had in Quincy.

The place was called Gambier Terrace; when I first came to Canning Street and Berta told me the name, it made me laugh, because I heard it as "Gambler Terrace." One morning, early, when no one was about, I turned in to it thinking of Toffee, whom we still knew very little about, only that she was "training well" and "looks promising." I paused, gazing along the length of the garden, thinking of tulips, and reminding myself to remember this moment when I was in bed that night, the sharpness of the morning sunlight as it spilled over the cemetery. I thought I saw something red, a possible tulip, and walked toward it. His voice said, "Miss Longbourn," so calmly, so agreeably. He was standing on Hope Street, gazing at me through a break in the hedge. What did I do? I breathed a sigh of relief that was echoed in the sigh of relief he also breathed. We both smiled. I said, "Mr. Hegarty, please call me Helen." He came to the hedge, held out his hand so that I would take it, and said, "I will. And please call me John." I took his hand. Our two hands fit together instantly, both the same size. We did not do the awkward thing, which would have been for one of us to clamor through the hedge, but we let go, turned, walked toward the end of Gambier Terrace near Huskisson Street, and then, together, on toward Upper Parliament Street. As we walked, me to his left, I glanced from time to time toward his face, and I thought that I had never seen such a well-molded and handsome visage in my life, the forehead, the cheekbones, the eyebrows, the bright-blue eyes, the prominent nose, the neatly trimmed mustache, the jawline, the way his neck swept toward his collar. He took my hand, put it under his arm, rested it on his forearm, laid his own hand gently across it as we walked. He said nothing; I said nothing. It was as if we knew that these few moments of sudden connection would and could never be repeated, that any words would end them by moving our attention toward something less remarkable and unique than what we were feeling now. I was ready, indeed, to thank God for answering my prayer, to recognize Jesus looking down upon us as we passed this window and that window. I looked at my feet stepping out from under the hem of my dress, at his, framed by the cuffs of his pants. I squeezed his arm. I was ready to accept that this was love.

II

As it happened, this feeling we shared that we wished and needed to be together didn't have much effect on how often we were together. Anne's new production began rehearsals, and Mr. Cunningham asked me to make myself of use with the animals, in addition, of course, to helping Anne with her lines and her costume. The animals were amusing, especially the donkey and the cat, which we would have called an "orange tabby" in Quincy, but which was called a "marmalade" in Liverpool. The donkey came from the countryside and lived in our stable, occupying Toffee's stall, and the cat wandered about the house for a day until finally choosing Anne's room for her abode. Her name was Tinker. Mr. Cunningham said that she was an experienced player and knew to stay where she was put on the stage and also could be counted upon to give out a loud meow if silence fell over the theater, which always sparked a laugh from the audience. The donkey was also female – a jennet – and was agreeable, though quiet compared to other donkeys I had known. I never heard her bray. Our stableman said that she – her name was Plum – was twenty years old and had been acting for fifteen years, not only in plays, but in street festivals and other sorts of events. She was about the size of a large pony and was somewhat better-looking than donkeys in Quincy or K.T., dark brown over her back and up her neck, with a white underside and nose. The insides of her ears were white, too. Her eyes were ringed in pale gray, and she had black markings here and there. I was not asked to lead her to the theater – the groom, Lester, and I went together, me carrying Tinker and him leading Plum. During the show, Tinker had to ride Plum, so part of my job was to give her rehearsals, setting her on Plum's back, letting them walk along, counting the strides, taking her off. Our goal was twenty strides. Tinker was a lazy cat – she didn't mind the ride or put her claws into Plum – so our goal was readily attainable. Lester and I chatted about Toffee, but we still hadn't heard much, so mostly we made things up or wondered if she was all right. Mr. Cunningham must have told Mrs. Cunningham about the production, because Evelina insisted on coming back to Liverpool and spending some time with the animals. She seemed in better health, so the Cunninghams allowed this. It was Evelina who told me that most "marmalades" were male, so Tinker was a bit of a rarity.

At the rehearsals, I sat quietly backstage, waiting with the animals until a player came to fetch whichever he or she needed. The only difficult one was the parrot, who would occasionally squawk at the wrong time, but his handler was good with parrots, and knew how to distract him; the parrot's name was Russell.

It seemed to me that I knew nothing about love, which was a sad thing to think when I thought of Thomas. Before we were married, my sisters had lost all hope for me – three local widowers had proposed, and I had declined to rear their populations of offspring, thinking of my own mother, who was perhaps seventeen when she married my father. For him, the rewards of marriage were to be that she would provide him with a son. For her, the rewards of marriage turned out to be repeated stillbirths or infant deaths – four before me, two after. Perhaps it was as a result of watching this that my favorite aunt, Miriam, had remained a spinster. Then Thomas and I met and were married. Alice and Harriet took my hasty marriage, followed by immediate departure to K.T., as a reason not to tell me a thing about marital obligations. Beatrice said that she "didn't wish to frighten me," but why would I be frightened? I had seen Roland breed sheep and a horse or two on his farm. I knew the difference between a fertile egg and an infertile egg. I hadn't seen a baby born, but I had seen puppies born at the farm when I was about ten.

Thomas, of course, was already on his way to K.T. when I met him, and as soon as the service was performed, we got onto the riverboat and went down the Mississippi. For our "wedding night," we stayed at a lodging in St. Louis called the Vandeventer House. We had a pleasant room, and we did laugh a lot about advice I told Thomas my sisters had given me – my favorite I attributed to Harriet – not to allow horses in the better rooms of the house, as they might kick over your most beloved set of china. Then I laughed about guns in the house, and was much astonished when we rose in the morning and I discovered that that was the very thing that Thomas had been tasked with transporting from Massachusetts to K.T. – that case of Sharps carbines, twelve of the newest and most efficient rifles. They were in our bridal chamber with us. We did not have a bad wedding night – it was the best one we, in our ignorance, knew how to have, with much fumbling and laughter. But somehow the carbines, the sight of them and the knowledge that we were smuggling them into K.T., overwhelmed those pleasures for me.

When we took the boat up the Missouri, it was a more nerve-racking trip than the one from Quincy to St. Louis. It took several nights, and the accommodations were not for the newly married. Even though we had a small space to ourselves, set off from the rest of the sleepers by a green curtain, the rolling of the packet or the shouting of the other passengers was distracting – if a fellow shouted on the other side of the curtain, it sounded as though he was right with us. We had to take to our beds by sunset, because there were so many people rolled up in blankets sleeping on the floor that the easiest thing in the world was to stumble over one of them and fall, which meant that we would be cursed at and threatened if we did so. And in part it was because of the carbines – how often did I think that that shouting man might push his way through the curtain, or even through the wall on the other side of what was called a stateroom, discover the case, pry open the lid, see the carbines? As it was late in the year and the river was low, there were frequent sandbars, and we had to disembark two times, both times, of course, leaving the carbines behind. The second time, somewhere west of Miami, I now remembered, there had been an altercation between a Missouri woman who slapped her slave girl hard across the face for misplacing a pair of shoes, and another woman, possibly from New York (though what in the world would a woman from New York be doing in Missouri?), who defended the girl, but did not accept the offer the slave-owning woman made – that she would trade the girl for the gown and the bonnet that the New York woman was wearing. Then, she said, she might be rid of the girl, and the East Coast woman could free her. She made this offer with such a disdainful sneer that my attention was momentarily distracted from the carbines. It gave me a shiver to think of this episode for the first time since I had witnessed it, now almost four years in the past.

But not a word was ever spoken about the feeling that I now experienced toward John, and it was also true that no books mentioned it, or, at least gave it to a woman character. How could I have understood the nature of love, the feeling of love, when, evidently, no one I had ever known, met, or seen understood it?

When I was with John, if only a walk from the Furnishes' to 2 Canning Street, what astounded me about our time together was that I could open my mouth and hear the very words I had been about to say come out of his: "Look at the chestnut blossoms" or "Was that lady peeking at us out of her carriage?" (followed by a laugh). I told him I had given up on *The Newcomes* – I liked the author's wit, but I couldn't follow the plot – and he said he had done the same, the previous summer. We both had enjoyed Mr. Dickens's novel *David Copperfield* (we said the title in unison), though he had read it three years before I had. He was not thirty, he was twenty-eight. I was not twenty-five (as he had thought), I was twenty-three. Oddly, our birthdays were exactly six months apart – his on September 15, mine on March 15. We both preferred apples to peaches, blackberries to raspberries, veal to lamb. He had passed the Furnishes' back garden many times and admired it. As May turned into June, we must have seen each other five or six times, without planning: Doing my errands, I would turn down a street that took me the long way around, and there he would be, having his boots blacked, almost finished. We both accepted that these moments were signs that we should pay attention to and enjoy. I didn't even tell Anne about him. I thought that if I kept everything to myself, my pleasures would last longer.

In the meantime, the rehearsals of Anne's melodrama turned into an opening night and then a lengthy run – three weeks longer than they thought, with plenty of profits. Lester and I had to take Tinker and Plum to the theater just before tea and stay there with them through the performance. I would say that, by this time, Tinker might have felt she could ride Plum over jumps. I hardly had to carry her at all. She meowed until I set her on Plum's back, and, indeed, our walk through the streets became an advertisement for the show. When we got to the theater, Tinker recognized where we were, and began standing up on Plum's back, stretching elegantly first to the front and then to the rear. That was when I had to grab her so that she wouldn't get away from me. As a result, people of all types, with money and without, would follow us to the theater and then, if they could afford it, purchase themselves admission. Miss Lucas had come for a week in late April, stayed with the Cunninghams, spent afternoons in Anne's chamber, giving her plenty of praise and some advice, which Anne listened to much more carefully than she did to Mr. Cunningham. Miss Lucas was not in charge of the players, but the man who was also knew whom to listen to.

Miss Lucas said that there were plenty of animal players in London, but that Plum and Tinker were "draws," and therefore they would be off to London in the fall, along with Anne. I wondered if I would go along, too.

During this time, we also heard from Mr. Denham, Toffee's trainer. I had found Mr. Denham to be an even-tempered fellow, and patient, so when he said that Toffee was "driving him off the rails," my first thought was that he would send her back, and she would be given to me, but it turned out that she was not misbehaving, or even having soundness issues, it was that she did not respond to training as other horses did. Mr. Cunningham mentioned that, early on, when they had her out on the course for the first or second time, she was moving along nicely, but the rider smacked her with the whip. She stopped dead, tossing him over her shoulder, though fortunately he curled up and spun so that he landed on his back, and then she walked over and looked down at him. The first thing he saw when he opened his eyes was her nose and her pricked ears. And so they learned not to use the whip but to show it to her – if the rider waved it, she took off. She also "detested" heavy ground, and since the spring was a rainy one, Mr. Denham not only hadn't raced her yet, he also hadn't galloped her through mud. He did get her out every day, but on muddy or rainy days, the rider simply rode her here and there, first early in the morning, then later, letting her look at this and that, letting her watch the other horses, keeping her moving and working but allowing her to satisfy her curiosity. As a result, there was nothing about the training area that she was uncomfortable with, and also as a result, when the ground firmed up, she was ready to run, and her works were impressive. He was casting about for the right race to start her in; that was the part that was driving him off the rails, because the likeliest races were far afield, and he couldn't make up his mind whether to chance putting her on a train or to chance putting her into a race that she might not be ready for. He was sure he would find something.

I told all of this to John. He enjoyed horses and said that he could drive better than he could ride, though he did not enjoy racing, which rather surprised me. However, he listened to my stories with a kindly patience, and that is what led me into telling him about Jeremiah. I hadn't intended to, but I wandered into recounting what happened the time that Frank spirited Jeremiah off to a spot outside of Lawrence where they were putting on a day of races, and when I finally found them, Jeremiah had won his heat and Frank talked me into letting him run another. In the middle of relating this, I saw a confused look on John's face (we were walking in the docking area), and I realized that he had no idea who Frank was, who Jeremiah was, or where those "heats" might have taken place, as that was not a feature of English racing. I closed my mouth and looked down. We continued walking, stopping at the ferry port, and then up the hill. When we got to Sefton Street, he said, "Please, tell me," in a kindly manner, but then, as we turned toward Park Street, a Negro man greeted him in a pleasant voice, and he responded, also pleasantly. The Negro man tipped his hat to me, and I fell into that swamp of complexity once again. I didn't say anything, or shake my head. A few minutes later, we resumed talking about books. We both liked this new book, *Doctor Thorne,* by Mr. Trollope – that was the book I had put aside the first time I saw it at the bookshop, but I had gone back and bought a copy for Mr. Cunningham. I had only read the first volume; John had read all three. John told me that he had heard that Mr. Trollope, who everyone knew worked for the Post Office, had gone to Egypt sometime during the previous year, which made John envious. Did I know that Trollope lived in Ireland, of all places? And so we walked back to 2 Canning Street, and I revealed nothing more about K.T.

That night, the fear that came to me was that John would see my behavior with regard to the Negro man in an unfavorable light, as if I were offended that he had not stepped off the walk for me. In K.T., and even in Quincy, everyone wanted others to see them as hard, intractable, or rough, so perhaps that was my natural behavior. In England, even the roughest, cruelest people smiled, said the proper thing. One result of this, for us, was that Anne had told me, early on, that she only discovered that she had been demeaned for her appearance or her acting when Mr. Cunningham explained it to her. She was now an excellent disdainer, but only if she had to do it in response to disdain offered to her. I was still, in most ways, myself. I rolled about, thinking of this, almost until daylight.

Over our morning porridge, Barnsby handed me an envelope. Inside was a single ticket to the show – not for me, since I'd seen it over and over, but, evidently, for John. Of course, Barnsby knew what there was to know, as he was an observant fellow, so observant that he might have seen us on the street without even leaving the house. Or perhaps he knew there might be someone, given that I was out and about more often and it took me longer to do my errands than it used to, but he didn't know who that someone was. He might be using the ticket to lure John out of his covert. Later that afternoon, I saw John very briefly at the corner of Canning Street and Hope Street. I was almost home, and he was going down Upper Duke Street. We squeezed each other's hands, smiling, and I gave him the ticket. I had noted the date, and the following Thursday, I placed myself backstage so that the audience was partly visible to me, though I was not visible to the audience, given that I was standing in the darkness. That was the night when the parrot, Russell, revealed for the first time that he knew words. The moment of silence came, in the second act, and Tinker meowed in her self-confident way, and then Russell, who was perched on a rack downstage from her (and tethered to the rack, which he didn't mind), called out, "Bugger off!" The audience not only laughed, they clapped. Russell didn't like it, and put his beak under his wing. I didn't see John.

But he had been there, and we laughed again when he told me how much he had enjoyed Russell's "instruction." That day was a

Saturday, so we had a fair amount of time. It was also a pleasant day; we walked along near the cemetery. I had to be home to lace up Anne and fetch Tinker for the evening show, but not for a few hours. We had nothing to do but wander around. We did pass a church on Rodney Street, not one I recognized, but I noticed that John glanced at it, and also lifted his eyebrow to a fellow who came out the front door, though the fellow didn't notice him, or us. He was carrying some books and looked as if his main concern was not stumbling down the steps on his way out. It didn't occur to me to ask a question, but it did occur to me to be grateful for one particular thing – that, in the weeks since John and I had taken each other's hands across the shrubbery in Gambier Terrace, we had not revealed much of ourselves to one another. It was not only that I knew that revelations had to be reciprocal and that I had too many things that I did not want to reveal, it was also that revelations were supposed to take you to a shared future as well as a shared past, and the last thing I wished to ponder was the future. Of course, it was lovely that Anne's play was a big success and that the theater in the West End of London had agreed to run it, but once she left for London in the care of Miss Lucas, what would be my role? No one had said anything, but I doubted that I was to accompany her. If I stayed here, I could continue to see John Hegarty, but I had no idea where that was going. I was now, or soon to be, what Barnsby termed "superfluous." I might relieve Berta and Barnsby of some of their tasks, but why keep me on for such paltry service? Mr. Cunningham could ship me back to Quincy any time he pleased, and how would I deny him? Was my only plan to get as much money from him as I could and then take myself to Wisconsin? No other spot in America was attractive in the least.

I glanced at John's "dashing," as they would say in England, profile, something I would certainly miss if I got sent back to Quincy. I knew that a proper girl would press herself upon the man that she felt drawn to, that in England, and to some degree in America, her relatives and friends would dig up information about his potential as a mate – not a friend, but someone who would take care of you, pay for you, have the funds to put up with you. Even so, I did think of our encounter with that Negro man and my response, and I felt uncomfortable. Just then, John turned down Upper Parliament Street, toward the dock area, and, putting my hand on his forearm, the light wool sleeve of his jacket, turned up St. James' Place. We walked along, and I attempted to appear relaxed.

It seemed to me that we were heading for the area I had walked around on my own in the early autumn, where most of the Negro folk in Liverpool happened to live, along with, according to Barnsby, Indians, Spaniards, French, and the filthy Irish. I remembered two things now – that I hadn't been aware of my own demeanor during that walk, either, only of my desire to eavesdrop upon the people I saw, which, because of their accents, had been nearly impossible, and, oddly, Helen, at Day's End Plantation, not long before Lorna and I escaped, telling me that it was the Puritans who started slavery in Rhode Island, and then sold off the slaves because it was cheaper to employ the Irish than to take care of slaves. I became aware of my demeanor – I pushed down my curiosity and made myself relax into a conscious stroll. John patted my hand. We arrived at Warwick Street, then Pickwick Street, and the longer we walked around, the more people of all sorts greeted John, either by smiling and tipping their hats or by pausing to greet him and ask him how he was. I smiled and nodded, but didn't dare say anything. I didn't want to reveal myself by speaking as an American (though events in America, according to the papers I glanced at Mr. Cunningham's, seemed to have settled a bit). The more we walked, the more I relaxed – certainly, we saw and greeted and were greeted by more people than on any previous walk we had taken. A few people addressed him as "John"; most addressed him as "Mr. Hegarty," or even "sir." This did make me curious about how he earned his living, but, once again, that was a matter I avoided. On Upper Warwick Street, a Negro woman was coming out of her small house. She pulled the front door closed, turned, saw us, and came running over. She looked about thirty-five, neatly dressed. Thanks to Evelina, I recognized that the collar of her dress was nicely tatted. She exclaimed, "John! How are you, my dear?" then walked over and kissed him on the cheek. He kissed her back, said, "I was hoping we would run into you, Susan. I haven't seen you since Easter. Let me introduce you to . . ." He paused, then said, ". . . Helen Longbourn." They turned to me. She appraised me, up and down. An eyebrow lifted, I assumed because of my height. She then smiled what looked to be a sincere smile, and said, "I am so sorry I can't have you in for a bit of something. I did make biscuits this morning, but I must be off to the school for a meeting." She rolled her eyes, which told me that she was a teacher and that some boy – like my cousin Frank, I thought – had been making trouble. She shook her head, said, "Do come back!," squeezed his hand, and hurried off. From this I deduced that John, too, might be a teacher, but I didn't ask and he didn't say.

We continued walking about, and I eventually realized that I was being trained exactly as I had trained Toffee – taken about the neighborhood until I relaxed and seemed entirely comfortable, no matter whom we might meet. Then he left me, with a squeeze of the hand and a touch on the cheek, at 2 Canning Street, and I did feel comfortable.

However, I hadn't realized how long we were out until I found Anne in her room with Tinker. Tinker was prowling about, and Anne was looking out the window. I was quite late for my duties, and in the end, rather than lacing her up, which takes a while, we opted to put her in a different gown, not as slender as the usual one. She was nervous about this, I must say, and she held herself erect as if she was laced up, but it was also true that her performance that evening was more active and energetic, and the audience quite enjoyed it – she got three curtain calls. She was so inflamed that, instead of being taken back to 2 Canning Street in the carriage, as she was every night, she walked with Lester, Plum, Tinker, and me. Many people greeted her, I must say, but more people paused to admire Tinker and Plum, which made her laugh. All in all, I would say that she fit the definition of "giddy" that night, and I did stay with her in her room for a long time, watching her pace and laugh.

We had been in England now for more than a year. She had had much praise and some successes, but it was as if now she finally believed it. What she said to me later, after the show closed and she was preparing to go to Bath for a respite with Miss Lucas, and then to London, was that somehow playing without being laced up made it not only more joyful, but also more believable, as if the lacing had served as a hiding place that she had been afraid to emerge from, and now that she had emerged, she felt utterly at ease. She had not been subject to stage fright, as most people thought of it. She knew that if she forgot a line she could fill in something else; she knew that if she turned the wrong direction she could spin around and thereby make her character more interesting; she knew that a surreptitious glance at the audience would lure them over to her side. She had been subject to a different sort of fear – our trip from Quincy was like a long narrow bridge over a deep gorge that could fall apart any minute, right before her eyes, dropping her into the gorge. Somehow, in that performance, she had gotten to the other side, and though the hills might be steep and the plains dry, she felt at ease making her way. Twice that night, she threw her arms around me, thanking me for being late, which I laughed at, but later came to understand.

A few days later, we got letters from my sisters. Harriet's and Beatrice's were as usual: a bit about politics – Mr. Douglas seemed to be doing a good job; a bit about Frank – he was working at Lorton and Silk, and though he was harum-scarum, well, most employees were during their first months; a bit about the weather – hot, humid, the stench rising from the river. Alice's letter was entirely about how she missed Annie, she couldn't do without her, she had hired a girl to help but she couldn't really afford that, and when would this whim of hers run its course? It was all very well to run off; hadn't Lidie done that very thing, along with Frank? (And, no, I hadn't run off – my sisters had been glad to be quit of me.) However, running off was all very well for a while, but what about responsibilities? Alice's joints were aching, she had terrible head pains, she now understood how well organized Annie had been, and if she hadn't seemed grateful at the time, well, now she was. In short . . .

We sent our responses. Anne sent some pound notes and something of an apology. We discussed whether those notes could be turned into dollars in Quincy, but we also thought that Frank or Horace might find a way. Without referring to Alice's letter, I sent two notices from the paper about Anne's performance, and my own thoughts about how gifted she was, and how much the audience admired her – compliments on the street and questions about her next performance, was it really to be in London?

One of my daily tasks came to be taking Evelina for walks. Mr. Cunningham and Evelina, together, prevailed upon Mrs. Cunningham to allow this, because, now that Evelina was sturdier, coughed less, and weighed a bit more, she was restless. Mrs. Cunningham agreed, but the caveat was that the walks had to be in the countryside – at least as far out of town as the botanic garden I had visited – and they had to begin short and lengthen gradually. I also had to carry some fruit and some sandwiches in case Evelina felt weak, but if she ever did, she didn't reveal it to me. Depending upon how busy the roads were, it took about half an hour to get to the garden in the brougham. As we went there, I did keep my eye out for Mr. Hegarty, but, as it happened, I didn't see him anywhere, and this went on for ten days. At the garden, Evelina and I meandered about, either among the flowers and well-shaped hedges or into the more open field, while Lester waited for us. I tried to talk him into walking with us, but he said that he would rather have a bit of a nap. Ten days was the longest period I had gone without seeing Mr. Hegarty since we had reached for each other across the bushes in Gambier Terrace, and after about seven days, I took to walking back and forth in the terrace, not exactly looking for him, but hoping for a bit of magic similar to the first one. In the meantime, I went back to arduously resisting any contemplations, good (how much I enjoyed his company) or ill (what accident might have befallen him) in the night. One morning, I was picking up this and that in Evelina's chamber while she was tatting, and she said, "Have you heard of the Gordian knot?"

I said I hadn't.

She held up her tatting and her wool, laughed, and said, "It was somewhere along the seaside at the bottom of Anatolia. The people who lived there told Alexander the Great that if he untied it he would be the king of the world." Now she pulled her wool apart a bit, and, indeed, it was tightly tangled. She said, "He looked at it and fiddled with it, but then he just picked up his sword and cut the rope. And then he got to be king of the world." Now she picked up her shears and cut her wool and laughed, tossed me the tangle, and went on with her tatting. I put the tangle in my pocket, and later, back in my chamber, under my pillow. If, against my will, I might begin thinking of all the things that confused me, I would put my hand under the pillow and finger the tangle. Once in a while, during the daylight (since I still refused to have a candle in my chamber, but, indeed, daytime lasted so long that I hardly needed one), I would try to unravel the knot, thinking of laying the long thin strand out on my table and then looking out the window at the sight of Mr. Hegarty passing by.

And then he did pass by – not by 2 Canning Street, but by the Furnishes', when I was there picking strawberries for Berta. I had taken a handful home the day before, when I was visiting Reggie, and Berta had been astounded by their flavor. She sent me back the next day with some money, but Reggie, and, indeed, one of the Furnish brothers, turned it down. This fellow, the one who had been to New Zealand, said that they were overrun with strawberries and dying to get out from under them, so he sent me home with a large enough basket for tarts and jams and whatever else Berta might want to do with them. I was walking down Huskisson Street, putting my third or fourth strawberry between my lips, when that voice, that melodious voice, said, "May I?"

I turned around, smiled, held out the basket. He took one, then walked me to the back gate of 2 Canning Street, squeezed my hand farewell. We said nothing else, for which I was grateful, as I hadn't untangled the wool yet, so I didn't know what to say, what to ask, what to propose.

Our next walk was two days later. He was across the way as I was getting out of the brougham with Evelina, helping her climb down from the carriage. He smiled, paused in his walk. I said nothing to him of her. I took her to the front door, handed her over to Barnsby, and turned around. John and I went down Hope Street, then to the neighborhood where we had walked two weeks before, this time straight to the house of the woman, Susan, and, yes, we were there for tea. She was prepared. We hardly knocked once on the door before she threw it open, gave John a hug, then took my hand and drew me into the house, down the corridor, past two rooms, and then out into the back garden. A table was sitting in the grass, with four chairs. On the table were a large teapot, several cups, and a dish of cherry scones. Susan (but I called her Miss Williams and she called me Miss Longbourn) seemed to be very fond of John. She smiled at him again and again, touched his hand, his arm, his shoulder, leaned toward him. I would have expected myself to be jealous, but I wasn't. Her friendliness was a good cover for me, and also an interesting display of how to interact with John. I could tell that he found her witticisms and her laughter more appealing than her affection, though he in no way put her off. The scones were excellent, and when I was taking my second one, I asked Miss Williams how she'd met John, well knowing that this question meant that I was approaching a tunnel I might not want to enter. She reached over and patted him on the leg. She said, "So long ago! At a church supper. He was just a wee thing then! I was twelve and what were you, John? Six, I believe. When you are young, those six years seem an impossible river to cross. I was very kind to you." They both laughed. John said, "She sneaked me half of her roly-poly, and I crawled under the table to eat it."

I said, "What is a roly-poly?"

Miss Williams said, "A lovely suet pudding nicely flattened, then spread with jam and rolled up. I still enjoy it. Miss Longbourn, what sorts of delicacies do they eat where you grew up?"

"Catfish. Crawdads. Creamed corn. My brother-in-law likes to shoot a raccoon, and then skin it and roast it."

Miss Williams said, "What is a raccoon?"

I paused, then said, "Imagine a giant hairy rat with a long tail and a sweet little face and tiny little hands, that can climb a tree and always washes his food." John burst out laughing, and I said, "I prefer catfish, myself. They have long whiskers, are ugly as can be, and bony, as well, but they taste good."

"My dear," exclaimed Miss Williams, "have you ever seen a flounder? Fish are indeed interesting."

I wondered how long we would be able to talk about food, but it is true that the English can keep any conversation going for as long as they wish. Miss Williams said, "I am amazed that you would eat a fish out of the river. In our own London, the Thames stinks so that no one would dare. I do hope that we don't see a repeat of the Great Stink." She waved her fan in front of her face, and wrinkled her nose. I asked what the Great Stink was.

John said, "Do you remember how hot it was last summer?"

I did not. Hot weather was routine for me.

He said, "The Thames, down in London, dried up so in that weather that all the refuse lying in the riverbed drove everyone out of town, even those who couldn't afford it. Well, they've been using that river as a sewer since the beginning of time. You have to wonder what they expected."

I said, "How wide is it?"

Miss Williams said, "Well, the tides go in and out, but the Tower Bridge is eight hundred feet."

I said, "They built a bridge across our river – " Then I remembered that I was from Chicago and said, "Not ours – down south, the Mississippi – several years ago, that was almost twice that. And then a steamboat ran into it and caught fire, and the company that owned the ship insisted that the bridge be taken down. Goodness me, they dragged that through the courts for over a year, and then the jury hung themselves in frustration." Suddenly I blushed at that word, "hung," even though Miss Williams and John were both chuckling, and said, "Of course, I mean that they couldn't agree. But in America no one agrees for more than a moment. At any rate, the bridge still exists, though whether another will be built somewhere across the Mississippi, I can't imagine. Over a mile wide down there." I continued, "That one does stink sometimes, and it is brown, not blue, like the Mersey." To remind myself that I was from Chicago, I said, "There is a lovely lake . . ." But I let my voice peter out, because I didn't want to be one of those folks you meet who tell you much more than you want to know.

After Miss Williams poured out another bit of tea, she and John discussed the plans for embankments and pumping stations that were being worked upon, and I said, "I hadn't realized why wealthy folk went to the countryside in the summer." They both nodded. I saw once again that we were fortunate to be in Liverpool, which, though by no means perfect, was much more agreeable than London, or St. Louis or Chicago or New York.

All in all, we had a pleasant chat, and Miss Williams was kindly when we departed, giving John a kiss and me a squeeze of the hand and then waving us on our way. John and I walked down the street.

I said nothing, just waiting. I did want to know about Miss Williams, but I wanted John to offer it up. He said, idly, "The Williams folk came to England because they were loyalists during your War of Independence. Or, I should say, their owners were. Some ships sailed out of Savannah; do you know where that is? I don't, but somewhere to the south."

I said, thinking of Barnsby, "Cavaliers."

John nodded. "Long ago, Susan told me that she knew that her great-grandfather was enslaved at one point, but her family never talked about it." So here was another pleasure of being in England – a man and his family could ease out of slavery without having everyone around them throw a fit and threaten to hang them. I pursed my lips to prevent myself from divulging anything more, but then I said, "What about sugar? I heard that . . ."

John said, "Perhaps that is the greatest sin, the cruelty of that. I don't eat sugar if I can help it. All these slaves carried off to the islands and forced to grow the plants and pound the stalks, and whatever." I saw him tremble with rage. Then he said, "You must have learned about triangular trade?" I shook my head. "Once this island began producing a lot of goods – cloths, household wares, weapons – ships were sent to Africa, and those goods were traded for slaves. The same ship that carried the goods from here, carried the slaves to the islands and to America. The sailors cared much less about the slaves than they did about the goods. In fact, the Africans were packed into the same shelves that the goods had been on. Chained. No place to sleep, little to eat, many deaths. It didn't matter to the kidnappers how old the Negro was – children were stolen from their parents, and parents stolen from their children. When they got to the islands, or Virginia, they were exchanged for tobacco, rum, sugar, some cotton, and those were brought to Liverpool. That is how this city became wealthy." I blanched. Thomas had never discussed this. I thought of Mr. Day's plantation and closed my eyes. I now understood a little bit more about how widespread the crime of slavery was. John stared at me, and I looked down.

After a bit, as a diversion, I asked about the Great Stink. He took a few deep breaths, and said that he had never been to London, and so he could only imagine it from pictures. I said, "Where have you been, then?"

"Belfast, here, Manchester, up north a bit. Around Ireland a bit."

"The Furnishes have been everywhere."

He said, "My dear, they are famous all over town for that very thing. It is as if you say a word about some distant spot and they leap onto a ship and go there. Once in a while, they prosper." Thinking of this returned him to a demeanor that was more jovial, more at ease. He touched my hand, then helped me across a mucky street. I decided to take this as evidence that I had succeeded in not offending Miss Williams. He said, "Have you met that lady, Elinor Furnish?"

I said, "The one who teaches at the school?"

"Indeed."

"I met her in their garden, months ago, then saw her guiding the girls at the school."

"There's a tale. Her father had some money, and he was a very manly and charming-looking fellow, and as a result, a young woman from Hampshire with a substantial dowry – Elinor, also – took him up, and the day after they married, they set out for the West Indies, and they met a fellow who talked them into going in on a coffee plantation, where they also grew indigo and some sort of rice – I gather that it was in a wet spot. But then they moved again, to, of all places, the Hawaiian Islands, so that is where she was born, in some lovely spot the name of which is entirely unpronounceable. I gather that the plantation they had there went bust, and they came home. But I have spoken with Elinor; I am fascinated by some of her earliest memories. She says that they pop in and then go away, that she knows what palm trees look like, and some of the flowers, though she hasn't seen them since she was three or four. I have no doubt she could still speak whatever tongue they speak there, because she is fluent in French and German." We walked along.

I approached that tunnel of revealing memories again, and said, "If you lived in Belfast, how did Miss Williams meet you when you were six?"

"My father and mother brought my sisters and me here for some months as they were deciding whether to stay in Belfast or not. I have heard that there was an offer of employment that was subsequently rescinded, but I don't know the details of that. I will say that, after bedding down with my cousins here, I was glad to go back. Two older boys. They were not kindly."

I didn't ask any questions. I said, "Older boys rarely are."

It was nearly teatime when I walked into 2 Canning Street, and I hurried to take off my bonnet and sort out my hair, then went to see if Berta or Barnsby needed anything. Barnsby handed me a corner of the table covering, and we then set out the dishware and the comestibles. I wasn't hungry, because of the cherry scones, but I did admire the cream cakes and hoped, to myself, that one or two would be left on the table, though I also wondered if I should feel shame for enjoying sweets so much. When Anne came in, and then Mr. Cunningham, Anne looked a bit flushed, and Mr. Cunningham looked unusually annoyed, which, I supposed, for Mr. Cunningham, meant annoyed in the slightest degree. There were a well-dressed pair of guests, a man and a woman, whom I did not know. As Barnsby and I walked out of the dining room, I heard a conversation commence about the London production of the show. Barnsby lifted one eyebrow, and muttered, "Investors."

I said, "When might the show begin?"

"Not before mid-October."

I now understood why: Londoners (the ones who could afford the tickets) leaving for the summer, and maybe, as well, some sort of stink.

After the guests left, I peeped in, not only looking to see if any of the cream cakes remained, but also to see if I might commence removing the plates, and I saw Anne and Mr. Cunningham were at it again, but in that English manner that Anne so perfectly imitated. Every word of their disagreement was polite – they smiled, they contained themselves, then lifted their chins, then looked away. The looking away seemed the most aggressive – rather like, in K.T., shooting off your pistol. Once, Anne looked toward me; then the two of them got up, laid their napkins very carefully on the table, and went out of the room. I ate my cream cake at once. It was heavenly.

That night, Anne told me the source of the disagreement: she did not want to go to Bath without me, though they had not argued, yet, about whether I would go along to London. As soon as she said this, I saw that my Gordian knot had even more tangles than I had realized, because the last thing on earth that I wanted to do was to go to the land of the Great Stink, and the second-to-last thing I wanted to do was to go to Bath. And yet, what better way to avoid that dark tunnel and to draw out my connection to John than to go away, taken against my will? I said, "Why is this a disagreement?"

"He said that Berta can't do without you now, but then, when I pressed him, he said that until the show goes on the boards he can't afford the expense of taking you along. And after that, he said, though as if regretfully, that I have cost him, as yet, more than I have profited him. Lidie! Can you please go to him and tell him that I can't do without you? Or, indeed, that you can't do without me? Whichever you think will be more effective." She gave me a pleading look, took my hand. She was not acting – her face was her Annie face, one that I remembered from a time long ago when there was something she wanted. A new rag doll. The one I'd passed down to her because I hated dolls had broken apart, and she wanted the same doll, which she thought I might have somewhere. A few days later, Beatrice brought in a new doll. Annie picked it up very gingerly at first, but then she got used to it, and carried it about for the next couple of years. She must have been three at the time, and I would have been five. Now, as years ago with the doll, I had no idea what to do. The last thing in the world that I wished was to leave this house, this neighborhood, John Hegarty, but I also feared for Anne, and I suddenly saw her for who she really was – a twenty-one-year-old young woman swimming in a deep body of water, staying afloat as best she could, but perhaps running out of the energy she needed to make it to some shore where she would feel safe and comfortable. Yes, I understood that she was a great performer, and also that her performance lasted all day and all night, and although she knew that it was her only alternative to the life of drudgery that she'd led in Quincy, she wondered if carrying on alone was beyond her strength. I said, "Evelina and Mrs. Cunningham liked it there. They say that there are so many things to do and people to see that they enjoy themselves the whole time."

She stared at me.

So: that, of course, was the problem. Not much chance to hide herself, not much chance to be herself.

I said, "I'll speak to him."

The die was cast, as they say in England. Or, as they say in Quincy, you've tossed the dice, now pay up, da — it!

Mr. Cunningham was in his study, a ledger open on his desk, though he was staring out the window into the darkness of the back garden. The window was slightly ajar, and I could hear a bird singing, and something else rustling through the bushes.

I don't know that he had been expecting me. When I knocked on the door, he'd called out "Enter!" but when he saw it was me, he sat up and sighed.

He said, "Helen. Believe me, I would like for you to go."

I said, in a low voice, "I would like not to go, but if I must, I must." He pushed his chair back, looked up at me, pursed his lips, nodded just a bit. That was all. When I got to my chamber, after I disrobed, I knelt at the windowsill again and prayed, this time for nothing; this time, for once in my life, I prayed to be told what to do, and then, after I got into bed, I allowed myself to think of John's visage, from the front, from either side – of his nose, his smile, his blue, blue eyes, his unruly hair, his gaze upon me. It did not put me to sleep, but somehow it was soothing. In the morning, just after I awoke, but before I rose, I closed my eyes and made the same prayer.

Sometime after the servants' breakfast, when I was helping Berta sort through the provisions to see what might be made use of for the evening meal and what I might need to go out and purchase, there came a banging at the front door of the house. Barnsby, of course, took about two moments to answer, and then there was some kind of talk that I couldn't understand and didn't pay attention to, until both Barnsby and the visitor burst out in a great laugh. Then I heard steps up and down the staircase. The Cunninghams, Evelina, and Anne were still asleep, or, at least, still in their chambers, but by the time I was peeping through into the entryway (and Berta was behind me, saying, "Ut's goin' on, 'elen?"), Mr. Cunningham was there, saying the same thing to the visitor. I didn't recognize the fellow, and he was not wearing the garments of an important man, but, indeed, he was important, for, as Barnsby told me when he came into the pantry and closed the door firmly behind himself, he had been sent by Mr. Denham to inform Mr. Cunningham that Toffee had won her first race, two thousand guineas was the prize, and, as the odds were long, twenty-five to one, Mr. Denham had also dared to put a bet down, ten pounds, for Mr. Cunningham. Barnsby lifted one eyebrow and said, "This Denham is a decent fellow. The bet he made offset the training expenses, and so Mr. Cunningham will get quite a return on his gamble."

I said, "I am sorry, sorry, sorry that I didn't get to see the race!"

"He told me all about it. Yes, she dawdled and even looked about early on, but when she saw the others leaving her behind, she simply stretched out and took them over, one by one. She passed the post with her ears flicking, as if it were the easiest thing in the world. Her jockey didn't even raise the whip."

I asked where the race was, and he said, "Kempton Park. Not far from London, and so a lot of punters. Denham went back and forth about starting her there in such a prominent race, but then decided that waiting was a longer bet than trying her out, and so he took a deep breath and tried her out."

By this time, the fellow had told Mr. Cunningham the whole story – I could hear him laughing, too, and I saw that I was doomed to go to Bath. But I was pleased about Toffee, and I did wonder if Bath was near wherever she was training: perhaps that would be my compensation.

12

You might call Toffee our savior, and if you did, you wouldn't be far off the mark. For one thing, it was a beautiful day – a brisk easterly breeze blew the smoke and the chill out to sea. The sky was a brilliant color, not so much blue as one of those more magical hues you hear about: azure, cerulean, indigo. I knew that I would take a walk, and I also knew that I would run across John, because everyone in Liverpool would be taking a walk on a day like today. After my walk, I would come back, I thought, and take Evelina out. Reggie would be in his garden and would give me a handful of something perfectly ripe and delicious, and the Furnishes would be chatting about their recent trips to Patagonia, let's say, and Scotland (which one would I prefer to visit?). Bath appeared to me not as a sinkhole somewhere to the south, but as a curiosity worth exploring, and who was to say that John might not take to the idea and follow us there for a bit? I must have been humming, because Jane, who passed through the library, where I was dusting some of the volumes, said, "Ah, 'elen, I am fond of that one!" and went away singing to herself, "The trees they do grow high, / The leaves they do grow green." And, yes, it is a sad song, one that I learned when I was growing up, but sad songs are the most haunting, and they tend to come to you when you are happy. And, yes, the song made me think of Thomas's death, but it also sent it away, into a world where such a thing is a common event that must be endured, turned into a song. It was true that I could go about my work with a song in my heart and a tear in my eye.

Just at the moment when I was looking out the window toward the garden and thinking of the lilies and the roses, Berta came to me and recited her list of comestibles – a rack of lamb, a small loaf of sugar, some black cherries for a tart, butter. She had not ordered these ahead of time, so she handed me two pound-notes and sent me out the door with a smile, saying, "Don't forget givin' yersilf a bitta somethin', as the streets'll bay crowded and slow. Maght I suggest a sausage roll? Nice puff pastry all round it."

I made up my mind to walk as quickly as I could all the way to the botanic garden, wander about there for a bit, then purchase the goods on the way home. According to the grandfather clock, it was half eleven, as Barnsby would say, so there was plenty of time. If you are destined to leave a spot you love very much, then you must explore it as best you can in your final days; that is to say, I now assumed that, once we returned from Bath, Mallory Cunningham would be shipping me back to Chicago.

The walk was not twenty minutes. I had to contain myself a bit, or I would not have walked, but skipped, trotted, cantered, woven in and out of the others on the street, thus attracting disapproving looks. The botanic garden, since it was before midday, was not as bustling as the streets, and I calmed myself by wandering among the beds. The flowers were indeed in full bloom, and very beautiful, but it was under the boughs of the trees that I found the strongest and most mysterious fragrances. It was a great pleasure to stand quietly and close my eyes, taking in deep breaths and doing my best not to work out what they were. And then I opened my eyes, and there was John, standing in front of me, on the walk, not under the tree, with an amused smile opening up his visage. He held out his hand, and I went to him.

At once he said, "Miss Williams liked you. She told me so when I saw her today." Then, "In the chapel."

I put my finger lightly on his cheek, told him nothing about Bath. As we walked toward a bed of roses, I said, "It's not Sunday."

He said, "She helps with the upkeep. We were turning the rugs."

I said nothing more, just gazed at his pleasant look and took in the fragrances. He asked me if I had finished that book he'd enjoyed so much, *Dr. Thorne,* and I said that I had better look for the second volume, as I suspected that I had pushed it under my bed, and perhaps the cat had dragged it away. This got a laugh. Mr. Trollope had moved back to England – did I know that? And Mr. Dickens – John had been reading the installments of his new book in *All the Year Round* (that was a journal he had begun, very profitable, but such a brouhaha was blowing up about Mr. Dickens's marriage, and every time Mr. Dickens said something, he made it worse) about the Revolution in France – did I know of that? Some ten years after the American war, much more violent in its way, but you could certainly understand . . .

He spoke in his usual manner, full of lively curiosity, and I did listen – I thought I might buy some issues of one of those journals for Evelina, and read a bit of the book – but, mostly, I reveled in his presence, in his hand on my hand, in my hand on his arm, in the way that our strides matched one another's, so that walking down the street, back to the meat market and the vegetable vendor's, was easy as floating. And we must have looked happy indeed, because the folks that we passed smiled as we went by, not to greet us, but because they couldn't help themselves. At the meat market, he bowed and gave me the sort of look a man gives you when he wishes he might kiss you, but cannot do so under the gaze of others. I thought of telling him that I was going to Bath, but I didn't know how he would respond. And the look he gave me was enough. I got home with the provisions in the mid-afternoon, passed them over to Berta, and was taking off my bonnet when Anne appeared, grabbed my hand, and pulled me into the library.

After she had walked around the room, looking here and there, she came to me and took my hand again. She no longer looked like a girl, much less the girl I had always known. She looked like Anne Revere, self-assured enough to be modest but direct in her demeanor. She said, "Darling, I don't know what got into me the other day. I've apologized to Mallory and stepped back from my insistence on your accompanying us to Bath. I was up all night pondering it. Do you remember when I started school? Goodness me, the schoolhouse was a block from Mama's house, and you were at Grandpa's, which was two blocks, but if you didn't appear first thing to walk me to the schoolhouse, I would toss myself under the dining table and hold on to the back leg so Mama couldn't pull me out. And then, one day, you were down with the croup or something, and I just walked out the front door in the rain and off to the schoolhouse as if it was nothing. I don't know why I'm like that, so hard to pull over the edge, but . . ."

I said, "I was thinking of the rag doll . . ."

She laughed. "Yes! I hated that new one for three days, then I hugged it to pieces."

"Good luck meeting your beloved."

She laughed again. "I'm sure I will know when he has arrived by the vigor with which I recoil from his presence."

"You got right onto the cars to Chicago, though."

"You came with me. And I did recoil, though perhaps you didn't notice. My plan, if I couldn't make myself do it, was to get you to push me up the train steps." She hugged me again. She said, "And I was glad you were carrying that" – she whispered in my ear – "pistol, because I knew that if you waved it in my face I would do whatever I was told."

I said, "My dear, I had no idea you were so peculiar."

"How else would I put myself in the minds of all those damsels that must collapse and die on the stage?"

And then we both laughed. Anne departed with the Cunninghams for Bath two days later, leaving behind the copies of *All the Year Round* I'd purchased for her, another pleasure for me. The plan was that the boys would join them for a week at the end of their term, then everyone would come back to Liverpool in late July. The surprise was that Barnsby, too, was taking some time for himself – and why shouldn't he? He got on the train to Durham, a town somewhere in the northeast, for a visit to his sister and her family, who lived not in Durham but on a small farm in another town, called Esh. Before he left, he walked me around the house and showed me how to close everything up for the night, and, given the fact that no one would be home, how to keep it mostly closed during the day. Berta would feed us – he left money for that – and he indicated that there should be enough activity about the place so that local thieves would not get any ideas. When the cab came to pick him up and take him to the railroad station, he squeezed my hand, told me that I had been very helpful, and said that the autumn races were always enjoyable, and he would see about arranging a visit, especially if Toffee might be running again.

The first day after their departure, when the house was clean as a whistle, as Alice would say, and very quiet, I loitered here and there for most of the afternoon, trying out *A Tale of Two Cities* and a piece by Mr. Trollope, but it was not the same Mr. Trollope as the one who wrote *Dr. Thorne,* so I threw it down, looked under the bed for the volumes, did not find them, looked for them in the library, did not find them, read ten pages of something else, then threw that one down and walked out the back gate and made my way to the Furnishes', looking for Reggie. The first thing I asked him, after he noticed me and invited me into the garden, was where the Furnishes were. He said, "The mister, 'e's in Austria, and the madam, she went back ta Glasgow for the month, and Elinor, she's up the street, and Laurence, 'e's in Sicily. Do ya know where that is? 'E's quite fond of that spot, especially this time of year, when it's muggy as can be. That's all I know, for sure. Ya never know altogether."

I hadn't met Laurence, but perhaps I envied him. I said, "Don't you ever wish to go along?"

He said, "I'd like ta see some plahnts. There are those fellas who go on sea voyages just ta bring home plahnts and set up gardens ta see 'ow they grow." He bent down and turned over his pile of vegetable dregs and horse manure, and the fragrance was enticing – I thought it smelled a bit of carrots. I lifted my skirt and stepped over a row of radish plants, then walked around among the berry bushes. I did resist taking the berries without permission, but the crop looked excellent. When I came back to him, I stood in front of him until he finished his task, and then said, "Who eats all of your delicious crops if no one is here?"

Reggie shook his head, and patted his belly, which wasn't much. He said, "Perhaps that's a raison ta seek diff'rent employment, but . . ." He surveyed his garden. Yes, how could he leave this, his very own Eden, behind?

It was taxing to have no errands, no daily purpose. Perhaps, in spite of the flowers and the fragrances and the harvests, this was what I envied Reggie for most: when he arose in the morning, he knew which tasks were most pressing, which could be put off, and also that his tasks extended into the future as far as he could see. It was lovely to me to have the leisure to wander in his garden, but awful to ponder where I would go next, what I would do – nothing. Anne was launched, Toffee was launched, Evelina seemed healthier by the day. I thought that if I were to meet up with John, I would ask him to take me to wherever it was that he and Miss Williams had turned the rugs and hand me a duster. Perhaps the chapel was a large one, and so the dusting would be an endless effort.

I was moved to consider Thomas in this regard, too (and this was easier as I stood gazing at Reggie, who was surrounded by plants, then at a cloud drifting by overhead that seemed to be floating on the blasts of horns from the docks). Thomas had been, of course, in no way prepared for his move to K.T. He was clumsy with one of those carbines, hesitant on the back of a horse, and mostly befuddled by the tasks of building or planting or foraging. But because of his strong abolitionist beliefs, there was never a moment when he doubted his course of action or, as far as I knew, regretted his journey. Even when I knelt down beside him after he had been shot, I could see, alongside the pain that his face expressed, an equal feeling of righteousness – the Border Ruffians had revealed themselves to him, and would, he knew, reveal themselves to the world. Because I married him and loved him, I did come to share his sense of purpose, and then the Border Ruffians themselves invested me with an even stronger sense of purpose – if I had, for all of my young life, been called "contrary," then the Border Ruffians would discover just how contrary I might be. I led Lorna away because she wanted to go, but I also led her away because her owner denied her desire to go. Now I had no mission, or, if I had one, then it was to do as I pleased, and here I had been for more than a year, doing as I pleased, and I had no idea what it pleased me to do.

After looking a bit more at the puffs of clouds in the sky wandering eastward, I went back to Reggie and asked if I might give him a hand. He said, "Ah, thank you, sister, but I've nothin' ta task ye with at the moment." I kissed him on the cheek for using that word "sister" and then wandered out of the gate. I had a few shillings in my pocket, and I rattled them around, wondering if there was anything I might purchase in the shops, and then I turned down a street I hadn't walked before; it was one of those short streets that lead nowhere other than to some trees and buildings, and so I had bypassed it numerous times – nothing to see or to purchase. Now, though, I noticed that the few buildings on the street were rather interesting, for the nature of the brick. Because of the sunlight shining on them from the east, I saw that the bricks were themselves glinting a bit, something I hadn't seen before, as bricks are always dark, solid, serious things. The three buildings were of modest size, one of them set slightly apart from the others, with a few steps and some grass. They were not quite the same style as the ones around 2 Canning Street, which Mr. Cunningham told me were called "Georgian" because they were built during the reign of one King George or another. These were a squatter, wider, humbler style, with modest windows, their only arresting quality the strange flashing bricks, which, as the clouds passed over the sun, went from almost black to almost flickering. A door opened in the one that was set apart, but I hardly noticed, and then John Hegarty was beside me. He said, "I see this as a sign."

I said, "Of the fact that I want to turn the rugs, or, preferably, dust the doorknobs? Please say yes, because I have nothing at all to do, as the Cunninghams whisked Anne and Evelina away to Bath." I didn't know if John knew Anne's name, but he had seen the show.

"I was hoping that you were looking for someone to walk with, as I have been inside since early morning, and I am starving for some sunlight and perhaps a bite."

"Of a sausage roll?"

"Ah! Don't laugh! That is indeed one of my favorite things." He took my arm and guided me toward the shops, and, in fact, the pubs, and when we entered the Ghastly Spirit, everyone there tipped their caps or gave him a smile. He said, "Shepherd's pie, black pudding, jellied eels – this is the spot. Pip Munt, who does all the cooking and preparation, is a true genius."

He kept me with him. At the bar he asked for the sausage roll and kippers. We went to a spot near a window onto the street. The sausage was nicely flavored, and the pastry was flaky. The kippers were a bit salty for me, not unlike what we called jerky in Quincy, something Roland made from venison as well as beef. We had not eaten together before. I minded my manners, but I saw that John had a hearty appetite, which surprised me a bit, since he had no gut. I tried to tread the line between evidently enjoying my food and eating the way a lady is supposed to in England, with discrimination and reserve. I did put two of my shillings on the table after we ate. He looked at me with some care, then nodded and took the money.

He now appeared satisfied and in a good humor, so I said, "What is that building where you spent the entire, and very pleasant, morning? I am impressed by the brick."

"It is the chapel where I am employed."

"As the caretaker?"

"Yes, in multiple ways. Our congregation is not large, so we mind the dust and the garden ourselves. But, in fact, I am the vicar, though we don't use that word, as we are not COE."

"Church of England?"

"Precisely."

I said, "Methodist?"

He smiled. "No."

"Baptist?"

"No."

"Roman Catholic?"

"No."

"Quaker?"

"No."

"Lutheran?"

"No."

"Presbyterian?"

"No."

I had now run through all the denominations in Quincy that I could think of. I said, "Minions of Satan?"

"Some would say so." He tossed back his head in a good-natured way.

"I gather that there are a plethora of churches in Liverpool." I enjoyed using that word, "plethora."

"Indeed, and a synagogue, too. Two blocks or so from the post office."

"And everyone lives peacefully together?"

"As a rule, yes."

"That is a pleasant thought."

We stood up. I touched my plate, to take it to the bar, but John nodded to a young boy who was waiting in the corner, and the boy trotted over to us. John gave him a sixpence and said, "Thank you, Silas."

"Ye like the kippers, sir?"

John said, "I did!"

We walked out to the street, and, without saying anything, turned toward the buildings I had been staring at. By the time we got there, the sun was behind the trees and the other buildings nearby, and the chapel, if that was what it was, though it had no steeple and no graveyard, looked more forbidding than it had. We went inside. It also had few windows – six in all – one on either side of the door, two on each of the side walls, none in the back, where there was a moderately sized cross, though no one being crucified upon it, and some benches. No altar, no tapestries, no choir, no organ, no rows of candles or silken fabrics. There were some rugs, neatly set out. I said, "I am sorry there is so little dusting to do."

"Miss Williams is very adamant about dusting. She gets all the spiders and all of the grime out of every corner and makes sure they stay out."

"This is a Negro church?"

"For all types. Whoever wishes to attend."

That would have been just the sort of thing that might have driven the Border Ruffians right off their heads, and so I appreciated it, but I did feel some reserve, and it was only later that I realized that it was the fact that it was a manifestation of *religion* that put me off, not that people of all sorts could join together there. But then I remembered my bets with God, my prayers, my vision, if that was what you wanted to call it, of Jesus walking down the streets of Liverpool unnoticed, helping others. I didn't know what to say or ask. As a rule, if you went into an English church, especially a Church of England building, which I had done, there were plenty of old statues and paintings to look at, many of them purchased and contributed to the church by wealthy members. The principal church in Liverpool was St. Peter's, which was a tall, stiff, rather rough-looking building that Mrs. Cunningham, in particular, found disagreeable. Once in a while, we had driven in a carriage past the oldest church, called All Saints, which was beyond the botanic garden and had a small cemetery crammed with old gravestones. An inn across the street was called Childwall Abbey, but, according to Barnsby, had never been a true abbey. The citizens of Liverpool enjoyed amusing names for their commercial establishments, and I did appreciate, for example, the Ghastly Spirit. Thinking of this, I said, "What is the name of your church?"

"Grove Chapel."

"Did you come to Liverpool to – "

"I did. That is, I lived here for some years, then in Manchester, and then I came back here three years ago."

"Where – "

"Oh, I live on the first floor in that building across the way." He pointed out the window to one of the two other buildings. The façade of that building was more forbidding than this one – a narrow iron staircase up one side, a small door, three tall windows that might get some sun in the summer but never in the winter. I was a little surprised that he lived there and yet was always so agreeable. I made an effort not to look judgmental. Just then, he said, "I cannot say that our chapel is a prosperous one, but we get by. Shall we walk toward the docks? I need to meet a friend." We went out the door, then ambled down Huskisson Street. The sunlight had disappeared, and clouds were gathering, some of them foamy but dark, promising a good wind, if not a storm. I pulled my shawl more tightly around my shoulders. John's demeanor was as usual. Perhaps I was the one who had tried very hard not to discover who he was – perhaps he didn't object one way or the other to who I was. Perhaps he thought he knew me; perhaps, indeed, he had asked around and gleaned whatever information he could about Anne and her minder, Helen. Perhaps he was a trusting fellow, who believed the evidence of his own eyes – if I laughed and chatted and walked along and gave him a ticket to an amusing show and told him about Toffee and was a friend of the Cunninghams and had gained the approval of Susan Williams, then that was enough for him. But, of course, that was not who I was, Helen Longbourn, and somehow, now that I had visited his chapel, I felt more strongly than ever both the need to hide myself and the opposing need to show myself. We walked on. At that public graveyard where I sometimes saw him, he bade me an easy and affectionate adieu. I turned toward 2 Canning Street and let myself in.

Berta and Jane were in the pantry, looking at supplies, tossing out the ones that had been shoved into corners and gone fetid or moldy. As I walked in, they were looking at some potatoes, which had perhaps been too small to use. Now they were green and had sprouted here and there. Alice had been a terrible housekeeper in the way of dealing with rotting food, so we often had a pile of moldy potatoes, which Roland took away to the farm, cut into pieces, and planted. I asked Berta if I could take them, and the floppy carrots and the softened beets and rancid flour, to Reggie, and they said I could, perhaps not knowing who Reggie was. But I liked the idea of expanding his pile. Berta brought out a basket, and we dumped everything into it. Then we went into the various chambers and took down the drapery, and so I had a few tasks to distract me for a bit, and then I took the basket full of dregs to Reggie. It was misting, not storming, but he was there in his garden, evidently unfazed by the weather. He rifled through my dregs, did take out a few of the potatoes, but not all of them; then he thanked me for them, and said, "More folks should be doing this, but ye can't train 'em." He tossed the dregs into his pile, turned it over a couple of times, shook the basket, then handed it back to me. When I returned to 2 Canning Street ten minutes later, we had an enjoyable supper of the very fish that Miss Williams had mentioned – flounder – with some drippings of butter and a Yorkshire pudding. Whatever that flounder might look like in the sea, it does taste much better than a catfish, and has fewer bones to pick at. And then Jane handed me the volumes of the Trollope book I had lost, which she said that she found among the bedclothes she was sorting through. I took them to my room, and read them well enough, since this time of year the sun was up and the light was good until almost ten, according to the grandfather clock in the hallway. Then, at last, I removed my garments, put on my shirt, got under the covers, and thought about John Hegarty.

What had I hoped he might be? How had I wished he would be supporting himself? I didn't know. As a teacher perhaps, since, in Liverpool, if you didn't manufacture rope or have a shop, and didn't go here and there on some ship, what else was there to do? He was always neatly dressed, his hands were not callused, he was clean but did not raise his eyebrows or flare his nostrils as Anne had learned to do when she consorted with the upper class. He was friendly in a way that seemed to me unique, as he acknowledged no boundaries of class, of race, of belief. In America, all boundaries were boundaries of belief – if you do not share my opinions, then I will avoid you if I am a peaceable sort, or I will shoot you if I've a mind to. According to one of those letters Anne had hidden from me, our Illinois senator Mr. Trumbull had declared that he wanted to send "free Negroes" to Central America, by which he was not referring to K.T., but to Mexico. He didn't want any Negroes in his party, or, I gathered, in his country. His great fear was that the slaves would be freed and then hurry north to work for businesses that would then throw the white laborers out on their ears. Of course, he wished them "God speed wherever they go." And then he said, "We believe it is better for us that they should not be among us." I remembered reading this, thinking of Lorna, being enraged. And, it was said, Mr. Lincoln did not disagree with him, but, indeed, did not dare to say so outright, because then someone would shoot him, for either agreeing or disagreeing.

I suspected that John wouldn't have darkened the door of a Catholic church, but I thought that he was, indeed, a saint. I also felt that something had been lost, though, some blithe ignorance on my part that allowed me simply to look at him and appreciate him and enjoy him.

As is usually the case, I sighed as I got myself to sleep and woke up in a perfectly fine mood – what had seemed undoable was now not much of a task. And it may be that I dreamed of that Jesus fellow that I had seen walking about in town, helping the old lady across the street, letting her lean on him, then the sun lighting up his face as he looked down on her when she thanked him. My dream wasn't sharp and detailed, as some dreams are, but a few images lingered even as I clothed myself and went to our morning repast (boiled eggs and bits of ham, along with pieces of a fruitcake that Berta didn't think would last until Yule). All right, I thought, let me take that as a sign and do as I am, evidently, being told to do. Since I no longer have a purpose, then John may give me one, as Thomas did, as most men would say that it is their right to do. I passed a mirror in the house, and saw that I looked something of a mess, so I stopped, for once, and straightened my gown, smoothed the skirt, did something with my hair, and then placed my bonnet more carefully than usual on the resulting tangle. How long would it take me to comb my hair perfectly? Maybe the entire afternoon, but I vowed that I would do it.

Sometime later, after I had been reading *Dr. Thorne* in the library, Berta came in and abruptly asked me if I would care to learn to cook? The look on her face was generous and pleasant, but my natural response was to say no. Even as I was opening my mouth, though, I recalled my new purpose, so I said I would, put down the book, and followed her into the kitchen. The first thing she did was to get out the makings for some scones – oats, currants, some pieces of sugar, some butter, and some light cream. She set them out on the table. My task was to grind the oats into meal, then pound the piece of sugar into grains. She showed me how she used her fingers to mix the butter in with the oatmeal, then she added the sugar and the cream, and when the batter was smooth but, as Berta said, turning to look at me and waving her hand, "not *too* smooth," she stirred in the currants, spread the whole batter out on a griddle, and cooked it in the oven over some coals. Then, since we had the oats out, she showed me how to make porridge, this time using some of that golden-colored sugar that was more tasty than the white, and some sheep's milk, which she said she preferred. Did I feel guilty, looking at the golden sugar? A bit, but I didn't say anything to Berta.

When the scone cake was well cooked and almost brown, she eased it off the griddle with a flat wooden paddle of the sort that my mother once used to spank me, and then cut it right away into eight triangles. Before the griddle cooled down, she brought out some black sausage, sliced it in pieces, threw them on the griddle, and left them on the coals until they sizzled and gave off some juices. Then she called in Jane, and we sat at the table, tasting the products of our efforts. Berta declared that the scones had cooked a bit too long, the black sausage was as it should be, and the porridge was better because of the golden sugar, and I should not let anyone tell me different. Jane seemed not to have much of an opinion – she repeatedly looked at Berta as if she was seeking permission to keep eating, and Berta must have given it to her, because she did keep eating. As for me, I liked the porridge best, and I thanked Berta for showing me how she made it, as the Cunninghams did all seem to love her porridge. She said, "Keeps ye going mosta the day, Ah'll sy that."

She went into the pantry. I brought in the water, and Jane and I cleaned up. I suspected she had begun with these items because she remembered I was clumsy with a knife, and so would put off having me try carving and chopping as long as she could. Once we had done the cleaning, I admit, I ran out of 2 Canning Street as if I was escaping jail, and went straight to the graveyard, where I walked about. Did Berta ever get out of the house? Not that I knew of. The room she lived in was next to mine, she was up long before I was every morning, and I had been told that she had no family. She was older than Mr. Cunningham, had worked for his father; and then I thought that perhaps she was training me to replace her, under Mr. Cunningham's orders. On the one hand, she looked healthy enough, and on the other, training me to replace her would take a very long time.

This got me wondering, not about Berta, but about Jane, who was closer in age to me – perhaps not quite thirty. She was not one to talk but, rather, to sing, and she did have a pleasant low voice. I made up a story in my mind that she had begun, like Mrs. Cunningham, as an aspiring actress, but, try as she might, she had not been able to project her voice past the members of the audience seated in the pit, and so Mr. Cunningham, or, let's say, Mrs. Cunningham, had taken her in, and now employed her about the house. I then left the graveyard (after marveling at some of the names, of a sort I have never heard in Quincy: Birdwhistle, Swem, and Trikelbank) and found Jane in the laundry area, sorting through the drapes. I watched her for a bit, then took one of those belonging to Mr. Cunningham's bed and imitated what she was doing with it – smoothing it out, folding it. She said, "Ye don't 'ave to 'elp me, but thank ye."

I said, "I was hoping you would sing me a song."

She glanced at me, smiled a bit, then commenced with a song

about picking thyme in the mountains, which I thought was a lovely one. I said, "Did you grow up singing that song?"

She said, "Nay. But I keep my ears open for a good 'un, and I always thought that was a good 'un."

I said, "I suspect you grew up around here?"

"Not exactly, but close enough." Then she buttoned her lips, and I thought she had something to hide, as I did. We continued, until all the drapery was in a stack. Then, suddenly and in a louder voice than usual, she said, "I was born in Ormskirk, and it is lovely there, but me da took to the ships, though me ma begged him not to, and, sure 'nough, his ship went down when I was twelve, and so me ma brought me here and a friend of hers found her work at a place on Percy Street, but I always looked at this one when I walked past it, so when me ma said 'twas time to go to work, I came knockin' on this door, and Berta took me in. And, indeed, the master is much more daicent than the one me ma worked for on Percy Street. When me ma was too old to do her work, that fellow put her out, and Mr. C. brought her here. She was in your room until she died, three years ago now. He is a lovely man, Mr. C."

"How do you know all those songs?"

"By keepin' me ears open. I dearly wish I could play that piano they have, and Mr. Cunningham don't mind, but Mrs. C. said it gives her a 'eadache, and, then, well, now I am too old to learn, because, even when she's gone, I can't get the tune right."

And now I remembered my vow, and so I went to my chamber, found my comb, which was under a volume of *The Newcomes,* and then I sat down on my bed and unpinned my hair. It was true that I unpinned my hair every night and pinned it up every morning, because, obviously, I wouldn't be able to sleep if I did not, but I never gave it a moment's thought, just gathered it between my hands, doing my best to grasp all of it, then twisted it several times, folded it over, and put in the pins. My entire goal was to keep it out of the way and make sure that stray hairs did not tickle my nose, which was something I could not bear. Now, sitting on the bed, I pulled it forward and looked at it. It was two years since I had cut it all off so as to pass as a fellow and unearth and destroy those Border Ruffians who shot Thomas and Jeremiah. I looked down, and saw it dangling below my shoulder. It was thick, as it had been, somewhat wavy, the same brown as Anne's was, and Harriet's and Alice's, and so the brown belonged to my father – my mother's hair had been reddish, which in Quincy was considered a bit suspicious. I ran the comb through the ends, and it went smoothly. I made my way up and behind, surprised that it wasn't a terrible tangle; when Toffee first came home with Peter, there was a knot in her tail that was like a solid ball, and it took me two days, off and on, to sort it out.

Once I had my hair combed, I went up to Anne's room where, of course, there was a mirror, and I looked at myself. Horse-faced hussy, indeed. Now I did my best to organize my hair into something more appealing than usual, with a small lock dangling on either side, the top pushed a bit forward, then my cap perched on top of the pile. I spent quite a while doing this, and I wondered how I could be one of those women, like Anne, who did this every day, sometimes more than once. And had I ever seen a man care about his hair? No, he put his top hat or his bowler on his head and left the house. His chin was what he thought about – there were those fellows who shaved everything off their faces and left a dark mass below their chins, around their necks, a style I could not fathom. Then it occurred to me that perhaps John knew exactly how appealing he was, since he combed his hair back and shaved everything off his face, and so revealed his features, and they were well worth revealing. All the other men I had known had found shaving themselves a pointless trial. Thinking these thoughts made me smile. I left the mirror, looked about Anne's room for some old issues of periodicals, and took them away.

I let myself out of the back gate, not forgetting to sort my gown and affix my bonnet in what might be a flattering way, and turned left down Canning Street to Upper Duke Street, toward the shops and the pubs. Neat as I was, I was not seeking John, though I wouldn't have minded his seeing me from afar and wondering what in the world had happened to me. It was more that I was trying out being looked at rather than looking at others, my normal mode of behavior. This made me think, as well, of K.T., where you did have to keep your eye out, even in Lawrence, that hotbed, as they said in Missouri, of d—ned abolitionists, because even among abolitionists there might be someone ready to snatch your purse or, at least, your satchel of potatoes. It had taken me a long time to push away my suspicions, to not start at every sudden sound and to not take offense at every scowl. In that regard, Liverpool had been a relief, since it seemed to be the task of every English man and woman to look pleasant, or, at least, inoffensive. Yes, there were gangs, but Mr. Cunningham had told me that they were in the older areas, closer to the river, and I had kept my eye out when I had to go there, though no one who looked like a member of a gang – let's say, carrying a knife or a pistol – had threatened me. But, then, when I stood up straight, I was taller than most of the men in that part of town, and my guess was that they had grown up with little in the way of nourishment – I remembered that when Thomas told me about one of the Dickens novels he'd left back in Medford, *Oliver Twist,* he'd said that it was mostly about starving children trying to survive.

Now, on Duke Street and Hanover Street, I did my best to appear personable and graceful, but also sturdy. I inhaled deeply several times and let myself relax. I let my steps stretch, but took them more slowly. I let my shoulders relax, and was glad I no longer had that stick hanging from my arm, reminding me that I could always whack someone over the head if I wished to. I remembered that fellow, Jesus, and the way he noticed waifs and strays. I gave a few pence from my pocket to children next to brick buildings with their hands lifted toward me. I did not smile, but I relaxed my face, too, so that it looked, I hoped, pleasant. The result was, well, not much, only that I felt more comfortable, more able to fit into the crowd. Two or three short men did look me up and down, but then they smiled pleasantly.

You may spend your entire life resisting being looked at, but, as I realized when I was strolling about, people do look at you, whether they call you a horse-faced hussy or not. It occurred to me, maybe for the first time in my life, to wonder whether Anne was prettier than I was. In fact, Alice, Harriet, and Beatrice had, over the years, often mentioned the resemblance between us, at least until I was about thirteen or fourteen, and got perhaps a head taller than Annie. For her whole life until she did that Christmas performance in Quincy, she had kept her eyes down, and for my whole life, I had stared around everywhere, curious or cautious, depending on where I was. In the reviews of her performances in the papers, she had gotten compliments on her beauty, but more often on her "intriguing demeanor" or her "expressive countenance." Were I to compare her to Miss Lucas, I would have said that Anne was prettier, but, then, not so pretty, perhaps, as Mrs. Cunningham, whose visage could be quite arresting. Indeed, as Evelina was getting healthier, she was coming to resemble her mother more and more. As I walked, my thoughts rambled through these ideas until I was quite out of my neighborhood – all the way to the Albany Building, above the newer docks (and, as it was high shipping season, the horns were bellowing). I walked down toward the pier, watched the ships being loaded, and also the few that were going out or coming in. Some of them looked very elegant to me, made me think of the library on the *Arabia,* and then of those two men, one of them named Dorsett, I thought, and our pleasant discussion of horse racing. In my current mood, I wondered not why I hadn't seen them at the races Barnsby had taken me to, but whether one of them might have seen me. And so a pleasant memory turned into an eerie thought.

I then turned south and walked along, enjoying the street

names – The Strand, Wapping – and not thinking of much until the mist rolled in, and then I thought only of stopping for a bite of something. I rattled the coins in my pocket. There were three of them, one of a decent size – a shilling, I was guessing, though I dared not take it out. I glanced here and there, and finally, up the hill, saw the Stormy Rest, a pub in the corner of a formerly elaborate but now somewhat ramshackle building. A boy who worked there was just closing the doors against what was now rain, but he stepped aside when I appeared, and I entered. It was not exactly mealtime, but it looked as though some of the comestibles had not sold, and, therefore, they were now laid out on the bar – slices of bread, some cheese, a few sausages, part of a tart that looked to be made of raspberries. I showed my shilling to the man behind the bar, and he waved his hand, saying, "Take what you please, miss. We're closing for the rest of the day, and it won't last overnight."

I said, "Why are you closing?"

He shook his head slightly, said, "A funeral service, miss." Then he handed me a plate and a knife and fork and turned away. I took a bit of each item, and maybe more of the tart than I should have. There were four other people sitting at tables. I went over and sat not far from two women who had finished their meal and were drinking tea. I always eavesdrop upon the English, because everything they say is interesting, if only for the words they use or the various accents; Mr. Cunningham often pointed out to Anne that the accent she mimicked in her roles had perhaps more meaning to a Liverpool audience than she realized, and she did try out the accents he showed her, much to her own amusement. But these two women sounded typically Liverpudlian (also an amusing word to a Quincyite), so I paid no attention until I heard the word "crack" and then the word "Hegarty." One more word, "chapel," told me that they were truly speaking of John, and I slowed and quieted my munching and leaned a little toward them. They were speaking softly, but I could understand them perfectly.

The woman nearest me said, "If, indeed, 'e 'as recovered from that, well . . ." She shook her head.

The other said, "'Twas assuredly an unexpected blow, but as 'is demeanor is always lively, I find it 'ard to know 'ow he truly feels."

Perhaps the grave below Hope Street was not that of his former teacher. I slowed my chewing even more.

The first one said, "It 'asn't been long, though. Six months. These things take a while."

"They were betrothed for a year, as I 'eard."

"And why, I ask ye, for so long? A fellow needs to act, not tarry."

From her tone, I guessed that John's betrothed hadn't died. A relief.

Then the second one said, "But, indeed, if Lord Scarborough 'ad come to ye – a man with an unencumbered estate and four thousand pounds a year, or that's what everyone says – 'ow long would it take for you to give up yar impoverished betrothed and 'urry off to France to do the weddin'? Don't ask me! When I was that age, I would 'ave done it."

Then the first one said, "Ow! She was a beauty. No question a that."

I stood up as quietly as I could and walked out of the Stormy Rest. As it was, indeed, now storming, I had to make my way back to 2 Canning Street as quickly as I might, but, even so, I was soaked from head to tail, and my hair was drooping and dripping. As I disrobed in my chamber, I acknowledged that a month ago, or even a week ago, I would have been relieved by what I had heard, and understood that what John cared for in me was what Reggie did – I was a sister. And I did kneel at the sill of the window, which was pounding with rain, and I did thank Jesus for his aid in revealing this to me, but I didn't mean it in the slightest.

13

THE NEXT MORNING, Barnsby was in the entry hall, quietly inspecting the front door, which was open, as routinely as if he hadn't ever left. I said, "I didn't realize you had returned! How was your journey?"

He continued inspecting the door for a moment, then said, "Ah, Miss Longbourn. It was as tedious as it could possibly have been. I came to wish for the Second Coming just because it might relieve my ennui."

I said, "What is 'ennui'?"

He said, "It is a French word for being so incapacitated with lethargy that when your cousin sees you in your chair, he wonders if you are dead."

I laughed. Barnsby's eyebrow lifted just enough to show me that he was jesting. I did know what the Second Coming was, because the pastors of the Methodist churches that I had occasionally attended with Alice or Roland had spoken of it, but of course the words stuck in my mind while the ideas that they represented had pretty much passed through my head and left nothing behind. I said, "I'm gathering you are glad to be back."

"Indeed."

"What are you looking for on the door?"

"Evidence of attempted intrusion."

"Did you find any?"

"Some muddy footprints on the step, but no evidence on the door."

"Why would you worry about footprints on the step?"

"They were indeed large, and there were several of them, as if the fellow in the boots was walking back and forth. That could be evidence that he was seeking a way in."

John had big feet and heavy boots, but I said nothing. I of course peeked out the door, but Barnsby had swept the step clean. He coughed slightly, then said, "Indeed, Miss Longbourn, I must commend Berta's fresh loaves and the very rich butter she said you procured a couple of days ago. Another reason for me to be grateful for my safe return."

I leaned toward him and pecked him lightly on the cheek, said I was glad he was back, too, then hurried to find Berta.

The loaves, two small ones, were indeed out of the oven, and Berta had cut one of them into slices. She gestured toward my seat at the table and set a plate before me, and Barnsby, as always, was correct – the bread was crusty and flavorful. Berta remarked that spring butter was always better because the cream was better, and did I know a thing about cows? Cows were very interesting, as they varied in their production of cream and milk, and a few years ago, they had bought some butter from a fellow who pastured his cows on a fertile hillside around that time of year when the herbs in the grass had matured, and Berta had detected some intriguing flavors, which was not to say that everyone had. She set two fried eggs before me and a bit of ham, and it wasn't until I was nearly finished that I thought of the conversation I'd heard at the Stormy Rest. I said, "The rain has stopped, I see. If you need me to go fetch anything."

"Indeed, it 'as, but you'd better be wearin' yer sturdiest boots, as there is muck everywhere. Barnsby will 'and you a paper. Just a few things."

In order to push away thoughts of John and the girl, I said, "Berta, don't you sometimes wish you could get out into the countryside?"

"Nay, 'elen. I don't like the countryside, to be 'onest. If ye grow up in a small village, which I did, then the first thing you learn is that the only thing folk 'ave to pass the time with is telling secrets about one another. When I got to Liverpool, I was sixteen, and 'ad 'ad enough o' that. Ye stay in your spot, no one cares about ye except people ye may trust, and everything runs smooth."

"I know what you mean, but I also envy how much you enjoy your daily round."

"I do, indeed, and that is another reason to enjoy this place. There is always someone 'oo 'as been somewhere, and not only France or America, 'oo 'as tasted this or that, and would like to taste it again, and so we cast about and do our best." She reached out and took my hand, then led me into the pantry. There, she opened one of the doors and said, "These are my 'erbs and spices, and I would say they are somethin' of a treasure."

The shelves were lined with small dishes, each covered with a bit of cloth. She lifted them one by one and said, "Thyme, of course. Bay. Cress. Fennel. Cinnamon – ah, that is my favorite." She took a deep breath. "Anise. Elderflower. Dill."

I said, "You put these in our food?"

"As many as I might. Mrs. Cunningham 'as me slip 'em into everything, as she says they boost Evelina. And, indeed, they must, given 'ow she has improved. When they returned from that town – "

I said, "Biarritz."

" – they brought me jasmine and saffron that they purchased there."

The pantry was indeed fragrant, like a garden boiled down and dried. But it didn't make me want to stay in the house, and within a few minutes, I had burst out into the back garden and was slogging through the gate. Muddy, indeed. However, the sky was blue and the air was crystal clear, and I made up my mind to go straight to John's chapel. Yes, I did look my usual mess, but it was true that I had not enjoyed my experience as a self-conscious, neatly done up female. It took me perhaps ten minutes, and when I got there, the bricks were flickering in the sunlight. The door of the chapel was open. I stepped inside, saw nothing, until my sight adjusted to the constant darkness of the room, and then I saw that John was there, kneeling in front of the cross. I must say that my heart instantly went out to him with a kind of softness and pity that I had not known before. I walked toward him, allowing my gown to swish. I did not want to surprise him, and he wasn't surprised. He lifted his head and turned, then smiled his smile and stood up, brushed his coat down a bit. He came toward me with his hand out. I said, "I wish you would come with me to the Furnishes' place. I know Reggie would give you some seeds. I would love to help you plant a bit of a garden, at least along the street. There is some sun there."

He squeezed my hand in his usual way, and off we went. It was only a few steps to Reggie's garden, and there he was, kneeling beside a newly dug S-shaped row, setting some sprouts one by one, and then mounding the dirt around them with his trowel. Without my even asking, he said, "Love-in-a-mist, they are. Pretty blue." He finished his work, as he always does, then rose to his feet, wiped his hands on his pants, and cocked his head in our direction. I said, "You know Mr. Hegarty, don't you, Reggie?"

"I do some'at," he said. "Ye 'ave that chapel."

John tipped his head. He said, "I do. Miss Longbourn says I need some flowers, and perhaps she is correct." Reggie said, " 'Tis a little late in the season, but I might come by and 'ave a look at the ground and the sun, just to get some thoughts about what would take 'old in such a spot. Do ye mind if I dig a bit here and there, to get a feel o' the dirt? As ye might see" – he waved his hand toward the pile of manure and dregs – "we 'ave a goodly lot of muck if it might need a lift, and it isn't far to carry a cartload or two."

He walked with us back to John's place, stepping lively with anticipation, once in a while tossing his trowel between his hands, and also, of course, keeping his eye out for the stray carrot or pile of horse manure that might be lying in the road. When we got there, it seemed to me that the spot didn't look promising – yes, there was some sunlight upon the area beside the walkway, but not a single weed voluntarily grew there. The walkways to the chapel and to the other two buildings were as hard as if they had been paved; on this muddy day, the water had simply run off into what was, on either side, only shadowed grime. I said, "How long have these buildings been here?"

John said, "Ten or twelve years. The chapel was originally a shop, and the other two were meant to be an inn and a domicile for the owner of the shop, but it was too out of the way to prosper, and, I suspect, too forbidding for guests. When the fellow died, he bequeathed the property to my predecessor, who could not afford not to take it, as the congregation had been meeting at his abode, which wasn't large, and his wife was . . ." He glanced at me and sighed, then said, "She died of the cholera. There was plenty of that."

Reggie looked up at the trees, and I sighed.

But Reggie was evidently excited, the way you are, let's say, when no one has managed to tame an especially unruly horse and now you have been granted the opportunity. He said, "Given the 'ealth of these Spanish chestnut trees, in particular, I would say that the soil isn't poor, only beaten down." He squatted, dug up a sample, rubbed it between his fingers. John and I looked at one another. John seemed pleased. I said, "It will give me a task to help him."

John cocked his head, an affirmative, and at any rate, how could one resist, here in England, the notion of a garden? There were gardens everywhere, reminding us daily of the pleasure of the natural landscape. I thought of Berta, and said, "You might grow some herbs and potatoes and, let's see, leeks."

This was a new thought for John—that he could supply his members with a few comestibles. I said, "Doesn't Miss Williams have a pleasant garden? She might—"

"She will, indeed, quite enjoy it."

I turned to Reggie, and said, "Is there enough sun, though?"

He said, "Primroses and foxglove grow nicely in the shade. Others, too. Mint. This 'ere is lemon balm. One of the Furnishes brought seeds back from a trip south. Lovely scent."

John said, "I see a feast." He squeezed my hand. I thought that if I stayed in the garden, arduously digging and weeding, I might be able to watch the members of the congregation enter the door, but not have to hear them discuss the Second Coming or the nature of sin or any of those topics I had heard back in Quincy. I might work for John as Berta worked for the Cunninghams, or as I did, for that matter, enjoying our tasks and keeping our thoughts to ourselves. What did I feel about the girl, the betrothed, who was now Lady Scarborough? I only wanted to see her passing along the street in her brougham, to look at the horses drawing the brougham, to see the visage of Lord Scarborough and judge whether it was as pleasant as John's. I thought that if I saw those few things, then I could gauge what her motivation might have been.

John stayed at the chapel, and I walked with Reggie back to his garden. On the way, he chatted about seeds he could gather, other plants he might grow from cuttings, and plants in his own garden that were getting too big for their spots and needed to be trimmed. I could see the wheels going about in his head. And when we got back to the Furnishes', he did get his shovel and a small bin and head toward the chapel to pick up the piles of manure we had passed. I went to 2 Canning Street, perhaps as calm as I had felt in weeks.

The following day was Sunday, and I got up early, because the sunlight through my window first awakened me, then reminded me of the garden. I did not think Berta had readied our morning meal by then, but I arose anyway, thinking that I might look in the pantry for a bite. Barnsby was already fully clothed, as neat as it was possible to be. When I passed through the entry hall, he said, "Ah, Miss Longbourn. You might accompany me to my church. If it was a lovely walk the last time you declined to go with me, it will be even more lovely this time." Then, as if reading my mind, he went into the pantry and returned with two scones and a dish of blackberries, and after I ate them, he went to the sideboard and brought out a small square, pale gold. He set it on the plate where the scones had been. He said, "Here is a bit of something I brought back with me. As you enjoy sweets, you might like it."

I said, "What is it?"

He said, "The Scots call it 'tablet.' It is concocted of nothing but cream and sugar – difficult to make, but my cousin's wife is adept. I do understand how fascinated you are by the peculiarities of the United Kingdom. This is one of them."

It tasted good enough, rather like a sweet that the boats sometimes carried to Quincy from New Orleans called pralines, something Beatrice and Horace loved to stock around Easter, and Roland enjoyed very much. I thanked him and said, "Your church is another. I will get my boots."

Barnsby said, "I've already cleaned them, Miss Longbourn."

For some reason, I had expected that we would walk east, toward the botanic garden, but, instead, we walked down Hope Street, past the cemetery, then toward the neighborhood where Miss Williams lived. I didn't expect to see her, as it was Sunday and she would be at John's chapel, but I did keep my eyes open. In fact, it was not a long walk – that Barnsby thought it was reminded me that he did not get out of the Cunninghams' house as often as I did. We walked briskly, and were there in a quarter of an hour. It proved to be perhaps the smallest, sparest church that I had ever seen, built of red-gold blocks of stone with tiny arched windows and doorways, no steeple. I soon understood why it was so unassuming when I saw that it was a Unitarian church. In Quincy, the Unitarians were also unassuming, though decided in their views, if someone can be decided in views that are kindly and skeptical, too. As far as I knew from what I had heard around the dinner table in Quincy, they were what I might have called "eye rollers" – if someone went on and on about the Holy Spirit, they would say nothing, but roll their eyes. If someone referred to the miracle of the Virgin Birth, they would cough a bit and look away. If someone talked about how God dictated the Bible straight to whoever was taking it down, they would mention how this bit didn't exactly agree with this other bit, and so, perhaps . . . The Unitarian church in Quincy wasn't far from Alice's house, and it was an open, agreeable-looking building, basically a large house with a lawn and a modest steeple. It was said that they were anti-slavery, but whether they had Negro parishioners was unknown – or perhaps, in Quincy, a secret, for obvious reasons.

Once Barnsby and I were inside the building, we were greeted by many of his fellow Unitarians, and there were several Negroes – three couples and one solitary older woman. We then seated ourselves. I looked around, and, yes, indeed, the spare cleanliness of the interior was pleasant, and whatever the pastor (who was neatly but not fashionably dressed, not nearly as well dressed as Barnsby was) said, he said it in an amused voice. He was perhaps the only pastor I had ever heard who seemed to think that God had a sense of humor, and was willing to put up with humans simply because He had created them, and, like a benevolent parent who often shook his head, and prodded his offspring in a different direction, nevertheless kept his despair to himself when they misbehaved, endangering themselves and others. The pastor's name was Mr. Riverton, and I thought that his God must be endlessly patient, but perhaps that meant that Pastor Riverton, himself, was endlessly patient. During most of the sermon, Barnsby's eyes were closed, and I did think he was listening, not sleeping, but how was one to know with Barnsby? He was simultaneously the most proper and most easily amused person that I had, perhaps, ever met. Nor was the service a long one. Two or three hymns, a pleasant talk, a good deal of chitchat, and then back out to Park Street. We turned left rather than right, and walked to Ullet Road. As we were walking, I remarked, "What must I do to join?"

"Come along with me. Be personable."

"One thing I don't understand is, where are all the screaming children?"

He lifted an eyebrow.

I said, "Have you ever been to Mr. Cunningham's church?"

He said, "Ah." We walked another half a block. He said, "Our pastor doesn't encourage procreation."

"Why not?"

"Perhaps for the very reason you have mentioned. The safety of his congregation." And, yes, I knew he was jesting. Then he said, "Have you visited this area before? It is called 'Dingle.'"

"I thought it was called 'Toxteth.'"

"That is just to the left, here. This is a wonderful town for small areas with evocative names." We kept walking, away from Canning Street, as far as I could tell, as the sun was now behind us. Barnsby had his bowler hat on; he pushed it back just slightly, and then straightened his gloves. To my mind, it was getting a bit warm for these sartorial flourishes – and his tweed coat was neatly buttoned up. He said, "Now we are coming to a worthy spot. Do you see that green area in the distance? It was once a deer park, and might be the most pleasant park in Liverpool if they would put it to use, but they can't make up their minds about it. I often have a stroll about the place on a Sunday."

"Pastor Riverton's service is mercifully short, isn't it?"

"Indeed. One of many things to appreciate about him."

There were others in the green area, a few on horseback, trotting here and there, some walking or standing beside a body of water, looking at the weeds and flowers. The grass was thick and unkempt, something I appreciated about it. Barnsby said, "There had to be deer to chase, and so a deer park was a place that was kept for them to breed."

"Why didn't they run off?"

"As the grass was thick and they were chased with hounds or arrows or lances, as this was very long ago, I doubt that the deer were in much danger. And then there would be the drink the hunters would have imbibed, causing them to fall should their equines become unruly."

"There are so many parks and gardens here. Where I came from in . . ." I paused, then said, ". . . Wisconsin, there was nothing of the kind. It was village or forest or partially cleared farmland. In . . ." I paused again. "In Chicago, it was muddy streets and a big lake and howling wind. I wish I had grown up in a civilized place like this one."

Barnsby said, "Indeed, but if you had grown up here, you might not appreciate it as you do." As if to underline Barnsby's point, we heard the distant cry of a ship's blast.

We walked a little farther, pausing to count ducks on the edge of the water, which was less than a lake but more than a pond, and in a brushy area where no one else was walking, I did see a buck and a doe in the shadow of a glade of trees. Barnsby, of course, noted them, too. He said, "Do you see the points on the stag's rack? I count ten, so he is a healthy old fellow. Evidently cautious."

A few minutes later, as we were walking across something of a hill, I stopped, turned toward Barnsby, and said, "Is Mr. Cunningham getting ready to send me back to Chicago?"

Barnsby was unfazed. He continued smoothly down the hill, neatly avoiding clumps of weeds and the occasional mole hole. He said, "Mr. Cunningham does not often know what he intends. He prefers to act upon impulse, and therefore, members of the household are frequently surprised by his decisions."

"Including Mrs. Cunningham?"

"Indeed. I would observe that this is a source of some disagreement between them."

I said, "Did she expect to receive me and Anne?"

Barnsby said, "Not at first, but he talked her over."

I lifted my eyebrows. Barnsby went on. "I would say that, once he knew the two of you were on the vessel, she accepted his decision."

And so I now came to see Mrs. Cunningham in a new light, also – she was not unfriendly, but, rather, repeatedly caught off guard.

Barnsby went on, "Mr. Gaitskill, Mrs. Cunningham's father, was an extremely orderly person who kept track of every sixpence."

We got to the bottom of the hill and stepped over some tall grass to a narrow path. I said, "Did you know him?"

"He was my mother's cousin."

I whipped around. Barnsby smiled slightly, then said, "Even in England, some families have always navigated the boundary between serving and being served. The Gaitskills have had, since the fourteenth century, a modest entailed estate in North Yorkshire. I have never been able to decide if that bit of property was a boon or a burden, as it is large enough to, perhaps, support a small family but requires considerable upkeep. My own mother, though related to the entailed owners, happily married herself to my father, who was the principal tenant farmer on the property, but by the time I was fourteen, I had had enough of mowing, turning, and stacking fields of hay."

I said, "You do seem to take to the orderly side of the family."

He said, "We all have our complexities," and, yes, Barnsby did enjoy the turf, and never shrank from a wager.

We walked back toward 2 Canning Street through neighborhoods I was not very familiar with, so I found them pleasant. They distracted me, for the time being, from thinking of John's chapel. It wasn't clear to me what I was supposed to conclude from Barnsby's remarks about Mallory Cunningham's impulsiveness. I had no sense of whether Barnsby had overheard, or, indeed, participated in discussions about whether to get rid of me or not. If he meant anything, I was sure he meant that I should save some money and be ready for whatever might happen. But, in fact, I did not know what I wished to be ready for. Even as I thought of this, I could feel Anne easing away from me, setting out on her own. I took off my boots, which were not as muddy as I had expected them to be, and went to my chamber and counted my funds. Five pounds, ten shillings, and twopence.

Late in the afternoon, when I was reasonably certain that the service would be over, I walked slowly toward John's chapel. In part, I wondered how he might be planning to get his dinner, but in general, I simply wished to see him. If, indeed, I was in love with him, then a sign of it was that I yearned for the sight of his face, though not necessarily for anything beyond that, because whatever we might say or do could always further tangle that Gordian knot that was still with the two or three shillings that I kept in my pocket.

Sundays were quiet days in Liverpool – no shops or pubs, and those who had caused a ruckus the night before were generally suffering from the aftereffects of the ruckus they had caused, and in this thing only, Liverpool was a bit like Quincy, where the wives were sure to serve Sunday dinner in the afternoon, mostly to settle the stomachs of their husbands and sons.

When I got to the chapel, I saw evidence that Reggie had already commenced his work: beside the walkway between the street and the chapel, two narrow beds had been dug and then raked over, though there was no evidence that anything had been planted, no cuttings or shoots. But it didn't surprise me that Reggie had jumped on the opportunity. I walked between the beds, and then sat on the step of the chapel. All was silent. I looked up. Spanish chestnut trees. Harriet was a great lover of chestnuts, and would gather us on the farm in the fall to pull the nuts out of the burrs.

For her birthday, which was in early November, she liked to pierce them, then roast them, then dribble some bits of precious molasses and melted butter over them, and, indeed, they were delicious. Yes, she was the sharpest of my sisters, but perhaps the most intelligent, too. If, indeed, Roland was a d— ned abolitionist, she might have been the one who saw to it that he wasn't detected. I looked at my feet and let thoughts run through my mind of their farm as a stop on the Underground Railroad (we all knew what that was), and it would have been a good stop – out in the country, shrouded in weeds and woodland, but not far off paths to the east and the north. If a man is known by his neighbors for his readiness to drive off any and all intruders, human and rodent, then the rumor gets everywhere, and even Border Ruffians might think twice about nosing around. Perhaps Thomas's fatal error had been that he looked, and was, approachable, defenseless, decent.

I sighed and rose to my feet. I surveyed the modest façade of the chapel, considered peering through the windows, as they were not shuttered, but I overcame the temptation, and instead walked about the grounds, doing my best to think of plants. There was no graveyard. In Quincy, graveyards were a normal feature of churches, and the part that, I had to say, I liked best, but this garden was too small for such a thing. This made me wonder what I might wish for my own burial. It was a startling thought. Even in K.T., watching as all around me d— ned abolitionists and Border Ruffians attacked one another, it hadn't occurred to me to wonder about such a thing. When I went back to Medford and saw Thomas's grave in the churchyard there, I was grieved, but it felt something like putting away a cherished possession in a safe place. Did his family wonder if I might, at some future date, join him? Since I had never thought of it, I noted no such ideas in their faces as they looked at me. They were kindly, reserved, afflicted, resolute. They dreaded the war they thought was coming, and said, among themselves, that the nation would be better off split in two, but then the slaves would be enslaved forever, and so the project of freeing them had to be followed through. His uncle, named Josiah, and one of the cousins, whose name I didn't remember, were decided in their view that those who did not actively combat enslavement were destined for Hell.

I wondered who John Hegarty thought might be destined for Hell. The Unitarians in Quincy thought that Hell was a place that people imagined for their own entertainment, rather like sitting by the fire on a dark evening and telling ghost stories until you were jumping out of your chair. Given Pastor Riverton's demeanor, I doubted that he hardly thought of Hell, and I wondered how I might begin a conversation about that with Barnsby.

I got all the way into the back of the garden behind the church, and looked for a moment at the houses across the backstreet. It was now evening. One house was already brightly lit, top to bottom. One was dark. I called one Heaven and one Hell, then went around to the front again. John was at the door, lifting the latch. I was afraid I might surprise him, but when I said his name, I saw him smile before he turned his head, and then he did turn his head, hold out his hand to me, and help me up the step. I remarked on Reggie's industry. He said, "My dear, if you want to help, you had better do so quickly, as Miss Williams and her young nephew, David, are panting with anticipation. Miss Williams told me to thank you for the introduction. She has walked past the Furnishes' garden and admired it many times, but never dared to introduce herself."

We entered the dark chapel.

It took a moment for my sight to adjust, and by the time it did, John had picked a lucifer out of a box that was sitting beside the door, then struck it on the stone wall and lit a candle. The light of the candle made the place look welcoming, not as spare as the Unitarian chapel, as there were pictures here and there that I hadn't noticed before. I stared at the one nearest to the door. It was of a ragged boy with a box in his hand. John said, "One of our members, Mr. Lacey, made that a year ago. It isn't so common now, even as it was then, for young fellows on the streets to be selling brimstone matches, or, I might say, making and then selling brimstone matches, but the depiction is a good reminder that they've got to be selling a bit of something in order to eat. That's why I hung it just here."

I said, "The boy's visage is neatly done."

"Mr. Lacey has a good deal of skill in that way. Come look at this one."

We crossed the room to the back corner, to the left of what in another church might be called the altar, and the humble wooden cross that was hung there. John held up the candle. This was a portrait of a Negro child staring over the railing of a ship that was heading into the blue of the ocean. His hands were gripping the railing, and he looked truly terrified. No adults or other children were in the picture, but there was the shadow of a large man falling toward the boy, as if the man was approaching him. Though the boy was not glancing at the man, it was easy to imagine that the journey and the man were equally frightful. There was something charged up about the boy, as if any second he might throw himself over the railing. I stepped back and then stepped forward again, looked at it more closely.

John said, "Mr. Lacey is, I believe, almost seventy. He has a strong memory of when the slavery trade was prominent in this city, and many a man made his fortune shipping slaves to the Caribbean. That he was not shipped out himself, he tells me, was purely a matter of luck."

"He is a Negro man."

"Indeed," said John.

I said, "You are unsound on the goose question."

John chuckled. "Well, true enough, it is not my preferred repast. Have you ever tried pheasant?"

When he said this, I knew I could back away from what I was

about to reveal, but I didn't want to. I said, "The goose question has nothing to do with fowl. It means, in America, how you feel about slavery. If you are sound on the goose question, you . . ." I paused, wanting to state this as honestly as possible. ". . . are willing to advocate for slavery. Or, at least, you deplore and detest those who advocate against it."

"I am certainly an abolitionist."

"A d—ned abolitionist, according to my relatives."

John blanched, and the tip of the candle trembled. Perhaps he had never heard a woman say that word, at least with the sharp American tone I had used. I said, "I believe I have a few things to tell you."

He said, "Come this way. There are several seats that are a bit more comfortable than the others." We crossed the room and sat not far from one of the windows, but the window was as dark as the wall. John set the taper on the sill, then turned his chair a bit toward mine, looked at my face, and took my hand.

The thing I left out was the plan my sisters made to marry me off to anyone they could find, just to be quit of me. I told him how Thomas and I met while I was doing the washing in a tub, how we left for K.T. only a few days later. I told him how K.T. was set up as a battleground by the slaveholders in the government in Washington along with the Border Ruffians, and how the abolitionists were ready and willing to take up the challenge. I told him about Thomas and the Biskets and Jeremiah, and then about Lorna and David B. Graves and my return to Quincy. I confessed that I had had no real feelings about slavery before Thomas came along, which was common in Quincy, and then, gradually, my feelings changed and got hotter. I told him that even now, when I read letters from my sisters about what was happening in America, my hands would tremble and my head would start throbbing. He continued to grasp my hand, nodded sometimes, shook his head sometimes, closed his eyes when I described Thomas's death, took a deep breath and swallowed hard when I described David B. Graves's betrayal of Lorna.

After I was finished talking – and, indeed, perspiring like a waterfall from the experience – he turned his seat directly toward me, took my other hand, and lowered his head. His lips moved, so I understood that he was saying a prayer, and perhaps I should have joined him, but my heart was pounding and my lips were trembling. It seemed to me that a prayer was beyond me. It was also true that I regretted confessing, because, now that we both knew of these events, I could never avoid them again. We would discuss them over and over, and even when we were not discussing them, he would be coming up with his own opinions and feelings about them. He would watch whatever events were set to unfold in America, and they would interest him, and so I would be less and less likely to be able to make them smaller and leave them behind. Looking at him now, I remembered that time when I was satisfied with simply looking at him. Two months ago or a bit more, just when winter was cracking into spring and the Furnishes' garden was turning green. I had known that that simplicity, that purity, of feeling was certain to be fleeting, but, looking at his face, which he had lifted toward me, I remembered it as well as I remembered any moment in my entire life, and as I gazed steadily at him, I gave it away. Was that a sadder moment than the ones I had just related to him? It felt as though it was.

I squeezed his two hands, sighed, and said, "Thank you, John, for listening."

And then we got to our feet, and he took me into his arms, held me close to his warmth, the side of his head pressed against the side of my head, and I felt my own self weaken and nearly collapse into his. We stood like that for a long moment, and then I kissed his hand, turned, and walked out of the chapel.

It was full dark now, still, amazingly to me, Sunday. The streets were quiet; many windows flickered with the candlelight from within. I stumbled a bit: as many times as I had been out after dark, it now felt threatening. I had to slow my footsteps and feel my way on the cobbles. It was, in some ways, an arduous walk. When I arrived at the corner of Catharine Street and Canning Street, I stopped, took my bonnet off, pushed my hair out of my face, and re-pinned it, then set my bonnet on top of it as best I could. I went straight to the back gate of 2 Canning Street, but there was Barnsby, evidently waiting for me. He said, mildly, "Ah, Miss Longbourn. I was beginning to feel a bit of concern. Berta and Jane have cleaned up, but Berta did leave you a portion of shepherd's pie and a biscuit."

While I sat on the bench and ate it, he was by the sink, polishing some silver. He said nothing, stood quietly, paid no attention to me. Bite by bite, I grew calmer. When I was finished, I stood up, took my dish to him. He set it in the tub, and said, "Oh, indeed, I do have something to show you. Please, stand by for a bit."

He went out of the room, returned with a piece of paper, handed it to me. It was from Mr. Denham. In the last week, he had transported Toffee and two of his other runners to Newton-le-Willows, a town up in the hills toward Manchester, and wondered if Mr. Cunningham would like to visit and watch Toffee do a workout. Barnsby said, "He writes nothing of running her in the Gold Cup, but, surely, he is thinking of that. I gather that he does not know of Mr. Cunningham's whereabouts. It is not a long distance from here to the course – something over an hour. I think that fellow who took us to Aintree would be happy to go to Newton, if only to eye the horses that are training there. The Gold Cup is run in July. It can be a prominent race."

I said, "I do long to see Toffee."

Barnsby said, "I feel that tomorrow is a likely day – it should be pleasant. There isn't much of a wind this evening, and what there is, is blowing from the southeast. I think we should seize the day, as it were – indeed, as you must do in the west of England if you enjoy sunshine." He smiled. "Mr. Denham will not know of our coming, but I suggest that we go early, so that we might be there when Toffee is out on the course."

I said, "Can we leave right now?"

Barnsby laughed.

And, no, I did not get a moment's rest over the night, but I spent my time persuading myself that I didn't care if I slept or not. I was up by six, the cab was there by six-thirty. The fellow who had the cab talked amusingly the whole way about how pleased he was to be getting out of the city – he had far too much business and was piling up more shillings than he could stow anywhere, yet he didn't have time to get his barrel-full to any of the banks and trade them in for pound notes. He was beginning to worry that his horse would break down under the burden of hauling all of these coins – certainly, he himself would break down under the burden of carrying them – and yet, if he asked any passenger for a note, that passenger would look him up and down as if he were a thief and run off without paying a thing. Barnsby indicated with his eyebrow that the fellow was intending to amuse us, and he did. He also went with us, once we arrived at the course just after eight, and walked here and there, surveying the horses. We found Mr. Denham and his son, and they seemed pleased to see us.

Toffee was fully filled out now, and well muscled. Mr. Denham's son led her from her stall, tacked up and as red and shining as a sunset. She was calm. Mr. Denham went over and tossed his son into the saddle. He picked up the reins, but then she spied us, tossed her head, and walked right over to where we were standing. The Denham boy seemed to have learned something, if only to control his temper, because he not only allowed it, it seemed to make him smile. Alas, I had nothing in the way of a treat for her, but I did bend down and pull out a tuft of grass. She ate it. I stroked her along the neck, as did Barnsby. Then the boy turned her, and they ambled toward a large flat area that rolled a bit but looked well tended and very pleasant. Evidently, their method of training her, which was to allow her to do as she wished, remained tried and true. What she wished was to walk about (and she was good at staying out of the way of the other horses and their riders), and then she wished to trot about, ears pricked, on a light rein, and then, when she got into the far corner of the field, which I heard people around me refer to as a "commons," she wished to canter. She cantered in a large circle, coming back to where she had first taken up the canter, and then the Denham boy took a tighter grip of the reins, and Toffee stretched into a strong and impressive gallop, one that showed off both how muscled up her haunches were and how sure-footed she was. I said to Barnsby, "It always amazes me that they can go so fast and never look down at their feet."

Barnsby said, "What amazes me about this filly is that I cannot detect her wings."

And, as I compared her to the other horses galloping over the ground, I saw that she did have a lightness to her stride that they did not have. Perhaps it was the long legs: I had noticed that she was maybe half a hand taller than the other horses, now fully grown – indeed, no longer a filly, as she was well into her fifth year.

The Denham boy did nothing with his reins except hold them. After perhaps four furlongs fully stretched out, Toffee came back to the canter, went another two furlongs, I estimated, then passed through a few strides of the trot until she was walking on a long rein, her head down, evidently completely at ease. Mr. Denham walked over to us with a pleased look on his face, and declared, "My boy knows to let her do what she wishes, and what you saw is what she wishes. With any other steed, I would hesitate to push him or her up into that gallop, but if he holds her back, she gets annoyed, so we let her do as she pleases." Barnsby asked nothing about the Gold Cup, and so I said nothing, as well. Barnsby only informed Mr. Denham that the Cunninghams were returning from Bath at the end of June, and he hoped they would be able to see Toffee.

Mr. Denham said that he had not realized they were in Bath. There was no more discussion about what Toffee might do.

On the way back to 2 Canning Street, the cabdriver was in an even better mood, and chatted about the bets he would be placing with all of his shillings, and how the odds on all of the horses he preferred would be very long, and so his plan was to wait until the races at Newton-le-Willows were over and all the punters were gone, and then he would haul his pile of coins to the commons and, in one dark night, shovel up a deep hole, and then he would call it a "mine-shaft" and sell the mining rights to some gullible toff, and insist on being paid in ten-pound notes. I said, "I would be sad to see you give up your cab," and he said, "Ah, miss, Ay would never give that up! How would Ay keep tabs on our citizens if Ay did?"

When we were eating our midday sandwiches, which Berta had made of black sausage, and which I had actually come to enjoy, as well as a cheese she got from a local farm, I realized that Barnsby had succeeded very nicely in steadying and calming me. My conversation with John the evening before now seemed not so dramatic, not even, in some ways, so important. I felt that I had allowed myself to be agitated by the darkness and the flicker of the candle. There should be no difference, I thought, between contemplating vile events and relating them to another person, and in the last two years, I had contemplated them many times, in anger, in sadness, in fear, then pushing them away, being filled with shame and regret. Perhaps, I thought, had I told John of them on a lengthy walk in a park, I would have related them with more sober wisdom than I had in the dark.

Once we finished eating, I performed a few tasks for Berta – rearranging her stock of cooking pots, sweeping the floor of the kitchen – and then I sorted my hair, my gown, and my bonnet and I went out, back to John's chapel, thinking that I would apologize, that my apology would be cool, rational, thoughtful.

John was there, standing at the top of the staircase that ran down the side of the building he lived in, and when he saw me, he shouted, "Aha! How are you?" and skipped down the narrow stairs as agilely as if he were a sprite, not the tall, solid man he was. I was impressed. One of the things I hate about women's dress is the clumsiness of the fabric – forever in your way, the hem getting dirty or wet or frosty, having to be held up so you won't step on it – always a bother when you are, as I often was, carrying parcels with both hands. I also had some difficulty watching Anne prance about upon the stage with petticoats, though she had told me that they do keep the fabric from between her legs, especially if they have a hoop. I had appreciated walking in Thomas's trousers when I was pretending to be Lyman Arquette – maybe that was the most enjoyable thing about it. Watching John descend the second flight made me wonder again in what ways my life would be different if I had been born a male. Then I thought of Frank. At least, I hadn't gotten into as much trouble as he did in K.T., enough trouble, it appeared, to abash him for the rest of his life.

John was a bit more reserved when he approached me. As he squeezed my hand, I put my other arm about his shoulders, and I felt him soften for a bit, then firm up. He said, "Perhaps we should go into the chapel. I have yet more cleaning to do, and at least there is light to do it by."

I followed him, turning over ways to broach my apology. It was that time of day when the bricks were sparkling, and the light in the chapel was clear and welcoming. I said, "John, I did not intend to – please forgive me for – I must say that I – "

He leaned toward me. "Are you tendering some sort of apology?"

I said, "I am."

"It is my belief that you are not responsible for your feelings before you have seen the light – or, rather, before the light has been shown to you. You have walked in darkness. But it is evident that your experiences in that place . . ."

I thought this was an odd way of putting it, but I smiled even so, and said, "Darkness doesn't usually affect me in that way. Sometimes, I am more disturbed by the flicker of the candle than – "

"Before I came to this city, this den of slavers' iniquity, I, too, did not have much of an opinion about the trade. We think most of the time of our own sufferings, and far too little about those of others and about what we might do to correct our world."

I said, "Oh, I wasn't referring to that. I meant – "

But he didn't seem to hear me. He said, "When I first began as a pastor, it was in a Methodist church that you might have seen on your walks among the shops. A large congregation . . ."

I remembered the man John had greeted that time we walked together, who was coming down the steps of a massive church, much concerned with not stumbling and therefore failing to notice John. I said nothing. He went on, "After I had been there about six months, I gave an impassioned sermon about these issues, and who had profited from them, who continued to profit from them, and I suggested that those profits be divided among those who had suffered from that trade. My superior was not offended, but he was concerned, and rightly so, from his point of view. Several of his wealthier congregants came to him and said I must either never speak in that way again or I must leave. Or, indeed, they themselves would leave. They did not expect to come to services for comfort and solace and then to be raked over the coals by an upstart from Belfast. I took my leave that very day, and then found this chapel, where the pastor was in, as I told you, I believe, failing health. Even he had heard of my sermon – it was that widely known. He welcomed me."

Now he grabbed my hand and led me past the sketch of the ragged boy and toward the altar. When we got there, he knelt on a piece of carpet in front of the simple cross, and tugged my hand so that I would kneel beside him. I did; then I glanced at him. His head was bowed and his eyes were closed. His visage was a bit flushed. He prayed to the Lord that we would find a way to spread the word and ease the suffering of enslaved peoples in America and elsewhere, and then he thanked the Lord that the Portuguese had come to their senses, and he hoped that the Dutch would, too. I was mostly silent during this prayer, saying "yes" from time to time, but I doubted whether the Border Ruffians would ever come to their senses, or the slaveholders below the Mason-Dixon Line. Then he thanked the Lord that he had been given me, his predestined helpmate in this all-important endeavor. His cheeks got wet with tears of gratitude, and just seeing those tears brought tears to my eyes, too. I could not resist this man. I edged closer, until our bodies were pressed against one another, and then, at last, I felt him soften. We knelt like that until we heard steps come up behind us. Whoever it was stopped, said, "Pastor," in a low voice. John straightened up and looked around in his customary welcoming manner.

The girl was small but not exactly a child – maybe thirteen or fourteen. Her eyes were wide and her hands were open. She said, also in a low voice, "Mama – " then stopped.

John jumped up. He bent toward the girl and said, kindly, "Emily, do you need me to go with you?"

Emily nodded.

John said, "Does your mama need . . ." But Emily had already turned and walked out the door.

14

On the way out of the chapel, we did stop in the third of the three buildings, which, apparently, John used as a storehouse. He handed me a loaf of bread and some cheeses in a bag. He himself took what looked like a bottle of brandy and some other curatives, as well as a bag of oat porridge. Emily had disappeared, but John evidently knew where she lived. He strode smartly down the street toward Toxteth, and I followed. I saw when we got there that the provisions were for the children, five of them. The youngest, a boy, looked to be about six. Emily was the oldest. The children were completely quiet; the only light in the small house came through one window and the open door, and the mother, emaciated, was stretched out on a narrow bedstead that had been brought into the front room. Her mouth and eyes were wide open, and she was dead. John went straight to her and pulled the coverlid, thin as it was, up to her shoulders. Very gently, he closed her mouth, but it dropped open again.

He took Emily and the girl who looked slightly younger than Emily by the hands, and they each took the hands of one of the other children, and then the six of them knelt beside the mother and prayed. I waited until they were finished. John cocked his head toward the provisions while continuing to comfort the children, though the little boy stood stiff in the corner, unwilling, or, indeed, afraid to approach anyone, even his sisters. I commenced making a large pot of porridge, doing my best to remember what Berta had taught me. John cut up the cheeses and the loaf with the least filthy knife, and one by one the four girls told me their names – Emily, then Mary, then Ruth, then Fannie. Fannie looked to be about seven. She said the boy's name was Alfie. I stirred and stirred. There was, of course, none of Berta's golden sugar to sweeten it up, but the children wolfed it down anyway, along with the cheese. While they were eating, John hurried away to find some of his congregation who would help in preparing, or finding someone to prepare, the body for her burial, and where that would be, I had no idea. It was a busy afternoon and evening. In the end, Miss Williams took Fannie and Alfie to her place, and John allowed Emily, Mary, and Ruth, who was eleven, to bed down in the church.

Given the cholera and the yellow fever that came up the river to Quincy on something of a regular schedule, I did keep my eye on the children for signs that they had gotten some infection, but they all looked healthy, just thin. After they were given coverlids and pillows and settled in the church, after we sang them a few songs and John said a prayer, he told me, without my asking, that the mother, Mrs. Briar, had suffered an apoplectic attack a year ago, and then another, brought on by no one knew what, other than fear and poverty. I said, "Where is Mr. Briar?"

He said, "Everyone has been wondering that for the last two years. He did have a good position as the captain of a merchant ship that sailed back and forth to Canada, as a rule, but in April of '57, the ship returned without him, and his first mate, who had had to take command, declared that no one had any idea of his whereabouts. Who knows if they were telling the truth? He didn't leave many debts behind, but he also didn't leave much in the way of savings. Mrs. Briar was sewing undergarments after he disappeared, and getting by, but then she lost much of the use of her right side. She could walk and see, but she could no longer sew. Emily and

Mary hired themselves out to do day work in a few houses, but they couldn't leave Ruth to take care of Alfie for very long. We helped when we could, and I did ask that fellow I was telling you about, at my old church, for some aid, which he kindly gave me. He tried to talk me into putting Alfie into an orphanage, and Fannie, too. Perhaps I should have done so, but I was very afraid of taking them away from Leonora – that is, Mrs. Briar. I feared it would do her more harm than good."

It was now quite late, and the sun was entirely gone. The air had been still and smoky all day, and I knew Barnsby would be looking out for me and wondering where I was. After I left John and was standing quietly, looking up and down the street, I felt, for the first time since I had been in Liverpool, that desire I used to have frequently in Quincy and K.T., for the smooth, cool feel of the pistol in my pocket. And then John appeared at my side, reading my mind once again, and he took my hand and put one of his walking sticks into it. He kissed me on the cheek and went back up his staircase. I gripped the stick and began my trek, but I saw nothing much to alarm me on my walk home – a man smoking a cigar in the corner between one building and another, who flinched when he saw me coming and looked more afraid of me than I was of him. Off in the distance, down another backstreet, I saw one man punch another and then get punched himself, but I looked away and hurried to 2 Canning Street, where it was as if I had conjured up Barnsby, because he opened the front door even before I rapped it with the handle of John's stick.

In his usual pleasant but formal manner, Barnsby said, "Miss Longbourn. If any other young woman were out and about at this time of night, I might have felt some concern . . ."

I showed him the stick. He said, "Maple. Very well made," took it from me, then helped me out of my wrap. I told him about Mrs. Briar and the children. He said, "Ah. Alfred Briar. I remember the tale. It was said that, on his previous voyage, he went off course toward Iceland, and not because of the winds but, according to the second mate, because of confusion, but he denied it all and insisted on helming the next voyage. As I remember, they docked in Tenerife, and he was gone by daybreak. They lingered, and several of the crew ran about looking for him, but no sign was ever found."

I lamented what might become of the children – I thought of those orphans who were sent to America and put to work on farms – but I said nothing of it, not wishing to suggest anything, even to Barnsby. I sighed. Barnsby went into the kitchen and came out with a cup of creamy warm chocolate, then helped me down to my chamber.

The next day dawned so brilliantly that I awoke at once, and in a much better temper. I knew what I would do. I clothed myself and left before Barnsby was out of his chamber, but I did not arrive at the Furnishes' before Reggie was in the garden – he was already planting something. I didn't ask what it was. I explained about the Briar children, and he handed me a very large basket. We then walked about the garden, picking whatever was edible – berries, carrots, small turnips, potatoes both sweet and white, greens – and I was at John's church when he opened the door. I told him that I had mentioned the children to Reggie, who said that he would send what he could as often as he could.

Here is what happened: The two older girls did go into service, within a day of the funeral. The woman who hired the older girl took her somewhere into the country, and that was the last we heard of her. The woman who hired the younger girl said she would keep her for a time, depending on her behavior – she had been occasionally disrespectful in the past. And a family in John's church – two sisters and their two husbands – took the younger children. Everyone acted as if there was nothing at all strange about this, for, indeed, they had not been to America, and did not know what people even in Quincy, much less in K.T. or Missouri, would have said about a white child's being taken up by a Negro family. The little girl did throw herself into the arms of the sister who claimed her and was warmly embraced. The boy was more wary, as, indeed, very young boys often are. But, as John said to me, the woman who took the boy was the more patient of the sisters, and he expected that she would do well with the boy. Somehow, John detected my surprise, though I devoutly hoped that he didn't understand the source of it. He reassured me – he had great faith in the two sisters. They were experienced mothers (one of them was already a grandmother) and would know how to cope. John was relieved at the outcome, and so I decided to be relieved also.

While this was going on, Barnsby came to me as I was eating my morning meal and asked if I would like to see Toffee again. He smiled before I even reacted, because he knew what my reaction would be.

He said, "The course is a bit of a way, but it is in a lovely spot, and we can go by rail. The races are tomorrow, and the first train is not likely to be crowded."

I said, "What time does it depart?"

"Just past seven. We would get there half noon, watch the races until perhaps four, then return by nine. Yorkshire. North Yorkshire, in fact. A spot like no other, I would say. I haven't gone there in five years or so, but I once went there each year, about this time. I am fond of going north during the solstice. Daylight seems to last forever there."

And when he said that word, "daylight," I thought what a pleasant escape it would be from the darkness of the poor Briar children, and, yes, John's chapel, which even at this time of year hadn't the windows to take in the everlasting light. Of course I agreed. In K.T., the weather at this time of year would have switched back and forth between thick heat and tornado thunderstorms, once again, of course, requiring any sane person to decide which way she might prefer to die – smothered or struck or blown away.

On our trip to the northeast, Barnsby handed me a hat I recognized from Anne's hat rack – black, flat, rather wide brim, two silk roses entwined into the hatband – and showed me a map he had copied by hand from a book. The railcar took us through mist and drizzles and some fresh wind, but mostly through sharp sunlight that made you think, even looking out the dirty window, that you could count the leaves on the trees and follow the path of a red-brown hare as he leapt into the shadows of a woodland. We passed through one city after another – stopping here and there, but only briefly. Manchester, Leeds, but also towns with odder names, like Huddersfield and Rochby. Barnsby would sometimes give me a bit of information about the names – "by" was an old Scandinavian term, from the Viking era, meaning village. "Field" did mean field, in some sense, but had begun as "feld," which meant a broad, open space. Any "chester" town had once been a Roman fortress. At one point, as we were passing a long verdant hill cut into squares by dark-green hedges and dotted with sheep, I said, "You strike me as a curious soul."

Barnsby said, "Perhaps it takes one to know one." We didn't talk for some time after that. Sitting beside him in the car seemed so normal that I didn't think two thoughts about it until I saw a pair of girls, perhaps fifteen, who got on in Rochby, glanced at us over and over, and then put their hands over their mouths to cover their smiles. Only then did it occur to me that one or the other of us, or both of us, were targets of speculation. I looked out the window for a moment, then looked down, checking my boots and the hem of my gown for dirt or blood or . . . I shook my head. Then, surreptitiously, I surveyed Barnsby. He, of course, was perfectly kitted out, his shoes shining in the sunlight, his gloves carefully tucked up his sleeve, his bowler hat resting in his hand, his hair and beard neat and perfectly matched in color – a dark hickory. My hat, of course, was sitting flat across my lap as if I didn't dare touch it. I decided that the girls were wondering how it came to be that this ideal male figure had taken on this rumpled miss. And, since the tops of our heads were even, was I indeed a miss? Or were we some sort of circus act, a man and his own personal clown? I smiled to myself and looked away.

We disembarked at another town with an interesting name—"Thirsk." After I stepped off the train, I paused and stared at the sign on the wall of the depot, and Barnsby said, easy as you please, "There was a similar Viking word indicating a lake somewhere, but the lake nearby is not much." He sniffed. I followed him out of the depot, and he summoned a taxi. This was a long trip, too, over an hour at a good trot, but the air was brisk and the horse was a lively chestnut, putting Toffee into my mind. I had not asked Barnsby why Mr. Denham would have brought Toffee so far north to run—farther north for him than for us, in fact, much farther. But, though the question was on my lips, I said nothing, because Barnsby and the cab man were chatting amiably about the race meet. I knew this because Barnsby was talking about ground and odds and riders and past performances, but I couldn't understand a word the driver was saying. It was not only that the words were different even from the ones I heard about town in Liverpool, but also that there was a halting moment as the words came out, as if, since we were headed to a racecourse, the driver's voice was jumping fences instead of galloping freely out of his lips. Sure enough, after some time, maybe a quarter of an hour or so, Barnsby, whom I had never known to be so talkative, began to mimic, or, perhaps, agree with, the driver's way of talking, so that I could hardly understand him, either.

When we were dropped at the course, the first race was set to run, so I picked up my skirt, and we scurried to where everyone was gathered. When we got there, Barnsby took my hat out of my hand and arranged it slightly askew on my head, not only to block the sun, of course, but also to give me a bit of style. He pressed it down hard. I hoped that it would attach itself to my hair-mess and stay on. The race was not Toffee's, and I did look about to see if I might detect her, or any of the Denhams. When we were relaxing afterward, taking a bit of a walk here and there, Barnsby said, "You must have noticed, Miss Longbourn, that our driver spoke in a perfect West Yorkshire voice. Anyone who travels in England is struck by how the voices diverge. It can be a bit of a challenge, but as my relations live even farther north, it is familiar to me, and I almost cannot prevent myself from dropping into it once I begin to hear it."

I said, "Yessir, Ah know jist what yure gittin' ai-ut. Ahv heard minny a voice in ma day, Ah must say. Here they cum, up the rivuh, and then thar they go, dan the rivuh, an' you kin hardly keep track o' thim."

And, for the first time since I had known Barnsby, he smiled, then burst out laughing, his mouth wide open and his eyes squinting, as amused as a man could be.

Now we went looking for a Denham, and also a bit to eat. We did find a young man selling some cheese sandwiches, and they were good – the cheese was flavorful and slightly different from the English cheeses I had eaten before. Barnsby said, "Ah, a smoked cheddar. Among the many reasons to make the trip. They have a breed of shorthorns up here . . ." And just then, off in the distance, but unmistakable, we saw Toffee, with the Denham boy mounted upon her back, wandering across a hillside, evidently looking for something – chamomile or, let's say, wild thyme – preparing for her race in her usual fashion. Even from a distance, I could tell that she was grown up now – tall, long-legged, but neatly proportioned, well muscled, her neck swooping from her ears to her withers in a nice curve, her tail switching back and forth. I was tempted to run toward her, but I held myself back, desiring once again to be a young boy, dressed in knickers, able to behave as I wished and not as I was expected to.

We circumnavigated the bookmakers and the ladies and gentlemen. I could see why many of the ladies had their lorgnettes in front of their eyes – the course itself was not terribly large, but it was set a ways off from where we might stand, not as accessible as the other courses Barnsby had escorted me to. It might have taken us a while to reach the Denham boy and Toffee, but Toffee saw us, pricked her ears, then whinnied. She turned; the Denham boy let her, and here she came. I bent down and plucked some bits of grass and greeted her with them when she arrived. What a lovely girl, and smart, indeed. After taking the grass, she nuzzled me on the hip, and I gave her a kiss between her nostrils, where a horse's coat is velvety.

Within a few minutes, Mr. Denham appeared, as if out of nowhere, pleasant as always. Barnsby said, immediately, "Good day, sir. Thank you for giving us the opportunity to visit one of my preferred courses."

Mr. Denham said, "Indeed, bringing horses here is a bit of a holiday. We brought three – Toffee, Abscoundrel, and Oolong. Oolong ran third in the first race, and as this is only his second outing, I am much pleased."

I said, "When does Toffee run?"

"As today is Ladies' Day here, they have put the fillies' stakes race off until the end of the day. Toffee will enjoy herself, as the course is rolling and the race is two miles. If she acknowledges the other fillies, I will be surprised. Lately, she has been treating the other runners like saplings in a glen, to be avoided and woven through."

I peered at him. Was he smiling? This comment seemed both resigned and amused, as if he continued to view Toffee as an entertaining puzzle.

He went on. "As this is her first stakes race, I thought the wise thing to do would be to bring her here, a bit out of the way." He and Barnsby smiled at one another, and I saw at once that the plan was not only to give Toffee a pleasant outing, but to keep her away from the gaze of the principal bookmakers. If she were to do well in this effort, then he would try something more prominent, but he wanted the odds on her to remain long. Barnsby evidently agreed with him in this, and it would not have surprised me to learn that

Mr. Cunningham had consigned the oversight of his racehorse to Barnsby.

We followed Mr. Denham back to the stabling area, which was bustling with horses and grooms and riders. He showed us Oolong, dark brown, almost black, with not a white hair anywhere, very sleek and a bit edgy, pawing the dirt in his stall and staring toward the trees nearby. Abscoundrel was a mild-mannered gray who did not seem to be either a scoundrel or an absconder, but, rather, a good eater who made sure every stalk of his hay was eaten, and who made his deposits in the corner of the stall, away from the door. As I looked at him, and I always like grays (but he was too small and dark to remind me of Jeremiah), I thought again how different horses are from one another, and from what we think of them. Mr. Denham was a good trainer, because he had an eye for idiosyncrasy as well as for profit.

It may have been Ladies' Day, and I saw that, here in the north, the ladies dressed as best they could, but they were not tightly corseted, and, while there were plenty of nice bits of lace around the collars and along the edges of the sleeves, it looked as though flounces were much reviled. The best thing about the way the ladies dressed was the flowers – all colors, all sorts, and plenty of them, tucked into their waists and their hatbands and the lapels of the men's jackets. I could understand what the ladies said a bit better than I had understood the cabdriver, but even the wealthy and the apparently educated talked in their own way. I was reminded of Thomas's family in Massachusetts – they, too, spoke differently than we did in Quincy. In other words, I had plenty of time for idle thoughts, and one of mine was about the passage of time. I looked up at the sky over and over, wondering where the sun was and why it didn't seem to be moving at all. Perhaps I was peering to the west for the umpteenth time when Barnsby cocked his head and said, "I am guessing, Miss Longbourn, that you have never been this far north before."

I said, "How far north are we?"

He said, "Were we to include Scotland, then we are just about halfway up our island. For North America, deep into the Canadian provinces. One time, when I was young, I went with my father to look at a piece of property in the Scottish Highlands. He took us, for a lark, by boat to John o'Groats, which he said is the farthest north spot on this island. It was about this time of the year, and there were but two hours of darkness all together." He said this, as he always did, in a neutral, informative way, and I thought of the Furnishes, wondering how far north they had been, if they had ever found what was called the Northwest Passage, what, indeed, might have been the strangest thing they had ever seen. Clearly, I had overlooked the many opportunities I'd had to engage one Furnish or another in some sort of conversation. I made up my mind to repair this omission when we got back to Liverpool.

In the meantime, we did have the opportunity to measure the day by races. Abscoundrel was brought out, tacked up, mounted. Barnsby watched him walk about, stared at his feet as they moved over the turf, then tapped me on the arm so that I would follow him. We made our way to one of the bookmakers, and I saw Barnsby hand the fellow a pound note – a considerable sum, I thought. I put my hand in my pocket and felt my coins and my knotted yarn. When he came back to me, he said that the odds on Abscoundrel were six to one. The longest odds in the race were ten to one. The bookmaker felt that the field would be tight and the race would be close. Abscoundrel was the only gray. As they approached the post, he seemed to stand out, and even twinkle in the sunlight. The horses lined up, Barnsby adjusted his bowler hat, and then he said, "I can hardly see them." Since I am long-sighted, I leaned close and related the race. The tape went down. The horses leapt out, or some of them did. One chestnut was left in the back, two dark horses ran along right in front of that one, and the others, with Abscoundrel clinging to the group like a burr, galloped in a tight bunch. The course wound up a hill and away from us, then went straight across a flat field, curved away again, then curved toward us, down a long and not very steep slope. There was a straight stretch, and then another curve, then a loop past the post. The race was a mile and a half, and the finish line was where the course curved toward us the first time. The officials and some of the bookmakers were gathered there. Because the finish line faced us, we could not see the order in which the horses crossed the line, but Abscoundrel was among them, with two to his left and two to his right. I told Barnsby this, and he rubbed his fingers over his ticket, then readjusted his hat, evidence that he was a bit agitated. How long did it take to learn the results? It seemed like another feature of that endless day. Abscoundrel ran third, as Oolong had, a head behind the second runner, a neck behind the first. Barnsby, always cautious, had spread his bet. He got his pound note back, plus another pound and a half. He put one pound note in the inner pocket of his jacket, and kept the rest of his funds in his hand for a few minutes as we walked about.

Barnsby said that it was now coming five. Our return train to Liverpool was to depart at eight, and that was the last departure of the day. It did occur to me to wonder if we would make it, but Barnsby seemed his normally reserved and composed self. When he returned to the bookmaker, to hand him the pound and a half for Toffee, I touched his elbow, and then, when he looked at me, pulled the coins out of my pocket. Four shillings. The odds on Toffee were fifteen to one. Part of me was offended that the bookmaker thought so little of her, part of me was pleased. Now the wind had picked up. I grabbed the brim of my hat and settled it more securely on the mess of my hair. I saw one woman's bonnet, silky light blue with a wide brim, blow right off her head. Her son, maybe a boy of twelve, laughed and ran to retrieve it. Other women saw it, too, and secured their hats by taking their hatpins out and putting them back in.

Now Toffee and her running mates were out of the stabling area, making their way toward the course. I counted twelve of them. They were all colors and sizes – it looked as though Toffee was the tallest. Two of the bays were nearly as tall, and also well muscled. Barnsby pointed out one of them. "Botany Bay," he said. And she was a bay. "By West Australian." He said, "She's the favorite. The odds are one to three. She had two wins in the spring. As I remember, she's run here before, because her owner lives outside of York." Toffee looked like her indifferent self. Even when one of the other fillies, ears pinned, nearly bumped her, she seemed not to care. She ambled along, tossing her head toward the grass. After a bit, they all picked up the trot.

Some of them were rarin' to go, as they would say in K.T., but not Toffee. She continued to look around, continued to weave here and there, and only at the last minute, when all the others were lining up behind the chalk mark, did she seem to understand where she was and the nature of her task. She at once stepped into her spot. The flag went up, the race began. Of course, two horses shot to the front, a small chestnut and a bay. Two miles is a long race, so the riders didn't push any of them – they seemed to be allowing their mounts to express their own opinions. According to the sheet of entries Barnsby had looked at, Toffee was the youngest of the twelve in the group – the oldest was nine, a nicely developed dark bay named Lurcher, who kept to the outside of the group and had a long stride. The odds on her were even longer than those on Toffee – apparently, she had run in fifty races, won only four. It was as if her owner had decided that, as she preferred horse racing to fox or deer hunting, why not let her do as she pleased? As I thought this, I smiled, and one of the two front-runners dropped back. Toffee was just behind the middle group. The course curved away and then back toward us. Toffee had moved up a bit, still looked relaxed. I related all of my thoughts to Barnsby, my hand on his forearm, my lips to his ear.

They came into the straight stretch, passed the starting spot, and headed up the hill again. The officials began to gather at the starting line, or the finish line – the "post," as they called it. By the time they got to the straight flat stretch again, which was perhaps two furlongs in length, the group was no longer bunched, and all of the horses and their riders seemed to be gathering energy and moving up to a more intensive effort. Toffee was still in the middle, but even from this distance, I could see that her rider was leaning forward a bit, and Toffee's long hind legs were gathering beneath her and pushing her toward the front with every stride. By the time they veered up the hill, she was by herself, in between the four horses vying for the first spot and the group in the back. I looked about. Many lorgnettes were focused on the race, and the crowd was quiet. Barnsby smiled and patted the back of my hand.

They came back down the hill, passed the spot where the post had been in the previous race, turned toward the post for this race. My estimate was that there were three furlongs left. Toffee moved up. One of the four in the first group dropped back. And then it happened – a light bay in the first group, not the one who had dropped back, stumbled and fell, exactly in Toffee's path. The filly lay flat, stretched out, and the rider huddled up against her. Toffee, the only one who couldn't avoid her, simply gathered herself together and leapt over her, as if over a fence or a ditch, apparently unfazed. By now, the rider of the fallen horse had crept forward, and he huddled by her head, perhaps stroking her, at any rate not letting her struggle to her feet until the entire field had gone by. The horses passed the post. Toffee came third. But when the riders had jumped off and the horses were led in front of the crowd of spectators, it was Toffee who got a round of applause. She didn't look fatigued, either. She looked as if she wanted some grass and a bit of a stroll. It was the rider who seemed affected. He was still taking deep breaths and shaking his head a bit. It turned out afterward, when Barnsby took me with him to give some of his winnings to the rider and to thank him for his composure, that the rider had not been afraid for himself, but for the other rider, who was a good friend of his, and, yes, that rider had, evidently, fractured his wrist, but the filly, whose name was Pleasant Dalliance, seemed to be well enough for now. Tragedy averted.

As for me, I was so filled with competing emotions that I had nothing to say, even to Mr. Denham, who was pleased with Toffee's performance, her self-possession, and her failure to win and, if she had done so, shorten the odds for future outings. He did say, "Some of them do prefer jump races," in a good-humored way, but that was all. And then we got the cab back to Thirsk. It is always the things that worry you the most that turn out to be of no consequence.

Barnsby had purchased some sandwiches and some strawberries for our journey home. He seemed pleased with his day out; I estimated that, because the odds were so long on Toffee, he had perhaps doubled his funds. I had another shilling in my pocket, now five. I thought I would donate it to John's fund for whatever it was that he was interested in now. I doubted that I would tell him where I had been all day, but I wasn't sure whether my answer to his inquiry would be a lie of omission or a lie of commission. I decided that I was too tired to figure that out at the moment, and that something would occur to me in the morning, over my . . . I imagined Berta's blueberry muffins – or blackberry, as there were plenty of those on the bushes. The farther we got from the racecourse, the more comfortable I became with what I had seen, the less I pondered the fallen horse, and the more I recalled Toffee's grace, good will, and, as Barnsby would say, "savoir faire" as she popped into the air and then galloped on. The driver of our cab was someone I could actually understand. He asked if we had won anything, said what he thought of the first three races, and that he wished he might have seen the later ones, but a man 'as to earn a living, don't 'e? Barnsby was personable, and agreed that, yes, a man did have to earn a living, but he wasn't talkative – back to his reserved, thoughtful self. We got to the station as the train to Liverpool pulled in, and, without seeming hurried in the least, Barnsby helped me up the step and found our seats.

As we rode on the railcar southwest, the light did change. It did not exactly dim, but it grew bluer, and occasionally, when we were on a downward slope, we could see a shade of pale pink in the distance, not to the west, but to the south, as Barnsby pointed out. We were on the right side of the railcar; I was beside the window, and I would say that simply looking out at the passing countryside, unlike anything I had ever seen before that morning, was a great pleasure, but one that prodded me to wonder whether Mr. Cunningham was going to be quit of me, and if so would I marry John, and if so would I fit into his life as well as I fit into his side when he held me against him in that warm, nonchalant way that he had.

I saw, and then felt, Barnsby's hand on my knee. I turned my head to glance at him, and there was a look on his face that I had never seen before, some hint of fear about it, and the first thing I did was glance out the train window, to see if there was a looming crash. But no, only a long green field and what looked like an apple orchard across a ravine, on another green hillside. Now I looked around the car. The nearest passengers were seated far toward the front. One of them was sleeping. I smiled. I said, "Thank you, Barnsby, for . . ."

And the look of fear on his face intensified, and he said, in a low voice, "Marry me. Marry me."

I looked around to see who he was talking to, as it could not possibly be me. I must have looked shocked, because he took his hand away and turned slightly toward the set of windows across the coach. We stopped at York. We stopped at Leeds. I opened my mouth to ask a question or two, but then maintained my silence. In both towns, as we rolled toward the stations, I could see a few interesting buildings, but each time I closed my mouth again, I thought a thought that I should not have thought, which was that perhaps, in some ways, Barnsby and I were more suited to one another than

John and I were; perhaps, were we married, we could go on just as we were right now, keeping the Cunninghams organized, talking about racing and Toffee and horses and books, laughing between ourselves at this or that, raising the occasional eyebrow, being of service while doing as we pleased. I thought these thoughts, but I simply did not know what in the world Barnsby might see in me, and then I remembered that time I asked him if he had ever been in love and he said, "Hasn't everyone?"

At the time, I had noticed what he said, then thought of the graveyard near 2 Canning Street, wondered if he had lost his love to an epidemic, but what I remembered now was that he went back to sorting the silver, as if my question meant nothing. Now, beside me, he was sitting in a perfectly upright position, his hat in his hand, his gaze shifting from one side of the car to the other, but never to me. At last, as the train pulled out of the Leeds station and the sun disappeared behind a tall building, I said "I – " and Barnsby said, in a low, insistent voice, "If you please, don't give me a reply." And so I did not let anything come out, even though I would have been as interested to hear it as I'd thought he was. But he didn't want to hear it. Perhaps that was more interesting.

Several passengers got on in Leeds, some of them loud and evidently staggering a bit. Two of them looked me up and down, looked Barnsby up and down, sat across from him. He fingered his stick. In the time it took us to get back to Liverpool, not quite two hours, and nothing to see out the windows but stars and darkness in the trees, a few houses with a light flickering in a window, I saw him reassemble himself piece by piece. When we disembarked from the train in Liverpool, he was brisk and normal, helping me down the steps, his facial expression pleasant and unrevealing, his smile unreadable. It was now truly dark. He was hailing a cab. I said, "What time do you think it is?" He glanced around, then said, "Half ten, perhaps. Nearly eleven." The cab pulled up, and the driver, as it turned out, was the same fellow who had taken us to Newton-le-Willows, for the outing Toffee had had there, and as soon as he saw us, he recognized Barnsby, and they fell into a lively conversation about Toffee and her adventure. The cabdriver remembered her well, congratulated Barnsby on his winnings, and regaled a story of his own: Just before picking us up, he had brought two fellows to the station from Wavertree, but he suspected that they had come there from farther away, perhaps Childwall, as they seemed fatigued and hadn't much in the way of funds, though they managed to put together enough to pay him. They were carrying a large wicker basket, which at first he didn't notice, but then he heard shuffling, and one of the fellows threw his coat over it. They kept on, saying they hoped not to miss their train to – and then, apparently, they couldn't decide where it was to, but the driver didn't stop, as their final destination was, he thought, a matter that should not concern him. "They were sixteen, thereabouts, old enough. I me-self was on me own when I was of that age." More shuffling, then a squeak, and then a piglet wiggled out from under the coat. "A Tamworth, 'twas. And a bright ginger, too, 'bout as big as a loaf o' bread, and one o' the boys grabbed it. Well, they were fearful o' me snatching it, I s'pose, because they pushed it back inta the basket, tossed me the fare, and jumped out o' the carriage before Rex here even came to a halt. Indade, lookin' into that little fella's eye did give me a pause about my next bit of bacon, I must say." He laughed. His story passed the time, gave Barnsby something to nod about, chuckle about, and a reason to ignore me, though he did help me out of the carriage with what seemed to be an unusual degree of thoughtfulness.

By the time I got down to my chamber, it was past midnight, and it was all I could do to get myself out of my gown, much less hang it up or do something with my hair, though I did carefully set the hat he had given me on the table. And then I fell into bed, and into a deep sleep.

15

I MIGHT HAVE SAID, back in Quincy, that I was up and out at the crack of dawn, partly because I could not be still and partly to evade Barnsby, but there was no crack of dawn the next day, as the sun was well up, though hidden behind the fog and the mist, and the horns from the docks were bellowing so often that I hardly noticed them. I left by the back entrance, wrapped in my shawl. As the mewses and the closes were busy, but the streets weren't, it was certainly before ten, perhaps before nine. I walked fast, to evade my thoughts.

Reggie, of course, was standing in his garden, looking down at something, a trowel in one hand and a hoe in the other. The garden surrounded him, brimming, or perhaps frothing, with flowers of all colors – red, white, pink, blue, purple, short and tall, nested in brilliant shades of green, overhung by branches of leaves – and, perhaps because he was still, he was also surrounded by birds, swooping here and there, cheeping, peeping, arguing among themselves, returning to their nests, and then flying into the luminous gray sky. I put my hand on the gate latch, and he saw me, tossed his head back with a welcoming smile. I unlatched the gate and walked in, careful to latch it again. I went over to him. He was staring at a tortoise that was making its way across the herb garden. It paused beside the thyme. I said, "Is it smelling the thyme, do you think?"

Reggie said, "Why not? 'Ow else would ya pass the hours for a 'undred years?" At the sound of our voices, the tortoise retracted into its shell, and Reggie carefully picked it up and carried it to a more remote part of the garden, among the blackberry bushes. Then he went to the patch of fruit trees, looked up at them. One of them looked a bit sickly, and so, when I wandered in his direction, I asked what it was. He said it was an apricot tree, something of a mystery. One of the Furnishes had brought him some pits from Morocco. He had planted four of the pits in pots and transplanted two into the garden, but one had died, and this one wasn't growing, though it was in the sunniest spot. Then he led me past the plum trees and the apple trees (full of tiny fruit) to a patch of gooseberry plants, red and green, that were tall and in some ways unkempt. "Close ta ripenin'," said Reggie. "Looks ta be a good saison. Plenty o' jam f'r the winter. Pie, too. That's me favorite, red gooseberry pie." He smiled. I liked gooseberry pie, too, something I had never heard of in Quincy. I hoped he would go on and on about the plants, but the next thing he said was that he had taken a goodly basket of root vegetables, principally turnips and swedes, over to John the day before and spent a bit of time, too, tending that garden and showing some of the members of John's congregation how to aerate the soil and apply bits of fertilizer. "They seem ta be takin' an int'rest in it." He looked pleased with himself, then went back to what he had been doing before I appeared.

Just now, a little girl ran past us, toward the blackberry bushes. An ugly little girl of about four, or, as Barnsby would say, "Not prepossessing." She looked to be shortsighted, which was, perhaps, the reason she didn't seem to notice us. She was only partially dressed – no socks, no frock, some knickers, and a wrinkled shirt. Perhaps it was indeed early, and she had only just gotten up. She went straight to the blackberry patch, and began plucking what berries she could reach, and then I heard her mother, or, at least, one of the Furnishes, call out "Mabel! Mabel! Where are you? For heaven's sake!" I might have done something, but the woman, evidently the mother, appeared, grabbed the girl, and dragged her back toward the house. She didn't seem to see us, either, and, indeed, Reggie was still as he could be. He said, "I did nab 'er yesterday, but the kicking and the screaming nearly knocked me off me 'ead." He went back to his work, and I made my way past the orchard and out the back gate.

Now there were more people walking the streets, carrying baskets and sticks, stopping here and there to have a word. I remembered that Anne and the Cunninghams were due back from Bath in three days, and I was surprised, I must say, at how that memory perked me up, instantly brought Anne's face into my mind. I would be glad to see her! What a thought that was! All these years, I had known what a kind and lovely girl she was, and in the last few, I had seen depths of talent and perception that no one had ever given her credit for. What else? Why, that she had opinions of her own about life, and relatives, and marriage, and political issues. I sped up a little, as if that would make time pass more quickly and cause her to return sooner. Once I thought of Anne, everything else fell back into place, and my experience of the day before returned to the many hours spent looking out the window of the train, then to talking with Mr. Denham, watching Toffee be herself, how amusing that was, and because the horse that fell had suffered no injury, I could reimagine her jumping over it many times, with the green slope and the blue sky behind her, and the halted bustle of the people around me as we all held our breath to see what might happen. Inside those hours, the moments where Barnsby revealed the unimaginable fell into a small place – regrettable, forgettable, as he would certainly return to his usual self, which, I now saw, was based on appearances, and why shouldn't it be, as that was his principal task – maintaining the appearance of the house, the Cunninghams, the social propriety of the family? This was something no one I knew back in Quincy or K.T. cared about, and look what the results of that were – endless threats and fights and grudges, and now, I was certain, some sort of looming conflict. Better to be here, where, yes, a man was occasionally tossed out of a saloon, but –

A few broughams and other carriages came along the road, one pulled by a pair of grays that caught my eye. I was making my way toward the shopping area. I did have some shillings in my pocket, and I thought that if I bought something good at the fishmonger's, Berta would be glad to have it, and would cook it up for supper. And nothing wrong with a tart, either. And there was John.

He was on the other side of the street, Grove Street. He didn't see me, though he was coming in my direction. He seemed to be chatting with someone, a tall fellow in a top hat, so thin that I could see sunlight between his upper legs. I would have thought him emaciated or impoverished, but he had one of those carefully groomed thick mustaches that curl to points. I smiled to myself, and stepped aside for a woman with flounces. I looked again at John's face, pleased to be long-sighted. Whatever they were discussing, it was not making John happy. His eyebrows were lowered, and just then he shook his head. I was getting closer, but even so, with the carriages and the bustling crowd (surely it was close to midday by now), it was likely that he would not see me, and I made up my mind to do nothing to attract his attention. I watched. He scowled. He stopped, grabbed the elbow of the other man, who shook him off and quickened his step. As I did mine. This was a John Hegarty that I hadn't seen before. We passed each other; I looked back one time, and saw the other fellow turn off and go up a set of stairs and into a building.

If Thomas had a temper, I never saw it. He could be indignant, of course, and he was, whenever the Border Ruffians committed some outrage, but all through our unexpected and irritating adventures up the Missouri River, he was never angry, and often amused. I have noticed that about people, especially Americans – a surprise might frighten anyone, but after that, it would be followed by amusement or annoyance, and even, for a few, rage. Harriet often said (since she was the one who was most likely, at Lorton and Silk, to encounter annoyance or rage) that it was drink that did it, but what to do about drink was a question that no one could answer. When I visited Thomas's relations in Medford, I saw that they were much like him – reserved and brimming with self-control, but also carrying their consciences and their indignation at the behavior of others about with them at all times. I stayed with them for several weeks, and I did, eventually, become uncomfortable. I felt no sense that they disliked me, but I did have the sense that some of them wondered what Thomas had seen in me. There was not a peep about any earlier love interest Thomas might have had, but, the longer I stayed there, the more I suspected that I was being retrained, and when I went back to Quincy, I felt a sensation that I was, at least a bit, fleeing Massachusetts, and not only because of the weather.

Now I imagined that young woman who had parted with John and married the well-endowed baron or duke or whatever he was. I wondered if perhaps making her fortune was not the only issue. Indeed, the unfortunate thing about eavesdropping is that you cannot often find the people you eavesdropped upon and request further information.

When I got back to Canning Street (and, yes, I did have a nice slab of swordfish with me), Berta, Jane, and Barnsby were enjoying their midday meal. Without my even asking, Berta took a plate from the cupboard and dished some up for me – she had made what they called "Cornish pasties" and she had also made a carrot soup. Both looked delicious. When I sat down, Barnsby gave me his usual smile, kind but reserved. They resumed their discussion of the Cunninghams' return: Were the rooms in perfect order? Might the windows need a bit of washing? What should be served on their first night home? Something festive, but not overwhelming, as they would quickly be off to bed – you never knew how taxing that sort of trip might be. " 'Ow far is it?" said Jane.

"Almost two hundred miles, I would say," said Barnsby. "I have wondered from time to time if the health benefits of the stay are offset by the filth of the journey. Not my favorite rail line." I listened closely to his voice, and looked at his face when I could, and I was relieved. He seemed to have put that proposal behind himself with an excellent degree of success.

All Jane said was "Two 'undred miles!" as if she could not imagine such a thing. It was at least twice that from Quincy to St. Louis and then up the river to Lawrence, and that aggravating and pointless journey had taken Thomas and me days. I agreed with Jane. Why would you bother? Then I wanted to ask how far we were from the Ripon racecourse, but I kept my mouth shut and continued to work on my pasty. I glanced at Barnsby. To me, he looked like his usual self. He was well dressed and personable. He did not seem fatigued or unhappy. I felt a bit relieved until he left the table, set his plate beside the washbasin, and walked out of the room. As soon as he closed the door, Berta said, " 'E looks some'at down to me."

Jane nodded, and said, " 'E sounded amused when 'e told us that bit about Toffee, but I've got ta say that 'e 'as more feelin's in 'im than 'e's willin' to admit to."

Berta nodded. She said, "Remember when the doctor said that that dog 'ad to be sent away? What was her name? Poppy. No matter 'ow much I cleaned up after 'er, still Evelina kept coughing and 'acking from the 'air and whatever else." She turned to me. "It was 'er dog. A black-and-brown spaniel, it was. She was sad to see it go, but Barnsby was the one 'oo wept."

I said, "Barnsby wept?"

"Aye," said Berta. "I caught 'im goin' at it in the pantry. 'E was the one 'oo trained the little beast, and of course 'e did a lovely job."

I said, "Did Evelina get better?"

"A bit, I will say." She sighed, and then said, "I am 'opin' she's thrived from this visit to Bath. If there's a place I'd like t' see, that is it."

I said, "Why is that?"

"Well, ya know that that is where the Romans built themselves a spot, and just for th' baths. They sy the salty water does aw'y with all yer ikes and pines, and, th'n, I am sure that the shops are somethin' t' see, as well."

She got up, went over to a little shelf where she kept her own things, and picked up a piece of paper. She came back and handed it to me, and said, " 'Ere's a nice walk for ya, 'elen, t'day or t'morrow, either is fine. Just a few things for when everyone gets back. Mrs. Cunningham will be after 'er oatmeal first thing, and she can tell if it's fresh. And she'll be wantin' some of that golden sugar to be sprinkled over the top. She likes that."

It was a goodly list, which pleased me no end. I gave her a little kiss on the cheek as I walked out of the room.

Well, it was evident to me, after my walk and my midday meal, that I had thought I knew John and Barnsby, but that I did not. I knew what they looked like – John, handsome and charming; Barnsby, meticulous and self-possessed. I had always considered myself an observant person – if there was a spider on the wall or a man with a threatening visage in the distance, I would be the first to see one or the other. When those Border Ruffians came out of the brush and shot Thomas and Jeremiah, I sensed their presence before Thomas did, and was in no way surprised, though I was shocked. Why did Annie bring me along if not to sense danger and protect her with my pistol or my stick?

I went to my chamber, took my pitcher of water from beneath the table, and poured some of it into the basin. I pushed back my hair and washed my face. It was then that I thought of my mother, Alice, Harriet, and Mrs. Cunningham. I, of course, did not know Thomas when we got ourselves wed and then on the boat to St. Louis. That I did not know him and he did not know me caused no comment at the time – he had a mission, we were in a hurry, and, really, I do believe that the standard view in Quincy, and maybe here, also, was that if a young man and a young woman were actually to know one another before they agreed to marry, then no one would ever get married. No doubt my mother, Alice, Harriet, Mrs. Cunningham would nod their heads and say that it is in the nature of marriage that you are to put up with whoever the fellow turns out to be, to hope for a bit of luck, and to give thanks because it might always have been worse – you might have ended up on your own relatives' hands until the day you died.

And then I recollected that John had not, in fact, asked me to marry him, unless referring to me as his "helpmate" in fighting slavery qualified as a proposal. He had taken my hand many times, most passionately across that hedge along Gambier Street, but the words themselves had never crossed his lips, and then I was more confused even than I had been. I looked forward again to Anne's return, and for the first time in my life, I made up my mind to ask her advice.

I was standing in the front hall, letting these thoughts roll around in my head, when Berta emerged from the dining room and said, "Ah, 'elen. With all that talk, I forgot ta make my request. There is a 'atmaker 'oo's bin making a new top 'at for Mr. Cunnin'ham, and 'e's bin at it for a while, I must say. At any rite, 'e sent round a boy 'oo said that the 'at is finally ready. 'Ere's the funds in this envelope. The address is on the front side." Normally, it would have been Barnsby who would send me on this sort of errand. She looked out the window. "Indeed, it might drizzle or worse. Don't forget yer umbrella."

The walk was about a mile – not right into town but a little to the east. I turned down Rodney Street, letting the umbrella swing on my arm. The streets were not terribly crowded, and I began to enjoy my walk – always the best way to regain one's balance, I thought. As happens in Liverpool, Rodney Street turned into Clarence Street, and then into Russell Street. I was wondering why this was, and also whom I might ask other than Barnsby, when a young fellow leapt out in front of me and shoved a paper in my hand. I took it without thinking, just as he expected me to, and looked about. There was a building nearby with a cross placed in the window. It did not look like a church, but many types of buildings housed many types of congregations. I might have tossed it, but when I glanced down at it, I saw "anti-slavery," and wondered if John had had something to do with it. I paused at the corner of Russell Street (where it turned into yet another street, Seymour), and began to read it. The group who had authored the tract called themselves "Wesleyans"; those were Methodists, according to people I knew in Quincy, and, as I remembered, the stricter believers. I hardly knew a thing about it, as I never paid attention in church, but there was something they believed in called "original sin," and somehow, no matter how hard you tried, you could not evade it. You were born with it and died with it. Perhaps the Border Ruffians were all Wesleyans who had decided that, if they could never get out from under the sins they were born with, best just to keep at them.

But these people were not Border Ruffians. They were much against slavery, and the tract the boy had handed me was saying that there were fifteen thousand slave owners in the United States who belonged to their anti-slavery religion and owned one hundred thousand slaves – no doubt an understatement, I thought. And I also thought, as I looked about for some sort of trash bin I might toss the paper into: Say whatever you please, they will not listen. If, as the tract proposed, congregations in England and Canada and Scotland and wherever else were to denounce and exclude them, they would consider themselves flattered and buy some more slaves. Did John, or whoever it was who wrote this tract, actually have any hope? I laughed, and then, for a moment, marveled at my own lack of hope. Nevertheless, rather than tossing the paper, I smoothed it, folded it, and put it into my pocket.

The rain continued to hold off. I found the hatmaker, and as soon as I announced myself, he leapt to his feet. When he brought out the top hat, he seemed quite proud of it. The brim was narrower than I had seen before, and the crown somewhat taller. It was as shiny as a mirror. I could see why the hatmaker was proud of it, but, in fact, I could not see why Mr. Cunningham would want it, though he was intent on staying at the front edge of fashion. I handed the man the envelope, and he set the hat very gently into a cylindrical box with a lid and a silk handle. He looked deeply into my eyes, as if to say, Do not damage my masterpiece! I nodded and walked out.

The trip back to Canning Street was slower, because there were more people out and about, and more horses to look at. Even so, I was home soon. I knocked on the front door, and no one answered. I went around to the back, and Berta came when I rapped on that one. She took the box out of my hand very carefully, as if it were a box of eggs, and carried it into the front hall. When she came back, she was shaking her head. She said, "Well, it seems 'e 'as a bit of a fever, as 'e is tossing about in 'is bed and asked me for water. I did put my 'and on his fore'ead, and I felt nothing, but I an't going to contradict 'im. We want no fevers about the place when Evelina returns. If 'e isn't better in the morning, I will send ye out to post a telegram t' Mr. C." I knew she was talking about Barnsby.

I nodded. And I didn't know what to think. I did ask if there was anything I might do to help him. I was thinking of a doctor I could go for, or some remedies from Reggie's garden, but Berta was already shaking her head. She said, " 'E an't got no faith in anything but stickin' it out. I niver saw 'im do so much as tike a cup o' chamomile tea, which is what I do when I feel down. You might ask 'im, but 'e will jest look away." She returned to the kitchen. I laid the back of my hand over my own head and looked down at my shoes. My head was cool. I felt utterly fine. I went out into the garden, then made up my mind, at last, to find John. A breeze had picked up, blowing the clouds back out toward the ocean, so I propped the umbrella against the wall of the house, right beside the door, where, I hoped, it would catch my eye upon my return. I didn't know what my plan was, but I trusted that walking toward John's chapel would provide one.

John was nowhere to be seen. The two buildings at this time of day were dark, almost black, and rather imposing. I walked along the edge of the little garden. I would not say that it was thriving, but it was doing well enough, considering the lack of sunshine. The soil was now dense and malleable (I rubbed some of it between my fingers), and there were some blooming flowers; the ones that were the prettiest were small purple blossoms clustered at the top of a stem. There were also plenty of ferns, and some white hortensia that Reggie had told me one of the Furnishes had brought him from somewhere far to the east. There were a few infant rosebushes doing their best in the sunniest corner, and I could see that Reggie, or someone, was tending them assiduously. John's voice said, "I did see you."

I spun around. He was smiling in his merry way, and then let out a laugh. "I could see that you saw me, and also that you were trying not to be seen. I must say, that was a good thing, because that fellow Cummins was calling out the worst in me, and it was all I could do not to give him a pop across the nose. Sometimes the Belfast in a man does surface."

I said, "I might have paused at the corner and waited for you."

He shook his head. "It took me till my midday meal to settle my temper. Isn't it the truth that the fellows who arouse the worst in you are those that you mostly agree with? But when they can't be won over concerning some issue, it's like a thorn in your back that you can't get rid of. You can't reach it and pull it out, and no one else can see it, so you are pricked and pricked and pricked." He shook his head, reached for my hand, and led me down the path toward the chapel. After a moment, I said, "Might I ask what the issue is?" We were at the foot of the steps.

He said, "Reparations."

"What are those?"

"Funds that the former slave-dealers, or their families, should repay to the former slaves. I will say that even the members of my congregation are divided about the issue. Those who are kind and hopeful suppose that the payments would square the bill and then the issue could be set aside, and those who are suspicious say that the ones who would have to pay would resent them even more."

I said, "You mean those who are realistic in their views."

He glanced at me, then said, "That is precisely what Cummins said."

I said, "Please, don't get angry with me."

And then we gazed at one another for a long moment. He was smiling, but I did see a new expression – annoyance – flicker over his brow. He said, a bit stiffly, "I was not angry with Cummins, and I am not angry with you. What is the word? Ah. I am frustrated, that's all. I understand that, where you come from, this issue of slavery has gone on for such a long time that each side must cling fast to its opinions. That is the nature of original sin, and whatever we might do to combat it, in our lifelong struggles, the results are, let us say, mixed."

I said, "Original sin?" just to see how he might respond, and he turned and sat down upon the highest step. I sat myself beside him. He did not exactly explain. What he did was sigh, and say, "A boy who grew up in Belfast must think about this perhaps forever. Every Christian knows what sin is, but no one agrees about how to contest it. My relatives in Drogheda, who are Papists – and I do have a few of those – say that our ancestors were drawn away from the true religion, and now they have returned to it. They would aver that confession, absolution, beginning again, kneeling before the altar, does the deed. Even if it erases only the most recent sins, they are erased, and one is moved to improve oneself. My relatives in Maghera, who are stricter in their beliefs than I am, would say that Satan himself walks behind them every step of the way, and they must be wary of what he might be guiding their hand or their steps toward. Do you know this fellow James Hogg?"

I shook my head.

He said, "He was a Scottish writer. My uncle knew him a bit. I was perhaps four or five when he passed, but there was a book of his in our bookcase, *The Private Memoirs and Confessions of a Justified Sinner,* or something on that order. I read it long before I would have been allowed to do so: I pushed it under my bed and only read it when I was alone. I saw at once that believing in original sin is more dangerous than believing in penance, even in penance that comes from your buying your way out of your transgressions, if you are wealthy." His eyebrows lifted.

I said, "What in the world is a justified sinner?"

"Ah. If God is all-knowing, then He knows who goes to Heaven and who goes to Hell from day one, as it were. Where you are to go is only a mystery to you. Ideally, you find out by behaving as well as you can – "

I interrupted. "Then virtue has no point."

He said, "There is that argument. But it is not one I would make."

It was a congenial discussion, and revealing, too. I had heard those expressions, though not from Thomas and not from my relatives. Roland and Harriet and Alice knew better than to make any attempts to convert one another, and they were wise in that. But that flicker of annoyance I had seen remained in my mind, not because I resented it, or even that it surprised me – what surprised me was that I had never seen anything like that in him before. John, after all, had an expressive face. If he was amused, he would smile or laugh; if he was concerned, his eyes would open and his eyebrows rise; his skin was pale, and often flushed red. I had never thought before how this contrasted to Thomas, who did smile, and occasionally laughed, and did speak about most issues, not only slavery, with sincere honesty, but, many times, his face went blank. If I annoyed him, if I pleased him, even if, upon occasion, I aroused him, his first response was to hide it, or, perhaps I should say, to keep it to himself. This was a quality I had appreciated, given that no one in my family kept anything to himself or to herself, and all over Quincy and in K.T., rage was on display.

We sat quietly for a moment; then I said, "Is there anything I can help you with in the chapel?"

He shook his head. "All cleaned up."

"Spick and span."

"As close as we could get."

"I should go back to the Cunninghams', then. It appears that Barnsby has come down with something. Is there anything going around? Do you have the yellow fever here? That came up the Mississippi to Quincy from time to time."

"Not recently that I've heard of. Some years ago, just before I arrived here, a ship set out for the South Seas full of Scots heading to Victoria, I think it was, because we had stopped sending the convict ships and the Scots needed the work." He shook his head. "Some of them were afflicted with typhoid fever, and a good many of them died on board, or so it was said."

"He doesn't seem to have a fever."

John said, "That may be a good sign."

We stood up. He patted my hand and walked me to the street. The light was still bright, and, as it had been a long day, I wondered what Berta might be offering for our evening meal.

I did retrieve my umbrella from beside the door, then carried it through the back of the house to the umbrella stand in the front hall. Everything was clean and quiet, frighteningly so. I walked about the rooms in the silence. All the windows were closed, most of the drapes drawn. I shivered. When I went back into the kitchen, Berta was there, and Jane came in. We sat down to a decent meal, mostly remnants of previous ones, but that was usual on a Thursday, because, if the Cunninghams were at home, they would be hosting parties on Friday or Saturday. Our remnants included bits of the swordfish, some decent potatoes, heated-up scones, and a piece of venison. I did ask how Barnsby was, and both Jane and Berta shook their heads. Jane said, " 'Ow are we t' know, but by list'nin' at the door? 'E 'as 'is crotchets."

I helped Berta with the dishware, and then went out into the garden. Now it was getting gloomy, a combination of dusk, clouds, and leaves. I stood not far from the window to Barnsby's chamber, which was closed, and thought of breaking it. If there was anything my sisters had insisted upon in Quincy, when someone was ill, it was fresh air, and the air was fresh – no fog or coal smog, hardly even any bellows from the docks. But if anyone understood the pleasure of refusing to do as one was told, it was Lidie Newton. I went to my own chamber, pulled out a book – one of those Trollope books – and tried to read. For once, I wished I was adept with my hands, so that I might lull myself to sleep by knitting or tatting or even sewing a seam. At last, the darkness fell, and I took off my frock, put on my nightdress, opened the window, got myself into bed. But there I lay and there I lay, and it got darker, darker, darker, and then some raindrops hit the window, and I rose and closed it, and after that, I crept out of my chamber, down the hall, up a few steps, and, without even knocking, I opened the door and went into Barnsby's chamber.

The first thing he said was, "Miss Longbourn, do not expose yourself."

I said, "Believe me, Mr. Barnsby, given where I grew up, I have been exposed to and survived just about every ailment there is." I went over to his bedside and knelt beside him. He looked away. My sight was well adjusted to the darkness of the room, and I saw that even in distress he was entirely organized – his coverlid pulled up to his chin, his arms straight against his torso. Even his hair was neat. There was a small jug of water on the table beside the bed.

He said, "That is not what I was alluding to. I have not come down with an illness, unless that is what you might term a bout of melancholia."

His head turned in my direction. I didn't know what to say, but, as always, he seemed to read my thoughts. He said, "You must not blame yourself, my dear. This is not my first episode by any means. I have kept a record. The first one came on twenty-two years ago, when I was seventeen. There was a fellow in London who put on frightening costumes and ran about town, surprising and abusing young women. They called him Spring-Heeled Jack, and he was thought to be a specter. It was in all the papers, as gory as the paper sellers could make it. My friends and I were fascinated by him, but then I began to think of him too often, and took to my bed. We did not live in London – were far away, indeed – but we also didn't know the fellow was a prankster. I truly believed he was a specter, and therefore might pop up anywhere. My mother was beside herself, and my father wanted to whip it out of me, but as spring came round, my melancholy eased, and I got back to myself. When it hit again, in the summer of 1841, and not for any particular reason that I understood, I gave myself a curative routine – to simply play host to the melancholy, to every fear and every sorrow, until they became too tedious to put up with." He smiled just the merest, I thought, ghost of a smile. Then he was serious again, and said, "It occurred to me, just after I expressed my wish to you in the railcar, that – and I don't know precisely how to say this – that it was the melancholy side of me speaking, that you are so tall and brisk and inquisitive, that you habitually have such a – how shall I describe it? – agreeably contentious look on your face, that I was seeking some salvation from the melancholy that has been creeping over me for the past few weeks."

I opened my mouth; he put his hand on mine; I closed my mouth. He said, "That is why I pleaded with you that you not answer me. Not because you might be uncertain, but because, I must admit,

I am uncertain." Now he stared at me and said, "My dear, there is nothing about you that I dislike, but there is plenty I dislike about myself, and I would not want to burden you with those aspects of my being."

And so, of course, now, kneeling beside him, his hand on mine, my eyes upon his thoughtful visage, my ears attuned to the cool, melodious quality of his voice, my memory full of all the things we had done together, all the amusements we had shared, all the things he had done for me since the first moment he opened the Cunninghams' front door and welcomed me into the house, I liked him better than ever. He squeezed my hand and I stood up, slipped through the door and back to my chamber. I was, in spite of the long day, wide awake. I took my taper to the kitchen, lit it on one of the coals still glowing in Berta's oven, carried it back to my chamber, and then pulled that Trollope book out again and began to read it. But it was of no use, at least for putting me into a sleepy frame of mind, as there were many characters in the book who also could not make up their minds what to think or how to act. I decided that this must be a feature of being English, and, having seen many a Border Ruffian, I admired them for it. It seemed to me that my countrymen had been busy over the years acting on impulse and then refusing absolutely to regret or apologize for whatever it was they had done, and now the evidence in the reports in the papers was that they were about to do it again.

When I finally laid the book aside and then blew out my taper, the sky was just beginning to lighten, and I slept far into the morning. Neither Berta nor Jane awakened me, so I understood that no telegram needed to be sent to the Cunninghams. When I did arise, I went to Berta and asked her how Barnsby seemed. She said, "'E's better. Still no fever. 'E says 'e'll be up and about by the time they return t'morra, and I must say, what else is there t' do but get the provisions for a light supper? Jane 'as kept the place — "

I said, "Spick and span."

Berta smiled and said, "Indeed. One of a kind, 'at girl. There was a time, two years ago, when Mr. Cunningham offered 'er a role in some production, a singin' role, which won't surprise you, but she turned it down flat, said she'd rather clean."

I said, "And I would rather fetch."

"Well, miss, ye can pick up the items on the list I gave you yesterday, and add a few. The first thought I 'ad when my eyes popped open was 'duck,' and that is what it'll be. And a goodly loaf of bread is already on the rise."

I said, "I thought they weren't coming home until tomorrow?"

"They are! But the longer that dough rises and the more you pound it, the tastier it is."

And I believed her.

Anne and the Cunninghams did not seem terribly exhausted when they arrived the next afternoon – even Evelina seemed perky and happy to be home when Barnsby, not quite his usual self but almost, held the door for them. I thought I was to accompany Evelina to her chamber, to help her with her traveling clothes, but Mrs. Cunningham lifted her eyebrow, and I retreated. I followed Anne to her chamber. She was voluble about the trip, by rail. She said, "I am so glad that we didn't do what I thought we were going to do, which was come back by boat. Mrs. Cunningham was fit to be tied when it turned out there were not enough tickets for the four of us. There were only two to be had, so at first she thought she would accompany Evelina, but then she got nervous about who else might be on the boat, so she thought Mr. Cunningham should be the one, but I could tell, as she talked about that, just by the way she glanced at me, that she preferred four hours on a train with yours truly! My goodness! So we all took the railcar, and the views out the window were beyond beautiful, not like anything I've seen before." She took a deep breath and plopped down on her bed.

I said, "Evelina seems well enough."

"She does, doesn't she? She thinks so, as well, and two or three times she did go off by herself without saying a word."

"Except to you."

Anne bit her lip, then said, "I knew she was safe and not by herself, if that's what you mean."

"Who was she with?"

"Another girl, slightly older, and her brother. All they wished to do was get away from their overseers once in a while. Evelina said they were from York."

I said, "We passed through York when we went to Toffee's latest race." And then I sat down beside her while she removed her boots, and told her of the incident. She displayed sufficient interest, though horses had never meant much to her, and then she threw her arms around me and said, "My goodness me, Lidie, I am so glad to see you!"

I embraced her, too, and we sat there quietly for some minutes, enjoying one another, until there was a knock at Anne's door, and Jane said that our meal was ready.

After the meal, it was as Berta had predicted – the tiresomeness of the journey came over Anne and the others, and they began to sigh and yawn, though it wasn't much past eight. I followed Anne back to her chamber and helped her put her things away. As we did so, she told me her news: Miss Lucas had spent about a week with them in Bath, working out the plans for the play they were to put on in London, in the West End, and Mr. Cunningham was in that state you get into before an opening – both thrilled and terrified. It was to be, for him, the biggest event of his career. The theater was a large one, and those financing it were enthusiastic. Three of them had come to Bath to look Anne over "from top to bottom," as she said. They had asked her to sing, and been content with her performance, and one of them had said, in her hearing, that her appeal wasn't in her looks, or even in her voice, though that was good enough, but in her grace. We both laughed. I said, "Nothing like a life of constant housework to show you how to move."

"And then dance lessons."

I nodded. I saw that, maybe for the first time, Anne believed in her gifts, that what I had watched her learn had become natural to her, or, I might say, as visible to her as it was to others, such as Miss Lucas. We had been in Liverpool for over a year now. It all seemed very long and very short at the same time. Anne pulled her nightdress over her head, yawned, and lay down. I tucked her in, as Alice had done with us when we were small, and kissed her on the cheek. She squeezed my hand, and I walked out of her chamber.

Over the next several days, Anne told me what they had done in Bath. It sounded like a very interesting town. It had been started by the Romans, not as a "chester" but as a spot where there were hot springs of different temperatures, and quite a smell, as Anne said, but she got used to it. She tried going to the waters four times. The odor of one of the baths reminded her of the Mississippi, so she avoided that one afterward, but it was the one that Evelina seemed to prefer, and Mrs. Cunningham would take her there every day, in the morning. Otherwise, the buildings were impressive, and there were parks and hills and every evidence of the history of wealthy people. Miss Lucas had told Anne that she visited Bath after the run of every show she happened to perform in, just to free herself from that character, good or bad, whoever she might be. Miss Lucas had given her a volume, *Northanger Abbey,* by Miss Austen, whose book, *Emma,* I had read on our ship, what was it, fifteen months ago? She went to her case, still partially full, took it out, and handed it to me. Miss Austen had lived in Bath, and was one of Miss Lucas's preferred authors. Evelina had read it in a day. I set it in my lap.

She was right about Mr. Cunningham. Over the next few days (now that they had returned, I had many errands, which I embraced with great pleasure), I noted that he did seem keyed up. The show was to have its first run in the middle of October, and so rehearsals were to begin, in London, on the first of September. He would take Anne there, put her up with Miss Lucas, then return for a week or so, until the boys went back to their school. He seemed to talk about the details in order to settle his temper and preserve himself from too many hopes. Barnsby, it looked like, was glad to get back to work, too, and began to partake of Mr. Cunningham's high spirits. He often looked at me kindly, but neither sought me out nor avoided me. As for me, I watched him more and more, found him more interesting, more alluring, kinder, more thoughtful.

This did not mean that I thought of John less frequently than I had. It was as if John and Barnsby, so distinct from one another, jostled about in my head like vegetables and cubes of meat in a stew, both fragrant, both utterly distinct from one another. But I also knew, even as I thought this, that no one was inviting me to enjoy the stew. I stewed through Sunday. Perhaps I should have gone to some service, and Anne did go with the Cunninghams to their church. But I kept to myself until they left, and until Barnsby left, and then I walked out, first to Reggie's garden, then toward John's chapel, then to Barnsby's quite distant Unitarian church. How appealing each of these men was! As differently as they acted, as differently as they looked, each of them had a sort of dedication and self-possession that I envied. John tended to his flock, Barnsby tended to the Cunninghams, Reggie tended to his garden, and for each of them, goodness was the product of their tending. As I walked about, gazing at buildings, at parks, at horses and carriages, at families, at flowers and trees and the clouds in the sky, I wondered what it was that I would wish to tend to, and I couldn't see a thing. The only thing I wanted to do was keep walking, keep looking. I knew, indeed, what I was, as a woman, supposed to tend to (a husband, a family), but it was not only that I had tried that and failed, but also that I had seen in my sisters what that came to when it was supposedly a success – frustration and conflict followed by resignation and old age. I turned down Dingle Lane toward the river. In my mind, I could hear my sisters discussing me:

"Well, she's done it her own way for far too long."

"We should have reined her in years ago. You see how well it has worked with Frank!"

"And then she led Annie astray!"

Much head-shaking.

"You ask me, it's the books."

Nodding all around.

Dingle Lane went along the river to Dingle Road, and that became Cockburn Street—not pronounced "Cock Burn," but, rather, "Coburn," which I whispered to myself, in that English way. Along Cockburn Street, there were quite narrow rows of houses, and when you looked between the rows, there was the sea, the river, the wind whistling into town. I was not far from the harbor. I hadn't been there in a while. It didn't take me long to make my way down to the docks, or, more precisely, a street that went along past the docks. There were several ships here and there. I looked at them, wondering which one might be leaving for New York, but I couldn't see the names of the ships, and had no understanding of how to ascertain which companies owned them. One ship, evidently transporting goods, not passengers, gave off a few bellows and then edged slowly into the river. Though it was slow, it was graceful. It gave off another bellow. At the far end, I then saw another ship, which looked rather like the *Arabia,* and I walked toward it, then went down onto the dock. I saw that it was the *Revelation*. It was a handsome enough vessel, roomier in the lower area than in the upper area. At one end of the dock, passengers were getting on, and at the other end, coal was being loaded into the lower area. A woman passed me, and I said, "Pardon me. Where is this ship going to?"

She looked me up and down, then said, "I believe Christiania."

"Where is that?"

"Norway."

No one in my entire life had ever mentioned that place! That made it interesting. The woman walked on, left the dock. Evidently, she was not going to Norway. I looked up the hill toward Canning Street – not visible, of course, but not far away. I had not asked Berta before I left if I was to do anything; sometimes there was something, even on a Sunday. I sorted my dress and my hat, preparing to go up to Nelson Street; it wasn't a long walk. And then something bumped into me from behind, almost but not quite knocking me over. I turned around and grabbed it – it was that girl I had seen at the Furnishes', the difficult, unappealing one. I picked her up – she struggled in my arms – and looked around. I saw no one. As I was not far from the edge of the wharf, it occurred to me that if she hadn't bumped me she might have flown into the water. What was her name? Ah, Mabel. I said, "Mabel."

She stopped struggling and looked at me. She said, "Who are you?"

I said, "I'm Reggie's friend. I'm . . ." I did pause, but then I said, "Lidie. I'm Lidie."

She laughed.

I said, "If I set you down, will you take my hand and not run off?"

She nodded. I set her down. I gauged that she was between four and five years old, and I suddenly remembered a similar episode when Frank was that age and he ran off. Roland eventually found him – after a long hour and a half of searching – by the bank of the river. Alice maintained that Harriet had never recovered from the distress of picturing him drowning.

Now the crowd, such as it was, parted, and two women came running toward us, the younger one in the lead. She was calling out, "Mabel! Mabel!"

Mabel stood beside me, staring, not waving or responding in any way. I said, "Is that your mama?"

Mabel said nothing for a few moments, then, as the woman got closer, she did nod and she waved her hand. It was then that I realized that Mabel could not see much. Her mother rushed up to us, picked up her daughter, hugged her. The other woman, who I saw was much older, was panting a bit. When she saw Mabel, she said, "Oh, thank the Lord!"

The mother whipped around, almost dropping Mabel, and said, "No! Do not thank the Lord. Thank this young woman for catching her!"

"I do, mahm, I do!" exclaimed the old woman, and then she walked over to where someone had set their traveling trunk and sat down on it, used her kerchief to wipe her forehead.

The mother took a few deep breaths. I said, as genially as I could, just to calm the situation, "Ah, madam. Haven't I seen you at the Furnishes'?"

She nodded, rearranged Mabel, and set her down, but kept her hand around Mabel's. She said, "Mr. Furnish is my father's uncle. We haven't visited before, but of course we've always wanted to. My husband and I are Victor and Elizabeth Kent."

I said, "Are you from Scotland?"

"In a sense. Just north of the boundary. In Gretna, not far from the Firth of Solway."

I had never heard of any of these places, other than Scotland. I said, "Are you going back there now?"

"Ah, no. Our time there is finished. But I think I've seen you, perhaps recently?"

"I often visit the Furnishes' garden, and pretend that Reggie is my long-lost brother, just so that I might get a few berries or apples."

"Ah, yes. Indeed. That Reggie is a treasure!" Now we smiled together at the very thought of him.

The horn of the ship bellowed, and Mrs. Kent started. She said, "Does that mean we are to board?"

I said, "I believe so."

Now we looked at the older woman, whose eyes were closed, almost as if she were asleep.

Mrs. Kent said, "That is our nanny, Florence. We are taking her with us, but in addition to the fact that she can no longer keep up with Mabel, I think her health is bad, though she won't admit it. I do not know what to do."

Now Mabel herself stepped forward, lifted her hand, and held it out to me. Clearly, she was an observant and thoughtful, if harum-scarum, child.

Mrs. Kent looked down at Mabel, then up at me. She said, "Would you like to go somewhere?"

I said, "Norway?"

"Yes, for now. But after that, Russia. My husband has gone on ahead, and we are to follow him."

My eyebrows must have popped off my head, because she chuckled.

I did not say no, I said, "How can I – "

And she said, "My husband has plenty of funds. We will give you a trunk and a wardrobe and a good wage. The war has been over there for two years. The treaty was unexpectedly amicable, so I think . . . Well, I have faith, let's say, that our stay will be both interesting and peaceful."

I must have looked a bit startled, remembering the few things Barnsby had told me about that war.

She said, "There was no fighting in St. Petersburg. It's almost as far from that city as it is to London, or, let's say, Paris. I have no fears." She leaned toward me, and said, "Part of my spouse's job is to assuage conflicts. He does it well."

We stared at each other, and then I looked down at Mabel. The horn bellowed again.

I imagined a conflict actually being "assuaged" rather than endlessly ramping up. I said yes.

And then Mrs. Kent hurried Mabel and me, with the nanny behind us, over to the gangway, chatted with the fellow escorting the passengers onto the ship. She pulled some notes out of her pocket and asked the fellow for a piece of paper and a pencil, which he went to find. Then she came over to me. She said, "Florence will deliver this missive to your friends. Look at her – she is over the moon!"

Florence did look pleased, I must say.

And so I gave her the address of 2 Canning Street, dictated some farewells to Anne and the Cunninghams, and asked Anne to communicate to John that I had left on a sudden voyage. And then Mrs. Kent handed Florence the paper, and we walked up the gangway and were shown to a rather spacious cabin on the upper deck. The horn bellowed again. The last thing I thought as we put Liverpool behind us was that Anne would not be in the least surprised.

A NOTE ABOUT THE AUTHOR

JANE SMILEY is the author of numerous novels, including *A Thousand Acres,* which was awarded the Pulitzer Prize, and the Last Hundred Years Trilogy: *Some Luck, Early Warning,* and *Golden Age*. She is the author as well of several works of nonfiction and books for young adults. A member of the American Academy of Arts and Letters, she has also received the PEN Center USA Lifetime Achievement Award for Literature. She lives in Northern California.

A NOTE ABOUT THE TYPE

Agmena was designed by Jovica Veljović for Linotype in 2012. Inspired by the forms and proportions of Renaissance fonts, Veljović created Agmena with the intent of making the perfect text face for books. Agmena was awarded a Certificate of Typographic Excellence by the Type Directors Club in 2013.

Typeset by Scribe,
Philadelphia, Pennsylvania

Designed by Marisa Nakasone